"Where is Kate?" Robert asked.

"She is giving away most of the contents of our food basket to a woman with three hungry children," Mrs. Kinnard said. "As she should. Now, about—"

"Excuse me," he said, pushing his way through the crowd again to get closer to the train.

He stood waiting on the platform, watching Kate progress all the way until she finally appeared. She was so…beautiful to him and had been since the first time he saw her in the downstairs hallway of his father's house.

Maria was right. He did want Kate to be a preacher's wife—*his* wife—and he didn't see how their situation could be any more impossible.

I love her, Lord.

He didn't know when it had happened, or how. All he knew was that it was so, that she was in his mind night and day—and now he was only moments away from breaking her heart…

Cheryl Reavis
and
Laura Abbot

An Unexpected Wife
&
Into the Wilderness

LOVE INSPIRED
INSPIRATIONAL ROMANCE

LOVE INSPIRED®

INSPIRATIONAL ROMANCE

ISBN-13: 978-1-335-44877-4

Recycling programs for this product may not exist in your area.

An Unexpected Wife & Into the Wilderness

CONTENTS

RITA® Award–winning author and romance novelist **Cheryl Reavis** describes herself as a "late bloomer" who played in her first piano recital at the tender age of thirty. "We had to line up by height—I was the third smallest kid," she says. "After that, there was no stopping me. I immediately gave myself permission to attempt my other heart's desire—to write." Her books *A Crime of the Heart* and *Patrick Gallagher's Widow* won a Romance Writers of America coveted RITA® Award for Best Contemporary Series Romance the year each was published. *One of Our Own* received a Career Achievement Award for Best Innovative Series Romance from *RT Book Reviews*. A former public health nurse, Cheryl makes her home in North Carolina with her husband.

Books by Cheryl Reavis

Love Inspired Historical

The Soldier's Wife
An Unexpected Wife

Visit the Author Profile page
at Harlequin.com for more titles.

AN UNEXPECTED WIFE

Cheryl Reavis

Be of good courage, and he shall strengthen
your heart, all ye that hope in the Lord.
—*Psalms* 31:24

For my mother, in honor of her birthday—
92 years and counting. Thank you, Mommy,
for always being my biggest fan.

Chapter One

Kate Woodard stood looking out the parlor window, more than content to be in her brother's finally empty house and do nothing but watch the falling snow. It was deep enough to drift across the veranda now, a barricade—she hoped—from any outside intrusion.

The house was cold; a strong draft at the window made the lace curtains billow out from time to time. She could light a fire in the fireplace—if only one had been laid on the hearth and she knew how. When she made her impulsive decision to deliberately miss her train, she hadn't for one moment taken into consideration that it was the dead of winter and she knew next to nothing about managing parlor fires, much less the one in the kitchen. Tomorrow she would do something about all that—hire someone or…something. Now she would savor the peace and silence of the house, and it would be enough.

She had come to Salisbury, North Carolina, to visit her brother and his family in the hope that a change of scenery and the rowdy company of his adorable young sons—two adopted, one his by blood—would redirect her mind. She was so weary of living the false life that had been foisted upon her when she was hardly more than a child herself. She needed…respite. She needed the privacy to *feel* all the emotions she had to keep bottled up for the sake of propriety. She wanted to weep—or not to weep. She wanted to pace and fret, if that seemed more applicable to her state of mind. She wanted the freedom to think about her own son. Her lost son. He was thirteen now, and the web of lies surrounding his birth had held fast. No outsiders knew young Harrison Howe was *her* child and not the child of her parents' closest friends, nor did they know his brother was not his brother at all.

John.

He had made a much better brother than father—at least before the war had changed him so.

All these years Kate had lived on the fringes of Harrison's life, watching him grow, being his friend but always carefully exercising the restraint it took not to make Mr. and Mrs. Howe or her own family think that she might be trying to get close to him. She was so good at it that she sometimes thought the people who knew the truth forgot that she was Harrison's real mother.

Her latest news of him was that he had been sent to a prestigious boarding school deep in the Pennsylvania countryside, the alma mater of many—if not all—the males in the Howe family and the one place Kate believed he would not thrive. He wasn't like the Howe men—John—or the senior Mr. Howe. He was more like *her* father—and her—thoughtful and observant and studious, and the fact that he required spectacles would make him even more of a target for boarding school jibes and pranks.

But there was nothing she could do beyond sending him small gifts of books and candy. He had sent her a *carte de visite* in return. She cherished it, but seeing his wistful young face staring back at her from the photograph only underlined her growing fear that he was miserable.

So she had come to her brother's lively household in the hope of forgetting at least for a time the helplessness she was feeling—only now she had put herself squarely into a different kind of helplessness. If she'd taken the time to think about it, she might have been discouraged by her lack of housekeeping skills. The original plan—her brother Maxwell's plan—had been that she would return to her parents' home in Philadelphia while Max and Maria and the boys and their nanny were away. There were no other servants in the house; Max relied on his soldiers to accomplish what few of the heavy chores Maria would allow them to do. He had even assigned one of his nervous young officers and his wife, who were traveling to New York City, to see her safely to her destination. But she had forgotten the basket of food Maria had packed especially for her to take on her long train journey. When she hurried back inside to get it, she realized suddenly that she didn't have to go. She was the last person to leave. She could stay behind; no one would be the wiser. Without a second thought, she had feigned a sudden "sick headache," dismissing the fainthearted lieutenant despite his legitimate fear of what her brother might do to him for not carrying out his orders. She had felt sorry for him and for his young wife, but she had still embraced the opportunity to have the solitude she had craved for so long.

She gave a quiet sigh and pulled her cashmere shawl more closely around her, caressing the softness of the wool as she did so. The shawl was not quite rose and not quite lavender, and it suited her coloring perfectly. It had been a birthday gift from her father, and as such, it was very much a symbol of her social status, especially here. Ordinarily she was mindful of the fact that she was Kate Woodard, of the Philadelphia and Germantown Woodards, the seemingly respectable sister of Colonel Maxwell Woodard, commander of the occupation army garrisoned in this small Southern town—and she behaved accordingly.

She was also the Woodard family's twenty-nine-year-old bona fide spinster, and at this late date, there was little incentive for her to learn anything domestic. There had been a time when she had thought she could—would—marry. During the early months of the war she had become engaged to Lieutenant Grey Jamison, an amiable young cavalryman who, unlike so many of his peers, was more interested in doing his duty to save the Union than in becoming a great military legend. She'd found him brave and honorable and optimistic—so much so that he had made her brave, too. For the first time in her life she'd actually believed she could dare to be happy.

But Grey had been killed in the battle of Bentonville in what would turn out to be one of the last throes of the Confederacy. She had been devastated when the news of his death had come, and then all over again when his last letter had arrived. In it he had seemed so…troubled. He'd asked her to promise that if he came home changed, she wouldn't coddle him. She would treat him as she always had, and if she should feel sorry for him, she would never let him see it.

But he hadn't come home, and when she had lost him, she had lost all hope that she could be someone's wife. There were too many secrets, too many lies, and she hadn't known then how hard it would become to maintain them, even the one that defined her very existence. Had she married Grey, at some point, she would have had to tell him about her son—because she loved them both.

"At least I was brave once," she whispered, and perhaps she was being brave now. She suddenly smiled. Wandering around in a cold empty house wasn't brave; it was foolish. Even she could see that.

But she made a determined effort not to second-guess her decision to stay behind. There was no point in dwelling on it—or perhaps she *would* dwell on it—later—because she was free to do just that, if she wanted.

Free!

She had a mèager basket of food and a cold hearth in the middle of a snowstorm—and she was happier than she'd been in a long while.

She began closing the heavy drapes in the parlor. She had no real plans beyond bundling up and going to bed. It occurred to her that it had been a long time since she'd eaten. She never ate much before a train trip. As a child she had learned the hard way that she was a far better traveler if she embarked with an empty stomach. But she was hungry now, and she picked up the oil lamp and stepped into the wide hallway that led to one of the two kitchens necessary for the running of her brother's household. The other one was outside, a summer kitchen with thick brick walls and a stone floor, and she hadn't the slightest idea how to manage either one of them.

It was so drafty in the hallway. And empty. Despite it being over five years since the war ended and the fact that Max could well afford whatever furniture Maria might want, the hallway was in serious need of some tables, a chair or two and perhaps a hall tree, the kind with marble shelves and a beveled mirror. According to her brother, many of those things had once been here—until General Stoneman and his men had raided the town. If Kate understood the situation correctly, the dearth of furniture and the mismatched sets of china, crystal and silverware still in use were somehow a badge of honor. Kate almost envied Maria the sense of pride she and the rest of the women here seemed to take in their years of deprivation.

In Philadelphia Kate had helped with the war effort, but she'd only done what was deemed proper for a young woman of Philadelphia's highest society. The truth of the matter was that the balls held to raise money for the Sanitary Commission and the gatherings where young ladies packed tins of cookies for homesick soldiers, or rolled bandages for the hospitals—none of which they actually believed would be needed—were as much an excuse for lively and supposedly patriotic socializing as anything. She hadn't gone into the hospitals to help with the wounded the way Maria and her friends here had. She certainly hadn't gone hungry or been deprived of new dresses or undergarments or anything else she might have wanted. *Wanted,* not needed. She sometimes wondered if she would have done anything at all if her brother and her fiancé hadn't been Union cavalrymen. And there was John, of course. He was the father of her child, and as such, he was on her very short list of males other than her son she cared enough to worry about. The war, the unbridled patriotism had been exciting—until Max and John had become prisoners of war and Grey had been killed.

She held the lamp higher as she made her way to the rear of the house, trying not to be disconcerted by the wavering shadows she cast as she moved along. This particular hallway always made her think of Max and John and their daredevil cavalryman tales of riding their mounts directly through the front doors of rebel houses like this one, just for a lark and with no thought that they could easily have been killed doing it. Back then, aside from the war, Max and John had been more than a little exasperating for the people who loved them. And who would have ever thought they would both end up completely domesticated, much less married to Southern women?

The door leading to the dining room was standing ajar and she moved to close it, hoping to interrupt the strong draft rushing through the house tonight. But then she stepped inside because she caught a glimpse of a toy lying on the floor—a small carved earless horse that belonged to Robbie, the youngest. The nanny, Mrs. Hansen, must have missed it when she packed up the boys' belongings for their trip.

Mrs. Hansen was yet another example of Kate's difficulty in understanding how the Southern mind worked. At first the woman's added presence in the household had led Kate to think that Maria was becoming more lax in her determination not to take advantage of Max's money. But then Kate realized that her wanting or needing help with the boys had very little to do with it. It was Mrs. Hansen who needed the help. She had been taking care of Suzanne Canfield, the adopted boys' sick mother, when Suzanne had been killed in a fire that also burned their house to the ground. The boys had barely escaped with their lives and then only because Max had braved the flames to go in and get them. Mrs. Hansen's grief and guilt at not having been there when the fire broke out had apparently been overwhelming, and Maria had deliberately given her perhaps the only thing that would ease her mind a little—the task of helping to take care of the little boys whom the fire had orphaned.

Kate picked up the wooden horse and put it into her pocket, smiling as she did so because Robbie's teething marks were all over it. He was such a dear little boy—indeed, they all were. Joe. Jake. Robbie.

Harrison.

"No," she said quietly. She wasn't ready to think about him just yet, not in the deep and intense way she wanted to.

She pulled the door firmly closed, and she saw the man immediately when she turned around. He wasn't wearing a hat, and his coat was still snowcovered, likely because it wasn't warm enough inside for it to have melted. Incredibly, he had taken the liberty of lighting not one but two of the kitchen lamps.

"Who are you?" he asked bluntly and with all the authority of someone whose business it was to know.

If her presence in the house had been authorized, she wouldn't have been so taken aback by the question, but as it was, she didn't reply. They stared at each other, Kate trying all the while to decide whether or not she was afraid.

"Why is the house so cold?" he asked next. He reached out as if to steady himself, but there was nothing in the hallway for him to grab onto. "There's plenty of wood…in the…box."

Kate eased backward, intending to make a run for the front door, snowstorm or no snowstorm. But she had the lamp. She couldn't run with it and she couldn't set it down without the man realizing her intent. The last thing she wanted was to light her unsuspecting brother's house ablaze.

"My apologies, miss," he said with some effort but in a slightly more genial tone. She tried to identify his accent. It was Southern, and yet it wasn't.

He took a few steps in her direction. "I didn't think…the questions were…that difficult."

"Who are *you?*" she asked finally, recovering at least a modicum of the snobbishness that was hers by birthright if not personality.

He took a few more steps, and she realized suddenly that something was indeed wrong. He was clearly unsteady on his feet now, and he seemed to want to say something but couldn't.

Drunk? Ill? She couldn't tell.

He suddenly pitched forward. She gave a small cry and jumped back in an effort to keep him from colliding with her and the lit oil lamp. He went sprawling face first on the parquet floor, his head hitting the bare wood hard.

"Sir," she said, keeping her distance. "Sir!"

He didn't move. She set the oil lamp on the floor and came as close to him as she dared. He was so still.

Someone rapped sharply on the front door, making her jump, and whoever it was didn't wait to be admitted. Sergeant Major Perkins, her brother's extremely competent orderly, came striding into the foyer and down the hallway, bringing much of the winter storm in with him.

"Miss Kate! I wondered why there were lamps burning— Who's that?"

"I don't know," Kate said, bending down to look at him again. He was still motionless.

"You didn't go and shoot him, did you?"

"No, I did not shoot him, Sergeant Major."

"What is he doing in here?"

"I don't know that, either."

"Then what are *you* doing in here? Colonel Woodard didn't say you were going to be on the premises."

"My brother doesn't know everything," she said obscurely.

"Well, you just go right on thinking that if you want to, Miss Kate, but if you want my advice, you'll revise that opinion, the sooner, the better. Don't much get by that brother of yours. Every soldier in this town can tell you that."

"Could we just address *this* first?" Kate said, waving her hand over the man still lying on the floor.

"That we can. Move the lamp so I can roll him over. I'm going to hang on to him. You see what's in his pockets."

Kate hesitated.

"We want to hurry this along, Miss Kate," he said pointedly. "While he's unaware."

"Yes," she decided, seeing the wisdom of that plan.

She slid the lamp out of the way and knelt down by him again.

"He's not dead, is he?" it occurred to her to ask.

"If he was dead, we wouldn't need to be hurrying. Go ahead now. Look."

Far from reassured, she reached tentatively and not very deeply into a coat pocket.

"I don't reckon he's got anything in there that bites," Perkins said mildly.

She gave him a look and began to search in earnest. He didn't seem to be carrying anything at all.

"You let him in?" Perkins asked.

"No," Kate said pointedly, moving to another pocket. "He was just…here."

"Kind of like you are, I guess," he said. He was clearly suspicious about the situation, and he wasn't doing much to try to hide it. "You miss your train?"

"I didn't 'miss' it. I didn't get on."

"Colonel Woodard know about the…change in plans?"

"He does not."

"I was afraid of that."

"There is nothing for *you* to worry about, Sergeant."

"And yet here I am. Down on the floor with an unconscious and unknown man, helping you riffle through his pockets."

"The riffling was your idea," Kate reminded him.

"So it was," he agreed. "Anybody else here?"

"Just him—as far as I know."

"You're not sick or anything, are you?" he persisted, the question impertinent at best.

She didn't answer. Her fingers closed around a small book in the man's other coat pocket—a well-worn Bible, she saw as she pulled it free. She opened it. There was some kind of…card between the pages. The texture felt like a *carte de visite*. She moved closer to the lamp so she could see. It wasn't a photograph. It was a Confederate military card.

"Robert Brian Markham," she read. She looked at Perkins. "Max's wife was a Markham. She had a brother named Robert," she said, forgetting how long he had been Max's right hand and how likely it was that he knew more details about Maria Markham Woodard and her family than Kate did.

But that Robert Markham had been killed at Gettysburg, along with a younger brother, Samuel. Kate had understood for a long time why Max tried to be elsewhere during the first three days of July. His wife's heart had been broken by her brothers' deaths, and he was the last person who could comfort her. He had been at Gettysburg, too, fighting for the other side.

Kate picked up the lamp and held it near the man's face so she could see it better. It didn't help. She didn't recognize him at all and she couldn't see any family resemblance. She'd never actually met anyone with his kind of rugged features. She thought that he might have been handsome once, but then his face must have gotten…beaten and battered somewhere along the way.

She realized suddenly that Perkins was watching her. "He's not bleeding," she said, moving the lamp away.

Perkins reached out and briefly took the man's hand. "Prizefighter, would be my guess," he said. "Men fresh out of a war can have a lot of rage still. And they have to get rid of it."

"By beating another human being for sport?" Kate asked.

"There are worse ways to live—especially if you need to eat."

Kate looked at the man's face again. How much rage could be left after that kind of brutality? she wondered.

Perkins took the card from her, then stood. "I want you to go upstairs and lock yourself in, Miss Kate," Perkins said.

"Why?"

"I need to take care of all this and I'm going to have to leave to do it. I've only got the one horse and the snow's too bad to try it on foot. You'll be all right if you stay quiet and keep your door locked."

"I don't think he's in any shape to do me harm," Kate said, trying to sound calmer and more competent than she felt. "I'm not afraid. Just go."

Perkins hesitated, looking closely at the man again. "All right," he said after a moment. "I'll be back as quick as I can. Find something to cover him with. He needs to be kept warm until we find out what he's up to—just in case."

Kate was about to ask what "just in case" meant, but then she suddenly realized that Perkins was considering the possibility that this man might actually be Max's—and her—brother-in-law, or at least have some information about him.

"Light some more lamps so I can see the house easier from the outside. It's snowing so hard it's a wonder I noticed anything was going on in here at all. Wouldn't hurt to light a fire, too."

Kate nodded at his last suggestion. She wholeheartedly agreed, but she couldn't quite bring herself to admit that she didn't know how to do it.

He helped her get to her feet, then picked up the lamp and handed it to her. She kept staring at the man on the floor.

"Miss Kate," he said as he was about to go, and she looked at him.

"If he starts stirring, you get away from him."

"Yes, I will. Of course I will."

But Perkins still didn't go.

"What is it?" she asked. She knew him to be a straightforward and painfully blunt man—it was the main reason Max relied on him so. But he was having some difficulty saying whatever was on his mind now.

"You're…sure you don't know this man?"

She was so surprised by the question that she could only stare at him. Then she realized that he was considering every possible explanation for the man's being here and that he actually wanted to make certain she hadn't missed her train in order to keep some kind of secret assignation. If she hadn't been so cold and so upset, she might have been offended. Or she might have laughed.

"I don't know him, Sergeant Major Perkins," she said evenly.

"All right then," he said.

"I'd appreciate it if you hurried," she said in case he had any more questions he wanted answered.

"My plan exactly, Miss Kate."

"No, wait. I need a telegram sent to my parents. Say I've been delayed. Could you do that, please?"

"Yes, miss," he said.

She expected him to leave then, but he didn't. He

was still looking at her in that sergeant major way he had. Not quite what her brother called a "sack and burn" face, but still…arresting.

"There is one other thing," he said. "My responsibility is to Colonel Woodard. I will do whatever is necessary to maintain his position and his authority in this town."

"Yes, all right," Kate said.

"Do you understand?"

"Yes," she said—which wasn't quite the truth. She understood that he made certain that her brother's life ran as smoothly as possible and that he wanted her to know something about that duty, which he felt was important. She just didn't know what that "something" was.

She had to turn away from the strong gust of wind that filled the hallway when he finally left by the front door. The man lying at her feet didn't react at all. She gave him a backward glance, then hurried upstairs to pull two of the quilts off her own bed because she didn't want to take the time to look through cedar chests for extra ones. He didn't seem to have stirred when she returned. She folded the quilts double, then knelt down to cover him, hesitating long enough to look at his face again before she went to light more lamps in the downstairs. One of his hands was outstretched, and she carefully lifted it. She could see the scarred knuckles, feel the calluses on his palm as she placed it under the quilt.

It was so cold on the floor. She couldn't keep from shivering, and she had to bite down on her lip to keep her teeth from chattering. For a brief moment she thought she saw a slight movement from him as well.

No, she decided. He wasn't waking. He was just cold. He had to be as cold as she was.

"I must learn how to build a fire. In a fireplace *and* in a cookstove," she said out loud as she got to her feet. "And that's all there is to it."

She went around lighting as many lamps as she could find—she did know how to do that, at least. She had no expectation that Perkins would return quickly, and after what already seemed a long time, she began to pace up and down the hallway in an effort to keep warm. She didn't know what time it was—only that it was nearly dark outside. She thought there had once been an heirloom grandfather clock in the foyer, but it, like the rest of the hall furniture, had become a casualty of the war, and Maria hadn't wanted another one. In this one instance, Kate thought she understood her sister-in-law's behavior. Some things were far too dear to be replaced, especially if all the replacement could ever be was a reminder of what had been lost.

Kate kept her eyes on the man as she walked the hallway, but she let her mind consider what she was going to tell Max about her being here instead of Philadelphia. After a time she decided that she wouldn't tell him anything. She would say the same thing to him she'd said to Perkins. She hadn't missed her train; she just didn't get on—and that was all these two representatives of the military occupation needed to know.

She suddenly stopped pacing. This time she had no doubt that the man had moved. She took a few steps closer because she couldn't tell for certain whether or not he was beginning to wake. If he tried to get up, if he seemed threatening in any way, she would do what

Perkins said. She would run to her room and lock herself in.

She could tell that his eyes were still closed, and she took some comfort from that, but after a long, tense moment, he began stirring again. He gave a soft moan and turned his head in her direction.

"Eleanor," he said.

Am I wounded?

He tried to open his eyes and couldn't. He needed to get up, but he couldn't do that, either. He could hear the voices swirling around him. Women's voices.

"Move aside!" he heard one of them say. She must have been some distance away. There were sharp-sounding footsteps coming in his direction.

"You!" she suddenly barked. "Get the parlor and the kitchen fires lit! This house is freezing!"

"Yes, ma'am," a young-sounding male voice said.

"The kitchen first!" she said, still yelling. "We need hot water and heated blankets! Now!"

He could hear the scurrying of a heavier set of footsteps, and then a different woman's voice.

"That way," she said kindly, and the scurrying continued past him down the hall.

"Have you made no preparations whatsoever?" the first woman demanded.

"No, Mrs. Kinnard, I have not. I don't expect he'll be staying."

He struggled to make sense of what he was hearing. *Mrs. Kinnard? Acacia Kinnard?*

It couldn't be her. Acacia Kinnard was…was…

He couldn't complete the thought.

"Indeed, he will be staying," this Mrs. Kinnard

said. "You cannot put Maria's brother out for all your thinking you've won the War. Shame on you, Robert Markham!" she suddenly barked. "Shame!"

"I don't think he can hear you," the younger woman ventured.

"Of course he can hear me! Robert Brian Markham! Where have you been!" Mrs. Kinnard demanded. "What would your dear sweet mother say! And poor Maria—if you'd bothered to come home, she might not be—"

Her voice suddenly drifted away, lost in the blackness that swept over him.

Chapter Two

Married to a Yankee, Kate thought. If Robert Markham had come home, as was his duty, then his sister might not have married a Yankee colonel. She was surprised that Mrs. Kinnard had stopped short of actually saying it.

Sergeant Major Perkins's plan to "take care of all this" left a great deal to be desired, in Kate's opinion. Her opportunity for solitude had completely disappeared when he'd returned with a number of soldiers, two hospital orderlies and Mrs. Kinnard, the indisputable Queen Bee of Salisbury Society. Mrs. Kinnard had an impeccable Southern pedigree, and she had used it to all but appoint herself head of just about everything, including the Confederate military wayside hospital down near the railroad tracks during the war. Mrs. Kinnard's word was still law in all matters not under the direct supervision of the United States Army, and, Kate suspected, in some of those, as well.

"Excuse me, Miss Kate," one of the hospital orderlies said.

She—and ultimately Mrs. Kinnard—moved out of the way so he could kneel down and assess the man's condition. It occurred to her that Robert Markham was going to have every bit as much trouble pacifying Mrs. Kinnard as her brother did.

"Is the doctor coming?" Kate asked the orderly.

"Just as soon as we can find him, Miss Kate," he said.

Kate stood watching as he uncovered the man and began to examine him, looking for a reason why he had fallen to the floor, she supposed.

"Well, can you do *anything* helpful?" Mrs. Kinnard said suddenly, and Kate realized she was once again in her sights.

"I…"

"*Exactly* as I thought. You do know where there is pen and paper, I hope."

Kate took a quiet breath before she answered. "Yes. I'll be happy to get it."

Kate escaped to Maria's writing desk in the parlor and returned with a sheet of paper and a short pencil. Mrs. Kinnard eyed the pencil, and Kate thought she was going to refuse to take it.

"The ink is frozen. I'm sorry," Kate added, because in a roundabout way, that could be considered her fault. "I assumed you were in a hurry," she said, still holding out the pencil.

Mrs. Kinnard gave an impatient sigh, then removed her gloves and bonnet and handed them to Kate in exchange for the pencil and paper. Kate had no idea what to do with them, given the dearth of furnishings in the hall. She held on to them in lieu of throwing them down on the parquet floor, then she opened the dining room door and went inside, ultimately placing the bonnet and gloves carefully on a chair next to the sideboard and nearly colliding with Mrs. Kinnard when she turned around to leave.

"They should be safe here," Kate said, because she hadn't realized the woman had followed her and concern for her finery was the only conclusion Kate could come to as to why she did. She could hear the front door opening and a number of footsteps in the hall. Several more soldiers passed by the dining room door, two of them carrying a stretcher.

Mrs. Kinnard sat down at the dining table near the oil lamp Kate had lit earlier and began to write—a list, from the looks of it.

"Mr. Perkins!" she cried when she'd finished, clearly eschewing Perkins's military title, probably because he belonged to an army she considered of no consequence.

"Yes, ma'am, Mrs. Kinnard!" he called from somewhere at the back of the house.

"Take this," she said, when he finally appeared in the doorway. "I want this list filled as soon as possible."

He looked at the sheet of paper, then back at her. "Mrs. Russell isn't going to welcome a knock on the door this time of night from the likes of me, ma'am."

"Whether she welcomes it or not isn't important. Taking care of Robert Markham now that he has returned from the dead, is. I won't see him hauled off to your military infirmary, and this young woman is of no use whatsoever that I can see."

Kate opened her mouth to respond to the remark, but Perkins cleared his throat sharply and gave her a hard look. His sergeant major look. Again. She suddenly understood what he had been trying to tell her earlier. Neither she nor her tender feelings mattered in this situation. Maintaining her brother's authority and his rapport with the townspeople did.

Very well, then.

She stepped around him into the hallway. If she was going to preserve Max's peace treaties, she'd have to get herself well away from this overbearing woman.

Honestly! she nearly said aloud. As she recalled, even Maria found the Kinnard woman hard going.

Robert Markham—if Mrs. Kinnard's identification could be trusted—still lay on the cold floor. The hospital orderly had lifted him slightly and was pouring brandy down his throat with all the skill of a man who had performed the treatment many times. Robert Markham eventually swallowed, coughed a time or two, but still did not wake.

"Miss Woodard!" Mrs. Kinnard said sharply behind her, making her jump. She closed her eyes for a moment before she turned around.

"Yes?" Kate said as politely as she could manage.

"We will put Robert in his old room," the woman said. "We have no idea what his mental state will be when he fully awakens. He needs to be in familiar surroundings. The bed must be stripped, new sheets put upon it—I'm sure Maria uses lavender sachet just as her dear mother did and he will no doubt recall that. And then the bed must be warmed and *kept* warm."

"The orderlies here will see to all that. Just tell them what you need, ma'am," Perkins said on his way out. "His old room is off the upstairs porch, Miss Kate. On the left."

And how in the world did Perkins know that? she wondered. It suddenly occurred to her that his room was also the one she was using—not that that would matter to Mrs. Kinnard. The woman had spoken, and Maria's brother was in need.

"Flannel," Mrs. Kinnard said, looking at Kate.

"I beg your pardon?"

"Flannel. We need flannel to wrap the heated bricks—you *are* heating bricks?" she said, looking at Kate hard.

"Yes, ma'am," one of the orderlies said for her. "The oven's full of them."

Undeterred, Mrs. Kinnard continued to look at Kate, now with raised eyebrows.

"I'll…see if I can find…some," Kate said, heading for the stairs.

Perkins hadn't left the house yet.

"Now try not to undo all your brother's hard work," he said quietly so Mrs. Kinnard wouldn't hear him. "He's finally got that old bat and her daughter where they don't set out to cripple everything he tries to do—and that's saying a lot. She's a mean old cuss and don't you go yanking her chain."

Kate sighed instead of answering.

"I'm telling you," Perkins said.

"I *don't* yank chains, Sergeant Major."

"Maybe not, but the Colonel says you are a strong woman, and it's my experience that strong women don't put up with much. This time it's important that you do, Miss Kate."

"Yes. All right. I'll…behave."

Easier said than done, she thought as he went out the door, but she was willing to try. She went upstairs and looked through the cedar chests, but there was no flannel in any of them. In an effort not to have to tell

Mrs. Kinnard that, she went down the back stairs to the kitchen, hoping that flannel for hot bricks, if she just thought about it logically, might be found there.

Somewhere.

She found them at last in the pantry on a top shelf, a whole basketful of double-thickness, hand-sewn flannel bags she concluded were the right size to hold a brick, hot or otherwise. She gave them to the soldier manning the cookstove, then ended up holding the bags open so he could drop a hot brick inside—once he stopped protesting her offer of help.

"Mrs. Kinnard," she said simply, and he immediately acquiesced.

When the job was done, there was nothing else required of her beyond standing around and letting the Kinnard woman use her for target practice. She had intended to get the bed linens for what had only moments before been *her* bed, but apparently one of the hospital orderlies—Bruno—knew more about where the sheets and bedding were kept than she did.

She went upstairs again, intending to remove what few belongings she still had in the room—yet another consideration that had escaped her attention when she'd made her bold decision to miss the train and stay behind. Most of her clothes had been packed up in her travel trunk and were by now well on their way to Philadelphia.

But she couldn't get into the room. It was full of soldiers trying to stay ahead of Mrs. Kinnard.

"There's a fire in old Mr. Markham's sitting room, Miss Woodard," one of them said. "You might be more comfortable in there."

"Yes, thank you," she said, more than grateful for

any suggestion that would keep her out of Mrs. Kinnard's way—for a while at least. But she could already hear the woman coming up the stairs, and she hurried away.

"The things I do for you, Max Woodard," she said under her breath. She was as intimidated as that young lieutenant who was supposed to see her safely to Philadelphia.

She slipped inside the sitting room and firmly closed the door, then thought better of it and left it slightly ajar. She didn't want Mrs. Kinnard sneaking up on her—not that the woman was given to anything resembling stealth. She was much more the charge-the-front-gates type.

A fire in the fireplace was indeed burning brightly. She savored the warmth for a moment, then moved to the nearest window and looked out. It was too dark to see anything but her reflection in the wavy glass.

Is that what a "strong woman" looks like?

She couldn't believe Max had described her in that way. She didn't feel strong. If anything, she felt…unfinished. What am I supposed to be doing? she wondered, the question stark and real in her mind and intended for no one. Clearly it wasn't going to be spending time alone thinking of her lost child.

Brooding.

Is that what she had actually planned to do? Perhaps, she thought, but she had never inflicted her unhappiness on anyone else, at least not consciously. To do so would have resulted in the decision to send her away—for her own good—and as a result, she would have had no contact with her son at all. She had worked hard to seem at least content with her life, so much so that she had nothing left over to nurture her better self. She always went to church, here and in Philadelphia, but the gesture was empty somehow. She felt so far away from anything spiritual and had for a long time. She still prayed for the people she loved, especially for Harrison. She had asked for God's blessing on him every night since he'd been born. But she never prayed for herself, and she had never asked for forgiveness. When she looked at Harrison, at what a fine young man he was becoming, she simply couldn't bring herself to do it. She might be a sinner, but *he* wasn't a sin.

Perhaps this was what living a lie did to a person—kept them feeling unworthy to speak to God. The best that could be said of her was that she had endured. Day after day. Year after year. In that context, she supposed Max was right. She was a strong woman.

She could hear the soft whisper of the snow against the windowpane. How much more pleasant the sound was when there was a warm fire crackling on the hearth behind her.

Is it snowing where you are, my dear Harrison? Are you warm and safe?

No, she thought again. She wasn't going to think about him now. She would wait until later. Until…

She couldn't say when. She gave a heavy sigh and looked around the room. It was no longer a combination sickroom, sitting room and library, but more a place to escape the domestic chaos of a household full of little boys. Even when Maria's ailing father had occupied it, it had been a pleasant place to be, with its floor-to-ceiling bookshelves, comfortable upholstered rocking chairs and windows that looked out over the flower and herb garden. She'd come in here often the first time she'd visited Max, shortly before he married Maria. Then the room had been a kind of *special sanctuary,* a place where old Mr. Markham had held court for the community and the conquering army alike, despite his doctor's orders. He'd been a witty and delightful man who'd enjoyed company—her company in particular, it had seemed—and she'd liked him very much. He'd been quite cunning, as well. He'd done his best to recruit her to bring him some forbidden cigars, and failing at that, it still hadn't taken him long to steer her into revealing all her misgivings about her brother's upcoming marriage to Mr. Markham's only daughter—some of which he harbored, as well.

She suddenly smiled to herself, thinking of Max and Maria and how suited they were to each other. "We were wrong to worry so, weren't we, Mr. Markham?" she whispered.

Or so she hoped. The chaos in Max's house tonight was of a completely different kind, the kind that had precipitated heavy footsteps and loud men's voices, Mrs. Kinnard barking orders like a sergeant major and some kind of commotion involving pots and pans in the kitchen. The house was annoyingly alive, and all because of the man who had collapsed in the downstairs hallway. If he was indeed Maria's brother, then it was no wonder he'd questioned Kate's presence here. He must have believed the house was still his home.

Where has he been? she wondered. *And why did he stay away?* She tried to imagine how she would have felt if Max had left her and their parents believing he was dead and grieving for him for years.

Kate suddenly realized that she wasn't alone. A

woman carrying a heavy-laden tray stood tentatively at the doorway.

"I— Am I interrupting?" the woman asked.

"No, no, of course not. Do come in, Mrs.—"

"Justice," the woman said quickly, Kate thought in order to keep them both from being embarrassed if Kate happened not to remember her name—which she hadn't.

"Yes, of course."

The woman came into the room, a bit at a loss at first as to where to put the tray. After a moment she set it down on a small table next to one of the rocking chairs. There was a plain brown teapot on the tray, a sugar bowl, a cream pitcher, spoons and a cup and saucer—and a plate covered with a starched and finely embroidered—but slightly worn—tea towel.

"I thought you might like some tea and a little bread and butter to eat," Mrs. Justice said. "I brought the bread with me—events being what they are tonight. I baked it early this morning so it's fresh. And I took enough hot water to make a pot of tea when it started boiling—Mrs. Kinnard didn't see me," she added in a whisper, making Kate smile.

"You're very kind—will you join me? I'm sure we can find another cup."

"Oh, no," Mrs. Justice said quickly. "They'll be bringing Robbie upstairs shortly and I must be on hand for that—though I'm not quite sure why. Mrs. Kinnard always seems to require my presence, but she never really lets me *do* anything. I can't believe dear Robbie has come home. He's so like Bud, you know."

"Bud?" Kate asked as she poured tea into the cup.

"Mr. Markham Senior. We grew up together, he and

I—well, all of us. Mrs. Russell, as well. You remember Mrs. Russell." It wasn't a question because Mrs. Russell was nothing if not memorable, especially if one happened to be associated with the occupation army in any way.

"I… Yes," Kate said. Maria had told her that the war was not over for Mrs. Russell—and never would be. She was as militant as Mrs. Kinnard was imperious, and she had single-handedly ended an alliance between her daughter and one of Max's officers. The disappointed young major had even reenlisted—much to Mrs. Russell's and his family's dismay—just to stay near her. So sad, Kate thought.

Together, Mrs. Russell and Mrs. Kinnard were a force majeure in this town, a walking, talking tribulation to all who had the misfortune to wander uninvited into their realms.

"Mr. Markham Senior was always 'Bud' to me," Mrs. Justice continued. "He was a bit of a rascal in his youth—and so was Robbie. You know, everyone says the love of a good woman is what turned Bud around, but that's not quite true. It's not enough that the good woman loves the rascal. The rascal has *got* to love the good woman, too. And if he loves her enough not to cause her worry or pain ever again, *that's* when it works out just fine. Or so *I* believe. And Robbie… well, before the war he was what you might call a regular brawler in the saloons and the…um…other places. Marriage to the right woman—somebody he loved— could have fixed him as well, I'm sure." She gave a quiet sigh. "Sometimes I think I can still feel Bud in this room. It's—" she looked around at everything "— nice. If only he'd lived to see this day and his older son come home again—or perhaps he does see it. His boys were everything to him. Everything."

"Mrs. Justice!"

"I do believe I hear my name," Mrs. Justice whispered with a slight giggle. "It's quite all right, though. I'd put my hand in the fire for Bud's son." She had such a wistful look on her face, and Kate suddenly realized that this woman had once loved Bud Markham beyond their having shared a childhood, perhaps loved him still, and Kate felt such a pang of loneliness and longing that she had to turn her face away.

"Oh, you should know our Mrs. Russell will be along shortly, too," Mrs. Justice said, turning to go. "Drink your tea, my dear," she said kindly. "You are likely to need it."

"Mrs. Justice!"

"Oh, dear," she whispered mischievously at Mrs. Kinnard's latest summons. She picked up her skirts and walked quickly toward the door.

"Mrs. Justice," Kate said just as she reached it. "Who is Eleanor?"

"Eleanor?" Mrs. Justice said, clearly puzzled.

"Robert Markham roused enough to say the name Eleanor. I think perhaps he thought I was she."

"Oh, that poor dear boy," Mrs. Justice said. "That *poor* boy. If *she's* the reason he's come home…"

"Mrs. Justice! We need you!"

Mrs. Justice held out both hands in a gesture that would indicate she couldn't linger because she was caught in circumstances far beyond her control. "Drink your tea!" she said again as she hurried away.

Chapter Three

❧

"**M**iss Woodard! Where are you!" The fact that the question was whispered made it no less jarring.

Am I in a hospital? Robert thought. He tried to move, but he couldn't somehow. Blankets, he decided, tucked in tight. Perhaps he was in a hospital after all—except that it didn't smell like a hospital. It smelled like…

…coffee. Baked bread. Wood burning in a fireplace. Lavender sachet.

His head hurt—a lot, he soon realized. He managed to get one hand out from under the covers and reach up to touch his forehead.

Yes. Definitely a reason for the pain.

He finally opened his eyes. A fair-haired woman sat on a low stool in a patch of weak sunlight not far from his bed, her arms resting on her knees and her head down. He couldn't see her face at all, only the top of her golden hair and the side of her neck. Was she praying? Weeping? He couldn't decide.

"Miss Woodard!" the voice whispered fiercely right outside the door, making her jump.

She turned her head in his direction and was startled all over again to find him awake and looking at her.

She took a deep breath. "I'm hiding," she said simply, keeping her voice low so as not to be heard on the other side of the door.

He thought it must be the truth, given the circumstances.

"What…have you…done?" he managed to ask, but he didn't seem to be able to keep his eyes open long enough to hear the answer.

Kate took a hushed breath. He seemed to be sleeping again, and in that brief interlude of wakefulness, she didn't think he had mistaken her for the still-mysterious Eleanor, despite his grogginess. She knew that the army surgeon had given him strong doses of laudanum—to help his body rest and to make his return to the living less troubled, he said. The surgeon hadn't known that Robert Markham had already made his "return to the living," and thus missed the irony of his remark.

She hardly dared move in case Maria's brother was more awake than he seemed. She watched him closely instead. He was so thin—all muscle and sinew that stopped just short of gauntness. Both his eyes had blackened from the force of the fall in the hallway, and there was a swollen bruise on his forehead. He hadn't been shaved. She tried to think if she'd ever been in the actual company of a man so in need of a good barbering.

No, she decided. She had not. She had seen unkempt men out and about, of course—on the streets of Philadelphia and here in Salisbury—but generally speaking, all the men she encountered socially were…presentable. The stubble of growth on Robert Markham's face seemed so intimate somehow, as if he were in a state only his wife or his mother should see.

But still she didn't leave the room. She looked at his hands instead, both of them resting on top of the latest warmed and double-folded army blanket the orderlies kept spread over him. The room was filled with the smell of slightly scorched wool.

His fingers moved randomly from time to time, trembling slightly whenever he lifted them up. She could see the heavy scarring on his knuckles, and she was sure Sergeant Major Perkins had been right. These were the kinds of scars that could have only come from fighting.

And rage.

I shouldn't be here, she thought, *Mrs. Kinnard or no Mrs. Kinnard.*

But it was too late for that realization. He was awake again.

Robert stared in the woman's direction and tried to get his vision to clear. When he finally focused, he could tell that she was the same woman he had seen earlier— in the same place—hiding, she'd said. Did he remember that right? Hiding?

She looked up at a small noise. She seemed only a little less startled to find him looking at her this time. "I didn't mean to disturb you," she said after a moment. "I'll go—"

"I wish you…wouldn't," Robert said, his voice hoarse and his throat dry. "I…don't seem to know…what has happened. Perhaps you could…help me with that."

"I don't think so," she said. "I'm somewhat bewildered myself."

"About what?"

"You, of course. You're supposed to be dead."

Robert looked away and swallowed heavily. He was so thirsty.

"Do you know where you are?" she asked, but he wasn't ready to consider that detail quite yet.

"Is there some…water?" he asked.

"Oh. Yes. Of course."

She rose from the footstool and moved to a small table near the bed. Someone had put a tray with a tin pitcher and a cup on it. She filled the cup with water, spilling a little as she did so. She hesitated a moment, before picking up one of several hollow quills used for drinking that had been left on the tray, then looked at it as if she wasn't quite sure how she was going to manage to give him the water.

Robert watched as she carefully brought the cup of water to him. He could see that it was too full and that her hands trembled, but he didn't say anything. As she came closer he could smell the scent of roses. How long had it been since he'd been this close to a woman who wore rosewater? He lifted his head to drink, his thirst making him forget the pain in his head. It intensified so, he couldn't keep still. Water spilled on the blanket, more of it than he could manage to swallow.

Appropriate or not, she put her hand behind his head to support him while he drank, but she took the cup away before he had drained it. "Not too much at first," she said. "As I understand it, when you're ill, what you want and what you can tolerate can sometimes be at odds."

"I'm not…ill."

"Not well, either," she said. She let his head down gently onto the pillow.

Robert looked at her, trying to decide if he felt up to arguing with her about it. No, he decided. He didn't. The persistent pounding in his head and the fact that he obviously couldn't manage something as simple as drinking from a tin cup on his own led him to conclude that, for the moment at least, he was some distance away from "well."

He watched as she returned the cup to the table and sat down again. He still couldn't decide who she was. *Not Eleanor* was the only thing he knew for certain— besides the fact that she was not a Southerner. Her diction was far too precise and sharp edged for her to have grown up below the Mason-Dixon Line. It was too painful to attempt any kind of conversation, so he kept looking at her. She seemed so sad.

Why are you sad, I wonder?

Since the war the whole world seemed to be full of women with sad eyes. She wasn't wearing a wedding ring; he thought she was far too pretty to be unmarried.

"My name is Robert Markham," he said after a moment because it seemed the next most socially appropriate thing to do.

"Yes," she said, watching him closely, apparently looking for some indication that she'd let him have too much to drink. "So I'm told. And you're sometimes called Robbie, I believe."

Robert frowned slightly. Incredibly, he thought she might be teasing him ever so slightly, and he found it…pleasant.

"Well, not…lately. How is it you know…who I am when I don't know you…at all?"

"I went through your pockets," she said matter-of-factly. "I found the Confederate military card inside your Bible. But three ladies who live here in the town actually identified you—Mrs. Kinnard, Mrs. Russell. And Mrs. Justice, of course. She's the one who calls you Robbie."

Robert drew a long breath in a feeble attempt to distance himself from the pain, but it only made his head hurt worse. Mrs. Kinnard. He certainly remembered that Mrs. Kinnard had identified him, and it was good that she had been correct in her identification. Mrs. Kinnard, as he recalled, was never wrong about anything. He nearly smiled at the thought that he might have had to assume whatever name she'd given him because no one had the audacity to contradict her. She would undoubtedly be the angry whisperer outside the door. It was no wonder this young woman had felt such a pressing need to stay out of sight.

He looked around the room, certain now of where he was at least, without having to be told.

Home.

In his own bed. It was so strange, and yet somehow not strange at all. It was the noise in the household that was so alien to him. Men's voices—accented voices and the heavy tread of their boots. Barked military orders and the quick, disciplined responses to them. What he didn't hear was his brother Samuel's constant racket; or his sister, Maria, playing "Aura Lee" on the pianoforte in the parlor; or his father and his friends laughing together in the dining room over brandy and cigars.

And he didn't hear his mother singing the second

verse of her favorite hymn, "How Firm a Foundation," as she went about her daily chores. Always the second verse.

Fear not, I am with thee,
O be not dismayed;
For I am Thy God,
And will still give the aid...

He had never had her kind of faith, and for a long time he had lost all hope that the words of that particular hymn might be true.

I'll comfort thee, help thee,
And cause thee to stand...

And what about now? Did he believe them now?

He had thought he was prepared for the shame of returning, but he wasn't prepared at all for the overwhelming sense of loss. That was far beyond what he had expected, the direct result, he supposed, of having been so certain that he would never see his home again. And yet here he was, despite his vagueness as to precisely how he'd gotten here, and that was the most he could say for the situation.

Mrs. Russell suddenly came to mind—and her son, James Darson Russell. He tried to remember...something. Jimmy had died in the war; he was sure of that, and yet the memory seemed all wrong somehow. He frowned with the effort it took to try to sort out what was real and what was not.

Jimmy had been several years younger than he, but he had had the self-assurance not often seen in a boy his age. Most likely it had come from having had to become the head of the household after his father's death. His mother and his sister had needed him, and he'd accepted that responsibility like the man he was years from being.

Robert smiled slightly as another memory came into his mind. Jimmy had been confident and self-possessed—until he'd gotten anywhere near Maria. Then he couldn't seem to walk and talk at the same time. He'd turned into an awkward, inelegant boy who couldn't put two words together without sounding like a dunce. It was strange what a certain kind of woman could do to a man when he ardently believed her to be unattainable. He himself had suffered the same afflic- tion when he'd been courting Eleanor and perhaps still would, had not a war intervened. But absence hadn't made her heart grow fonder; it had made it grow more discerning. So much so that shortly before the disaster at Gettysburg, she had written him a letter—her final letter to him—telling him plainly that she had decided that their reckless personalities, hers as much as his, would make for nothing but misery if they wed. He had been stunned at first, and then resigned—because he couldn't deny that their relationship was as volatile as she said it was. He'd lost the letter along with all the rest of his belongings somewhere on the Gettysburg battlefield, where it must have lain, who knew how long, soaked in blood and rain, and unreadable.

"He was killed at…" he said abruptly, aloud with- out meaning to.

"Who?" the woman sitting on the footstool asked. He had forgotten she was there. She was looking at him intently.

"Mrs. Russell's son. James Darson—Jimmy," he said with some effort, not remembering if she knew who Mrs. Russell was or not. "She was one of my mother's friends. Mrs. Russell and Mrs. Justice. And Mrs. Kinnard," he added as an afterthought. He deliberately called up the women's names because he'd lost his place in the conversation—if there had actually been a conversation—and he didn't want her to think he was any more addled than he was.

"Jimmy Russell had red hair—the good luck kind— a carrot top. I used to chase him down and rub his head before every card game and every horse race. He was always threatening to have his head shaved— just to break me of my gambling habit. Once, though, he hunted *me* down—because he heard I was going to play poker with Phelan and Billy Canfield's Up North cousins—do you know the Canfield brothers?"

"No—except by reputation," she added. He thought there was a slight change in her tone of voice, enough to signify something he didn't understand.

He looked at her for a moment. Yes. Her eyes were sad.

"Harvard men, these cousins were," he continued without really knowing why he should want to tell her—or anybody—about any of these things. Perhaps it was because he was starved for the company of another human being. Or perhaps it was the fact that she seemed to be listening that made his rambling recollections seem—necessary. "You could say they were arrogant."

"I can imagine," she said.

"Almost as arrogant as I was," he said. "It was important—a matter of honor—to win, you see."

"And did you?"

"I had to. Jimmy said he'd shave *my* head if I... didn't. Billy and Phelan would have helped him do it, too. I can't believe he's gone...so many of them..." His voice trailed away. He had to force himself to continue. "Jimmy's life was full of burdens, but he was always laughing..." He trailed away again, overwhelmed now by the rush of memories of the boy who had been his friend. He shook his head despite the pain. He had something important to do; he had to pull himself together. "I can't seem to recall where it happened—what battle. Early in the...war, I think. He was Mrs. Russell's life. It must have been...hard for her."

"It still is," she said quietly.

Footsteps sounded in the hallway again, but they continued past the door toward the back of the house. "I always...liked Mrs. Justice," he said when it seemed that they were safe from any outside intrusion.

"I believe the feeling is mutual."

"I liked all my mother's friends...but it was a little harder with... Mrs. Kinnard." He supposed that she must know about Mrs. Kinnard and her bossy nature—unless things had changed radically, everyone in this town longer than a day would know. But he only made the remark to see if she would smile. It pleased him that she did.

"All your mother's friends vouched for you. If they hadn't, I suspect you would have awakened in the stockade rather than in your own bed."

"I...don't look the same."

"Even so, they didn't hesitate."

"I'm most grateful, then."

They stared at each other until she became uncom-

fortable and looked away. It was time for her to identify herself, and he wasn't sure why she didn't. He
supposed that hiding was one thing, and introductions
were something else again.

"Miss Woodard," she said finally.

Robert frowned, trying to remember if he'd ever
known a Woodard family. "Miss Woodard," he repeated. Half a name was not helpful. He still had no
idea who she was. "And that would be the… Miss
Woodard who…hides."

"The very one," she said agreeably. "I do apologize
for intruding. I didn't intend to come in here at all, but
I thought you were still unaware, and I was quite…
trapped. My only excuse is that I've been charged not
to upset the occupation by offending Mrs. Kinnard.
I'm finding it…difficult."

"Yes, I can…see that. Tell me, do you often…go
through men's pockets?"

"Thus far, only when Sergeant Major Perkins insists," she said.

"If he's like the…sergeants major I've known, he
does that on a…regular basis. Insists."

"Well, he is formidable. They say my brother knows
everything that goes on in this town and in the occupation army. If that is true, I believe the sergeant major
is the reason." She stood and smoothed her skirts. "I
must go now and tell him you're awake."

"Your brother is…?" he asked, trying to keep her
with him longer, though why he wanted—needed—
to do that, he couldn't have said, except that she was
an anchor to the reality he suddenly found himself in.

She looked at him for a long moment before she answered. "Colonel Maxwell Woodard. Your brother-in-law. Which makes us relatives, I suppose, by marriage."

Robert heard her—quite clearly. He even recognized the implication of her brother's military title. He just didn't believe it. Maria married to a Yankee colonel was—impossible. It would have been no surprise to him at all to learn that she had wed during his long absence, but she would never have married one of them. Never.

And then he remembered. *Never* was for people who had viable options, not for the ones who found themselves conquered and destitute and occupied, especially the women. He should have been here. Who knew what circumstances had pushed Maria into such a union, and he had no doubt that she had been pushed.

A sudden downdraft in the chimney sent a brief billowing of smoke and ash into the room. He realized that his alleged sister-in-law was more concerned about him than about the possibility of a singed hearthrug. She was looking at him with a certain degree of alarm, but he made no attempt to try to reassure her. He stared at the far wall instead, watching the shifting patterns of sunlight caused by the bare tree limbs moving in the wind outside. It was his own fault that he was so ignorant. He supposed that some might find the situation ironic, his little brother dead at Gettysburg and his sister married to one of the men directly or indirectly responsible.

"I'm sorry to have put it so bluntly," she said after a moment. "I should have realized that the news might be…difficult to hear."

He dismissed her bluntness with a wave of his hand. "Your brother and Maria…?" He couldn't quite formulate a question to ask; there were so many. Seven years' worth.

"They live here," she said, apparently making a guess as to what he might want to know despite her misgivings about him. She couldn't know if he had been so uninformed by choice or because of the circumstances he'd found himself in.

He had to struggle to keep control of his emotions. He hadn't expected to hear that the Markham household as he knew it was essentially gone. Finding out that Maria had married one of them was hard enough, but it was even more difficult to accept that this Yankee colonel had taken up residence in the house where his family—especially Samuel—had lived. Lying here now, he wanted to hear Samuel's boisterous presence in the house just one more time. Samuel, running down the hall, bounding up the stairs, whistling, dropping things, sneaking up on their mother and taking her by surprise with one of his exuberant hugs. Robert smiled slightly. It had cost the household a whole dozen eggs once when Samuel in his joyful enthusiasm had made her drop the egg basket she'd been carrying.

His smiled faded. There was nothing now but the tread of enemy soldiers.

No. The war is over. We aren't supposed to be enemies anymore.

"And you live here, as well?" it suddenly occurred to him to ask.

"No. I'm only visiting."

"Visiting," he said, because it all sounded so…normal. Only it wasn't normal at all. Nothing was normal anymore.

His head hurt.

"Are you—" she started to say, but he interrupted her.

"Is he good to her?" he asked with a bluntness of his own. "I want to know." He turned his head despite the pain so that he could see her face. The question was disrespectful at best, and far too personal under the circumstances. He knew perfectly well that she would likely be the last person to give him a truthful answer, especially when the question in and of itself suggested that he had no faith whatsoever that her brother could behave well toward a Southern woman.

But it couldn't be helped. She was his only opportunity, the only person who might actually know.

She didn't seem to take offense, however. "He is as good to her as she will let him be," she said. "He has to be careful of her Southern pride."

"And you see…that as a…problem?"

"No, I see it more as a token of his regard for her. He was quite smitten."

"Was. He isn't smitten now?"

"The word suggests to me a transient kind of emotion, Mr. Markham," she said, clearly trying to explain. "I believe what my brother feels for Maria is a good deal more than that. Maria has made him happy—when he thought he would never be happy again. The war…"

"Yes," he said when she didn't continue. "The war."

"He was a prisoner," she said after a moment. "Here."

"And now he's the…?"

"Occupation commander."

"That must be…satisfying, given his…history."

"If you're talking about an opportunity for revenge, it might have been just that, but for Maria. He loves her dearly. And it isn't one-sided, Mr. Markham."

"What do the townspeople think of the marriage?"

"That would depend upon whom you ask, I believe."

"Has she suffered for it—for marrying a—the colonel?"

"The fact that Mrs. Justice and the others are here in the house ready to take care of her brother, and have been since you arrived, would suggest that she hasn't."

She was still looking at him steadily, trying to decide, it seemed to him, precisely how much he should be told of his sister's situation. At this point he was certain there was more. Perhaps Mrs. Justice would know. Asking Mrs. Russell and particularly Mrs. Kinnard was out of the question.

He loves her dearly.

And Maria apparently loved him in return. That was the most important thing, wasn't it? He couldn't want more for Maria than that. But, whether she was happy or not, he still had to face her—and his father. He closed his eyes. He dreaded it, almost as much as he dreaded facing Eleanor. He had never answered her letter, but even after all this time, there were things still to be said.

He took a wavering breath. The things he'd done—and not done—had become overwhelming and indefinable. His sins were so many he couldn't separate them out anymore. They had all melded into guilt, into sorrow, into a relentless sense of regret. There would be no fatted calf for his homecoming, nor should there be. He didn't deserve one, not when he'd abandoned what was left of his family the way he had, and the worst part was that, despite the progress he'd made, he was still lost in the relentless apathy that passed for his life.

I need Your help, Lord, he thought. *I have to make*

this right if I can. If I haven't waited too long. If the damage can be undone.

"Who is here in the house?" he asked abruptly.

"Right now? Mrs. Kinnard—she comes and goes. Mrs. Russell and Mrs. Justice are here on a more permanent basis for propriety's sake. And Sergeant Major Perkins. Several soldiers from the garrison who are usually assigned to the infirmary—they've been taking care of you. The army surgeon is in and out. And there are one or two other soldiers whose job it is to keep Mrs. Kinnard happy."

"And my father?" he asked. "Where is he?"

She looked surprised by the question. "I'm sorry, Mr. Markham. Your father died not long after Maria and Max were married," she said.

He took a deep breath, and then another, trying to distance himself this time from a different kind of pain. Coming home, getting this far, had been the hardest thing he'd ever done in his life. He had known that the old man might not still be alive, but he had hoped—prayed—that that would not be the case. Incredibly, he hadn't realized how much he was counting on his father being here.

Dead and gone. Like Samuel. Like Jimmy Russell. Like so much of his life. His faith was strong enough for him to believe that they would all meet again; in his heart he knew that. But surely he hadn't thought he could come home after all this time and find that the important things would have remained the same? The sorrow he felt at this moment told him that he had.

He knew she watched him as he tried to process the information she had given him so ineptly. He was grateful she hadn't just left him to try to understand all the things she'd told him on his own.

"My father— Do you know...what happened?" he asked after a moment.

"He was very ill. It was his heart," she said. "They had to hurry the wedding on account of it—at his request, because he wanted to see Maria as a bride. And his doctors advised that there could be no delay."

"My father approved of the marriage, then."

"Yes. He was quite fond of Max, and he…" She hesitated, apparently uncertain as to whether he was up to hearing the details of his sister's marriage to a Yankee colonel.

"Go on," he said. "I need to know."

"He made sure that Maria could live here as long as she wanted. It was in his will. He was worried that something might happen with the occupation and the house might be confiscated if Maria owned it. So he left it to Max. Your father trusted him to take care of her—they had long talks together about it. The ceremony was held here in the upstairs, the wide hallway right outside his room on the other end of the house. He could see and hear everything. Maria looked beautiful—she wore the earrings you and Samuel gave her before you left for the war—"

"We thought she would marry Billy Canfield. Where is he? Why didn't she?"

"You would have to ask her about that," Kate said.

"My father was pleased about her marrying your brother," he said. It wasn't a question, but the whole idea of such a thing was hard for him to believe.

"Yes. He was. I think it was a very enjoyable day for

him. Lots of food and drink and good company, and I'm certain he sneaked at least one cigar."

Robert smiled briefly at hearing that his father's love of cigars had never waned. At least he had had something pleasant to focus on at the end of his life. "An enjoyable day. That's good. I'm…glad."

"I liked Mr. Markham very much," she said after a moment. "We would talk sometimes."

"Did he ever—" He suddenly stopped, unable to bring himself to ask the question.

"What were you going to ask?"

"I— Nothing."

"He spoke of you once," she said, and once again he thought she was trying to second-guess what he might want to know.

"He said you were his warrior son. And Samuel, his poet."

Robert looked away. He had thought he was ready to hear these things, but he wasn't. Had he not been such a hotheaded "warrior," Samuel might be alive today.

He forced himself to push the conversation in a different, but no less painful, direction.

"The colonel—isn't here?" he asked.

"He and Maria and the boys left for New Bern three days ago."

"Boys? There are…children?"

"Three. Two are adopted. One, the youngest, is their birth child. My brother had military business to attend to in New Bern and he wanted his family with him. And Mrs. Hansen."

He looked at her sharply. "Mrs. Hansen?"

"She helps Maria with the children. The boys are quite a handful."

"You're talking about Warrie Hansen?"

"Yes. You would know her, I think."

"I did," he said. "A very long time ago."

So, Robert thought. Now he knew where he could find Eleanor's mother at least.

"How…long have I been…?" He couldn't quite find a word to describe his current condition. He felt as if he had slept a long time, but he didn't know why or how. He reached up to touch his forehead again. It still hurt.

"You arrived the day they all left," she said.

"Poor…timing on my part. Or perhaps not," he added after a moment, primarily because of the look on her face.

"Given the circumstances," Kate said, "it would have been alarming for Maria to suddenly come upon you the way I did, but, given the state that you were in that day, I think it would have been even worse. When you fell in the hallway, you hit your head on the parquet floor. Hard. The army surgeon says your collapse was caused by hunger and exhaustion from trying to travel on foot through the deep snow. That, and the wound you received, I assume, at Gettysburg. He says it left you—"

"I know how it left me," Robert said. He lived with the pain every day and with being less than he'd once been both physically and mentally. He was thirty-three years old, and he felt like an old man.

But he suddenly remembered. "Mrs. Kinnard was there—when I was on the floor."

"Yes," she said.

"I remember…bits of it. She was upset with me. It was like…when the Canfield brothers and I tipped over…one of her outhouses."

She looked at him with raised eyebrows. "I can see why Maria thinks Robbie may demonstrate a mischievous streak when he's older."

"Robbie?"

"Max and Maria's little boy. He's named for you. The other two, Joe and Jake, are Suzanne and Phelan Canfield's sons. Max adopted them after she died."

Robert closed his eyes, his mind reeling. A nephew named after him? Suzanne Canfield dead? And Eleanor. What had happened to Eleanor?

"I shouldn't be in here," she said suddenly. She moved quietly to the door, opening it slightly and peering into the hallway for some sign of Mrs. Kinnard.

"I think you should rest," she said over her shoulder. "The night you arrived, you were in no condition to either get or give explanations. You're better now, and you're going to need all the strength you can muster if you intend to try to make Maria understand why you did what you did. I don't think it will be easy. I know how I would feel if I were in her place and Max had suddenly come back from the dead. Truthfully, I don't envy you the attempt."

Robert didn't say anything. She was quite straightforward, this new sister-in-law of his.

"I have a favor...to ask," he said, despite the inappropriateness of doing so. "Two favors."

"All right. Ask."

"Would you tell the sergeant major that I'd like to talk to an army chaplain. Tell him I want to talk to one who has seen the elephant. Someone who's fought in battle and survived. Will you do that?"

"Yes," she said without hesitation.

"And I would consider it a kindness if you would find

out whatever you can about Miss Eleanor Hansen—
where she is."

He expected her to ask him for explanations, but she
didn't. She nodded, and after one final cautious look
into the hallway, she slipped away.

Chapter Four

What is wrong with me? Kate thought as she made her way to the kitchen. Hiding from a woman she had every right to challenge in her own brother's house. It wasn't like her to hide. Keep silent, yes. Endure, yes. But not this.

She gave an exasperated sigh. She knew perfectly well that it wasn't the hiding alone that had her so disconcerted. It was that she had willingly engaged in a prolonged conversation with a strange man—albeit a relative by marriage—in his—*her*—bedchamber.

She wasn't really certain why she'd tarried so long with Robert Markham—except that he wasn't like any man she'd ever met. He was literally her enemy, of course, an active participant in the war responsible for Grey's death and for Max's nearly fatal imprisonment, and yet there was something…else about him, something she couldn't begin to define. Perhaps it was the contrast between his rough physical appearance and his quiet demeanor. Or seemingly quiet demeanor. Even that was an intriguing puzzle to her. His eyes weren't quiet at all. They were so intense and intimidating—a look she thought he might have perfected in the prize-fighting ring.

And yet he'd seemed perfectly willing to have her take refuge from Mrs. Kinnard at his inconvenience. She had immediately sensed that he would have given her whatever help she had required, if he could, whether he knew her or not. She decided that perhaps it was the knight-in-shining-armor quality Southern men were purported to have, but she had no experience in that regard and therefore couldn't possibly know with any certainty. All she knew of the group as a whole was what Maxwell and Grey had both told her—that they were worthy enemies and excellent horsemen, things soldiers—cavalrymen—apparently found time to note and admire despite their determination to kill one another.

"It is *Tuesday,*" Mrs. Kinnard suddenly announced behind her, once again making Kate jump. And the woman made it sound as if *Tuesday* was a very bad thing to be.

Kate waited as patiently as she could to be enlightened, but so did Mrs. Kinnard. And the impasse it created continued to the point where poor timid Mrs. Justice and the two orderlies who would have walked past them in the downstairs hallway immediately changed their minds and went back in the direction they had just come.

"How may I help you, Mrs. Kinnard?" Kate said finally, capitulating once again for Max's sake. But it wasn't just her need to keep the peace that made her try to be agreeable. She couldn't help but think of Mrs. Russell's lost son, and she intended, by keeping Mrs.

Kinnard pacified, to be able to write her letter to Harrison at some point without interruption, a very long letter, whether John's parents would interpret it as intruding into his life or not.

John's parents.

She never thought of the Howes as Harrison's parents.

There was a good chance that the trains would be running again after the heavy snow. If so, she wanted to make sure her letter would go out today. Her son was still in this world, and even if she couldn't be with him, couldn't see him, she could still have written contact and through his return letters know how he fared.

"I have had no communication from your brother," Mrs. Kinnard said, interrupting Kate's thoughts. "None. I should have heard from him by now."

"I'm afraid I couldn't say why you have not, Mrs. Kinnard. Perhaps the heavy snow has brought the telegraph lines down—or some other…incident regarding the telegraph has occurred," Kate added with enough significance to make her point. Diehard Rebels were still known to disrupt the telegraph messages in any way they could, and Kate had no intention of taking the blame for that or the weather. "Whatever the reason, he won't return until his military duties are satisfied."

"Well, I need to hear from him," Mrs. Kinnard said, clearly not placated by mere logic.

"And I'm sure you will. When he is able."

"And if Robert Markham dies without seeing Maria? What then?"

"He's awake now," Kate said. "Perhaps he won't die."

"Awake? Why was I not told!"

"I've just told you, Mrs. Kinnard. And I've carried out his request—"

"What request?" Mrs. Kinnard asked, immediately seizing on the remark as if something underhanded was afoot. And her tone suggested that she already knew she wasn't going to be happy with Kate's answer.

"He's asked to see the army chaplain—I've just advised Sergeant Major Perkins," Kate said—or tried to.

"What utter nonsense! Robert Markham has his own pastor! If it's spiritual comfort he needs, I can send for Mr. Lewis right now!"

Mrs. Kinnard made an abrupt about-face and headed toward the main staircase—apparently because she suddenly realized she could go directly to Robert Markham's room and have this whole matter straightened out in no time.

Kate watched her go, feeling more than a little guilty that she'd unleashed the woman upon him without warning. Unlike Kate, he couldn't hide.

But the sergeant major intercepted Mrs. Kinnard at the bottom step and stood firmly between her and her obvious desire to ascend.

"I *will* see him, Mr. Perkins," Kate heard Mrs. Kinnard say.

"Yes, ma'am, you will. But not now. He's asked to talk to the chaplain and with us not knowing how much strength he's got at the moment, he's not going to use it up on anything but that."

"*She* says he has asked for *your* chaplain," Mrs. Kinnard said, swinging her arm around to include Kate.

"Yes, ma'am. He has."

"Well, I don't believe it! Clearly, he's not himself!"

"Just the same, he's not going to be bothered until after we get him the kind of chaplain he says he wants—"

"And what kind is *that,* pray tell?"

"He wants one who's seen the elephant. He's the colonel's brother-in-law so that's what he's going to get. In the meantime nobody is going to be seeing him but the hospital orderlies assigned to look after him. I saw that tongue-lashing you gave him when he was down on the floor, Mrs. Kinnard. He doesn't need any more of that. He is going to be just as calm and rested as he is right now when the chaplain gets here. After that, *then* we'll see."

"Indeed we will!" Mrs. Kinnard said. "You should be mindful that Robert Markham is one of *our* people. He's not *yours* to direct as you please. Elephants, indeed!"

"And I remind you, ma'am, who won this war. It would be better for us all if you went somewhere and waited until I send for you. And right *now,* if you please. I don't want to take exceptional measures, but I have the authority to do just that if I see fit."

Kate stayed well out of the set-to, advancing only after Mrs. Kinnard had turned on her heel and headed for the dining room in a huff.

"How is it *I* have to maintain the peace for my brother's sake and you don't?" she asked the sergeant major.

"I am maintaining the peace, Miss Kate," Perkins said.

"It sounded more like you might shoot her."

"What I'm doing is trying to make sure that *Mrs.* Colonel Woodard finds her brother in the best state of mind and health possible when she gets back here. I'm thinking Mrs. Kinnard isn't going to be much help when it comes to either of those things. And I'm thinking if the colonel's lady is happy, then the colonel will be too. Which means, so will I. And probably you, too," he added for good measure. "If you remember, he's not going to be expecting to find *you* in the middle of all this."

Kate frowned at his annoyingly perfect logic. No. Max definitely wouldn't be happy that she wasn't where she was supposed to be. "As much as I hate to admit it, I think I have…things to learn, Sergeant Major," she said.

Sergeant Major Perkins was only too happy to take her at her word. "Yes, Miss Kate, you do," he said without even a token regard for her feelings. "For example, now would be a good time for you to go and apologize to Mrs. Kinnard for my very disrespectful behavior. Tell her your brother will hear of it, after which I'll be disciplined accordingly."

"I don't see how that will help."

"As you said, you have things to learn. It's time to start learning. If you please," he added respectfully.

"I am not going to lie, Sergeant Major," she said, despite having lived in a huge web of untruths for more than half her lifetime. The fabrication regarding Harrison's birth had been foisted upon her; she'd had no choice. In this matter she did.

"There is no lie in what I want you to do. I gave you the easy part. It's going to be harder to get the colonel's brother-in-law the chaplain he's asked for. It might take a while. We have to find him and then we're likely going to have to sober him up. The man gets into the O Be Joyful every chance he gets."

Kate frowned. "Then I don't think he's going to do."

"He's the only one we got who fits the bill," Perkins said matter-of-factly. "What would be very helpful now is for you to go and mend the fence I just knocked down. If you please," he said again, tilting his head in the direction Mrs. Kinnard had gone.

She didn't please. She didn't please *at all*. But she went.

"Miss Kate," he called as she reached the dining room door. "The company baker has made up a big batch of those shortbread cookies you like so much. They're locked in the pantry. Maybe you and the ladies would like some of them. They'd go nice with a pot of tea."

"You are bribing me with cookies," she said incredulously.

"That I am, Miss Kate."

She shook her head in exasperation, then took a deep breath before she opened the dining room door and went in. She was surprised to find Mrs. Justice and Mrs. Russell sitting at the long mahogany table, as well.

And the gathering felt more like a planned meeting than a happy coincidence. She wondered if she was to have been included, if that was the reason Mrs. Kinnard had been so determined to find her.

"What are you doing here?" Mrs. Kinnard said immediately, her rudeness causing Mrs. Justice to make a small sound of protest.

"This is my brother's house," Kate said calmly. "And if by *here,* you mean this room, I…wanted to ask if you might like some tea and shortbread cookies while we wait for Mr. Markham to see the chaplain—"

Mrs. Kinnard bristled at the mention of the clergyman she hadn't approved.

"Robert Markham has his own pastor, one who has known him since he was a boy," she said. "I can't imagine why he would want anyone else."

"He didn't say why. I believe he wants to speak to someone of faith, but he also wants someone who has been in battle, as he has. That's what 'seeing the elephant' means, that one has fought the enemy and survived."

The women looked at each other. Mrs. Kinnard must have more questions, but apparently she had no intention of asking Kate.

"I would like some tea," Mrs. Justice offered timidly from her seat at the far end of the table. "And cookies. I dearly love cookies. Mrs. Russell and Mrs. Kinnard do, too."

"I have no interest in…cookies," Mrs. Russell said, but Kate heard "*her* cookies."

"Nor I," Mrs. Kinnard assured her.

"Of course you do," Mrs. Justice said, stopping just short of blatantly insisting. "Remember when all three of us got into trouble for eating the cookies that were left cooling on the windowsill at old Mrs. Kinnard's house? I can still smell that wonderful aroma after all these years. Don't you remember? We were all three riding on my brother's decrepit old brindled mare. We got a whiff of those cookies and off through the spirea hedge we went. And we made the poor old nag go tree to tree and shrub to shrub until we got close enough to snap those cookies up—I don't know what that horse must have thought. Now *these* cookies we won't have to…um, borrow."

Incredibly, Mrs. Russell smiled. "We did do that, didn't we?"

"I don't recall any such thing," Mrs. Kinnard said. "The very idea. *I* certainly never took cookies from my mother-in-law's windowsill."

"Oh, for heaven's sake, Acacia," Mrs. Russell said. "She wasn't your mother-in-law then. We were only seven. You do remember being seven, I hope."

"Six," Mrs. Justice said. "And already well on our way to a highwayman's life—just as soon as we got a better horse."

Mrs. Justice and Mrs. Russell looked at each other, then burst out laughing, and Kate couldn't keep from smiling. Mrs. Kinnard, however, remained unmoved.

There was a polite knock—kick—on the door, and Kate went to open it. A young soldier stood in the hallway, struggling to hold on to a large silver tea tray laden with a matching teapot and a mound of cookies and mismatched china cups and serving plates.

"Sergeant Major Perkins asks if you would like tea and cookies, Miss Woodard," he said as if he'd re-hearsed the line any number of times. Clearly, Perkins wasn't taking any chances that Kate wouldn't carry out his plans for fence mending.

"Do we?" Kate asked, looking over her shoulder at Mrs. Kinnard, giving her the final word.

"Wouldn't it be rude not to accept Miss Woodard's hospitality?" Mrs. Justice said behind her hand to Mrs. Kinnard—as if Kate couldn't hear her. "I believe all three of our mothers taught us how to behave in some-one else's home, no matter what the circumstances might be."

"Oh, very well," Mrs. Kinnard said, clearly exas-perated. "Since it's here. Bring in the tray," she said to the soldier. "Put it there. Will you pour or shall I?"

she asked, clearly startling him to the point that even she realized it.

"Good heavens! Not *you*," Mrs. Kinnard snapped—to the young soldier's obvious relief. *"Her."*

"I would much prefer that you poured, Mrs. Kinnard, if you would be so kind," Kate said, assuming that she was the target of Mrs. Kinnard's remark. "Unfortunately I haven't had that much practice. My mother always chose to use the Woodard heirlooms rather than storing them, and she was always worried I would break something—with good reason." She was telling the truth, but she was also trying to do as Perkins wanted and lay some groundwork before she made an attempt to soothe Mrs. Kinnard's decidedly ruffled feathers. Besides that, she wanted to focus her attention on what was happening upstairs with Robert Markham.

"Indeed," Mrs. Kinnard assured her. Believing that a catastrophe would be imminent if anything breakable found its way into Kate's hands was clearly no hardship for her at all.

Mrs. Kinnard frowned at the mismatched cups and saucers on the tray, and for a moment Kate thought she was going to comment on it. But then she must have remembered what had likely happened to the set. "Maria went to such great trouble to hide her mother's things when the house was looted," she said. "We must do our best to preserve her tea service, after all."

"My thoughts exactly," Kate said, smiling. She understood perfectly that she was supposed to cringe at the insinuation that she had political and regional ties to the looters, and that as a hostess, she left much to be desired. But being able to preside over the pouring of tea didn't matter to her in the least and hadn't since

Harrison was born. She gave a soft sigh at the sudden thought of him. She wanted desperately to be away from Mrs. Kinnard and the others so she could at least write to him. She had been so faithful in her correspondence to him that she liked to think he might even anticipate the arrival of her letters. She always tried to make them as interesting as she could in the hope that he would look forward to the next one. Perhaps she would tell him about the strange return of the man upstairs.

The tea pouring proceeded in silence and without mishap.

"Tell me, Mrs. Justice," Kate said at one point in an attempt to foster enough mild conversation to carry out her mission. "What other adventures did you have when you were a little girl?"

Mrs. Kinnard gave her a warning look. She clearly didn't want any more disclosures regarding her childhood. Kate tried not to smile again at the mental image of the three of them riding an ancient horse and trying to make it to those cookies on the window ledge without being seen. Somehow she couldn't get past imagining them dressed just as they were now.

But Mrs. Justice was saved having to answer by a loud commotion in the foyer. Kate thought for a moment that Mrs. Kinnard was going to get up and go see what was occurring for herself, lest the chaplain get by her without her having the opportunity to give him both his instructions and her opinion of his being brought here in the first place.

"Well, how drunk is he!" they all heard Perkins say.

Kate couldn't make out the reply. She worked on looking as if she had no idea what that comment might mean.

"Get him in here and sober him up! Stick his head in a bucket of snow if you have to!"

"Soldiers do seem to have unusual solutions to their predicaments, don't they?" Mrs. Justice commented mildly as the commotion intensified and moved past the dining room door toward the back of the house. She took another sip of tea and looked at Kate. "What did Robbie say, my dear? Did he mention where he'd been at all?"

"I didn't ask him anything about that," Kate said.

"Oh! Of course not," Mrs. Justice said, apparently alarmed that she'd dared suggest such a rude and thoughtless thing. "That wouldn't have been a good idea at all. But you did talk to him?"

"He had…questions. He didn't seem to remember what had happened to him." She took a quiet breath. "He didn't know his father had died."

"Oh, that poor, poor boy," Mrs. Justice said.

"And did he know about Maria's marriage?" Mrs. Kinnard asked.

"No. He didn't."

"I'm sure he was upset about *that,* as well."

"He is Maria's brother. He would naturally be concerned about her. Fortunately I could reassure him."

"Indeed yes," Mrs. Justice said. Mrs. Kinnard and Mrs. Russell both gave her a hard look.

They could hear a second arrival in the foyer and then heavy footsteps going up the stairs.

"That must be the chaplain, don't you think? Poor Robbie," Mrs. Justice said again.

"Poor Robbie, indeed," Mrs. Kinnard said, setting her cup down hard despite her desire to keep Maria's mismatched tea service safe. "He'll get no spiritual comfort *there*."

"Sounds like their army surgeon to me," Mrs. Russell said. "For a thin man, he has a very heavy tread. But then they *all* do."

Kate took a breath and tried not to consider what in the world could have been behind the remark. Her head was beginning to hurt, despite the tea and the excellent cookies. No matter what Sergeant Major Perkins thought, there were some things cookies just wouldn't fix.

"I'd like to say a prayer, if I may," Mrs. Justice said.

"For *whom?*" Mrs. Kinnard asked, as if prayers came under her jurisdiction, as well.

"For our Robbie, of course," she said. "If you would bow your heads please." She waited a moment for them to comply, then continued. "Dear Lord, we don't know where Robert Markham has been or what kind of trouble and heartache he's had, but we ask you—now that he's home again and safe—please guide us so we can know what to do for him, and please don't let us do anything to add to his worries and make them worse. Amen."

Mrs. Justice smiled and looked around at each of them. "There. I feel so much better now."

So do I, Kate thought. Incredibly, Mrs. Justice, with her gentle, forthright prayer, had reminded all of them that Robert Markham would likely need help—but none of them should arbitrarily decide what that help should be. She wondered if Robert had any idea what a staunch ally he had in this kind and pleasant woman.

Someone knocked softly on the door, and without

waiting to be admitted, Mrs. Kinnard's daughter Valentina swept into the room.

"Ah! Here you are, Mother," she said. She looked… stunning. She would have been perfectly at home in any salon in Philadelphia.

"Imagine my surprise when I arrived home—*finally*—the snow on the road from Mocksville was terrible—Aunt Matilda and Uncle Bart send their love, by the way. And here I discover you're nowhere to be found and the servants tell me you're in the middle of all this excitement about Robert Markham—and my word, there are soldiers all over the place. How is it that this house is *always* overrun with soldiers?"

"Perhaps because a colonel lives here," Kate said mildly.

"Oh. Well. Yes. Hello, Miss Woodard," Valentina said, smiling. "You're looking very…fine today."

Kate was well aware that she didn't look fine at all. She'd been alternating the same travel dress with a plain calico morning dress she kept at her brother's house specifically for getting down on the floor and playing with the boys. The fact that most of her wardrobe was likely sitting in the Philadelphia train station meant she might be alternating the two dresses for some days hence, turning whichever one she'd just worn wrong side out and hanging it on the rack in the airing room next to the nursery each night.

"You're very kind, Valentina, but I'm not at my best, I'm afraid. What a lovely dress and hat you have on," Kate said truthfully, openly admiring the bright orange shantung day bodice Valentina wore above a pale blue skirt with a pleated cream underskirt showing beneath it, and cream-colored lace at her throat and wrists. "Would you like some tea?"

"Yes—"

"No," Mrs. Kinnard assured them both.

"No," Valentina said dutifully. "I'm very apt to spill. Or break," she added, completely ignoring the look her mother gave her.

"So am I," Kate said. "I was only just telling your mother I ought not pour the tea because of it. Do you suppose there is anything we can do about it?"

"Perhaps there's hope for you, Miss Woodard," Valentina said. "As for myself—I am quite useless. Or so my mother tells me. You wouldn't believe the number of dresses and tablecloths and teacups I've wrecked."

Kate couldn't keep from smiling. For the first time in their numerous encounters since Max and Maria had married, Kate found herself coming very close to liking this young woman. Today she seemed to have no guile at all, despite what must have been her mother's diligent tutelage.

"So tell me. Is it true that Robert Markham has returned?" Valentina asked the room at large.

"Yes," Kate answered, because no one else seemed inclined to.

"Is he very changed— Oh, that's right. You wouldn't know. Is he changed, Mother?"

"I couldn't say. *I* haven't been allowed to see him," Mrs. Kinnard said, and Valentina actually laughed.

"Oh, dear. Someone is going to suffer for that." Valentina was openly teasing her mother—and somebody was going to suffer for *that,* too, Kate thought.

But Valentina didn't seem to be worried in the least. She was so different from the Valentina Kate had grown accustomed to, and she couldn't help but wonder why.

"Miss Woodard, I believe we were trying to ascertain whether or not Robert said anything sensible. Are you or are you not going to enlighten us?" Mrs. Kinnard said.

"He said he was grateful to you, Mrs. Kinnard—and to Mrs. Justice and Mrs. Russell for establishing his identity," Kate said.

"As he should be," Mrs. Kinnard said, not about to give an inch. "Certainly we will have to find out where he's been all this—"

"Why?" Kate asked, daring to interrupt. "There's no need for him to justify his whereabouts to anyone, except perhaps Maria. She is the one he has hurt the most."

"Well, there's El—" Mrs. Justice started to say.

"And *that* is not fit for civilized discussion," Mrs. Kinnard snapped. "What she became is clearly what she always was." She looked at Kate. "Or perhaps things are done differently where you come from and there is no accountability for bad behavior."

I'm too tired for this, Kate suddenly thought. What little sleep she'd had had been on one of the boys' cots in the downstairs nursery wing of the house. Mrs. Kinnard had more than proved that she intended to go to any length necessary to be offended, and Kate just couldn't endure another round of verbal sparring.

She stood instead. "I believe I'll go see if the sergeant major can tell me what is happening with my brother-in-law," she said, hoping that the term "brother-in-law" would induce Mrs. Kinnard to understand whose claim on Robert Markham took precedence. This was a family matter. No one could pacify Mrs. Kinnard at this point, least of all Kate, and she had no intention of allowing the woman to meddle where she didn't belong. Kate had no intention of coming back, either, whether she gleaned any information from Perkins or not. She had to write her letter to Harrison and she had to get away from Mrs. Kinnard before she said something to unravel Max's fragile hold on a peaceful military occupation altogether.

"I'll come with you," Valentina said.

"That's not necessary—" Kate tried to say, but Valentina ignored her and her mother's protests.

"Oh, but I want to. You must tell me about the dresses in Philadelphia—after you speak to Sergeant Major Perkins, of course. I get so lonely for my own kind sometimes. We can have a real conversation."

"Valentina. I require you here," Mrs. Kinnard said firmly as Kate stepped into the hallway. She could immediately hear raised voices coming from the upstairs. Sergeant Major Perkins stood at the bottom of the staircase, alert but not yet ready to intervene.

"What's happening?" Kate asked. "Is that the chaplain yelling?"

"Could be. Or it could be your brother-in-law," Perkins said. "Not sure who's preaching to who."

"Aren't you going to intervene?"

"Not until I hear furniture breaking," he said calmly. "Most of the time two soldiers yelling at each other won't mean a lot."

"Miss Woodard! Wait!" Valentina called behind her, and the sigh Kate had been suppressing for some time got away from her. Clearly her life would have been much simpler if she'd just gotten on that train.

Chapter Five

Where is she?

Robert kept listening for the sound of his sister-in-law's footsteps in the hallway outside his door. He had only seen her once since the hiding episode, when she'd brought him his Bible and his Confederate enlistment card, and that was two days ago. He didn't think she'd been driven to hide again because he hadn't heard Mrs. Kinnard's distinctive voice for some time now—or if she had concealed herself, she'd found a more obscure place to do it.

He was feeling much stronger; he was awake and dressed and seated comfortably in the rocking chair by the fire, like the old man he had seemingly become. His appetite had returned—much to Mrs. Justice's pleasure—but ever since he'd awakened from his laudanum-induced stupor, he'd found himself in the middle of a crossroad. Not a spiritual or an emotional one, but one that literally involved all manner of comings and goings in the house. People arrived in a steady stream at the front door, or they made their entry into the house at the back via the kitchen. However they managed to get inside, they all apparently had the same goal—ostensibly to deliver food and drink as a "welcome home" for him, but actually to satisfy their curiosity about his return. There was no surprise in that, of course; he had essentially come back from the dead. What surprised him was that the parade of would-be visitors continued despite the fact that none of them were ever allowed to visit. He had his brother-in-law's sergeant major to thank for that, and he was grateful. It was a great relief not to have to talk to anyone. Unfortunately the one person he actually wanted to talk to was prone to hiding.

Kate.

He had learned her given name by overhearing snippets of conversation in the house. "Miss Kate," the sergeant major called her. It would seem, too, that she actually did have a certain responsibility for keeping Mrs. Kinnard pacified, and he didn't envy her that.

He was also learning more about the soldiers assigned to the house—Bruno, who had cared for his father during his final illness and who clearly had a fondness for the old man. Private Castine, who was suffering the torture of being a young man surrounded by attractive Southern young ladies nearly everywhere he went, most of whom never deigned to speak to him and the ones who did weren't nearly so prized. Admiring someone from afar was a decidedly lonely pastime.

It came as a surprise to Robert that he rather liked Sergeant Major Perkins. The very first question the man had put to him had seemed offhand and innocent—even humorous—but it had been straight to the point: "Did you get the chaplain straightened out or not?"

It was a question for which there was likely no answer, but by asking it, Perkins had made it known that he—if not the entire household—had heard the heated exchange during what everyone had assumed was an occasion for giving and getting spiritual comfort. But he hadn't asked Robert for any details, as Robert had expected. Instead he had established that, at some point, he might, and at that time he would expect an answer.

Robert had managed to endure a short one-sided conversation with Mrs. Kinnard—she'd talked about the suffering she had endured at the hands of the occupiers; ostensibly, he listened. He'd also had a visit with Mrs. Justice, but she had cried so when she had seen him awake, sitting up and mostly himself again, that he couldn't find a way to ask her about Eleanor. Mrs. Russell didn't come to talk to him at all, and he supposed it was because he was too much of a reminder of Jimmy.

What with the influx of food into the house and the weeping, it was as if he'd died rather than come home again. He was certain of one thing, however. It had to be significant that Mrs. Justice did not once mention Eleanor. He was not so certain that Kate Woodard was going to be able to grant him his second favor and bring him the information he wanted.

He looked up at a sound out in the hallway. The sergeant major stood in the doorway.

"You sent for me, sir?" he asked.

"I… Yes. I was wondering if Miss Woodard was available. I'd like to speak to her."

"She's about to leave the house, sir, if she hasn't already," he said.

"Do you know when she'll return?"

"Couldn't say, sir. She had some letters she wanted to mail, and then Miss Valentina—Mrs. Kinnard's daughter, that would be—she kind of swooped in and pounced on her about wearing the same dress all the time. Anybody would have thought the fur would fly after a remark like that, but off together they went. Miss Woodard's got her hands full trying to keep the peace with the Kinnards. You probably already know things will run a lot smoother for a lot of people if she does," he added significantly, and Robert didn't miss his implication that whatever affected Colonel Woodard would also affect Maria, and ultimately her newly resurrected brother, as well.

"If Miss Valentina intends to address this wardrobe situation, she'll likely keep Miss Woodard hostage until she's got everything the way she thinks it ought to be. It's going to be interesting to see how this turns out, what with both of them being as determined about things as they are."

"Why is she wearing the same dress all the time?" Robert asked, commenting on the one thing in the sergeant major's report he found intriguing. He hadn't actually had the opportunity to notice her dresses, but he did understand enough about women to know that while such a situation might not be troubling to a farm woman who only had one everyday dress, to someone like Kate Woodard, it could be a catastrophe.

No, he decided immediately. It wouldn't be a catastrophe to her at all. Valentina might think it was the end of the world, but not Kate.

He frowned because he had no idea how he had arrived at that opinion.

"Well, she doesn't have much choice. All her trunks went on the train to Philadelphia. I guess you could say they went and she didn't."

"Are you saying she didn't go because I turned up?"

"No," he said bluntly. "I'm not. Anything else, sir?"

"Would you tell Miss Woodard I'd like to have a word with her when she comes back."

"I'll tell her—but I can't say for sure what she'll do about it. Like I said, she's a determined kind of woman."

"Sergeant Major," Robert said as Perkins turned to go. "Is there any word about my sister's return?"

"Not yet. Telegraph lines are down in places east of here. You would know how that goes."

Robert looked at him. It took him a moment before he understood what the sergeant major meant. In Perkins's opinion at least, and on some level, the war was still going on.

When Perkins had gone, Robert walked to the window and looked out. He didn't see Kate or Valentina—which likely meant that she was still here after all.

He took the back stairs down to the kitchen. Mrs. Justice was just putting loaves of bread into the oven.

"Dear Robbie," she said when she saw him. "Can I get you something?"

"I...was just looking for Miss Woodard."

"She's gone to army headquarters and then, I believe, on an emergency quest to the dressmaker's with Valentina. All her trunks went to Philadelphia without her, you know."

"Yes. I heard about that."

"It's terribly inconvenient," she said. "She has her valise, thankfully, but they only carry so much. I'm still not sure why she didn't go. The colonel had everything arranged. It was a good thing she didn't, though. Heaven only knows what might have happened if she hadn't been here to help you."

"Yes," Robert said, but the truth was that it hadn't occurred to him before, how timely Kate Woodard's being in the house that night had been.

"Robbie?" Mrs. Justice said, and she looked so troubled. He waited for her to ask the question she so obviously wanted to ask. She was frowning, something she rarely did in his experience.

"What is it, Mrs. Justice?"

"I— Oh, it's nothing. Here," she said opening the warming oven and taking down a plate. "Have a ham biscuit."

"You have such *adventures,*" Valentina said as they walked the distance to… Kate didn't quite know where. All she knew was that Valentina had insisted that they leave the house immediately and just go, that it wasn't too far for them to walk and that they would both enjoy an outing on such a sunny—if somewhat blustery—winter's day. Sergeant Major Perkins, in the meantime, had done some insisting of his own. He had assured Kate that she would not be going anywhere without being escorted, and he'd promptly assigned the same hapless and perpetually startled young private who had brought the tea and cookies to the dining room to trail along.

The sun was indeed shining—albeit a weak sun— but the snow was still on the ground and there were icy patches where it had melted and frozen again. The wind cut sharply at times, and the private's nose was soon red with the cold. He kept sniffing as they walked along. It was clear to Kate that he considered this duty to be some kind of torture, but she didn't think it had anything to do with the walk or the weather. She thought it was primarily because he wanted to admire Valentina openly and he couldn't, not with the firm knowledge of what Perkins would do to him if he were accused of gawking at Mrs. Kinnard's daughter. Valentina looked especially impressive this morning in her blue velveteen coat and pert little hat covered in black net and emerald-green feathers.

"I wouldn't say that," Kate said, turning her attention back to Valentina. *Adventure* was not a word she associated with any aspect of her life.

"Well, *I* would. I don't know *anyone* who ever got stranded without her dresses. You couldn't have worn any of Maria's, I suppose."

"Not and maintain any sense of propriety," Kate said, trying not to smile because the topic of conversation had apparently made the young private's ears turn as red as his nose. "I'm a good two inches taller than she is."

Valentina suppressed a giggle. "Can you imagine what my mother would say about *that?*"

Kate had no problem imagining it at all, but she didn't say so. "I must go to the army headquarters first. I want to make sure my letters get sent out on the next train. And then where is it we're going?"

"To the dressmaker's of course—Mrs. Russell's sister, that would be. She's the best dressmaker in town. She does beautiful work. I think her business is quite prosperous now that more of the officer's wives have come to share their husbands' occupation duty. I wonder if they find it lonesome here—hardly anyone talks to them, you know. Just at church and one has to be civil there. Anyway, we can hope Mrs. Russell's sister will have a few dresses mostly finished to carry you through until she can sew you some new ones. It's sad how her husband died in the war—not in the fighting—from the measles. It seems very inappropriate for a soldier, doesn't it? Dying of a child's disease, like that— Were you very afraid?"

"Afraid? When?"

"When you found Robert Markham in the house that night. I would have been terrified, especially since I thought he was dead."

"Well, he wasn't conscious long enough to be threatening, and I didn't know who he was."

They walked for a time in silence, and at one point, because the ground was so icy, the young private had to offer them his arm as they maneuvered over the spot.

"What is your name?" Valentina asked him as she accepted his help—which caused his ears to redden again.

"Private Castine, miss," he said.

"Thank you, Private Castine. You are a very diligent escort—for a Yankee boy."

The private clearly chose to hear the compliment and not the insult in her remark, and blushed in earnest this time. Kate wondered if surviving an encounter with someone as dazzling as Valentina constituted yet another version of "seeing the elephant."

The closer they came to the wide main street and the army headquarters building, the more soldiers there were on the sidewalks and in the alleys and doorways. Some of them seemed to have a purpose in being there—keeping watch for signs of trouble around the saloons, guarding army supply wagons waiting to be unloaded, directing the movement of various buggies and carriages through the deep mud and fresh manure—and some did not. And those were the ones Kate dreaded to encounter despite having an escort. She knew that Max had strict rules regarding the military's behavior toward civilians, but she also knew Max was in New Bern and that even when he was not, there had been drunken incidents like the one involving the young officer who was in love with Mrs. Russell's now officially forbidden daughter. Since her talk with Robert Markham, Kate could almost understand Mrs. Russell's unyielding position. She had lost her beloved son to the war; she wasn't about to lose her daughter, too.

How hard this all must be, she suddenly thought—for ex-Rebels like Robert. His town, his very home—his sister—had been taken over by the enemy. And perhaps worse, all his suffering for the Confederacy had been for nothing. His prolonged absence had perhaps been driven by his need for solitude and freedom from other people's expectations. If so, it was much like her own decision to miss the train, only on a much grander scale.

How strange, she thought, that she and an ex-Rebel soldier, though their situations were profoundly different, might feel the same.

Kate and Valentina continued their way toward the army headquarters, and apparently Max's authority held fast today. Soldiers promptly stepped aside for her and Valentina whenever necessary, and none of them had anything coarse to say. She was able to deliver her letters to the sergeant on duty with no difficulty whatsoever.

When they came outside again, Valentina insisted on leading the way to the dressmaker's, which, as near as Kate could understand from Valentina's convoluted explanation, was somewhere near a church and less than a block off the main street. At least they were out of the wind much of the time now, and that made the going easier, but Valentina took so many shortcuts, Kate lost track of exactly where they were. Eventually she realized that the dressmaker was actually near the church she attended with Max and Maria every Sunday.

"I always wonder what kind of tree that is," Kate said of the tall, spirelike evergreen growing in the churchyard.

"Do you? I never wonder about things like that."

"What do you wonder about, then?"

"Oh, about husbands—finding mine, that is. Don't you do that?"

"No," Kate said truthfully. "Is there anyone in particular you have in mind?"

"Oh...no one suitable," Valentina said with such nonchalance that Kate wondered if someone had caught her eye who shouldn't have. "There aren't that many men to marry since the war. The ones who did come back are so...*changed*. Mother really wanted me to marry Colonel Woodard—she thought *he* was very suitable even if he did fight on the other side—but that didn't work out."

"No," Kate said, somewhat taken aback by Valentina's candor. She wondered if the girl had somehow forgotten that she was talking to Colonel Woodard's sister.

"I should like to pick my own husband," Valentina said wistfully.

"Perhaps you can," Kate said, despite the fact that they both knew Mrs. Kinnard wouldn't stand for such a thing—ever. She looked again at the unusual tree, but it was Harrison she was thinking about. Harrison would have wondered about the tree just as she had. He was blessed with such a wonderful curiosity about everything.

What are you doing today, my dear Harrison?

He was probably in the classroom, she decided. She wished she'd asked him about his daily schedule so she'd have a better idea of what his life was like now that he was away at school. It would be…pleasant to know what was happening in his world hour by hour.

Comforting.

She would ask him about it in her next letter.

"They say he's gotten religion," Valentina was saying.

"Who?" Kate asked because she hadn't been paying attention.

"Robert Markham, of course. He must have if he asked for a *chaplain*."

"Yes, but their meeting sounded more like an out and out argument than anything that had to do with his getting religion."

"Well, if he *is* religious now, I suppose it's because he was so wild before the war—he hardly *ever* went to church. Mother said at the time that a war was the best thing that could have happened to him—because his love of brawling might actually be useful for a change. But that was before Samuel was killed. Samuel was such a sweet, sweet boy. Robert was supposed to watch

over him—and I'm sure he did—but poor Samuel was
killed, anyway. That would make him sad enough to
try to change his ways, don't you think? People used
to say Eleanor Hansen would make him settle down,
but look how that turned out."

Kate stopped walking. "How did it turn out?"

"Oh, dear," Valentina said, putting her neatly gloved
hand to her mouth. "It's so confusing. I keep forgetting
you don't know anything."

"Then tell me."

"I couldn't! It's one thing to mention such matters
in the company of someone who already knows the
particulars, but you can't discuss it with someone who
doesn't—oh, no! There's my mother's carriage. I'm
sure she's sent it to get me. I'm afraid we'll have to see
about the dresses another time. I enjoyed our walk so
much. Truly. We must do it again soon."

A carriage was indeed headed down the street in
their direction. Valentina gave Kate a little wave and
hurried to meet it, likely because Mrs. Kinnard didn't
just send the carriage to fetch her daughter; she'd come
along. Kate wondered if Mrs. Kinnard had approved
an outing at all. Her best guess was that she had not.
Mrs. Kinnard was nothing if not diligent in her quest
to find Valentina a rich and prestigious husband, and
once Max had married Maria, he was no longer important. Mrs. Kinnard certainly wouldn't want Valentina
wasting her time and energy on an unavailable Yankee colonel's sister. Poor Valentina. Kate and Valentina both were firmly ensnared by the expectations of
society and family.

Kate gave a quiet sigh and wished yet again that
Max would get home. Bearing even a small part of the

responsibility for the federal occupation of this town was beginning to weigh heavily.

"I'm going to step into the church for a moment. I won't be long," Kate said to Private Castine, because the Kinnard carriage was still sitting on the street in plain view—much to the private's pleasure—but the last thing Kate wanted was yet another prickly encounter with Mrs. Kinnard.

Still hiding, she thought with a sigh.

She found the church unlocked, and she went quickly inside and took a seat on one of the back pews, thankful that the church had been so handy. She suddenly smiled. What must God think of the things Kate Woodard found to be grateful for.

But I am grateful, Lord, even when I'm not running away from something. Truly...

Her son was alive and well, even if she did worry about him, even if he was far away from her. It was only in one moment after Harrison's birth that she'd despaired so and wished herself dead. But she hadn't felt that hopeless since. She'd been sad and worried and afraid more times than she cared to count, but all of that had always been overridden by the fact that she was Harrison's mother.

She took a silent breath and looked around the sanctuary. No one else seemed to be about. It was so peaceful here. Despite her longstanding estrangement from God, she liked this church. Perhaps it was the extraordinary tree outside, or the pleasant smell of lemon oil and beeswax used to polish the pews and the wood paneling or the way the sun shone through the sparkling clean windows. She had always felt that church buildings had personalities, and this one had such a comforting air. She could almost feel the prayers and praise of generations swirling around her. After a moment she bowed her head and recalled the part of Mrs. Justice's prayer for Robert Markham that had resonated with her so.

But her prayer was for her son.

"Bless Harrison, Father, and keep him safe. And please—*please*—guide me so I can know what to do for him. And whatever situation he may find himself in, don't let me ever do anything to make things worse for him…" She stopped for a moment, then continued, "And watch over Robert Markham. Help him with whatever he needs to do to find his way home again. Amen."

The private was waiting where she'd left him when she came outside again. He kept glancing at her as they walked along the still snowy path toward Max's house. Clearly he had something on his mind, but she didn't say anything to push him into making a revelation.

"Thuya," he said finally.

"I beg your pardon?'

"Thuya. It's a thuya tree, miss. *T-h-u-y-a*. Thuyas come all the way from China. That's what Mr. Markham says—Mr. Robert Markham what's staying at the colonel's. He says it's planted in the churchyard to show that no matter where you come from, in God's house, you're welcome."

"That's…very interesting," Kate said, but she was thinking what a complex man Robert Markham was turning out to be.

"Yes, miss, it is."

The conversation ended, and by the time they reached the house, Kate was feeling the cold. Her toes and her fingers burned and prickled with it. She entered with nothing in mind but getting warm.

"Miss Kate," Perkins said as soon as he saw her. "Mrs. Justice saw you coming. She's got some good hot tea waiting in the dining room."

"Thank you, Sergeant Major," Kate said with a smile. She couldn't think of anything she would like better than tea with Mrs. Justice "Still no word from my brother?"

"No, Miss Kate. Not yet. I sent off another telegram. I don't know how much longer I can put off Mrs. Kinnard without having to lock her up."

Kate couldn't keep from smiling.

"What did you do with the other one?" she heard Perkins ask the young private as she walked toward the dining room door.

"Her mother came and got her—in this fancy carriage."

"How mad was she?"

"About like usual, I reckon, Sergeant Major. She didn't yell at nobody. Of course, Miss Woodard, she hightailed it into the church before Mrs. Kinnard got close enough. By the time she did, there weren't nobody left to yell at but me, and I had a couple turns yesterday. I reckon she decided to rest up before she gives me what-for again."

"Go see why that wagon's stopping out front," Perkins said, and Kate heard the front door slam again.

Mrs. Justice looked up from pouring the tea as Kate opened the dining room door and stepped inside. "You look frozen," she said. "Come sit close to the fire. I've got your cup ready for you."

"Bless you, Mrs. Justice," Kate said, removing her

gloves and shawl and sitting in the chair closest to the hearth. She hesitated, then took off her wet boots as well, determined to savor the heat from the fire on her cold feet. It felt wonderful, and it reminded her again that she still didn't know precisely how to build one. "Is Mrs. Russell joining us?"

"No, she's overseeing the soldier who is cooking blancmange for the evening meal—or trying to. I believe he is balking at the addition of rosewater. Did you find yourself some dresses?"

"No," Kate said, taking the cup of steaming tea Mrs. Justice offered her, holding it in both hands rather than pretending she was a lady and not cold at all. "Mrs. Kinnard came and fetched Valentina before we got to the dressmaker's."

"Hmm," Mrs. Justice said.

"My thoughts exactly," Kate assured her.

"Did you see Robbie when you came in?"

"No, why?"

"He was asking after you earlier," she said. "He may still be in the kitchen. He was visiting with Mrs. Russell in there a little while ago." She gave a heavy sigh. "It was hard for them both."

"He told me about Jimmy Russell," Kate said.

"Did he?" Mrs. Justice said, clearly surprised. "I think Mrs. Russell had her hopes revived that Jimmy might turn up, too. But that's impossible, of course. A number of his comrades were with him when he died."

They sat for a time in silence, sipping their tea.

"I believe something is worrying him," Mrs. Justice said after a time. She looked at Kate. "Robbie."

"I— Mrs. Justice, Robert has asked me to find out what I can about Eleanor Hansen," Kate said, deciding to speak plainly. It was her first opportunity to actually talk to Mrs. Justice alone about the favor he had asked her to do.

Mrs. Justice frowned. "That seems— Why do you suppose he would ask *you* to do that? You don't even know Eleanor. Oh, I know. Robbie trusts you to tell him the truth."

"Does he? I can't imagine why."

Mrs. Justice smiled. "You have a way about you, my dear. There is something you carry with you that inspires trust. It's probably the reason he talked about Jimmy Russell."

"I don't think Mrs. Kinnard would agree."

"Ah, well. Acacia and I have been friends since we were children so I can truthfully say—without malice—there aren't many things Acacia finds agreeable. I've always thought it was a sad and fearful way to live one's life. We should pray for her whenever we say our prayers, don't you think?"

Kate smiled without answering. She had just prayed for Robert Markham, whom she barely knew, and yet that hadn't seemed nearly as ill-fitting a task as the idea of saying a prayer for Mrs. Kinnard. She continued to sip her tea and stared at the fire in the fireplace, thinking about the train heading north sometime today. How many days would it take her letter to arrive? One could never be sure. A week? Or much longer? In her mind's eye she could see Harrison's shy smile when it was delivered to him. Or so she hoped.

Please watch over him...

"My dear," Mrs. Justice said gently, and Kate looked up at her. "It doesn't go away," she said. "The sadness. But it does get better."

Kate attempted a smile, to reassure Mrs. Justice if nothing else, but she couldn't quite make it. "Mrs. Justice, do you know where Eleanor is?" she asked, hoping to change the subject and to satisfy the quest Robert had given her.

"I know she left town. Warrie—her mother— doesn't talk about her. Even so, she is the one Robbie should speak to. Perhaps you could tell him that. She will have the information he needs."

"I can't remember meeting anyone named Eleanor. Did she come to Max and Maria's wedding?"

"She wouldn't have come to the wedding even if she'd been invited. It wouldn't have been…proper, and Eleanor would never have done anything to ruin Maria's lovely day. So you wouldn't have met her. And if you heard mention of her at all, you would likely have heard her called Nell."

"Nell—yes. I do remember someone named Nell. Oh," she said as her memories of the woman called Nell unfolded. "Oh," she said again.

"Just so, my dear," Mrs. Justice said.

There was a sudden sharp whistle outside the door, the kind one might use to summon a horse or a dog, and it heralded a great commotion in the hallway, a running and assembling of all the military personnel on the premises—along with Mrs. Russell, who was apparently still very concerned about the blancmange.

"Perkins! What are you doing here!" Kate distinctly heard her brother ask—demand.

"Sir! You didn't get my telegrams, sir!" Perkins said.

"I did not—why are these soldiers in my house?"

"Well, it's one of those long stories, sir—"

"The short version, Perkins!"

"Sir, I wish I could oblige, but this is going to take a while to explain. And we need to keep Mrs. Colonel Woodard out of the way somewhere until I do."

"Why? What are you talking about!"

There was an added disturbance in the foyer—the boys and Warrie coming inside. And—surely not—Mrs. Kinnard and Valentina.

"Colonel Woodard, I will *not* be put off any longer!" Kate heard Mrs. Kinnard say.

Oh, please. Do not tell him the day of the week, Kate thought, remembering Mrs. Kinnard's earlier fit of pique when Max hadn't met her deadline for addressing her long list of complaints. It hadn't mattered to her in the least that he had been attending to army business in New Bern some two hundred miles away. Kate had worked too hard to preserve the occupation; she didn't want Max in his present state of mind to unravel it all.

"Our Maria's back," Mrs. Justice said happily, despite the escalating confusion beyond the dining room door.

Oh, no! Maria!

Kate scrambled to put her cup down and get to her feet, then ran for the door shoeless, but Mrs. Justice reached it ahead of her and threw it wide as she stepped into the chaos in the foyer. Kate was left staring directly into her brother's astonished face.

"Kate—?" he said incredulously. "Mrs. Justice—?" But whatever else he was going to say got lost in a long and terrible wailing sound coming from someone behind him. And it didn't stop. It went on and on. The boys began to cry, and in the sudden shuffling of people, Max ended up holding his youngest son. He thrust the baby into Kate's arms and turned to help Mrs. Justice ease Warrie Hansen down so she could sit on the bottom step of the stairs. Joe and Jake were clinging to her skirts, and Mrs. Kinnard kept insisting on having Max's attention.

And Maria—

Maria was standing just inside the front door, staring past Kate toward the rear of the house, her face ashen. And then her eyes rolled upward and her head tilted back. She grabbed for Valentina's arm as she sank into a heap on the floor. Valentina's squawk of alarm added to the din, and Max moved her bodily out of the way so he could get to Maria. Perkins was barking orders, sending a runner for the army surgeon and the rest of his soldiers to either help clear the foyer of unnecessary people or get out of the way.

And Warrie Hansen was still sobbing.

"Joe! Jake!" Kate said to the boys, holding out her free hand. "Come here!" Surprisingly, they ran to her, and she took them back toward the kitchen, carrying Robbie, leading Joe and essentially dragging Jake, who held on to the folds of her skirt with both fists. Her only thought was to get them out of the melee, but Mrs. Justice and Mrs. Russell decided to bring Warrie Hansen down the hallway to the nursery wing so she could lie down. Kate and the boys were decidedly in the way. Mrs. Justice kept trying to soothe Warrie, but it was having no more effect than Kate's trying to soothe the boys. Their crying escalated, and Kate felt like crying right along with them.

Kate stopped short as she realized that Robert Markham was standing in the kitchen doorway, much as he had that snowy night he'd arrived home. But she knew more about him now, and when she saw his stricken face, she understood immediately what had happened. He must have been standing there when Warrie and Maria came into the house, and both women had seen him, not knowing anything at all about how he came to be there. Warrie was still so distressed, she didn't seem to know that she was passing right by him.

"Robert," Kate said, but he was looking at his sister being carried into the parlor. "Robert," she said again because she thought he was only a moment from going to her.

"This is my fault," he said.

"Yes," Kate said. "It is. But right now isn't the time for you to try to talk to Maria. My brother has to be told what's happened so he can prepare her. I told you how it is with them. He's not about to let you make things worse. Please," she said because he was clearly determined to handle this himself, but she knew her brother, and she knew she was right. "I need to get the children upstairs," she said, but he wasn't listening. She moved around to where she could see his face.

"I need to take them upstairs."

He finally looked at her. "Give me the baby," he said.

She hesitated, then handed Robbie over to him. He took the baby gently, skillfully, and held him against his shoulder. Kate managed to get Jake to release his grip on her skirts. She took him by the hand and led both boys through the kitchen and up the back stairway.

She looked over her shoulder at one point to make sure Robert was behind her. It suddenly occurred to her that he might be too unsteady still to carry a baby, but he seemed to be maneuvering the stairs without any difficulty. When she reached the big open upstairs hallway, she considered going into the sitting room on her right, but then she kept going, leading the way to the room Robert now occupied, primarily because she could hear what was happening downstairs better from there. Once inside she gave Robert a look of gratitude for being reasonable and tried to catch her breath, then she bent down and put her arms around both boys.

"It's all right," she whispered to them. "Don't cry."

"Maria fell down!" Jake wailed, and Kate could hear Robert's sharp exhalation of breath behind her.

Joe had nothing to say. At some point, as the older of the two, he had decided to leave the actual asking of whatever questions the two of them might have to Jake. For reasons known only to him, he didn't want anyone to know he might be in need of information. He especially didn't want to be laughed at because of something he didn't understand. Kate leaned back to look at him. He was trying so hard to stop crying and be brave.

"Max will come and tell us all about it just as soon as he can," she said, moving his hair out of his eyes. "We're going to wait right here so he won't have any trouble finding us."

Kate glanced at Robert again. The baby was still crying despite his gentle swaying and soothing words. Kate gathered the boys to her again.

"I found Robbie's horse. It's on the mantel in the sitting room. Will you run as fast as you can and get it?"

They both whirled around and ran out of the room, delighted in spite of their distress to have permission to run free *in* the house. They were back in no time, both of them clutching the horse and holding it out to her.

"Thank you," she said, smiling. "You were so quick! Robbie," she said softly, moving to where Robert stood so she could caress the baby's soft curls. "Robbie. Look what Joe and Jake found. See? Look, Robbie."

After a few more moments of crying he turned his head in Kate's direction, and seeing the horse, he took his fingers out of his mouth and reached for it. But he dropped it on Robert's chest in the process. Robert retrieved it and let him take it again, smiling slightly as the baby began to bite on the horse's head.

At least one problem is solved, Kate thought. Clearly she should address the few things she could actually accomplish. She began to help the boys off with their coats.

"Joe. Jake," she said. "Do you know who this man is?"

They shook their heads, still sniffling.

"This is…" She hesitated, ostensibly to help Jake get his arm out of his coat sleeve, but actually because she didn't know how she should explain Robert to them. He was Robbie's uncle, but she didn't know how he would feel about suddenly having two adopted nephews.

"I'm your uncle Robert," Robert said for her. Both boys looked at him doubtfully.

"We belong to Maria and Max," Joe said after a moment, his voice full of suspicion.

"Yes. And I'm Maria's brother, so that makes you my nephews—"

"Maria's brothers died. Everybody knows that. Maria cried and cried. Maria's brothers and my mama—they're all in heaven. Warrie said so."

"I was wounded in the war, but I didn't die," Robert said. "And I'm here now."

"Is my mama coming back, too?" Jake asked hopefully.

"No, Jake. What happened to me isn't what happened to your mama."

The boys looked at each other, and for once, Kate thought Joe might pose a question of his own. But then he sighed and said nothing, clearly disappointed that Robert was so certain that their mother wouldn't return.

"Papa went to Texas," Jake offered after a moment.

"Did he?" Robert said. He glanced at Kate, she thought for some kind of validation. He must have assumed that both the boys' parents were dead if Max had adopted them.

Kate gave him a slight nod. This was yet another change he didn't know anything about.

"I didn't know that," Robert said to the boys.

"And Uncle Billy, too. They couldn't stay here anymore—because of the Yankees. Have you been to Texas?"

"I have. Once, before the war."

"Do you know my papa and my uncle Billy?"

"*My* papa and *my* uncle Billy, too," Joe said, giving him a push.

"Yes, I know them. When Phelan and Billy and I were just about your age, we were best friends."

"Did *you* ever get in trouble?" Jake wanted to know despite Joe's pushing.

"Yes," Robert said. "I did."

"Papa and Uncle Billy, too?"

"Yes."

"Me, too," Jake said solemnly. "And Joe," he said, careful not to leave his brother out this time.

"Well, it's hard not to sometimes," Robert said, glancing at Kate again. She came and took the baby from him and moved to sit down in the rocking chair.

"We wanted to go to Texas, too," Joe said. "But nobody wanted any boys along. I could go to Texas. I could go right now. I could go *easy*."

"Can not," Jake assured him. "We like it *here*. Maria and Warrie would cry and cry if we—" He abruptly stopped, Kate thought, because current events had suddenly given him some insight as to what that might look like. Joe leaned forward and whispered something in Jake's ear.

"Where did *you* come from?" Jake asked, looking at Robert hard.

"New York City," Robert said. He sat down on the side of the bed and patted the folded blanket next to him as an invitation for both boys to join him—which they did, Jake sitting next to him and likely still full of questions, and Joe well apart from them both.

Kate looked down at Robbie. The rocking and the quiet turn of the conversation seemed to have put him on the verge of sleep.

"Did you ride on the train?" Jake asked.

"No, mostly I walked," Robert said. "Sometimes I hitched a ride with a mule skinner."

"Well, *I* would ride on the train. I wouldn't be *walking* or riding with a mule," Joe assured him. "You should have thought of it. We rode on the train to Raleigh. Then we rode on another train to New Bern. I like New Bern. Warrie took us to see the boats. Boats and boats and *boats!*"

"I guess there were a lot of them."

"Yes!" the boys cried in unison.

"I think—" Robert suddenly stopped because Max stood in the doorway.

"I want to talk to you," he said. "Now."

Chapter Six

So. This is Maria's husband. Once his enemy, and perhaps he still was.

Robert got to his feet; he had no intention of letting the man tower over him. They stared at each other, and Robert found himself clenching and unclenching his fists as if he were about to step into the ring again, about to beat some hapless opponent bloody and reeling until he fell to the ground. He had thought he was done with all that, but how easily it had come back to him. He'd had to struggle hard to let go of his need to always respond with anger, and apparently he still did.

Watch ye, stand fast in the faith... Be strong. Blessed are the peacemakers.

"I think my brother means me, Robert," Kate said behind him. He thought she couldn't help but see the sharp contrast between the two of them—Robert raggedly dressed, disheveled and still in need of a shave, and her brother, all military spit and polish.

"Indeed," Max said. "But you'll have your turn, sir.

I require at least some explanation as to why my house has been turned upside down."

Robert didn't actually flinch when Max Woodard said "my house," and he was grateful for that.

"Sergeant Major!" Max snapped. "Gather up these boys and see if you can find them something to eat."

"Yes, sir!"

"Come on, men," Perkins said to Joe and Jake. "You heard the Colonel. I happen to know we've got cookies around here someplace. If we can find them, I reckon you can put away one or two. What do you think?"

Both boys nodded vigorously.

"And take the baby to Mrs. Kinnard," Max said.

"Mrs. Kinnard, sir?" Perkins said, clearly thinking he'd heard wrong.

"Tell her I need her help. Say I know she's very busy, but I've asked if she'll take Robbie into the dining room and keep him there for a bit. Say I'm sure she'll know what to do for him."

"Yes, sir. If anybody can settle that woman down, I reckon our Robbie can. Come on, Little General," he said, taking the baby from Kate. "Let's go see the elephant."

"Kate," Max said, holding his hand in the direction he wanted her to go

But Robert had her attention now, and he thought his brother-in-law knew it. Kate was looking at him with such…concern, but he saw no pity in her eyes. It was more a kind of understanding, and he was grateful for that, as well. But there was something else, something he recognized easily because of his wild younger days and because he'd had a sister like Maria. Kate Woodard was fervently hoping that the men around her—

her brother and he—would at least make some effort to behave in a civilized manner.

"I trust you'll stay here—where I can find you," Max said to him. And while the statement, on the surface, was at least somewhat cordial, it was by no means a request. This Yankee colonel didn't want him doing anything without his knowledge and approval, and the two armed soldiers standing in the hallway assured that he wouldn't.

"You do know the war's over," Kate said to her brother as she passed by him on her way out.

"Only for a select few," he said, and Robert certainly knew the truth of that. The Reconstruction held both sides captive and would for the unforeseeable future. And then there were the individuals like himself and like the colonel, if he had been a prisoner of war—soldiers for whom the war would never end.

Surprisingly Kate and her brother didn't move very far down the hallway, and Robert could hear them both quite clearly. He made no pretense that he wasn't listening, standing where both the soldiers left to keep him in line could see him. Neither of them apparently considered overheard conversations any of their concern.

"What are you doing here?" he heard Max ask his sister bluntly. "How did you get tangled up in all this?"

"One thing doesn't have anything at all to do with the other," Kate said. "So don't suppose that it does."

"Perkins told me what he knew about *him* being here, but he was less clear about how it is you're not in Philadelphia."

"I didn't go," Kate said.

"Yes, I can see that. The question is *why?*"

"I didn't want to go. So I didn't."

"Just like that."

"Exactly like that," she assured him.

"And why would that be, I wonder?"

There was a long pause.

"Sometimes…" Kate said as if searching for the right words. "Sometimes one gets weary of other people's arrangements." Her voice was calm yet full of significance. Robert had no idea what she might have meant, but the silence that followed suggested to him that the colonel did.

"Kate, you can't just—"

"That's all I have to say about it, Maxwell," Kate interrupted. "I mean it."

"You do understand that I worry about you."

"Yes. And I appreciate it—sometimes. Now tell me what's happening with Maria."

"The doctor and Mrs. Justice are with her."

"And?"

"And I was ordered out of the room. So I came to find out what kind of cataclysm I've walked into."

"Perhaps it's not that dire," Kate said.

"Any situation that has Perkins wearing his sack and burn face *and* Mrs. Kinnard firmly established on the premises is dire. If this man really is Maria's brother—"

"He is. Mrs. Justice, Mrs. Russell and Mrs. Kinnard have all vouched for him."

"Which counts for nothing with me."

"Then Maria will settle it."

"Yes. She will. And assuming he is who he says he is, then what? Is he going to stay around or is he going to go off and play dead just when she's used to the idea that she has the last of her family back again?

She loved her brothers, Kate. If what I've heard of this one is true, his staying isn't going to do much for Maria's peace of mind—"

Robert had heard enough. He stepped out into the hallway, causing both the soldiers standing by to move toward him.

"I want to see my sister," Robert said. "Now."

"And I want you to stay put until I tell you otherwise. I would hate to have to shoot you, Markham," Max said in response.

"I've been shot before," Robert said.

"So have I—"

"Oh, for heaven's sake!" Kate said sharply. "What is wrong with the two of you! It doesn't matter what either of you wants. I know you're used to being in charge, Max, and you, Robert, you need to make things right with Maria—but she—and Mrs. Hansen—have had a terrible shock. At least give them a chance to get their footing before you start squabbling over who's going to do what when. Honestly! Sometimes I can't—"

"All right!" Max said, holding up both hands. "Your point is well taken. Any particular reason why you're so…prickly?"

"Yes," Kate said.

"I don't suppose you'd care to enlighten me."

"Very well. *I* am not a member of your occupation army—and I don't have any dresses."

"Or shoes, either, from the looks of it. If I'm meant to understand that remark—" Max stopped because Maria was coming up the stairs.

"Here you all are," she said calmly, but she was looking directly at Robert. Her mouth trembled slightly, and she bit down on her lower lip to stop it.

How pretty she still is, Robert thought, realizing that he hadn't expected her to be. He'd seen too many Southern women completely worn down by the war, their youth and their health gone. She looked…fine, like the grown-up woman she was meant to be. But she was yet another one of the many with sad eyes, and the difference this time was that *he* was directly responsible for the sorrow he saw there—and the disappointment.

A sudden cascade of memories filled his mind. Maria, the happy and smiling baby sister who'd toddled around after him just so she could give him hugs and kisses and who'd had him wrapped around her little finger from the day she was born. Maria, dancing the evening away in her white summer dress with gardenias in her hair—while he had made certain her enthusiastic beaus knew precisely whose sister she was and what he would do to them if they happened to forget. Maria, standing on the upstairs veranda, her heart breaking as he and Samuel rode blithely off to war.

Maria.

Sweet. Funny. Strong. He'd always been so proud of her.

Yet he had deliberately let go of his life here just so he would never have to face her again. His throat ached as he realized, perhaps for the first time, what he'd given up. She was all he had left, and he could see how hard she was struggling now to rise above the pain *he* had caused her.

He stepped forward, and so did his brother-in-law.

She held up her hand. "I want to speak to Kate," she said, looking directly into his eyes.

"Me?" Kate said, clearly surprised.

"Mrs. Justice told me you were here when Ro—when my brother arrived," she said, still looking at him.

"Yes—"

"Maria, I'm the one you need to talk to," Robert said with every intention of pushing past his guards to get to her.

"No," Max said sharply. "Not until I know how you are, Maria."

"Max, I am myself now. Truly. And I know you won't understand this, either of you, but sometimes a woman just needs to speak with her own kind."

Robert looked at his brother-in-law. He strongly suspected that in this one matter they could agree. They didn't understand, not in the least.

"Will you just…stay here, please?" she asked. "Or go spy on Mrs. Kinnard. She has our boy giggling in the dining room. This is apparently a day for…extraordinary events."

"Maria," Robert said, and she looked at him for a long moment. Then she shook her head and went down the stairs.

Kate didn't wait to hear what her brother and Robert decided. She maneuvered around them and followed after Maria, despite being in her stocking feet. Halfway down the steps Kate realized what Maria had meant by "her own kind." It wasn't just that they were both women with a common interest—Max. It was that they were women with exasperating older brothers. Surprisingly they had been able to sit together on the upstairs veranda on warm summer nights after her marriage to Max and compare their experiences as "little sisters" on more than one occasion—until her sadness at

Robert's loss came rushing back again. No one in the house would understand what Maria was feeling at this moment better than Kate.

Maria put her hands to her face as soon as Kate closed the parlor door.

"Oh, Kate," she said, close to tears. "My brother is back from the dead and all I want to do is—*shoot* him! What's happened to him? His face— I don't—"

"Sergeant Major Perkins thinks he's been fighting—prizefighting."

"Prizefighting! Well, why not! That's so much better than coming home to the people—who—love—you—" She was weeping now, and Kate came closer and put her arms around her.

"We—*I*—needed him. And my poor father—he loved Robert so, Kate."

"I know," Kate said. His warrior son.

Maria took a deep breath and stepped away, crossing the room to open a box on the writing desk. She removed a small, framed daguerreotype and brought it to Kate. It was of a Confederate soldier—Robert Markham, Kate realized after a moment, before his features had been battered so.

"You see? You see how much he's changed? Mrs. Justice says you've talked to him. What did he say?"

"I did most of the talking, I'm afraid—he didn't seem to have any information about what had occurred while he was gone or after he collapsed in the hallway. I told him you and Max were married. I told him about your wedding—how much I thought your father had enjoyed it—and that he'd likely managed to sneak at least one cigar."

"He smiled at that," Maria said, but it was more a statement of hope than one of fact.

"Yes," Kate said truthfully. "He did."

"But where has he been?"

"I...didn't ask him. He told the boys he'd come from New York City."

"New York City. Prizefighting—"

"The army surgeon says the wounds he received at Gettysburg were severe. He had to have spent a long time recovering."

"But all this time he let us think he was dead!"

There was nothing Kate could say to that.

"Perhaps..."

"What?" Maria asked.

"He must have had a reason, don't you think? And it must have been...unbearable."

Maria wiped at her tears with her fingertips and began to pace around the room, apparently lost in her own thoughts until she suddenly stopped and took a deep breath.

"I thought I was ready to see him, but I'm not, Kate. The boys—Perkins is good with them, but they're so afraid something is going to happen to me like it did with their mother. I've gotten myself together enough to reassure them, but if I see Robert now, I'm just going to—come—undone. I'm going to stay down here. Will you tell Max I'm in the parlor? And tell Robert—oh, I don't know what to tell Robert. It's— I just—"

"I'll tell him you need a little time before the two of you talk—but I don't know if he'll listen." She offered the daguerreotype she was still holding.

Maria nodded and wiped her tears from her cheek again before she took it. "Tell him—ask him—if he'll wait for my sake, then. I can't bear to have him and Max at each other, and you know they will be if I can't be calmer than I am now."

"If it comes to that, Perkins will step in."

"Perkins. Yes. I forgot about Perkins. Kate," she said as Kate opened the parlor door. "Has Robert…asked about Eleanor Hansen?"

"Yes," Kate said.

"Did you tell him anything?"

"I don't really know anything to tell him. Nothing firsthand."

Maria gave a heavy sigh and looked down at the daguerreotype as if she didn't quite know how she happened to be holding it.

Kate hesitated, then stepped into the hallway and closed the door quietly behind her. And she didn't have to worry about telling Max anything. He was already coming down the stairs. He went into the parlor without stopping, brushing past her without saying anything.

Kate stood in the middle of the now empty hallway, at a loss as to what she should do next. She suddenly looked down. Shoes. First things first.

She walked quietly to the dining room, remembering that Mrs. Kinnard and Valentina were in there with Robbie only after she'd opened the door.

"I…need my boots," she said because she had no choice, quickly crossing the room to get them.

Mrs. Kinnard was sitting near the fire. Robbie stood happily in her lap, bouncing from time to time on her crisp, dark blue taffeta skirts and making them rustle in a way that was clearly appealing to an almost-ready-to-start-walking baby boy. Valentina opened her mouth to say something, but Mrs. Kinnard cleared her throat sharply, and her daughter stayed silent. Kate braced herself to hear a lecture on being seen in her stocking feet and her utter—but typical—lack of social decorum.

"Is Maria all right?" Mrs. Kinnard asked instead.

"She's...distressed."

"Yes," Mrs. Kinnard said. "And she will remain so until she's had a real opportunity to speak with Robert without interruption. This won't do. This won't do *at all.*" She stood and handed the baby over to Valentina, who was surprisingly pleased to have him.

"Hello, handsome," she said to him. "*Where* have you been? I've been looking for you *everywhere*. Yes! I have!"

Robbie grinned and removed his fingers from his mouth and tried to stick them into hers, making Valentina laugh. "No, thank you, young master Woodard," she said. "I've had my baby fingers today."

"Mrs. Kinnard—I don't think—" Kate tried to say. She was more than alarmed that Mrs. Kinnard had apparently decided to execute one of her heavy-handed plans—when the situation was precarious enough already. The last thing any of them needed was an unfettered Mrs. Kinnard in the middle of it.

"Miss Woodard, I am sure you will agree that there are some things about us here that you cannot begin to understand. I will be back in a moment," Mrs. Kinnard said firmly.

Kate sighed. Short of trying to restrain her bodily, there was no way to stop the woman. She would just have to leave that to Max.

And she still needed to find Robert and tell him as tactfully as she could that his sister was refusing to see him. She sat down heavily in the chair close to the hearth and reached for her boots, but she didn't put them on.

"You're tired, aren't you?" Valentina said after a moment.

"I... Yes."

"Well, it's been a very tiring hour."

Hour? Kate thought. Had no more time passed than that?

"Valentina, what do you think your mother is going to do?"

"Why, something for Maria, of course."

"I'm not at all sure that's a good idea."

"My mother knows what she's doing," Valentina said, smiling again at Robbie, who wanted to bounce. "Believe me. My mother *always* knows what she's doing."

Kate looked at the dining room door, listening hard in an attempt to determine in which direction Mrs. Kinnard had gone, but the exasperating woman would pick now to go about quietly.

"My guess is she'll be talking to Maria and the Colonel," Valentina said. "Where are they?"

"The parlor," Kate said. She sat for a moment longer, then began putting on her boots, but she stopped every few seconds to listen again for Mrs. Kinnard. The house was so *quiet* given the intense emotions that had just been unleashed. There was nothing, no sound whatsoever to tell her what was happening.

"Sergeant Major Perkins thinks of everything, doesn't he?" Valentina said suddenly.

"I think he has to," Kate said, but she had no idea

what had precipitated the comment and no desire to learn.

"Mother thinks I should know how to do all sorts of things for babies. The War, you know. She said there was a lesson in that terrible event for all of us—one never knows when one will have to fend for oneself."

"Yes," Kate said. She had already realized the wisdom of that, especially if one happened to deliberately choose to go it alone. "You're very comfortable with Robbie."

"Mother thinks she taught me how to handle him, but she didn't. She'd be very surprised if she knew who did. It was Sergeant Major Perkins," Valentina said, whispering now. "He told me not to drop him and to just *talk* to him like I would anybody—as if he actually understood. He said babies like that because they don't know they're babies— Ups-a-daisy!" she said suddenly, because Robbie began to bounce in earnest. "He told me about this, too. He said be ready for the jumping—babies Robbie's age love to jump. That's what he said," she added to Robbie, who grinned.

Kate turned her head sharply because she thought she heard rustling in the hallway. But if it was Mrs. Kinnard, she kept going, past the dining room toward the rear of the house.

Kate looked at Valentina, who was preoccupied with Robbie and apparently hadn't noticed anything.

"I wish there was a rocking chair in here," Valentina said. "Robbie is ready to nap, I think."

But in lieu of rocking, Valentina began to walk around the room with him, humming softly—and telling him all about a new dress Mrs. Russell's sister was making for her, down to the last detail. In a short time

Robbie began to rub his eyes and his head began to nod. He fretted for a moment, then lay his head down on her shoulder. She made a few more rounds, then walked over to Kate and turned around so she could see Robbie's face.

"He got very heavy all of a sudden. Is he asleep?"

"Quite asleep," Kate said. "That was nicely done."

"Oh, I think it's Robbie, not me. Or so Mother says. She says young master Woodard is 'unusually pleasant.' I understand I wasn't like that at—"

There were distinct footsteps in the hallway now—a lot of footsteps. Kate moved quickly to open the door and peer out. Perkins was getting the boys' coats on, and Mrs. Russell was coming along the hallway supporting Warrie Hansen, whose eyes were red from weeping. Mrs. Justice and Mrs. Kinnard followed directly behind them; Mrs. Kinnard was clearly in charge.

Maria stepped out of the parlor just as Warrie reached the front door.

"I can't stay here tonight, honey," she said to Maria. "I just can't. He ruined my girl. I can't stay here."

Maria didn't say anything. She reached out and briefly clasped Warrie's hand, then she bent down and kissed both boys. "Be good for Warrie and Mrs. Russell. I'll see you tomorrow," she said, and kissed them again.

"Is Warrie going to cry again?" Jake asked, frowning.

"I don't think so," Maria said. She reached into a pocket and took out a neatly folded handkerchief. "But if she does, you can give her this."

He nodded solemnly. Having a remedy of sorts in

his hand and ready if he needed it seemed to give him courage.

Kate moved out into the hallway closer to Mrs. Justice. "Where are they going?" she asked quietly.

"Warrie and the boys will stay at Mrs. Russell's house tonight. Mrs. Kinnard thought it would be better for them if they weren't here while Maria talks to Robert. Better for Maria, too. I imagine that's how she put it to Colonel Woodard."

And apparently Max had been convinced. He picked up both boys and carried them out to Mrs. Kinnard's carriage—an exciting prospect apparently. Her carriage hadn't reached the eminent status of a train or a New Bern boat, but as far as the boys were concerned, it clearly had its merits.

"Valentina!" Mrs. Kinnard called loudly. "Let's get this baby bundled up. Mr. Perkins! Where are his things?"

"He's all packed and ready to go, Mrs. Kinnard."

"His cup? He will only drink from his silver cup, you know."

It also happened to be the cup Mrs. Kinnard had given him at his christening, and Robbie's eventual fondness for her gift had probably done as much to keep the peace in this town as anything. It was Max's droll opinion that he liked it because he could see himself in it.

"Yes, ma'am. It's in the basket."

"Valentina!" Mrs. Kinnard called again. "Take Robbie and let his mother kiss him good-night."

"Yes, Mother," Valentina said. "Just let me get my coat."

"Robbie is going with the Kinnards?" Kate whispered to Mrs. Justice as the sergeant major, Johnny-on-the-spot as always, helped Valentina into her coat.

"Yes—and the sergeant major, too," Mrs. Justice said. "Just to make certain all goes well. I'm staying here in case Maria needs something. Or you, my dear," she said kindly and, incredibly, Kate felt the sudden prickle of tears behind her eyelids.

She stepped back out of the way as Mrs. Kinnard and her entourage trooped out into the cold winter dusk. After a moment Max came back inside. He stood with Maria, but they weren't talking, his unhappiness with the entire situation clearly visible on his face. Kate continued to wait by the dining room door. It seemed as good a place as any until she determined where she should go to be out of the way. But as strained as the atmosphere was, she was grateful that Mrs. Kinnard hadn't decided she should be relocated to another house, too.

Even so, Kate had to fight down the urge to wring her hands and pace. It wasn't as if she hadn't experienced a family crisis before—indeed, she'd even been the cause of one. But this was different. This had nothing to do with trying to stay ahead of a monumental scandal. This was about hurt and anger and forgiveness—and who knew what else.

"Sergeant Major Perkins has put a campaign table and the latest army dispatches in Bud's sitting room," Mrs. Justice said. "He thought there should be some tea and buttered bread on hand as well—just in case you and the Colonel find you're hungry while you're waiting."

It seemed that the Sergeant Major truly did think of everything. It wasn't difficult to guess what he likely had in mind. Max would be both out of the way and close by in the sitting room—and occupied if he chose to be.

"Oh," Kate said without meaning to when she saw Robert coming down the stairs. He looked tired, so much so that she wondered if he were up to this. He stopped near the bottom step.

Max barely looked at him. Instead he said something to Maria and caressed her cheek, then walked in Kate's direction.

The sack and burn face, Kate thought. Clearly Perkins wasn't the only soldier who had one. She looked past him to where Maria stood waiting for her brother to come the rest of the way down. Tears were running down her cheeks, but she made no attempt to wipe them away. Maria had earned her tears, and thanks to Mrs. Kinnard's impromptu rearrangement of the entire household, she didn't have to hide them from her sons.

"I'm going to sit myself down by the fire in the kitchen and do some knitting now, Colonel Woodard," Mrs. Justice said softly. "If you need anything, that's where I'll be."

"Thank you, Mrs. Justice. You have been a great help to me this day," Max said, but Maria still had his attention. He clearly didn't want to leave her on her own to hear whatever Robert Markham was about to tell her.

"You're welcome, Colonel Woodard," Mrs. Justice said. "Maria is as dear to me as if she were my own. Don't forget the tea," she added as she walked away.

"It's upstairs," Kate said to Max. "I think perhaps we should go drink it."

Max took a deep breath, stood for a moment then led the way toward the back stairs.

He's too used to being in charge of everything, Kate thought. She glanced over her shoulder as she was about to follow him. Robert was looking in her direction. She gave him the barest of nods, hoping he would understand that she wished him the best in his endeavor to make amends.

Hoping.

And praying.

Please help him, Lord. And help Maria and my brother. Help them all to put this family back together.

She turned and quickly followed Max up the back stairs. When they reached the sitting room, he looked at the campaign table and the leather pouch full of dispatches, but he made no attempt to read any of them. He sat down in the nearest rocking chair instead.

"This—homecoming—has been the—"

"I know," Kate interrupted, hoping to keep him from dwelling on the chaos he'd found on his arrival, not to mention her presence in the middle of it.

He sat and stared at the fire. After a moment Kate poured two cups of tea. Serving tea informally—with a brown glazed pottery teapot instead of a monstrously ornate silver one—she could handle. But neither of them drank it. They sat in silence, listening for some sound that would tell them what was happening in the parlor downstairs.

At one point Kate got up, intending to walk the length of the hallway to the head of the stairs to see if she could hear anything.

"No," Max said. "I gave Maria my word I wouldn't interfere. I think eavesdropping is included in that."

"Oh, all right," Kate said with a sigh, sitting down again. She looked at her brother, then at the dispatches. He didn't take the hint. He continued to sit, and so did she. Despite their extreme attentiveness, the only noticeable sound in the house was Mrs. Justice stirring around in the kitchen below from time to time.

Kate leaned her head against the back of the rocking chair and closed her eyes. Every now and then she sighed. With the last one Max kicked the rocker on her chair with the toe of his boot, startling her enough to make her jump.

"Max!" she said in annoyance, and he gave her a hard look.

Then he stared at the fire again—and she had to suppress another sigh.

"What do you think of him?" he asked after a moment. "Robert Markham."

"I think he wants what's left of his family back," Kate said without hesitation.

"He abandoned Maria when she needed him most."

"There must have been a reason."

"He's asking a lot of her!"

"He's her brother," Kate said simply, because that particular kinship would erase a lot of sins. "He's yours, too, regardless of how this turns out."

Max made a noise of annoyance and moved to the campaign table, apparently deciding to read dispatches after all. He dumped them all out, paying no attention to the ones that slid off the pile and landed on the floor. He read. He stopped to sign his name from time to time. Then he read some more, but like Kate, he was still waiting.

Kate closed her eyes again, only to promptly open them.

Someone—Maria—was playing the pianoforte—or attempting to. There were several false starts and stops before Kate could recognize the song. It was "How Firm a Foundation."

Chapter Seven

"Oh! I'm sorry. I didn't know you were—anyone—was— I'll go," Kate said.

Robert was sitting there in the dark—the last person she expected to find in the nursery. Both her hands were full, and she struggled to keep from dropping everything.

"Wait," he said as she turned to leave, apparently without considering whether her brother might object to his having a conversation with her, too. Kate strongly suspected that Max would do just that because, thanks to the events of the evening, he was now set to object, without rhyme or reason, to anything associated with Robert Markham, no matter what the situation might be.

She stood there, unsure whether or not she should stay or go. It seemed that she was destined to keep losing her space in the house to him.

"I don't want to disturb you," she said.

"You aren't. I was just thinking about a passage from Isaiah."

"Isaiah?" Kate said, and he actually smiled.

"Yes. I'm not as unchurched as I might look, Miss Woodard."

"No, I—didn't mean—"

"You aren't the only person who would be surprised," he said, still smiling.

He stood and crossed to the fireplace to add another log and waited until the sparks had settled. Kate looked around the room for a place to put the unlit candle and candlestick she was holding without dropping her book, some paper, an inkwell and a pen.

"I'll light the candle," he said.

She managed to hand it to him, and the candlestick, but she dropped the book on the floor in the process. He bent to pick it up and her *carte de visite* of Harrison fell out. He retrieved that as well and held them both out to her. She took them from him quickly, clutching them tightly while trying to put the rest of the things down on the small, well-used oak table in the middle of the room.

"My mother brought that table with her when she married my father," he said. "It wobbles. See?" He reached out to show her how uneven the legs were. "It was a keepsake from her girlhood, her 'something old.' I suppose it's a place for Maria's boys to have their meals with Warrie Hansen now—and whatever else little boys might want to do with their books and toys and treasures." He looked around the room for a moment as if he were searching for something else familiar.

"I see you're writing another letter," he said as he lit the candle and set it securely in the candlestick. "When I was looking for you earlier today, Sergeant

Major Perkins told me you'd gone to mail some letters," he added.

"Oh," Kate said. "I…didn't feel sleepy, so I thought I'd just have this handy—in case—" She stopped because she was running out of inane things to say. She had no idea what had passed between him and Maria tonight, but whatever it was, seeing him now, she didn't think he was the better for it.

"It's good that you keep in touch."

"I…suppose so. What was the passage?" she asked, hoping to steer the conversation to a better topic. "From Isaiah."

"'This is the rest wherewith ye may cause the weary to rest. And this is the refreshing,'" he quoted. "I think I need that—the refreshing."

"Why were you looking for me?" she asked when he didn't say anything more. She thought that it likely had something to do with his request that she find out whatever she could about Eleanor Hansen. She did have some information now, most of which she wouldn't share. She could tell him that Mrs. Justice had said that Eleanor left town, but she wouldn't say that Mrs. Justice had also told her—without actually telling her— that Eleanor Hansen was Maria's childhood friend Nell, the one who had lost her honor and reputation—or had thrown it away. And, based on Warrie Hansen's remarks as she'd left the house tonight, in her mind at least, Robert Markham was the one responsible for her daughter's downfall.

"Is it very late?" Robert asked instead of answering. "I don't have any idea what time it is. The big clock in the hallway seems to be missing."

"I understand it didn't fare well—when General

Stoneman raided the town." Kate paused, but he seemed disinclined to make any comment regarding the fate of the Markham grandfather clock. "It's just after midnight, I think," she said.

She could feel Robert watching as she moved the sheets of paper on the table a little to the left with her free hand.

"Would you…stay for a while?" he asked. The request was simple enough, and he made no attempt to justify it.

"Yes, all right," she said after a moment.

Kate sat down in the other rocking chair, which was closer to the one he had been sitting in than she would have liked. But she didn't want to make a point of moving it. She really didn't mind the proximity. What she minded was Mrs. Kinnard somehow finding out about it. Kate could hear him sit down in the other rocking chair, but she didn't look at him. She stared into the fire instead. The log he'd just put on the andirons began to pop and hiss. She wouldn't ask him about his talk with Maria. She would just leave him to his thoughts.

They sat in silence; the silence was not uncomfortable—at least not for her.

"This was Samuel's room," he said after a time. "Our father decided to take out a wall here and there to make a bigger space for one of us. We played poker for it—much to our mother's dismay. Or she would have been dismayed if she'd found out about it."

Kate turned her head to look at him. "And you let him win."

"What makes you think that?"

"Phelan and Billy Canfield's Harvard cousins make me think that."

He smiled. "How did you know about them?"

"You told me."

"I don't think I remember."

"You were heavily dosed with laudanum at the time."

"Ah. That would explain it then," he said.

"You were a good brother," Kate said, daring to glance in his direction. She wanted to know how he was. She had been too direct in her conversation with him before, and now she couldn't seem to find that kind of directness at all.

"Not good enough," he said, his voice flat. "I'm not very good at putting the things I've broken back together again."

"You were—are—a good brother," Kate said firmly. She believed that to be true even without knowing whether his remark pertained to his distant past or to whatever had happened when he'd talked to Maria tonight.

Once again the silence between them lengthened. Somewhere in the distance a dog barked. Kate held on to her book and waited, thinking of Harrison and of Joe and Jake and Robbie, all of these boys asleep tonight in a place that was not their home.

"I...don't know where Samuel is," Robert said, his voice quiet and devoid of emotion. He might have been telling her the day's date or the correct time. She could see that his hands were clenched tightly on the arms of the rocking chair.

"I know he died," he continued. "I was with him when he died. I saw the wound. I saw the light...go out of his eyes. It was there, and then it wasn't. He was gone and I knew it, but I still couldn't...

"I tried to get him to the rear, but I couldn't carry him. I couldn't get him up off the ground. I kept trying and trying. Somebody dragged him away from me. Somebody else carried me the way I was trying to carry him. I thought he must have been brought off the field, too. But he wasn't. I kept asking, but no one could tell me—" Robert stopped, and Kate could almost feel him struggling to remember. "And then I was on a wagon full of wounded men, in retreat with our tails between our legs. We couldn't believe it—Bobby Lee had let us down. It rained for days after the battle, and Samuel was still out there. In the rain. I don't even know if he was…buried. I remember the rain, but after that, it's all blank. I just—can't remember. I try but I can't. It's…gone."

"You can't blame yourself when you were wounded, as well," Kate said. She had heard the army surgeon tell Perkins how severe Robert's wounds had been. But she knew the moment she said it that he wouldn't accept that reason as an excuse for whatever had happened, no matter how rational it was.

Grey's last letter, the one that had arrived weeks after she knew he was dead, suddenly came to mind.

If you ever feel sorry for me, don't let me see it…

She took a hushed breath. Why was she feeling his loss so strongly tonight? "Perhaps some of the men in your old regiment will know, men who were there," she said.

"I think not. Samuel was—" He stopped for a moment before he continued. "He was the company favorite. Everybody loved him. They would have told our father and Maria where he was, if any of them had known. Father would have moved heaven and earth to get Samuel home so he could be buried here beside our mother. I…was supposed to take care of him and I…"

"Did you tell Maria any of this?"

He didn't say anything. "Yes" would have been an easy enough answer had he done so, and from his ensuing silence, she could only conclude that he hadn't. She felt instinctively that this one event was at the heart of everything, the prize fighting, his not coming home and perhaps Eleanor Hansen, as well. And not telling Maria about it now could only prolong both their misery.

"Don't—" Kate began, than stopped.

"What? What were you going to say?"

Kate leaned forward in the chair so she could see his face. "I was going to say don't spare her. She won't thank you for it. You said you weren't any good at putting the things you'd broken back together. If you can't find the solitude you need to sort all of this out—if it gets too difficult being home when it's not home anymore, and you can't find the…courage to tell Maria the worst of what happened to you and Samuel—don't just up and disappear again. At least tell her that you're going, even if you can't say why."

He was looking back at her. "Are you always so certain about things?" he asked.

"No," Kate said. "But when I am, I don't want to ever regret not having said so." She stood. "I'll take my leave now. Good night, Mr. Markham."

"I'm not going anywhere," he said when she was in the hallway. "You can tell your brother that."

Kate kept walking.

"Miss Woodard," he called, and she stopped and turned to look at him.

"Thank you."

"For what?"

"For praying for me."

"I—I'm afraid I'm…not someone who offers prayers on behalf of other people very often," Kate said, not quite denying that she had done exactly that.

"But you prayed for me. I could feel it. I want you to know I'm grateful. I'm often in need of prayers. I hope you will keep it up."

She stood for a moment longer. "Good night," she said without acknowledging his gratitude, and she continued down the hallway.

"My dear," Mrs. Justice whispered as she passed the kitchen door. "Will you join me?"

Kate hesitated, then followed Mrs. Justice into the kitchen. She was surprised that Mrs. Justice was still up and dressed. At this late hour she would have expected that the woman would have been fast asleep by now in the room off the kitchen she'd been sharing with Mrs. Russell ever since Mrs. Kinnard had essentially ordered them both here.

The kitchen was warm and quiet and still smelled of the bread that had been baked earlier in the day— yesterday. She was so hungry suddenly; her stomach rumbled.

"You've been neglecting yourself," Mrs. Justice said. "I don't believe you've eaten all day. Sit down at the table. I'm going to find you something. We can't have you getting sick on top of all this upset."

Kate would have protested, but she was too hungry. "Thank you, Mrs. Justice," she said instead. "Bread and butter would be nice."

"We've plenty of that. And some nice strawberry

jam. One of the soldiers brought it—young Private Castine, I believe. I'm not going to wonder where or how he got it. We'll just open a jar and have a bit of a feast. Sit—sit," she urged.

Kate sat. In no time at all Mrs. Justice had the strawberry jam on the table and had fetched the milk and butter from the cold shelf in the cellar and then sliced some bread she took from the warming oven in the cookstove. She sniffed the jug before she poured them each a glass.

"Hasn't turned. *Eat,*" she insisted. "No need to wait for me."

Kate began to eat, while Mrs. Justice went into her bedchamber. The bread was warm, warm enough for the butter to grow soft and delicious. Kate's face was sticky with jam by the time Mrs. Justice returned.

"I've made up another of the beds," she said. "You must come in with Mrs. Russell and me—at least until…the house is more settled."

Kate looked at her. Mrs. Justice had said "house," but Kate suspected that wasn't what she meant at all. She meant Robert Markham.

"I don't—"

"We must do what is proper, my dear. It's late. You can't sleep in the nursery while Robbie is sitting there—he may be in there some time. And you can't go to the room you normally use because he's so at loose ends he may turn up there, as well. You'll find the room down here warm and comfortable. There's hot water in the ewer, and I've laid out a fresh nightgown for you—one of mine, so it'll be too big, of course, but still comfortable enough for sleeping. I believe tomorrow may be every bit as trying as today has been. If it is, you will need your rest."

"Mrs. Justice, I—" Kate hardly knew what to say in the wake of the woman's kindness. "Thank you."

"You're welcome, my dear. I'm only acting in dear Bud's stead. He would want you to be comfortable in his house despite everything that's going on. Of that I am certain. Run along now, if you're finished. I want to speak to Robbie before I retire—if he'll let me."

Kate hesitated, thinking she should at least help Mrs. Justice clear the table, but the woman shooed her away.

"Sleep well, my dear," she said. "And don't forget your prayers."

The gentle reminder made her sigh heavily.

"What is it, my dear?"

"I— It's— I want to pray but I'm so—" Kate shook her head. "What do you do when everything is just a—"

"When your worries are all jumbled together and you don't know where to start?"

"Yes," Kate said. "That's it exactly."

"Well," Mrs. Justice said. "For me, two words always take care of it."

"What two words?"

"Thy will. *Thy* will. And then you take a deep breath and…let go." Mrs. Justice smiled, and Kate couldn't keep from smiling in return.

"Thank you, Mrs. Justice."

"You're welcome, my dear. Good night now."

Kate waited, listening as Mrs. Justice walked toward the nursery wing. It was good that she was going. Perhaps she could give him the emotional comfort Kate had been too afraid to offer.

"Afraid," she whispered. And she only just this moment realized it. She couldn't say why exactly. She only knew that she was and that she shouldn't have been. They had no connection beyond Max and Maria's marriage. Yes, Robert had confided in her, but it didn't mean anything. Their long conversation, when she was hiding from Mrs. Kinnard, had set some kind of precedent, she supposed. And it was always easier to tell a stranger something because they couldn't be hurt by the revelation. He was simply—

Kate gave a sharp sigh. She didn't know what he was doing, and perhaps he didn't, either. Her only certainty at the moment was that she was exhausted and she wanted to go to sleep. But first she crossed the kitchen and quietly looked into the hallway. She didn't see Mrs. Justice, but she could hear a quiet murmur of voices coming from the nursery, and she felt at least a little hopeful.

She had never been in the room the Markham family apparently kept available for visiting friends and relatives or, as in this case, people like Mrs. Justice and Mrs. Russell, who came to help when some emergency arose. Kate had always used the room upstairs whenever she'd stayed here, the one she now knew had been Robert's. When she opened the door, she could see that a fire burned brightly on the hearth. There were four beds of varying sizes, one against each wall, and a braided rug had been placed on the floor beside each of them.

Warm. Comfortable. Just as Mrs. Justice said.

Kate walked to the bed she assumed was hers—the

one with a nightgown draped across the foot. She sat down on the edge, trying to gather her wits enough to get undressed. She really wanted to lie down just as she was and feel sorry for herself. She had presumed too much in her remarks to Robert. He had revealed to her something terrible, something personally dev-astating, and she'd given him no real words of comfort at all. She'd only heavy-handedly suggested that no one—*she*—didn't particularly expect him to follow through with what he'd started by returning home, and that Maria would be the worst for it if he didn't.

She gave a heavy sigh and moved to the washstand despite the impulse to forgo everything but sleep. There was indeed hot water in the pitcher, and Mrs. Justice had laid a clean piece of flannel, a towel and some rose-scented soap next to the basin. Kate made some attempt to wash away the stickiness of the jam from her face and fingers. She would have liked to wash away the worry she felt as well, but there was nothing she could do about that or about the ache in her heart. She couldn't stop thinking about Robert Markham and what had happened to him and to Samuel.

The warrior and the poet.

What would she do if something like that happened to Harrison? Mrs. Russell—and Grey's mother—how did they bear the loss?

She pushed the thought out of her mind and finished washing up. She took the pins out of her hair and shook it loose, then put on the nightgown. It smelled of sunshine and fresh air and lavender sachet, and it was decidedly too big—but comfortable, just as Mrs. Justice had predicted.

"Bless Mrs. Justice's heart," she said aloud, borrowing the phrase she'd heard many times during her visits here and never once heard in Philadelphia. For the first time she actually thought she understood what it meant. She climbed into the bed and stretched out, savoring the lavender smell of the crisply ironed sheets, as well. It felt so good to lie down.

I laid me down and slept; I awakened; for the Lord sustained me.

She closed her eyes, but her mind raced from one worry to another unabated.

Don't forget your prayers...

She kept thinking of Harrison. Was he lonely? Worried? Afraid? And then she thought of Robert again.

Robert.

What a struggle it must have been for him to get this far; she believed that, *knew* that, she supposed, the same way he had known she had asked God to help him. It was so disconcerting to have him know that she had prayed for him—when she hadn't the right to pray for anyone except Harrison. She was Harrison's mother, and offering prayers on his behalf was perhaps the only privilege she had where he was concerned.

Don't forget your prayers...

"Thy will," she whispered. "But please help him."

And she lay there listening to the sounds of the house settling and the wind outside, knowing the prayer she had just spoken had been as much for Robert Markham as it had been for her son.

Chapter Eight

"**I** wouldn't go up there," Perkins said.

Kate wasn't close enough to put her foot on the bottom step of the staircase, but the sergeant major still presumed to know what her immediate plans were. And, of course, he was right—but at least he didn't know the nature of her business, *why* she was in such a hurry to see her brother this morning.

She had awakened sometime during the night thinking it was dawn, but a full moon had lit the room, not the sunrise. She'd lain there in the moonlight, and she had finally acknowledged something she had been well aware of for some time. She was becoming far too involved in Robert Markham's troubles. She was simply too…concerned about him, and she didn't want to be. She didn't want to worry about where he was. She didn't want to look into his eyes and see the anguish there. And she could only think of one remedy for all those things she *didn't* want. She would have to leave and return to Philadelphia as soon as possible.

Having made that decision, she had slept very late,

and she felt the better for it. She'd had a quiet breakfast with Mrs. Justice—Mrs. Kinnard, thankfully, wasn't yet on the premises. The last thing Kate needed was to squander her newfound energy crossing swords with her.

Or with the sergeant major, for that matter.

"Why shouldn't I go see my brother?" she asked him anyway.

"Your brother-in-law's up there. With the Colonel."

"Whose idea was that?" Kate asked, trying to ascertain just how distressing this encounter might turn out to be—for everyone.

"Your brother-in-law's."

"Do you know why?" Kate persisted.

"Well, Private Castine said he went out early this morning—the sun was barely up. He stayed gone a long time, and when he came back, he went out there to the summer kitchen and he was banging around in there for a while, doing nobody knows what. Then he wanted to see the Colonel, and he wouldn't take maybe for an answer."

Kate frowned. "Has he been up there long?"

"Not long. I reckon they're still in the staring each other down stage."

Kate had no doubt that Perkins was right. It occurred to her—belatedly—that he was no longer at Mrs. Kinnard's house, and she wondered if that was good or bad.

"Have you seen Mrs. Woodard this morning?" she asked, trying to discover yet another aspect of the situation if she could, hopefully without seeming to do so.

"I have. She sent for the Little General first thing. They're in the parlor."

"Thank you, Sergeant Major," Kate said. She headed to the parlor, then immediately changed her mind. She was far more concerned about what was happening upstairs between Max and Robert at this particular moment. She walked as quickly as she dared toward the rear of the house instead, through the kitchen to the back stairs, looking over her shoulder at one point to see if Perkins might have guessed that she was all but running because she was about to shamelessly eavesdrop. He apparently hadn't, and she quietly climbed the steps to the first landing.

She could hear Robert quite plainly.

"—to ask a favor."

There was a long pause before Max answered.

"What kind of favor?"

"Permission to live in the summer kitchen. I want to be here—on the premises—it's my family home. But I don't want to distress Maria by being underfoot when she's not…used to the idea of my being back. I think it would be better for both of us."

Again, there was a long pause. She could almost feel Max considering the consequences of having Robert out of the house, but still so close, good and bad.

"I'll speak to Maria about it," Max said finally.

"I've already spoken to her," Robert said.

"When in blazes did you do that!"

"When she was waiting downstairs for Perkins to bring the baby home. I didn't think I needed your permission to have a conversation with my sister."

"Well, think again!"

"Maria doesn't need you to tell her what to do!"

Kate hurried up the rest of the stairs, but Perkins was already there ahead of her.

"Excuse me, Colonel Woodard. Urgent dispatch," he said, stopping just short of breaching military protocol by barging all the way into the room and putting himself between the two men.

Kate couldn't see her brother, but she could imagine the look Perkins was getting about now. She didn't doubt that the dispatch was "urgent," but she wondered if Perkins had been holding on to it longer than he should have in case he needed to derail an impending brawl.

"It's urgent, sir," Perkins reiterated in the unlikely event that his superior officer hadn't heard him the first time. "I'll handle this," he said under his breath to Kate, but it was apparently loud enough to cause Robert to look in her direction.

Oh, Kate thought. He looked so sad and so weary. She had been asleep when Mrs. Justice had returned from her attempt to talk to him, and she wondered how late their visit—if it could be called that—had lasted. Or perhaps they hadn't talked at all. Perhaps, after Mrs. Justice had left, the candle had burned down and once again he'd sat in the dark until he'd left the house this morning.

She sighed and turned to leave the way she'd come. Clearly this was not the time to talk to her already annoyed brother.

"Kate!" he said loudly.

"Yes, Max," she answered.

"Did you want something?" His tone suggested that he wasn't likely to be receptive if she did.

"I did—do—but I'll wait until you're a little less… truculent."

"I'm a colonel," he said. "I'm *supposed* to be truculent."

"Indeed you are. And the nonmilitary members of your family find it ever so endearing. I'll be back later."

"I need to talk to you, Kate!" he called after her.

"And so you shall!" she called back as she reached the first landing. She didn't go any farther. She stood there, assuming that he meant for her to wait her turn.

It's worse than I thought.

Looking into Robert Markham's eyes just now, she was more convinced than ever that she should *not* stay here. Robert Markham seemed to want her company, but even that might be more than she could give. His body had been seriously wounded—and so had his soul. That aside, he couldn't find the woman he obviously loved, and when he did, he would likely be gone again, hopefully not in the dead of night without Maria knowing.

Eleanor.

She could still hear the longing in is voice that night when, in his delirium, he had thought she was Eleanor Hansen.

But none of that was any of her concern. Her focus needed to be on her son and not on her unbridled curiosity about her brother's family situation, a curiosity that was piqued every time she encountered this enigmatic ex-Rebel...*prizefighter.*

She looked around at the sound of footsteps behind her. To her dismay Robert was coming down the stairs. She thought he would just go on by, but he didn't. He stood on the landing with her, apparently giving no thought to decorum or her brother's current mood.

She looked at him with all the directness she could muster, hoping to seem calmer than she felt.

"Did Max say yes or no?" she asked, making no attempt at pleasantries.

"Neither. He gave me a curt nod. I'm taking that to mean he's handing the summer kitchen over to me—against his better judgment."

She couldn't help but smile. In her opinion that was exactly what the nod meant. She continued to look at him, and she was beginning to regret this direct approach. She couldn't seem to look away, and if he had second thoughts about having spoken to her so frankly about Samuel's death, she couldn't tell it.

"I think I've remembered something else," he said after a moment. "About the night I got here."

"What is that?"

"I remember hearing you say that you had to learn how to build a fire. It's rather a strange comment, especially given the circumstances, but nonetheless the memory seems real. Is it?"

She frowned, not wanting to say.

"That's what I thought," he said, despite her silence. "You don't have to worry about it anymore. I intend to teach you. It's the least I can do for someone who saved my life."

"I didn't save your life."

"Mrs. Justice maintains that you did. She thinks something very bad would have happened to me, had you not been here. I'm inclined to agree."

"I was only—" She stopped because it occurred to her that he could be teasing her, despite the seriousness of his face. There was something different in his eyes now. Amusement? Mischief? She didn't quite know.

"So, Miss Woodard, prepare yourself to learn. I'll let you know where and when."

With that, he continued down the stairs into the kitchen.

"I don't think my brother's nod included that," she called after him, and she actually thought she heard him laugh.

"Kate!" Max suddenly barked at the head of the stairs, making her jump. Between his *and* Mrs. Kinnard's penchant for abrupt summoning, it was a wonder she had an ounce of serenity left.

"I need to talk to you," she said ahead of whatever pronouncement he was about to make. She climbed the stairs and edged past him to lead the way into old Mr. Markham's sitting room, and she closed the door firmly as soon as he was inside.

"I'm going home," she said without prelude.

"I want you to stay here," he said at the same time.

"What?" she said.

"I said I want you to stay here."

"No. I'm going home to Philadelphia—"

"You're not listening to me."

"You haven't said anything!"

He sighed. "No. I guess I haven't. It's… Maria."

Kate waited for him to continue, but he now seemed disinclined to do so.

"What about Maria?" she said to prompt him.

"I have to go back to New Bern. I think I'll be there for…a while. I want you to stay here with her."

"Max, I'll be in the way. Maria needs to reconcile with her brother and not have to deal with one of her in-laws perpetually underfoot."

"No," he said firmly.

"What do you mean, *no?* I was headed home, anyway."

"We'll get to that at a later time," he said. "I want—" He stopped and took a breath. "I *need* you to be here. Maria's going to have another child—"

"Oh, Max," Kate said, smiling. "Maybe a little girl this time. You need a little girl."

"I'm leaving Perkins behind again—because of this brother situation. But there's only so much he can do where Maria is concerned. I need you here to make sure she doesn't…overdo."

"Did her talk with her brother go that badly?"

"I honestly don't know. She was…upset afterward. She didn't really give me any of the details. If there are more talks, I may need you to referee—I have no doubt that you can handle it."

"Well, I'm not sure I like that remark. You make me sound like Mrs. Kinnard."

"I meant it as a compliment, Kate. You're very… astute. I think you will see early on if things aren't going well and intervene. I won't be easy about leaving if Maria is here alone. Will you do this for me?"

Kate looked at him, more than a little amazed that he was actually asking rather than telling.

"Kate?"

"Yes, all right. I'll stay until you get back," she said, watching yet another of her so-called plans dissipate.

"You just found out about this, didn't you?" she asked, because she was certain that Max would never have allowed Maria to confront her brother last night if he had known.

"The army surgeon told me this morning. It seems

my wife is very…persuasive when it comes to when I may and may not know what I ought to know."

Kate couldn't help but smile.

"This is not cause for amusement," he said pointedly, and her smile broadened.

"She loves you," Kate said.

"She loves that wayward—prodigal—ex-Rebel brother of hers," Max countered.

"Yes. She does. And that's what makes her Maria."

"I can count on you, then?"

"I'll do my best. I don't think I'm very good at refereeing. My first impulse is always to flee."

"That's not what Perkins tells me. He said you did a fine job placating Mrs. Kinnard and keeping her in hand."

"Oh, yes—except for the small fact that Perkins and I both have been ready to shoot her—on several occasions. Besides that, he doesn't know about the times I went into hiding— You won't go yelling at the lieutenant who was supposed to see me to Philadelphia, will you?" Kate suddenly asked. She thought she had seen him in the house earlier, and it seemed the least she could do for the man—intervene on his behalf since she'd deliberately put him in an untenable position with his superior officer.

"I expect I will," he said. "Why? Feeling guilty?"

"Just a bit," she said. "He tried his best to dissuade me. He and his wife."

Max was looking at her steadily. She could tell the moment he decided that despite the opportunity she'd inadvertently given him, he didn't want to discuss her refusal to board a northbound train when she was supposed to.

"It's been a long time since you've seen Harry," he said quietly, indicating perhaps that he understood more of the situation than she thought. She looked away. Max was making an observation, not asking a question, so she said nothing.

"Does he write to you?"

"Sometimes," she said, deliberately keeping her response to his question to a minimum. She didn't trust herself to be able to enter into a conversation about Harrison, not even with Max, who knew everything there was to know about her downfall. "He…sent me a *carte de visite.*"

She wanted to tell Max how worried she was that he might be unhappy at his boarding school and how unsuitable she thought that particular institution would be for a quiet boy like Harrison, despite its being the alma mater of the Howe men. But she didn't. Max had enough worries of his own.

"Perkins has retrieved your trunks, by the way," he said after a moment. "They may have already been delivered to the house."

"Hmm. I think I can see how disingenuous your 'request' for me to remain here was just now."

"I can assure you it was sincere, Kate. No matter how it sounded, I was asking, not ordering. But I admit I was willing to do whatever it took to get you to agree to do this for me. Now. Go away. I have things to do."

Whatever those things were, Kate soon realized that it required a good deal of military activity. Max apparently had chosen not to go to army headquarters. Instead he had headquarters come to him. Soldiers— officers mainly—arrived en masse and congregated noisily in Mr. Markham's sitting room. Kate had no idea where Robert had gone. He wasn't in the house as far as she knew, and she didn't see him anywhere around the summer kitchen whenever she looked out the window—which was more often than would have been seemly had anyone noticed.

Truthfully she was glad he wasn't here at the moment; the last thing he needed to see was how completely his family home had been taken over, not just by Union soldiers, but by her, as well. Apparently she had already been reinstated as the occupant of the bedchamber upstairs. Max had lost no time taking Robert at his word that he wanted to move out of the house. Sergeant Major Perkins informed her on her way back downstairs that the room had been "readied," and that her trunks would be taken there as soon as they arrived from the depot.

She couldn't keep from smiling. The thought of having more than two things to wear was pleasurable indeed. She went looking for Maria. If Kate wanted to know how her sister-in-law's meeting with her brother had gone last night, she was clearly going to have to ask the source—if she could figure out a tactful way to do it.

As she headed for the parlor, she encountered Maria and the baby coming in the opposite direction. The baby immediately reached for her, and she took him gladly, smiling as she remembered Valentina's remark regarding Mrs. Kinnard's opinion of him.

"Yes," Kate told him earnestly. "You are definitely pleasant."

Maria gave her a quizzical look, but Kate didn't explain.

"Are you all right?" she asked instead, watching

Maria closely for some indication of her well-being, regardless of what she said.

"I'm...better," Maria said. "In fact, I was looking for you. We're all going to have a special dinner in the dining room tonight—in honor of Max's last night home."

"All?" Kate asked, a bit taken aback by the idea.

"Yes, all. I've told Robert I expect him to be present, as well."

"And what did he say to that?"

"Actually he asked me if someone had dropped me on my head while he was gone."

Kate didn't mean to laugh, but her amusement got away from her. It was so like something Max might have said. She was beginning to think that these two men were far more alike than she—or they—might have realized.

"Does that mean he'll be here?" Kate asked.

"I wish I knew. All I can do is set a place for him and hope for the best."

"What about the boys and Warrie?"

"They'll be at Mrs. Russell's another night. I was afraid Mrs. Russell would find Joe and Jake being there too much of a reminder of her lost boy, but that doesn't seem to be the case. She asked to have them another night and they were begging to stay, so I agreed—for Warrie's sake as much as anything. Mrs. Kinnard and Valentina are also invited here tonight."

"Max's idea, I imagine," Kate said. She couldn't help but marvel at his presence of mind when it came to maintaining his peaceful occupation. She had shared a sit-down meal with Mrs. Kinnard before, on the occasion of Max and Maria's very rushed engagement announcement, and she could do it again if she set her mind to it, only this time she understood the necessity of preserving Mrs. Kinnard's sense of her own importance better than she had even a few days ago. No, it wouldn't do at all for Colonel Woodard to have a farewell dinner without her present, especially after all she'd done for him in his absence by maintaining a semblance of propriety in his household.

"Max's soldiers are doing the cooking—he was adamant about that. I hope we won't have a table full of army food."

"If one of the cooks is the soldier who makes the cookies Sergeant Major Perkins keeps bringing, I believe you need not worry."

Robbie was becoming rambunctious, and Kate handed him back to his mother.

"I think I'd better see about my trunks," Kate said.

"And we are going into the nursery. This young man's mother needs for him to take a nap."

Maria turned to carry him to the back of the house, but then she stopped.

"Thank you, Kate," she said.

"Whatever for?" Kate asked, returning Robbie's uncoordinated but very enthusiastic wave goodbye.

"For...being here when Robert came home. Things might have turned out very differently if you hadn't been."

"I didn't do anything, Maria. Truly. Sergeant Major Perkins and Mrs. Kinnard are the ones who—"

"That's not what Robert says. You're the one who talked to him so straightforwardly. He says your candor helped his state of mind a great deal."

Kate didn't know what to say. "I...like your brother,"

she said finally, because it was the truth. "It was no hardship."

Maria smiled. "Anyway, I thank you for that, and I'm glad you're going to be here while Max is gone," she said, switching her wiggling baby boy to her other arm. "I—" She stopped, apparently because of the commotion on the back stairs—soldiers leaving, and from the sound of it, Max was among them. Apparently he was going to headquarters after all.

"They sound like boys being let out of school," Kate said.

"Don't let Max hear you say that," Maria said, and Kate laughed.

Maria continued toward the nursery wing, and Kate stood for a moment, trying to decide whether or not she was annoyed that her brother's wife had assumed she would be staying even before Max had asked her. But of course she would. Kate was the Woodard family's official spinster. Still, there was a lot to be said for being needed. Max and Maria and the boys were her family, and she would just have to work around the growing concern she had for Robert and for Harrison. It occurred to her that Mrs. Justice would likely be staying here during Max's absence as well, and she was comforted by that thought. Mrs. Justice's presence in the house was as soothing as Mrs. Kinnard's was unsettling.

The dining room door was slightly ajar, and as Kate passed by, she could hear voices—Mrs. Justice's and Robert's. He was here in the house after all.

She hesitated, concerned for a moment that he might have overheard the admission she'd made just now. It was better that he didn't know what she'd said about liking him. She didn't look in, and as she passed the door, she realized too late that one of Max's officers— a major whose name she didn't know—was coming down the front staircase instead of following the rest of his fellow soldiers out the back way. When he saw her, he immediately headed in her direction rather than the front door.

"Miss Woodard!" he said with far more enthusiasm than was appropriate. "What a pleasure it is to see you again. May I be the first to offer you whatever assistance you may require while the Colonel is away?"

The major continued to advance, crowding too closely for her liking. She tried backing up, but it didn't help the situation. She glanced over her shoulder. Except for Mrs. Justice and Robert in the dining room, the downstairs was completely deserted.

"Thank you, but that won't be necessary. Excuse me, sir," she added firmly, but he didn't seem to register that she meant for him to get out of her way.

"I will plan to stop by every day," the major persisted. "You are a stranger here, just as I am. I'm sure you will enjoy the company of a fellow Northerner."

"That won't be necessary," Kate said again. "Mrs. Woodard and I will be well cared for." He was close enough now for her to smell the whiskey on his breath.

"Just in case you require anything of a more personal nature," he continued, reaching out to put his hand on her arm. "I feel it's my duty—"

"Actually it's *my* duty," Robert said behind her.

"And who are you?" the major asked, truly overstepping his authority now.

"This is Robert Markham," Kate said. "Mrs. Woodard's brother. My brother-in-law."

She watched the major's face as it occurred to him that *her* brother-in-law would also be the brother-in-law of his commanding officer.

"I'm afraid I don't know your name, Major," she said, hoping to defuse the situation before it got any further out of hand. "I must tell my brother how…accommodating you are."

The major looked as startled as she hoped he would, and as she expected, he didn't offer to identify himself.

"Kate, where is Maria?" Robert asked, using her given name, she thought to establish that he was indeed her family—and her protector—and therefore he had the right.

"She's in the nursery wing, putting the baby down for his nap."

Kate briefly met his gaze, and she was not reassured by it. He was working hard again to control his emotions, his rage at one of the enemy.

"I believe you know your way out, Major," she said, but she made no attempt to leave the two men unattended in the foyer. She knew enough of how the occupation worked to know that the unsubstantiated word of an ex-Rebel soldier wouldn't count for much against that of a Union officer—whether he had been drinking or not. She wasn't about to walk off and leave Robert without a witness. Max had assigned her the task of "refereeing," but she doubted that even he thought she would need to begin this soon and under these circumstances.

The major stood for a moment longer.

"Miss Woodard," he said finally—with great formality. He gave Robert a hard, narrowed-eyed look meant to intimidate him, then he turned and left by the front door.

"Why did you do that?" Robert said as the major slammed the door behind him—hard.

"Do what?"

"You know what. Did you think if you didn't intervene, I'd be in the stockade about now?"

"Only if you'd hit him."

"I wanted to."

"Yes. I know."

They stared at each other. It suddenly dawned on her that he was actually angry that she *had* intervened. "You are my duty as well, Mr. Markham. As I understand it, a peaceful occupation is the utmost priority in this house. You'd do well to remember that."

She walked away, without looking back, and she went straight into the parlor for no reason whatsoever, closing the door behind her and leaning against it for a moment. It was incredible to her that he couldn't see where an altercation with an officer in the occupation army would have led, regardless of the circumstances. It wasn't that she didn't appreciate his stepping in on her behalf. She did. The fact that she'd encountered this kind of behavior in her brother's house suggested that the major wouldn't have been daunted by her protests, no matter how firmly she'd made them.

She heard Mrs. Justice say something and Robert answer. Then she heard the front door slam again. She moved to look out the window. Robert was striding down the gravel path toward the street—but then he apparently changed his mind and veered off to his left. He disappeared from her view, and she moved to a window on the side of the house to look out. She could see at least part of the summer kitchen without difficulty, and after a while, she could see Robert, as well. He was carrying an ax, and after some preparation, he began splitting logs and stacking the pieces near the summer kitchen door, working in his shirtsleeves despite the winter cold. She wondered if this was a necessary chore or if it was something he needed to do in lieu of hitting a Union officer.

And here he was again, she suddenly thought—in the forefront of her mind where she didn't want him to be. She tried to convince herself that it didn't matter whether he was present at the dinner table tonight or not—except that it did, and she knew it. She just wanted him there. She wanted to be able to talk to him if she felt like it. And she could do that without consequence—socially. It would be quite safe because a table full of people and her brother would be present.

Safe.

Because Robert had abandoned Eleanor Hansen and was therefore untrustworthy and unsuitable? Or because his loving Eleanor meant Kate wouldn't have to keep up her guard? It wouldn't matter what *she* might feel when there was no chance of such feelings being returned. It would be pleasant to be his friend—if he weren't still annoyed with her. Pleasant. Uncomplicated. Meaningless.

And safe.

She looked out the window again. He was still chopping wood, but he had to stop and rest from time to time, as if his strength had been quickly depleted by the exertion. The house was quiet; Kate was free to go see about her trunks, but she didn't. She continued to watch him work. He was no longer the man who had collapsed in the hallway, but he was not yet as strong as he wanted to be perceived. And he was troubled. He was also, by all accounts, wild. Had the war and Samuel's death taken the wildness out of him? She knew that love had changed both Max and John Howe, but did sorrow have the same effect? She didn't know.

She gave a quiet sigh. She had told Maria the truth. She did like him, regardless of the fact that she barely knew him.

Private Castine came trotting up and handed him a piece of paper. Robert read it, imbedded the ax in the chopping block and left, apparently with no intention of returning any time soon. It was only then that she finally quitted the parlor to go upstairs.

The sergeant major had once again thought of everything. There was no sign whatsoever that Robert Markham had ever occupied this room. It was completely hers again. Her trunks were sitting at the foot of the bed—with the keys in the locks. The small tables that had been removed to give the hospital orderlies room to carry out their duties had been returned, as had her books. She unlocked the trunks and then removed from the large one the brassbound mahogany writing box Grey had given her. He had teased her that he wanted to make sure she would have no excuse for not writing to him, but he had also known that she was…scholarly, that she liked to read and make notes, and he had simply wanted to give her something she would enjoy.

She smiled slightly at the memory, touching the fine wood of the box with her fingertips. But that memory was fleeting at best, and she was suddenly thinking of Robert Markham again. That he had lived here in this house, grown up here, left here most likely in the same flurry of duty and patriotism that Max and John had left their own homes. And he had loved his family, just as they had; she was certain of that—which made his choosing not to come home all the more inexplicable.

"What is *wrong* with me?" she said out loud.

What with her recent penchant for hiding and her preoccupation with a man who had been her country's enemy *and* a prizefighter, she hardly recognized herself.

She began lifting her dresses out of the trunks and spreading them on the bed until she decided which one she would wear to dinner tonight. Her anxiety regarding the upcoming evening seemed to be growing, likely because neither sequence of events was desirable—that Robert wouldn't come, and his chair would sit there empty for the entire meal, or that he *would,* and she would see the look in his eyes and likely feel a pressing need to worry about him even more than she already did.

She eventually decided on a dress, a plain pale beige one with a blue iridescence to the fabric and blue edging on the collar, cuffs and bustle. No ruffles. No pleats. No lace. It would do nicely. She had no doubt that Valentina would arrive in all her splendor, and in this dress, Kate could all but disappear into the background, where she would happily remain for the duration of whatever social torture was about to unfold. She knew Max would try hard for Maria's sake, and she thought that Robert—if he came—would, as well. But they were, after all, men, and bitter enemies at that. Who knew what would happen, especially with

Mrs. Kinnard in the mix? It would be so easy for any one—or all—of them to take offense.

She took a long bath and even longer to arrange her hair and dress. She ultimately decided on leaving her hair "careless," pulling the front and sides back into a topknot and allowing the blond tresses to fall free down her back. The simplicity of no padding and no false hairpieces suited the dress and her mood.

It was growing dark outside, and the noise level in the house rose as did the aroma of baked bread, apples and roasting meat coming from the kitchen. She continued to look out the window from time to time for some sign of Robert, but she didn't see him.

She stayed upstairs as long as she could—until it was absolutely necessary that she be on hand to greet Mrs. Kinnard and Valentina when they arrived. As she headed downstairs, she smiled slightly to herself, wondering if Private Castine would be on hand somehow to see Valentina.

Max was standing in the foyer, resplendent in his uniform.

"Very handsome and military," she said as she reached the bottom of the stairs, knowing her teasing him about the way he looked would annoy him.

"I see you're not wearing *your* uniform this evening."

"No," she said, trying not to smile. "I am not." For a moment it was like the old days, she, joyfully on the verge of becoming the woman she hoped to be, and he, the big brother who teased her unmercifully and yet was always kind.

"You look very nice, anyway," he said, making her smile in earnest. She was on the verge of asking him if Robert had returned, but then she didn't. Having *all* the women in the house fixated on Robert Markham would do nothing for his mood this evening.

She turned her head sharply at some commotion on the porch, but it was only Private Castine, stamping his feet to stay warm. She left Max with a sympathetic pat on the arm and went into the parlor, leaving the door ajar and sitting were she had a good view of the foyer. Maria stood by the window, tense with the effort it took not to wring her hands.

"I don't believe Robert will be here," she said. "He's gone off somewhere, and I have no idea where that might be."

"Private Castine brought him a note earlier. Maybe he would know."

"I'll ask," Maria said, heading for the door.

"He's on the veranda," Kate called after her.

Maria was gone only a moment.

"He says the note was from Reverend Lewis, but he doesn't know what it was about. Max told me about Robert asking for an army chaplain. I simply do not understand my brother's sudden interest in the clergy."

"Surely there are worse things he could be doing, don't you think?"

"It's the *reason* he's doing it that worries me. It's not like him. At all."

Kate looked at her without comment, thinking how changed Max had been when he'd come home. She thought it was to be expected, but she didn't say so.

They sat for a time in silence—until Kate suddenly made up her mind to ask what she wanted to know.

"Maria, when you and Robert talked, were you able—"

But the question was interrupted before Kate could

finish asking it. Mrs. Kinnard and Valentina were arriving, much to Private Castine's obvious delight. Kate could see him through the window as he bounded off the veranda to hurry and open the door of Mrs. Kinnard's carriage.

But his obvious pleasure must have been short-lived. Valentina had no time to pay him even a backhanded compliment this evening. She disembarked from the carriage and swept past him with barely a glance in his direction.

"What a chilly evening," she said to Max as she entered the foyer. "But I'm sure it's colder in Philadelphia."

"Much colder," Max said. "Miss Kinnard, Mrs. Kinnard—and Mrs. Russell—I am very glad you could join us this evening."

He might be glad, Kate thought, but there was something in his voice that suggested he hadn't known Mrs. Russell was on Maria's guest list. Somewhere along the way, Kate suspected, it had become Mrs. Kinnard's guest list. If there were any more additions, Max was going to be decidedly outnumbered at the table.

"I understand there are *soldiers* cooking the meal," Mrs. Kinnard said bluntly.

"Yes—and I would be very glad if you would give me your opinion of the food. Secretary of War Belknap—when he was here making his inspections—found their efforts too Southern for his liking."

"Too *Southern?*" Mrs. Kinnard said in a tone that all but guaranteed that whatever showed up on the dinner table tonight, it would be—in her opinion—exceptional.

"I'm afraid so," Max said. "Thanks to Maria's fine

cooking, I am quite partial to Southern cuisine, myself."

Kate could hear that Private Castine was still attending to his duties and was now on hand to take the ladies' wraps. He carried them to the chairs that had been brought from somewhere and placed in the hallway just for that purpose and carefully draped each one over the back as if his life depended on it.

"Miss Woodard!" Valentina said as soon as she spied Kate. "You have dresses! Or a dress, at any rate." She was wearing a bustled frock in a shimmering blue color—"Independence Blue," it would be called in Philadelphia, and likely "Bonnie Blue" here. It had a ruched overskirt with a smooth long skirt beneath it. Two rows of deep ruffles adorned the hem. There were ribbons of a lighter shade of blue at her wrists and a large bow of the same color over white lace at her throat. Her hair was elaborately arranged in two large chignons. She was—as always—stunning.

"I do. My trunks have found me again," Kate said, but she was thinking, *Poor Castine.* She was also listening for some sound inside or outside the house that would indicate that Robert had returned.

"Everyone, please do sit down," Maria was saying. "Valentina, what a beautiful dress. You look lovely. If you'll excuse me, I must check on our dinner—"

"Kate can do that," Max said over Valentina's demure thanks, looking at his wife hard. In her condition and after the emotional upheaval of last night, he did *not* want her tiring herself out—and that was that. "Kate?"

"Yes, of course," Kate said, happy to have a reason the leave the gathering in the parlor. She walked quickly down the hallway, thinking as she went of the leather-bound, handwritten book of etiquette her mother had made her read—study—so that she could at least supervise the running of a household. She remembered a particular notation that said that the number of dishes served at a sit down meal with guests didn't need to be many—but they did need to be excellent.

She wasn't the least bit worried about Max's soldier-cooks; it was the atmosphere at the table that concerned her. According to the book, such a meal wasn't to be hurried on any account—and that alone was a major drawback to her way of thinking. The sooner this evening was over, the better. But the worst departure from the rules was that one should make certain that the invited guests were "compatible." Mrs. Kinnard and Mrs. Russell, because of their strong personalities, were barely compatible with each other, despite their highwayman history, and if Robert managed to get here in time, even a modicum of harmony would be unlikely, if not impossible.

Kate stood for a moment in the kitchen doorway before she interrupted the bustle of food preparation that seemed to be going on everywhere at once. Every soldier in the room seemed to be busy at some cooking task, except for the one who held a happy Robbie on his knee while he ate a mashed up...potato, it looked like—with the wrong end of a spoon.

Little General, she thought. She doubted he would have any of the prejudices associated with the war that must afflict both his father and his uncle.

"Good evening," she said, startling everyone except Robbie, who waved his backward spoon in her direction. "Is your spoon broken, Robbie?" she asked him, making him grin.

"Aye, miss," the soldier holding him said. "I believe it is. He doesn't like the big end, and he's a clever lad. He finds his own way."

"The Colonel's lady would like to know when you will be ready to serve," Kate said to the group at large because she didn't really know which of them held the highest rank. A grizzly-looking man with a large piece of food-stained muslin wrapped around his waist stepped forward.

"Twenty-five minutes, miss," he said. "No sooner. No later, if it's all going to come out right."

"Excellent," Kate said. "Thank you… Sergeant. Is that apple pie I smell?" she asked.

"It is, miss."

"My very favorite," she told him. "I shall look forward to it."

On her way back to the parlor one of the lower ranked soldiers called to her. "Miss!" She stopped and waited for him to catch up.

"Mr. Markham says for you to come to the summer kitchen, miss," he said in a rush. "Now, if you please."

"What?" Kate said, thinking she'd heard wrong.

"Brother to the Colonel's lady, miss. He says for you to come now—and hurry, if you please."

Kate frowned because it was disconcerting to realize that she wasn't even going to hesitate. She immediately followed the soldier back into the kitchen, sidestepping the cooks, and boxes and baskets, and waving to Robbie again as she made her way to the back door.

A lantern hanging from a post lit the slate path that

led to the summer kitchen door. She had no difficulty seeing where she was going. *Why* she was going was something else again.

She didn't knock, and she didn't stand in the cold and wait for Robert to open it. She pushed the door open and went inside. There was a fire burning on the hearth, and the stone structure was not nearly as frigid as she might have expected. There was also a man lying flat on his back on the long harvest table Maria must use for food preparation and preserving.

"I need you to bring me some things from the house," Robert said immediately, standing in her way as if he didn't want her coming any closer.

She could still see the man, and the most significant thing about him was that he was obviously in the Union army.

"Who—?" she began.

"It's the chaplain," he said, heading her off.

"The one who's 'seen the elephant'?"

"Yes. He's in a bad way."

"Drunk, you mean," she said because she could smell the whiskey on him from where she stood.

"No— Yes. And he's used up all his second chances. They'll put him in the stockade this time. He's a friend of Reverend Lewis's—they were in the seminary together. Reverend Lewis doesn't think the man is well enough to be hauled off to the stockade. Mrs. Lewis is temperance in the extreme and won't have him in the house. He's asked me to hide him until he sobers up."

Kate stared at him. "Well, you picked the worst possible place I can think of to do it," she said. "Mrs. Kinnard's in the house. And Mrs. Russell. I don't know where Mrs. Justice is—"

"Will you help or not?" he asked, apparently trying to hurry this along.

"Yes, I'll help. What do you want me to do?"

"Can you get out of the house with some coffee and blankets?"

"No," she said with some trepidation. "But I will. Somehow."

And that turned out to be much harder than she anticipated. When she opened the summer kitchen door, Valentina, in all her blue shimmering splendor, fell into the room.

"What's happening?" she asked as she righted herself, clearly not concerned that she had been caught spying. She kept bobbing up and down on tiptoe, trying to see for herself.

"There's a problem," Kate said, and she knew from experience that there would be no getting rid of Valentina now. It would be impossible to fob her off with some concocted story, even if Kate had been so inclined—which she wasn't. The only thing left was to recruit her. "I have to get some hot coffee and some blankets out of the house. It's important that my brother doesn't see me," she said, keeping the details to a minimum.

Valentina kept trying to see the man on the table. Clearly this was not what she'd expected to find.

"We have about twenty minutes before dinner is served. I will need you to either help me or stay out of the way," Kate said, and Valentina finally stopped bouncing up and down.

"Oh. All right. Yes. I'll help," Valentina said. "What do you want me to do?"

"Go back to the parlor, tell everyone that dinner will

be ready in fifteen minutes time. And don't look like there is anything going on."

"I can do that," Valentina assured her. She suddenly grinned. "This is wonderful! I can't tell you how long I've been waiting to have adventures like you do."

"Then hurry," Kate said, shooing her out the door.

Kate glanced at Robert. He was almost on the verge of smiling.

"You have adventures?" he asked.

"So it seems to Valentina."

"She knows about the hiding, then."

"No, she does not," Kate said pointedly. "No one knows about that."

"I do," he said. The man was teasing her, she suddenly realized. In the middle of all *this*.

She exhaled sharply and turned to go.

"Kate," Robert said, and she looked back at him.

"What?"

"I…appreciate your help."

"I haven't done anything yet."

"Maybe not, but you've kicked over the traces."

"Is that another…soldier saying?" she asked. "Like the elephant?"

"It is."

"Well, I'll have to wait to find out what that one means—and hopefully you and the chaplain won't end up in the stockade. The chaplain is stirring," she added, looking at him for a long moment before she hurried out the door.

I'm doing this for Max, she told herself on the path back to the house. So he won't have to step on an urgent request from Reverend Lewis. It would mean nothing to Mrs. Kinnard and Mrs. Russell if he put a drunken chaplain in the stockade, but for the Reverend.

She had formed a plan of sorts by the time she got to the house, one that involved Private Castine. But just as she was about to corner him, the sergeant major stepped into the foyer, and her hope that Private Castine would likely do anything if he thought it was for Valentina evaporated.

"Is there something you need, Miss Kate?" the sergeant major asked, looking at her closely. Kate was trying hard to hide her agitated state, but from the expression on his face, she knew it wasn't working.

In for a penny, in for a pound, she thought.

"Yes," she said hurriedly, whispering to keep anyone in the parlor from hearing. "The chaplain—the one who has 'seen the elephant'—is drunk in the summer kitchen with Mrs. Woodard's brother—*he's* not drunk, just the chaplain. Reverend Lewis and the chaplain were friends in the seminary, and the Reverend wants the chaplain hidden until he's sober because this time he's going to end up in the stockade and the Reverend thinks he's not well enough for that kind of punishment. I need coffee and blankets and somebody to mind him—so Ro—Mrs. Woodard's brother can sit down at this dinner—so *my* brother won't have to risk the occupation peace by having to address any of this with Mrs. Kinnard *and* Mrs. Russell here—because it all comes down to Reverend Lewis's request, you see, and they will surely take exception if it isn't carried out. And we definitely don't want Mrs. Woodard all upset because her brother's in the middle of it." She stopped to breathe and found she didn't have anything more to say.

"Miss Kate," he said after a long moment. "I can tell you right now, I'm going to think long and hard before I ever ask you a question like that again. Castine!" he whispered sharply, making the private jump despite a much-less-audible-than-usual summons. "You and Giles get coffee and blankets out to the summer kitchen *now*. Send Mrs. Woodard's brother back to the house and you two stay there with this…problem until I tell you different. Go!"

Castine scurried toward the kitchen just as the dinner guests poured out of the parlor on their way to the dining room.

"There you are," Valentina said as if she hadn't just seen her. "It's time to be seated." And she followed Max and Maria to the table with a great sense of importance—and mischief—which was not lost on Max.

He gave Kate a pointed look; she ignored it. She lingered in the hallway, trying to see if Robert was going to come back to the house.

"Kate? What are you doing?" he asked when she didn't immediately join the rest of the guests.

"Oh…nothing," she assured him.

"Then could you do it in here? Somebody's got to sit between Mrs. Kinnard and Mrs. Russell," he added in a whisper.

Kate smiled sweetly and took her place between the two women, noting with some dismay that Robert—if he came—would be seated directly across from her. As usual the table was set in mismatched china. It immediately set Mrs. Kinnard and Mrs. Russell to reminiscing about the occasions they'd attended when this set or that set in its entirety had been used—Maria's christening, Samuel's birth. There seemed to have been no occasions regarding Robert.

Kate made the mistake of looking at Valentina, who raised her eyebrows and looked at the empty chair next to her, then back at Kate—with the subtlety of a broad ax. Kate wasn't quite sure whether Valentina was simply enjoying her "adventure" or whether she was trying to ask a question—which Kate could not have answered because she had Max's full attention. She sat there, trying her best to effect a certain air of nonchalance and hoping that for once, his reputation for knowing everything wouldn't hold.

Soldiers began bringing the food in and placing it on the sideboard—beef, pork, chicken, buttered potatoes, shell beans, sweet and sour beets, cooked cabbage, pickles, bread and butter, cold milk and coffee. Everything looked and smelled wonderful, and the soldiers selected to do the actual serving clearly had had practice. Kate accepted a few spoonfuls of everything, but she had to force herself to eat. It didn't help that she could see Sergeant Major Perkins walk past the open dining room door carrying Robbie more than once.

Kate looked down at her plate and concentrated on the food, bite by bite. Neither Mrs. Kinnard nor Mrs. Russell seemed interested in conversing—with her—to Kate's relief. Maria included all three of them in conversation from time to time, as a good hostess should, but Mrs. Kinnard stayed disengaged, until Max introduced the topic of civic pride, especially the possibility of beautifying the area around the train station where visitors gained their first impression of the town.

Beautification, after so many years of hardship and deprivation, was obviously dear to Mrs. Kinnard's heart, and she was full of ideas and suggestions—and criticisms of the occupation. Valentina, who had likely heard them all before, fidgeted in her chair and looked at the ceiling from time to time.

Kate glanced toward the dining room doorway again, thinking she had caught a glimpse of someone in the hallway.

It wasn't Perkins pacing to keep Robbie happy. It was the baby's namesake himself. Robert stood just in the doorway until he caught his sister's attention.

"Robert!" Maria said, as surprised as she was pleased.

"I apologize for my lateness," he said. "I thought it better to be tardy if it meant showing up presentable."

There was at least some truth in that. He'd clearly been to see the town barber at some point, something Kate hadn't noticed in the dimly lit summer kitchen, and he was wearing a white shirt and a dark suit, both of which looked new.

Yes, Kate thought. *Presentable.*

He greeted Mrs. Kinnard and Mrs. Russell; they both seemed pleased to see him.

"Miss Woodard," he said as he took the seat across from Kate. "Are we missing Mrs. Justice this evening?" he asked, causing Mrs. Kinnard and Mrs. Russell to look at each other despite Kate's being in the way.

"She is visiting someone in need," Mrs. Kinnard said after a moment.

"That sounds very much like Mrs. Justice," he said, finally glancing in Kate's direction. Once again she looked down and concentrated on her plate.

The meal continued pleasantly enough, punctuated by succinct but informed comments regarding

the weather—from Mrs. Kinnard and Mrs. Russell—
and how the recent snow affected train travel— from
Max. Maria kept staring at her brother, as if she still
couldn't believe he was here.

Kate thought that Max was making every effort not
to say something that might lead to the topic of wars
lost and subsequent martial law and reconstruction.
Robert chatted with Valentina, asking her where the
little girl Samuel used to tease so had gone. Kate could
sense the tension in Maria at the mention of Samuel's
name, but it soon passed, likely because of the gentleness with which Robert spoke of him. There was
no evidence of the agonized pain Kate had witnessed
last night, but she would have guessed that it was not
easy to mention him. Perhaps Robert's talk with Maria
had helped after all, even if Kate still suspected that
he hadn't told her the full details of Samuel's death.

When the dessert—apple pie, as promised—arrived
and had been served, there was a slight commotion in
the foyer, but it was loud enough to catch everyone's
attention.

"Just the mail pouches," Max said, looking at Kate,
because he knew the degree of her expectancy when a
train bringing the mail from the north arrived. She took
a quiet breath, aware that Robert was looking at her
as well. She didn't count on there being a letter from
Harrison, but she hoped for one all the same.

"I would like to make a request—it's more of an invitation, actually," Robert said. "To all of you."

Neither Mrs. Kinnard nor Mrs. Russell had finished eating, but his remark caused both their half-
lifted forks to return to their plates.

"What is it, Robert?" Maria asked, clearly wondering if this was going to be something worrying. She glanced at Max in what Kate thought was a request of her own.

Whatever it is, let him be.

"I want to ask all of you to be in church tomorrow," Robert said.

"I am *always* in church on Sunday, Robert," Mrs. Kinnard said. "Surely you remember that."

He smiled. "Yes, ma'am. So I've always heard. And you must remember that despite my dear mother's best efforts, I *wasn't* always there in the Markham family pew on Sunday."

"I believe *never* would be the more apt word for it," Maria said, and his smile broadened. Kate watched as it quickly faded. It was as if he couldn't—wouldn't— let himself enjoy even the smallest pleasantry, and if sometimes the enjoyment overtook him, he had to push it quickly away.

He doesn't think he deserves it, Kate thought. And no one understood that better than she.

"Even so, I wanted you all to know that I am extending my personal invitation, and I earnestly hope you'll be on hand."

"*Your* personal invitation," Max said.

"Are you going to tell us why?" Maria asked.

Robert looked around the table and then directly at Kate.

"I'm preaching the sermon."

Chapter Nine

Robert watched their faces. If he had to assign an emotion to each of the people present at the table—the ones who had known him before the war—it would have been the same emotion—incredulity. And he would have to include his brother-in-law as well, because the Colonel, who had likely heard a great deal of what Maria's brother had been like, was nothing at the moment if not incredulous.

"And who has approved this?" Mrs. Kinnard wanted to know, clearly intending to interrogate him, as was her self-appointed duty.

"Reverend Lewis," he said. "I had a long talk with him. It's all arranged," he added.

Mrs. Kinnard opened her mouth to say something, but then didn't. She was clearly undecided about the appropriateness of such an event. She, like everyone else in the town, knew that he had lived "a man's life" before the war, and "all arranged" was not a term she was inclined to recognize, especially when she had had no part in the arranging.

"Well," she said after a moment. "I simply do not know what to say."

"It won't be my first sermon," Robert said. "If that helps."

Clearly, it didn't because she looked even more startled than she had at his initial announcement. And Maria. Maria was openly bewildered by it all, and he couldn't fault her for that. He was still somewhat bewildered himself.

"I take it you have had some kind of Saul-on-the-road-to-Damascus experience, then," Max said finally. The remark was rude; everyone at the table recognized that fact, just as everyone wanted to hear Robert's response.

"Nothing nearly so dramatic," Robert said, looking at his brother-in-law directly. "I will talk about that tomorrow in church."

"I see," Max said.

There were no more comments and the silence at the table grew more and more uncomfortable.

Robert looked at Kate. He couldn't read her expression at all—because she was avoiding his eyes. He expected her to be surprised—and doubtful. Given their conversation last night, *doubtfulness* was the one emotion he was most prepared to see. But when she finally did look at him, he saw neither. What he found there in her eyes was understanding, as if the things he'd just said, to her way of thinking, explained everything: his coming home again, the effort he was making to mend his relationship with Maria—and the chaplain in the summer kitchen.

Two are better than one, he suddenly thought. *For*

if they fall, the one will lift up his fellow...a threefold cord is not quickly broken.

He gave her a slight nod and stood, and he thought for a moment she was going to ask him to sit down again. It was clear to him that she didn't want him to go, not yet, and that she was a woman with questions, who apparently saw no reason in this world why he shouldn't answer them.

"If you'll excuse me now," he said. "I'll take my leave. Maria—Max, thank you for inviting me. The meal was excellent. The best I've had in a very long time. Ladies, it was a joy to spend this time in your company. I am most grateful."

He shot a look in Maria's direction.

See? I haven't forgotten everything our mother taught us.

"Robert—" Maria began, but then she seemed to realize that whatever she needed to say, she couldn't say here. "Good night."

He smiled and left the table, waiting until he was out of sight to sigh in relief. It was over. He had done it, and now he was committed to this new life he was about to embark upon.

Be strong and of good courage...for the Lord thy God... He will not fail thee.

I'm trying, Lord...

He looked around at a sound. Kate had come out of the dining room. He watched her now as the sergeant major approached her, holding a letter in his hand. She thanked him and took it, barely glancing at it, as if she had no real interest in where it had come from or who had sent it. But then, when the sergeant major was walking away, she looked down at it and, holding it with both hands, briefly pressed it to her lips.

"Oh!" Valentina exclaimed as she came into the hallway. "There was a letter for you in the mail pouch! I love to get letters. I don't care to answer them, though," she said with a laugh. "It's so tedious. Is it from someone special?"

"Just a young friend of the family," Kate said. "He's…away at boarding school."

"Not that exciting, then. Not like when it's from an admirer."

Kate said nothing to that. She put the letter carefully into her pocket. Robert had hoped to speak to her— about what, he hadn't decided. He just wanted to look into her eyes again. He wanted to know if he had been mistaken earlier and perhaps to ask if she would be at tomorrow's service. It would help him a great deal if she were, but he wouldn't tell her that. To do so would be inappropriate, and he'd done enough inappropriate things where she was concerned already. Valentina's presence precluded any exchange between them at all, but Valentina wasn't the only reason. Standing here and being privy to that one intimate and heartfelt gesture regarding her letter had suddenly made Kate unapproachable. He wondered suddenly if the letter was somehow connected to the photograph she kept hidden in her book. She was such a mystery to him, and he had no wish to intrude.

He turned and left the house, heading down the slate path to see how the chaplain fared. If the man was sober enough now, he would likely either be belligerent or embarrassingly remorseful, neither of which would be a true measure of the man. In any event Robert would have done all that Reverend Lewis had asked him to do—with Kate's help. She had taken care of what he couldn't—at least not without a stint in the stockade. It was possible that the chaplain could be sent back to his barracks now, hopefully in the company of soldiers who wouldn't let him make any detours along the way. Or he might still be deep in his whiskey-induced oblivion. Either way Robert had a sermon to write. He would do that and he would not think about Kate Woodard.

"Robert's leaving," Valentina said. "It takes some getting used to, doesn't it?"

"What does?" Kate forced herself to ask. It would perhaps be another hour before Mrs. Kinnard and the rest of them left, and it was all Kate could do not to go upstairs now, without a word to anyone, and read Harrison's letter. But Valentina was here, forcing her to participate in what was supposed to be an enjoyable evening.

"The way he looks— Oh, I keep forgetting. You didn't know him before."

"Maria showed me his photograph," Kate said, glancing at Max and the rest of the guests as they passed by on their way to the parlor. "I could see that he is…changed."

"He's still handsome, though, don't you think? In a rough and dangerous kind of way—like a *pirate* or a *highwayman*. I wonder how the man is?"

It took Kate a moment to realize that Valentina likely meant the chaplain.

"I was so surprised when Robert came to dinner, weren't you? This evening has been more exciting than any evening I've ever had—well, except when there was a bread riot during the war. Or when the prisoners broke out of the stockade—Mother and I both were quite afraid. Oh, and when General Stoneman raided the town. But those involved *everybody*. They weren't very…personal. Not like tonight when I was able to actually participate. I've decided I quite like adventures. It will be hard to go back to the dull everyday things. Excitement seems to follow you, Miss Woodard. I must visit you every single afternoon in case there is more."

"No, I don't think so," Kate said, meaning the daily visits as much as the idea that events like tonight's escapade somehow followed her about.

"Oh, dear," Valentina said, looking past her. "Mother wants us. We'd better go in."

Us? Kate thought. But she didn't argue. She followed Valentina dutifully into the parlor, her hand resting on the pocket where Harrison's letter lay safe and hidden.

"Play for us, please, Valentina," Mrs. Kinnard said.

"Of course," Valentina said with the assurance of someone who was completely secure in both her appearance and her accomplishments.

Valentina sat down at the pianoforte and began looking at the piece already open on the music stand. Kate intended to take the chair by the window, regardless of the cold draft.

"Remember where you are," Kate whispered to Valentina, who looked at her blankly for a moment before she realized that it wouldn't do to play either Southern or Northern songs.

"I brought these with me from Philadelphia," Kate

said, retrieving a stack of sheet music from the book-shelf nearest the pianoforte.

Valentina looked through them. "I don't know any of these—'Little Brown Jug'?"

"They're quite new," Kate said. "I believe you'll enjoy playing them."

Valentina looked at them doubtfully, then selected one.

"'Sweet Genevieve,'" she said over her shoulder to her mother and began to play as easily as if the song were part of a well-rehearsed repertoire.

Kate sat down by the window. She could see that a lamp burned in the summer kitchen and that from time to time someone—Robert, surely—moved about.

Valentina worked her way through the sheet music, and after being cajoled into an encore, began to sing the lyrics the second time through. She even managed to get Mrs. Kinnard and Mrs. Russell to join in on "Little Brown Jug."

Kate might have found this a most enjoyable eve-ning if she hadn't had Harrison's letter in her pocket. And she felt a little sorry for Private Castine because he couldn't hear Valentina play and sing. Mrs. Kin-nard had clearly done her work well in preparing Val-entina for whatever bride fair she might find herself participating in.

Kate glanced out the window again. The moon was high, and the night cold and still. She saw the lamp in the summer kitchen go out, and someone leaving, but she couldn't tell who. All must be well with the chap-lain, she thought. For now at least. But despite the Rev-erend Lewis's good intentions, it seemed to Kate that they were only delaying the inevitable.

Out of respect for Max's departure tomorrow, the evening ended early despite Valentina's desire to keep playing. Kate said her good-nights to the women, and she intended to go straight upstairs to her bedchamber.

"We're almost all accounted for," Maria said when Kate was about to take her leave. "Sergeant Major Perkins says Robbie is fast asleep in the nursery, but Mrs. Justice hasn't returned yet."

"I'll stay down here and let her in," Kate said. "I'm not sleepy and I want to read awhile." She was telling the truth on both counts, and it didn't matter to her where she read Harrison's letter, only that she be alone.

She waited for a little while after Maria had gone because she wanted to make sure that she wasn't interrupted. When the house was quiet, she removed the letter from her pocket and turned it over to read her name in Harrison's painfully meticulous handwriting. Mrs. Howe had insisted upon that, that he achieve the penmanship of a gentleman. Kate had seen him practicing many times—struggling—to accomplish what Mrs. Howe had asked of him.

Miss Kate Woodard.

She took a deep breath and opened the envelope.

Dear Kate, it began.

She looked up because of a slight rustling in the hallway. Mrs. Justice was standing in the doorway, and she was clearly distressed.

"What is it?" Kate asked immediately.

"My dear," Mrs. Justice began. She gave a heavy sigh. "I need your help. I've done a terrible thing."

"What?" Kate said, growing alarmed now.

"I've been at Mrs. Russell's house—talking to Warrie. It didn't help. It didn't help at all. She blames

Robbie for everything that happened to Eleanor. Mrs. Russell told her that he's going to preach tomorrow, and she's—she's—oh, she is just not herself. I think she's going to disrupt the service. I couldn't talk her out of it—and poor Robbie—I thought he should know, so I told him."

"About the disruption?"

Mrs. Justice stood wringing her hands. "And about—Eleanor, too," she said, her chin trembling. "Oh, my dear—I just didn't know what else to do. And now I've made things worse. Now he's so— Will you talk to him?"

"Me? Mrs. Justice, I couldn't possibly."

"You have such a good effect on him—"

"How could I? I barely know him."

"I don't know how. I just know that you do. He knows it, too."

"Mrs. Justice—"

"You're the only one who can help. Please, my dear. He's in the kitchen."

"The lamp isn't lit in the summer kitchen."

"No, no. Not out there. The kitchen in here. Just… go. Sit with him for a time. Let him have someone to talk to if he needs to—the way you did before. It will help him. I know it will."

Kate closed her eyes and sighed. She did *not* want to do this. If she was certain about anything, she was certain that he would much rather be alone.

"Hurry, my dear!" Mrs. Justice whispered, looking down the hallway. "Please!"

Kate folded Harrison's letter and put it back into her pocket. Then she took a deep breath and stood.

"I'll…go," Kate said. "But I don't think I'll stay."

"That's all I ask, my dear," Mrs. Justice said. "Even if it's just for a moment, it may be all in this world he needs."

Kate walked steadily down the hallway, the soft-soled shoes she was wearing making very little noise. She saw him long before he saw her. He was sitting at the worktable near the cookstove. He looked up sharply when he realized someone was there.

"Go or stay," she said bluntly.

He looked at her for a long moment before he answered.

"Stay," he said finally.

Kate walked to the stove and looked into the coffee pot. It was half full, so she got down two cups from a nearby shelf, poured them each a cup and brought them to the table.

She sat down in one of the chairs at the side of the table so she wouldn't be across from him.

"Did Mrs. Justice send you?" he asked.

"Yes," Kate said, and he nodded.

He didn't say anything more, and neither did she. After a time he picked up the coffee cup and took a sip.

"Did you make this?" he asked, for the sole purpose, she knew, of making her smile. He already had at least a notion of her domestic shortcomings.

"I pour it much better than I make it," she said, smiling.

"Something to add to the list."

"List?"

"The one with learning to build a fire on it."

"Oh. *That* list. How…is the chaplain?" she asked, thinking it was a safe enough question.

"He's sober and able to walk on his own two feet.

He is likely to fall down at some point, but Castine is in charge of monitoring that."

"I've been wondering…" she said, tentatively taking a sip of coffee. It wasn't bad at all. She'd had much worse in some of Philadelphia's best restaurants.

"About what?"

"About the day the chaplain came here to see you. I've been wondering what you were arguing about."

"I had the impertinence to comment on his highly inebriated state. Men who already know they drink too much don't like having the fact that they aren't sober when they should be pointed out to them. It didn't help that I was in the wrong army."

"I see," Kate said.

"Did you…know?" he asked quietly, and Kate looked at him, knowing full well that they were on a different topic now.

"Yes and no," she said. "I knew about the woman, Nell. But I didn't know until just recently that she and your Eleanor were one and the same."

"Would you have told me about her?"

"No."

"Why not? I've come to think of you as being straightforward."

"Because I only knew some of the details and those were secondhand."

"Do you know if they…drove her out of town? Mrs. Kinnard—did she make Eleanor leave?"

"Not that I know of. It helped a lot that she—"

"She what?"

"Max told me that Eleanor…made sure Maria got her earrings back. The ones you and Samuel gave her.

The previous military commander had confiscated them as contraband of war."

"And how did she do that?"

Kate looked at him directly. "I don't know," she said truthfully. "I think that her being shunned by the people here was more...self-imposed, at least where Maria was concerned. Maria didn't—wouldn't—cross the street to the other side if she saw her, and Eleanor wouldn't let her sacrifice her own reputation to keep up their friendship. Thinking about it now, I seem to remember that the reason Max and Maria hired Warrie to help with the boys was because Eleanor asked them to—because the fire that killed the boys' mother happened when Warrie was away from the house and she was taking it very hard. Eleanor didn't want her mother to know that it was her idea."

"Yet another broken thing that can't be fixed," Robert said, more to himself than to her.

"Are you ready?" Kate asked. "For tomorrow's service." She meant for Warrie's interruption, but for all her straightforwardness, she couldn't quite bring herself to say it.

"No. I expect it to be...difficult."

"Because of Warrie Hansen?" she asked after all.

"No. Because I need to...speak to the congregation first—before I presume to speak to them about God."

Kate looked at him thoughtfully.

"What?" he asked after a moment.

"Maria—and Valentina—say you were never...interested in religion."

"I wasn't. But when a man goes to war, it changes him. I've seen two things happen. He can either lose his faith or he can find it. I found mine."

"Yes," Kate said, because she believed him. She thought this must be the explanation for his being... comforting, despite his warrior-like intensity. She looked toward the windows. The bright moonlight was no longer in evidence. It was raining.

"I've been wondering something, as well," he said.

"What is that?"

"I was wondering who wrote the letter Perkins gave you this evening."

The remark took her completely by surprise, and after a moment, she decided there was no reason why she couldn't tell him the same thing she'd told Valentina.

"A young friend of the family. He's away at boarding school. His name is Harrison. Some people call him Harry."

"But you don't."

Kate looked at him, wondering what had made him decide that.

"No," she said. "I don't. He's always seemed like such an old soul to me, even when he was a little boy. Harry just didn't fit."

"So what does Harrison have to say about boarding school?"

"I don't know. I haven't had a chance to read his letter."

"Read it now," he said. "You won't be interrupted."

Kate could feel him looking at her. There was no reason why she couldn't do that. She felt perfectly comfortable here—with him—despite her early reluctance. But she still hesitated until finally she removed the letter from her pocket, smoothing it carefully and leaning toward the lamp hanging over the table so that she could see it.

She had to force herself to read slowly, to make it last. She couldn't keep from smiling at the familiar handwriting, but then—

She shuffled the pages to backtrack and started over, reading quickly now, straight through to the end. Then she sat there, holding the letter in her hands, trying to understand. After a moment she held it up to the lamp in an attempt to decipher crossed out words at the bottom of the last page.

"What's wrong?" he asked

"I can't tell what this last part is," she said, hearing the tremor in her voice despite her determination to sound calm and in control.

"Maybe he didn't mean for you to."

"And that is why I need to see it. Something isn't right with him. He said the same thing twice."

"Boys sometimes lose track, I think."

"Not this boy. But it's not just the repetition. It's what he said. He said that being there was good for his character and he would be strong when it was over, as strong as his brother was when he escaped from the prison here. And then a few paragraphs later, he wrote the same thing again, as if he'd forgotten—only I know he didn't." Kate stopped. She could feel him trying to understand her concern—and failing.

"John—his brother—wasn't strong at all. He was half-starved and his mind was—if it hadn't been for his love for the woman he married, I think he would have never recovered. Harrison knows that. This is not like him. It's not like him at all," she said.

"His is the photograph you carry in your book," Robert said. It wasn't a question.

"Yes." She held up the letter again. "I think the last word is *me*."

"May I?" Robert asked and she handed it to him. "The word before that would likely be *for* or *to*. Perhaps *with*." He held it up to the light as she had done. "Three words," he said. "Something ending in the letter *y* and then *for me*. I think I know what it is."

"What?" Kate asked. "What is it?"

"I think it says, 'Pray for me.'"

"Pray for me? Oh!" Kate got up from her chair and began to pace the room.

This! This is what it feels like to be a mother, she thought wildly. *This is what it feels like to love your child and be able to do nothing to help him.*

"He crossed it out—"

"Yes, but why? *Why?* That's the question. Maybe he was afraid he'd said too much—because of what he wrote about John. It simply wasn't true, and he knew I would realize it. John was in terrible shape when he came home. And maybe he—oh, I don't know what to do!"

"What kind of school is he in?"

"A legacy school. All the Howe men went there—he's not like the Howe men."

"What kind of boy is he?"

Kate looked at him. "Quiet. Scholarly. Sensitive."

"An old soul," Robert said.

"Yes! I don't know what to do!" she said again.

"Is there no one who might understand your concerns?"

"No," she said. Then, "Yes. His...brother might."

"Then you must let him know. Can you do that?"

"I could write to him. I can't explain this in a telegram without making him think I'm—" She stopped and forced herself to take a deep breath. She was close to weeping and that wouldn't help anything. "John lives here, but he and his family have been in Philadelphia for several months—some kind of family legal business that had to be dealt with—and then his mother fell ill. The letter would go out on the train tomorrow—yes. I'll do that." She took another deep breath. There was something she could do after all.

Robert stood and moved her chair around. "Sit down," he said.

"No—I must write the letter."

"I think it would be good if you—we—did what Harrison asked first."

She looked at him blankly.

"I think we should pray for him."

"I— Yes," Kate decided immediately. No matter why the words had been marked out, Harrison had written them.

She sat down. Robert moved his chair facing hers and sat down as well.

"Give me your hands," he said.

Kate hesitated, then she bowed her head and placed her hands in his outstretched ones, feeling their warmth and strength, seeing the scars. It was raining still; she could hear it beating against the kitchen windows. She took a wavering breath.

"Kate needs Your help, Lord," he said quietly, and she looked up at him. This was not at all what she was expecting. There was none of the formality she was accustomed to. It was if he were speaking to someone there in the room.

Robert's eyes were closed; she bowed her head again.

"She's afraid for Harrison. You already know that, just as You are privy to his situation, while we are not. I know You are always with us, but if there is cause, if he's in trouble, I ask that You help him to know that You are there. *Help* him. And help her—us—so we can be ready to do whatever we can for this boy who means so much to her."

In spite of all she could do, Kate could feel a tear sliding down her cheek. She watched as it fell onto the back of his hand.

Chapter Ten

Kate was late for church. Robert had all but relinquished his hope that she was coming when he saw her standing tentatively in the vestibule, as if she still hadn't made up her mind as to whether or not she would attend this morning's service. He thought she hadn't slept because she looked so pale, so weary. He had no doubt that her letter to young Harrison's brother had been written—he'd seen the lamp burning in her window late into the night. It was likely already in the mailbag, awaiting the next northbound train.

Kate waited until the ushers were taking up the collection before she came into the sanctuary. The Yankee major who had accosted her in the hallway was sitting next to the aisle midway down, and he watched her intently as she passed by him. Joe and Jake, who were sitting with Maria, did, as well.

"Kate!" one of the boys called, only it sounded more like "Cake!" She smiled at them and put her forefinger to her lips, a gesture both of them returned, grinning from ear to ear all the while.

The only vacant places were on the front pew, and Kate continued her way down the aisle to take a seat. Robert watched as she took a deep breath and then looked up at him. He gave her the barest of nods, and she returned it with such subtlety that he might have only imagined that she had.

She's nothing like Eleanor.

And yet she was. They both had this…fierce quality about them that was not in the least offensive and definitely to be admired.

Eleanor.

He had to believe what Mrs. Justice had told him, albeit without her actually saying the words that would have left no doubt in his mind as to what she meant. But the fact was, he didn't. He couldn't. Eleanor was… *Eleanor*—laughing, headstrong and defiant. She was his first love. Some part of him, no doubt, would always love her. He simply didn't understand what could have made her become what people—Mrs. Justice— hinted she had become. What he did understand was that Eleanor would let the good people of this town think whatever they wanted to think, whether it was actually true or not, and enjoy the joke, no matter the consequences. He realized now that Warrie Hansen believed that he was the cause of her daughter's supposed downfall, despite the fact that it was Eleanor who had ended their engagement. He could only suppose that she had never told her mother about the letter she'd written to him.

But no one knew better than he did how a person could do things they never thought they'd do and then find themselves trapped in the consequences with no way out—and never once understand how they had gotten there.

He gave a soft sigh.

Bewildered again, Lord.

He looked out over the congregation. This morning's service was well attended, and he didn't doubt that he was at least one of the reasons. It surprised him that his brother-in-law was here. Apparently he had delayed his departure, most likely for Maria's sake if this church service proved too upsetting for her. Robert hoped that that would not be the case, but if it was, then he would be glad that Max was here.

Aside from his brother-in-law, the military was well represented—officers, mostly—and the decidedly openhearted Private Castine. He liked Castine—because he reminded him of Samuel.

He saw people he recognized from his childhood—Mrs. Kinnard and Valentina, Mrs. Russell and Mrs. Justice, of course, but many others, as well. How long ago it all seemed now. A number of his comrades had come. As boys he'd led them on more than one foray into what they all considered a lark and what Mrs. Kinnard considered the end of civilization as she knew it—the turning over of any number of residential privies. When they were young men, they had gone drinking and gambling together, and eventually, full of patriotism and pride, they had gone off to war.

And look at us now...

Until this day he had lost track of all of them.

The Reverend Lewis accepted the offering and blessed it; the choir sang the doxology. Mrs. Kinnard scowled at one of Max's officers, who was openly staring at Valentina. Then Reverend Lewis said a few words of introduction, and suddenly it was time.

Robert rose to his feet and walked to the lectern, surprised that his hands didn't shake. He felt the familiar restlessness, the kind he always had before a bare-knuckled fight in the ring, but he was not afraid.

He stood quietly looking down at the open Bible on the lectern. He could hear the creaking of the pews as people shifted in their seats. He could hear the whispers. Before he spoke, he wanted to give them enough time to look at him, to satisfy their curiosity about whether it was really Robert Markham standing up there and whether he did or didn't look like himself.

"There's Wah-but!" Jake called out, as if he'd only just that moment realized that his brand-new uncle was standing where the pastor normally stood. He had no doubt that Maria would put her finger to her lips just as Kate had done.

He looked up, first at Kate, and then slowly at the rest of the congregation. He didn't see Warrie Hansen.

"What am I doing here?" he said, his voice strong. "I believe that is what everyone is wondering—including me."

There was a ripple of laughter through the congregation. He waited until it subsided.

"I had a conversation with a friend last night. In this conversation, the fact that I was never known for my church attendance came up."

He could see Mrs. Kinnard straighten up and sit taller as she concluded that the friend he referred to was she.

"I said the rumors were undeniably true," he continued. "I didn't go to church as I should have. As my mother wished. But I also said then that when a man has been to war, he is changed. I said that I had seen two things happen. Some men lose their faith, and some men find it. I am here today to tell you that I have found mine.

"My experience was nothing like Saul's on the road to Damascus. It was more like Cleopas's on the road to Emmaus. Cleopas and another disciple did not recognize the resurrected Jesus as He traveled along with them, I think, because they weren't looking for Him.

"And so it was with me. I was not looking for Him. I was too lost in my own guilt and rage. I had failed the people I loved in the worst way possible. My brother, Samuel, was killed on the battlefield when I had promised my father to keep him safe. Samuel, with his poet's heart, was the best of us hardened soldiers, you see—"

"Amen," someone in the congregation said—a comrade who had been at Gettysburg.

"And yet it was he who died. It was beyond my understanding. All I knew was that I had broken my promise—"

"We all did, Rob," another veteran said. "Not just you. We *all* did."

Robert hesitated. It had never occurred to him that there might be men in the company who had felt the same sense of responsibility for Samuel that he had. He looked at the man who had spoken, and nodded, grateful for his candor.

"I was wounded, and it was many weeks before I knew where I was. My only strong memory of what had happened on the battlefield that day at Gettysburg was Samuel—alive and then dead. I know that there were men who pulled me to safety, but all of that is a blur.

"My wounds were such that I was thought to be dying as the army retreated back to Virginia. I'm told that when that was the case—when the ambulance wagon or whatever conveyance was being used—had a dying man in it, the driver would stop at a house along the way and ask the people who lived there if they would give the dying soldier a decent burial. A Maryland family—one that did not believe in war, but did believe in the parable of the Good Samaritan—took me in, with the intention of giving me whatever ease they could and then a place in their family cemetery. Living—dying—it didn't matter to me—but it must have mattered to God. I tried to let go of this life, but He wouldn't let me. When I became aware enough, I realized no one there knew my name. My identity had gotten lost in the battle and in that terrible retreat south. In my shame and in my rage at Samuel's death, I didn't tell them who I really was." He paused to look at Maria, who was openly weeping now.

"I said there was no one they could write to. It was a way out, a way to escape from a thing I could not bear, and I took it. I took it and I *lived* it, until the day came when I couldn't live it any longer.

"There is a church mission in New York City—in an often violent and unruly part of the city known as the Bowery. The mission is called Rising Hope, and it is their vocation to reach out to men like myself. The lost ones. The hopeless ones. The war-scarred ones who survived but know they don't deserve it and can't understand why.

"I was making my living by prizefighting there in the Bowery—illegal, bare-knuckle fights on the river barges beyond the reach of the law, where poor men and powerful men alike—and their women—came to gamble on my ability to beat another human being into the ground. I was good at this…trade, but I was not good at anything else. I knew that what I had become was despicable, but I didn't stop.

"A man can live by the sword only so long, and then he will die by the sword. Men who had bet heavily on one of my opponents took exception to my ability to win, and they did their best to keep me from ever winning again.

"The churchmen from Rising Hope found me. They picked me up out of the gutter, and they took me in. They looked after me until I could look after myself. And all they asked in return was that while I was there, I try to help the men around me who were worse off than I was.

"And so I did. Little by little. I helped in the kitchen at first, because I couldn't bear the company of others. And then one day I saw a man there who was trying to hide from his pain just as I had been trying to hide from mine. I *knew* what he was feeling—his despair and his anger—because I had felt the same. I was also coming to realize how pointless running away from it was. It was always there. Nothing took it away. Not drink. Not violence. Nothing.

"I spoke to him. Later, I spoke to another despairing man. Then another and another, until—

"It was like the hymn. I 'was blind, but now I see.' In reaching out to others, I found a way to live again. I had been on a long and terrible journey to get to that very place without even knowing it, and I thought I was alone every step of the way. But I wasn't alone. *He* was there—and had been all along. He was on the battlefield when Samuel died. He was on the river barges and He was with me in the gutter. Only I couldn't see Him because I wasn't looking for Him. My awareness of His presence came so slowly that I barely noticed—but it was no less profound to me than Saul's having been struck blind. Like Saul, I had been traveling this world with death in my heart until one day it was gone.

"I have asked God for His forgiveness for my many sins, and I believe I have received it. But before I can begin my new vocation, before I can presume to help others, I need to ask for your forgiveness as well. I want all of you to know—especially you, Maria—that I am truly sorry for the pain my weakness and my deception has caused you. And I want to thank those of you here who helped to take care of my family when I could not. I'm home now—truly home in body and in spirit—and it is my hope that I can begin to repay the debt I owe.

"For the time being, I will be staying in the summer kitchen—" he looked at Max "—on Colonel Woodard's property. We have all suffered through a terrible war, and we must continue to help each other as best we can. I want you to know that my door will be open.

"Now I want to ask you to remember God's words from a passage from the Book of Joel," Robert said, knowing that for some present in the congregation, what he was about to quote would no doubt border on an act of sedition. He looked at Kate again before he read it. She was looking up at him and clutching her handkerchief. Had the sad tale of his past seven years affected her that much? No, he decided. He could hear the long wail of a train whistle approaching, and her letter was waiting.

"'And I will restore to you the years that the locust hath eaten...'" he said, his voice once again strong. "'And ye shall eat in plenty, and be satisfied, and praise the name of the Lord your God...and my people shall *never* be ashamed.' May all of us recall these words and have hope."

Robert stepped down from the lectern, but instead of taking his seat, he walked down the center aisle. He had said what he wanted to say, and he had every intention of leaving now, but men and women alike reached out to him as he passed. Some of the women were crying. Maria came out of the pew where she was sitting and embraced him. Joe and Jake grabbed him around his legs.

And Warrie Hansen stood in the vestibule.

He would have gone to her, but more and more people left their seats and crowded around him. He shook hands, accepted the pats on the back and received, with as much dignity as he could muster, the unrestrained hugs from people who still saw him as the boy they'd once known.

When he finally reached the vestibule, Warrie was no longer there. He could hear Reverend Lewis hurriedly end the service, which for all intents and purposes had already ended. Maria waited just outside the church doors with Joe and Jake chasing each other around and around and Robbie soundly asleep on her shoulder. He expected to see his brother-in-law as well, because the Bible passage from Joel must have sounded to him like a call for the South to rise again. But it hadn't been that at all. He had wanted to encourage the people he'd known all his life to have hope and to let go of the past and build again on the ruins of the country they had loved.

Maria reached up to touch his cheek. "I'm very proud of you," she said. "Father would have been, too."

He nodded, but he was still trying to see if Warrie was somewhere in the crowd.

"Will you escort Kate and Mrs. Justice home?" she asked. "The children and I are going to wait with Max at the train station until he leaves."

She was looking at him so hard.

"What is it?" he asked.

"It's going to be better now," she said. "For us both."

"I need to talk to Warrie," he said. He was not yet ready to consider "better" as a possibility.

"Yes, you do. There's Kate. I think you'd better catch up with her."

He gave her a half smile. "And I think you're afraid I'm in trouble with your husband and you want me several yards in the other direction."

"Robert Markham," she said in mock surprise. "Whatever do you mean?"

He kissed her cheek, and walked toward Kate and ultimately Mrs. Justice. The weak sun that had been evident earlier this morning had completely gone. The sky was heavy and gray, and a cold wind blew out of the north. Spring would come quickly here, once it gained a foothold, but that time clearly hadn't arrived yet.

"Are you not going to see your brother off?" Robert asked Kate when he caught up with her.

"No, I've said my goodbyes. He needs some time with Maria and the children before he goes."

They both stopped to wait for Mrs. Justice, but she shooed them on, and they began walking again. In silence.

"Thank you," Kate said when they were nearly in sight of the Markham—now Woodard—house.

"For what?"

"For not asking me…anything. I don't think I could bear any questions."

"There's nothing I need to ask," he said. "I can see how you are."

She looked at him quizzically.

"You haven't slept. And you aren't going to rest easy until you know how Harrison is."

She gave a hushed sigh. "It was a job well done," she said after a time. "Your sermon."

"Well, it wasn't quite a sermon. It was more a belated confession."

"It must have been very hard for you."

"I've done harder things."

"I doubt that," she said.

"Does Mrs. Justice know about Harrison's letter?" he asked quietly.

"No one knows—except you."

Kate didn't say anything more. She walked along, completely lost in her thoughts. She dreaded the long afternoon that stretched before her. She dreaded the slow crawl of days it would take for her letter to reach John in Philadelphia and then to hear something in return. All she could do in the meantime was worry—that John wouldn't take her seriously, that something bad was happening to Harrison and her letter would arrive too late to prevent it. And all the while she was completely aware that just being with Robert Markham brought her a kind of ease and that it would be much worse for her if he were not here.

She realized that he had dropped back to speak to Mrs. Justice, and she stopped and waited for them both.

"It's time," Robert said when he and Mrs. Justice caught up.

"Time?" Kate asked.

"For you to learn to build a fire."

"What?" she said, thinking she had to have misunderstood.

"It's time for you to learn to build a fire. Right now—when the boys are out of the house. We wouldn't want to give them any ideas. Mrs. Justice agrees. Don't you, Mrs. Justice?"

"I do, Robbie," she said, smiling at them both.

"See?" he said. "If you would both be so kind as to bear with me, you, Miss Woodard, will soon learn everything there is to know about managing a hearth. The cookstove comes later."

"I think not," she said, certain that she wasn't about to participate.

"It won't take long."

"Robert—"

"I believe learning something is the best way to pass the time when it hangs heavy. And…"

Kate waited for him to continue. "And what?" she asked.

"And this is something you yourself said you needed to learn."

Kate looked at him, then frowned. "I think I'd do better learning not to talk to myself around seemingly unconscious men."

"I agree," Robert said. "But since you did, and I now

know about this terrible shortcoming and I am fully prepared to remedy it, what else can you do?"

"What, indeed," Kate said. "Where will this fire building take place?"

"Where do you think, Mrs. Justice?"

"I think Bud's sitting room would be a good place. The logs have burned out and need to be redone and a new fire started. Maria will likely want to be in there once the Colonel has left for New Bern. It gives her comfort, you know."

Yes, Kate thought. *And Mrs. Justice, as well...*

The three of them trooped into the house and up the stairs to old Mr. Markham's sitting room.

"Come over here," Robert said, motioning for Kate to come close to the hearth.

She took off her hat, her coat and gloves and did as he asked.

"It looks as if the fire is out. But it isn't. That's because the embers were covered in ashes, so when I stir them up again, I'm going to find they're still smoldering and will flame up when I—you—add kindling. Pay attention now. This is how a fire should be laid. Ashes at least an inch or two past the andirons—you don't want a draft of air getting under the logs."

"Why not?"

"A draft of air will make the logs burn through too fast. That's better than no fire at all, but you have to keep tending it. You want a fire that will burn slow and steady and keep the room warm without making it too hot and risking a fire in the chimney."

"What if there aren't any ashes?"

"Then you use sand. Not dirt—sand."

Kate had no idea where to find sand, but she didn't

say so. She heard the train whistle suddenly give one long blast, and her thoughts went immediately to Harrison.

"You see the logs here in the wood box are different sizes? Kate?" he prompted because her attention had wandered and she wasn't listening.

"Yes. I do," she answered, forcing herself to look at the contents of the wood box. The train whistle blew again.

"A large log goes in the back, up against the brick. A smaller one goes on top of it. A third log, one that's not as big as the big one or as small as the small one, goes in the front, as far forward as you can get it and still keep it on the andirons."

"Wait!" Kate said when he was about to lay the logs on the hearth. "If I'm the one learning, I'll do it."

"You'll get your dress dirty," he said.

"I have more than two now. Kindly move aside."

She had to struggle to get the largest log into place—somehow she'd never realized how heavy wood could be. But she managed. Placing the other two was much easier.

"Now what?" she asked.

"Now we start the fire—between the back log and the fore log. Get some kindling—those small flat pieces there. That's kindling. Take the shovel and uncover the coals, put a few pieces of the kindling on it. Give it a puff of air from the bellows. Keep adding kindling, a little at a time, until the fire is burning well enough to add a small log. Then place some more kindling so the log will catch fire. Then situate another log. Let it catch fire, too, then put on another one until you've got several logs burning in the middle. And that's it."

"How do I keep the fire going?"

"Just add whatever size log has burned up—that will be the ones in the middle mostly. Then the fore log and the small one on top of the back log. It'll take a while for the back log to go. Use the poker to get a new back log into place so you don't get burned."

"Anything else I need to know?"

"Don't set the house on fire?" he suggested.

"What an excellent idea. Anything else?"

"Wash your hands after you've handled the logs. Sometimes they've had poison ivy vines wrapped around them and it will get on your hands. You don't want that."

Kate looked at him. "No," she said, agreeably. But she realized suddenly how sad they both were. She also realized what he'd been doing by insisting that she have this household lesson. He was trying to keep her occupied, trying to give her at least a few moments respite from her worry about Harrison. She abruptly looked away, and she began to follow his instructions to the letter, cajoling the flames with kindling until she had four small logs burning brightly in the center. When he was satisfied that everything was as it should be, they both stood.

"That's a very fine—"

"Robbie," Mrs. Justice interrupted from where she had been standing by the window. "There are men waiting at the summer kitchen. There must be a dozen."

Robert looked out. It had started to rain steadily. "I said my door would be open. I'd better go down."

"Wait, Robbie," Mrs. Justice said. She pointed off to the side.

When he looked out the window again, he could

see Warrie Hansen standing among the trees, the rain beating down on her.

"I'm going to go speak to her," he said, but Mrs. Justice caught him by the arm.

"You wait here," she said. "If she's here to talk to you, I'll bring her to you."

Mrs. Justice gave Kate a worried look and hurried away. In a moment Kate heard the front door open and Mrs. Justice calling Warrie Hansen's name.

"I'll go let the others into the summer kitchen," Kate said. "Before they follow Warrie in."

"Yes. Good," Robert said. "And build them a fire."

"What?"

"You know how, so do it."

Kate stood looking at him. He was challenging her to put her brand-new skill to good use—already—and she was going to take him up on it.

"All right, I will."

"And don't forget to wash your hands."

"I'll remember," she said. She hesitated a moment longer, then went downstairs; Warrie Hansen was just coming in the front doorway with Mrs. Justice, her face haggard, her eyes red from weeping.

"I'm wanting to talk to him," she said to Mrs. Justice, and Mrs. Justice nodded.

Kate stood out of the way as they walked toward the stairs.

"Maria and the boys will be home before long," Mrs. Justice said.

"I ain't planning on taking long."

"I think you should take as long as you need, Warrie," Mrs. Justice said with a firmness that was surprising. "And I think you should plan on staying. You have a job to do here with those rascally boys. I just wanted you to know that the children aren't here now. Robbie is in Bud's sitting room. Close the door when you go in, if you will."

Kate could hear Warrie's progress down the hallway, and Robert must have come out to meet her.

"What about my girl?" Warrie said. "I didn't hear you say you was sorry for what happened to her. Why ain't you sorry for *that,* Robert Markham? When you decided you'd play dead, you all but took her with you, you know that, don't you? And you don't say one thing."

The door closed, and Kate couldn't hear any more. She stood for a moment, then headed for the back of the house. She hurried through the back door to the path that led to the summer kitchen, all but running because the rain was coming harder.

The men were clearly surprised to see the colonel's sister running around in the rain. She opened the summer kitchen door for them. "Do go in," she said. "Please," she added when they hesitated. "Robert should be here soon. I hope you won't mind waiting."

"No, miss," one of them said. "Being in the army gets a body used to that kind of thing."

Kate followed them in. There were only a few chairs, but the men didn't seem to mind. After a moment most of them began sitting on the floor. Kate looked around as Mrs. Justice came in with a bag of coffee and a tray full of stacked tin cups.

"The coffee grinder's over there on that shelf, Wiley," she said to one of the men. "If you'd fetch it for me." She sat the cups and the sack on the table where the chaplain had lain earlier. "I understand soldiers have their own way of making coffee, so I'm going to turn it all over to you. Here are the beans. Wiley's got the grinder—"

"He don't know what to do with it, though, do you, Wiley?" one of the men said, making Wiley grin.

"The pot is over there," Mrs. Justice said, smiling. "And there's the water bucket and plenty of cups..."

She gave Kate a pointed look, and Kate went immediately to the hearth. She recognized the configuration of the logs and ashes immediately. She could do this; she was certain.

Mostly certain.

She supposedly didn't have to worry about anything but resurrecting the smoldering embers that were presumably under the ashes.

And so they were. There was plenty of kindling, and in no time at all she had a blaze burning. She smiled to herself, feeling more useful than she had since—ever. But her sense of satisfaction only lasted a moment until her worry about Harrison returned.

"Now," Mrs. Justice said. "There's a nice fire for you. If you'll excuse us, Miss Woodard and I will go back to the house now. Robbie should be here soon."

"Much obliged, Mrs. Justice, Miss Woodard," they said, more or less in unison.

"I made a big batch of buckwheat cakes yesterday," Mrs. Justice said as they walked down the slate path to the house. "I'll give them time to get their coffee going, then I'll take a platter and some molasses out to them."

"No, I'll do it," Kate said. "You shouldn't be out in the rain."

"Oh, thank you, my dear. I would appreciate that. This kind of weather makes these old bones ache."

They both stopped just inside the kitchen and listened. Kate could hear a murmur of voices coming from old Mr. Markham's sitting room, but no actual words.

"I hope—" Kate said. She stopped, because she didn't know quite what she hoped. She could only imagine what a difficult day this must be for him, and it was far from over. She sighed. She just wanted everything to work out all right for him.

And Eleanor, she thought. She had no business forgetting about Eleanor.

She realized suddenly that Mrs. Justice was watching her closely.

"Come let's sit in the kitchen," Mrs. Justice said. "It's warm there, and we'll be out of the way. There's coffee left from breakfast on the stove. And my buckwheat cakes are in the warming oven. Let's have ourselves another feast."

"Yes," Kate said, forcing herself to smile. "Let's."

After they'd eaten, Kate took the remaining buckwheat cakes—a heaping platter—more than enough for the men in the summer kitchen to have at least one—and headed out the back door, struggling to hang on to a jug of molasses as well. She could smell the aroma of hot coffee before she was halfway down the path.

Fire must still be burning, she thought, pleased.

One of the men saw her coming and held the door open for her. All of them were clearly happy to see her bringing something for them to eat.

"If you see Robert, you can tell him to take his time," one of the men said as she set the buckwheat cakes and the molasses on the table, and she and the others laughed.

She was still smiling as she made her way back to the house. Robert was standing by the well, apparently waiting for her. He looked so…resigned—she supposed that would be the best word for it. It was as if he had encountered a formidable situation he could not change, and he had no choice but to accept it.

She didn't ask him if he was all right. She didn't ask him about Warrie or if she had told him where Eleanor had gone.

"They're still out there, I take it," he said when she was close enough.

"Yes. They're eating Mrs. Justice's buckwheat cakes and molasses."

He gave a slight smile. "We used to talk about her buckwheat cakes on the march sometimes. Hers were the best in the county. We'd remember all about when and where we'd eaten them and how many we had—and make ourselves miserable."

He looked toward the summer kitchen. Kate could feel him trying to gather his thoughts—or perhaps let go of them. Whatever had happened with Warrie Hansen, she thought that he didn't want to take it with him when he talked to the men who were out there waiting.

"Thank you for doing this, Kate," he said quietly.

"I built a fire," she said, hoping to make him smile.

He did, and Kate felt as if he had given her a small but incredibly special gift.

Then he took a deep breath and stepped out into the rain. She watched him go, waiting until he went inside the summer kitchen. In only a moment a loud cheer went up. Robert Markham was home at last, and he'd gotten a hero's welcome.

She was on her way upstairs when the carriage

bringing Maria and the children home arrived. Sergeant Major Perkins came in carrying the baby in one arm and the civilian mail pouch that would contain the family's personal mail in the other. Private Castine had Joe and Jake slung over each shoulder as if they were sacks of flour, running the last few steps to the door to make them giggle as only little boys can.

"Send them young'uns over here to me," Warrie Hansen called from the far end of the hall. "We got to get them out of their Sunday best while we still can."

Castine deftly put both boys on their feet, and they dashed down the hallway to Warrie.

"Sergeant Major, bring that one along, too," Warrie called.

Maria was just coming in the door, and she stopped dead.

"What?" Kate asked.

"Well, I hardly know where to start. Warrie's here, for one thing…"

"She came and talked to Robert a little while ago. I didn't realize she hadn't left—he's out in the summer kitchen."

Maria was still looking at her. "And you're…"

"I'm what?"

"Well, you don't look like you did at church," Maria said, trying not to grin.

"Why?" Kate asked. There was no mirror in the downstairs hallway where she could see for herself.

"You haven't been shoveling coal, have you?"

Kate looked down at the front of her dress. It was heavily streaked with wood ash.

"Face, too," Maria advised her, grinning openly now.

"It's your brother's fault. He has been teaching me how to build a fire," Kate said.

"Why?" Maria asked.

"Mostly because I didn't know how—and please don't look at me as if my sanity was suspect. It's not my fault I was brought up useless."

"Kate, you are the least useless person I know," Maria said kindly.

"Then I've certainly got you fooled. Anyway, a vote was taken and I lost. Robert and Mrs. Justice outvoted me, so I had a lesson. I'm happy to say I can now officially build a hearth fire."

"I should hope so," Maria said, still teasing. "Given the way you look."

"Actually I've lit not one but two fires since the church service," Kate said. "And the fire brigade hasn't had to be summoned—so far," she added in an effort not to tempt fate, and they laughed together when—Kate was certain—neither of them felt like it. But she and Maria knew the importance of at least trying to find a better humor. Doggedly making the effort had likely gotten them both through difficult times in their lives. This would be a somber house until Max came home and until Kate knew for certain that her letter had reached Philadelphia.

A train whistle sounded in the distance, and they both turned their heads in that direction, the brief respite from the disquiet that threatened to overwhelm them rapidly fading.

The boys—shoeless and half-undressed now—came racing down the hallway despite Warrie's objections. It was clear that they had no intention of returning to her. They ignored her as long as they dared, giggling

as they circled Maria and Kate both, and then running
back in the direction they'd come. Kate couldn't help
but smile at the audacity of young male children. Had
Harrison done things like this when he was their age?
Had he ever had the opportunity for exuberance? She
had always wondered. John very likely had, because
he was as recalcitrant as they came, but Harrison was
nothing like John. Mrs. Howe had wanted him seen
and not heard and he would always have done his best
to please her—until now.

"I think I'd better put on my play clothes, too," Kate
said, and she went upstairs to repair what damage she
could to her face and her dress—but not before she
checked on the fire in old Mr. Markham's sitting room.
It was burning just as Robert said it would—slow and
steady—and the room was warm and comfortable.

She smiled slightly when she returned to her room.
A fire burned there, as well. Castine had beaten her
to it.

Kate washed her face and hands, then she changed
her clothes, deciding she really would put on the dress
she always wore whenever she played with the boys—
or whenever her trunks went somewhere without her.
She stood for a moment looking at her sad reflection
in the washstand mirror, then closed her eyes.

"I'm afraid again," she whispered. "I want to believe
You're here, just the way Robert says You are. He be-
lieves You're always with us, no matter what. I want
to believe that, too. Help me."

She sighed, and turned away.

The house had grown quiet, and Kate assumed that
Mrs. Justice, and Warrie and the children, were all
settling down to take their customary afternoon naps.

Maria would likely be napping, as well. She was going to have another child, and Kate knew from experience how fatigued Maria must be in these early days.

Kate moved to the window where she could see the summer kitchen. After a moment she thought she could hear…singing.

Yes, she decided. Robert and the men in the summer kitchen were singing a hymn—"Amazing Grace." She could hear the melody quite clearly now, if not the words. They had sung together before, she thought. Perhaps as boys, and as young men and as soldiers.

She took a deep breath, her mind suddenly filled with the most disturbing aspect of Harrison's letter.

Pray for me.

"I am, sweet boy," she whispered. She moved to the bed and stretched out. She had been so long without sleep that it was a relief to lie down, and yet she still wanted to get up and pace the room, as if that would somehow help. Eventually she reached for the quilt at the foot of the bed and pulled it over her, and—incredibly—she slept.

Chapter Eleven

"Robert has company," Mrs. Justice whispered to keep Warrie from hearing her.

Kate kept stirring finely chopped onion and bacon into the cornbread batter Robert had Mrs. Justice teaching her to make. Kate was fully aware that Robert was bent on keeping her busy as a way of making time pass, and in the interval since her fire-building lesson, she had learned all manner of things pertaining to the kitchen and the household. Or so it would seem to the casual onlooker—and there were several. The most diligent observer had been Valentina, who seemed to pop up at the most unexpected times without ever saying why. It seemed to Kate that she only wanted to know what Kate was doing, and where Robert was while she was doing it.

Kate didn't have to ask Mrs. Justice who Robert's company today might be. Men came to the summer kitchen all the time, sometimes just one and sometimes a half dozen or so. She had even seen the chaplain arrive under his own power—twice. Robert always spoke with them, and when he did, Kate and Mrs. Justice would bring coffee. Today it looked as if some of the men's wives or sisters or mothers had come along, as well. Robert's reputation was growing, and so was the strain on the household schedule. There were constant disruptions to the sergeant major's routine—and therefore everyone else's—despite Robert's best intentions. After the second week he sat up specific times for prayer meetings—Thursday and Saturday early evenings so as not to conflict with the other churches in town. And, aside from just bringing the refreshments, Kate found herself staying to hear him speak, keeping well in the background so as not to be a distraction. Her brother was the occupation commander, something very few people in this town would be able to ignore if she were too obvious.

Thanks to Mrs. Justice, Kate was beginning to know, at least by sight, many of the people who showed up—and how they figured into Robert Markham's early life. They were merchants he'd run errands for after school, church friends, distant relatives by marriage, old classmates, Sunday School teachers who had thrown up their hands more than once at some of his antics, but all of them were apparently finding some degree of comfort and good sense in what he had to say.

Surprisingly—or perhaps not—Valentina had shown up for a recent meeting, but whether it was for a personal spiritual need or whether she was bent on finding herself another "adventure," Kate couldn't say. Or perhaps Valentina had come on her mother's behalf, to keep Mrs. Kinnard informed so that she would know if—when—she needed to put a stop to all this.

A much bigger surprise was the evening Mrs. Rus-

sell came. After the service many of the Confederate veterans who were present gathered respectfully
around her, speaking to her of James Darson and their
regard for him. It was as if they had been wary of doing
so before, because of her intense grief, but now that
she had come to hear Robert—and in her lost son's
absence—she would henceforth belong to all of them.

Kate made a point of spending time with Maria in
old Mr. Markham's sitting room in the evening because she had promised Max she would be available
to his wife, and because—if she were truthful—she
knew that Robert might come to visit with his sister
before she retired for the night. Maria felt better when
he was near, and so did Kate. Stronger somehow. More
hopeful.

But this night Maria had gone to bed early, and
only Kate was sitting by the fire when he came up the
back stairs.

"Your handiwork?" he asked, nodding at the hearth.

"It is, actually," she said. "I'm afraid Sergeant Major
Perkins finds my new skill very unsettling."

"He hasn't forbidden you to do it?"

"Well, not yet. And so far I've been able to beat Castine to it enough to keep my hand in."

"Poor Castine," he said, and she smiled. She was
looking directly into his eyes, and she shouldn't. She
knew that, but she didn't look away.

"I was…surprised," she began, because this was
the first opportunity she'd had to speak to him alone.

"About what?"

"About Warrie—that she decided to return to the
house."

"I coerced her into doing it."

"How so?"

"She's a good woman—a kind woman—and your brother told me that Maria was having another child."

Kate frowned, and managed to refrain from saying how surprised—shocked—she was that Max would have told him such a personal thing.

"He wanted to make sure I understood what my responsibilities were while he was gone," Robert said as if he had read her thoughts.

"And do you? Understand?"

"I do. And I passed some of them on to Warrie. I told her that Maria needed her—which she does—and that she and I had to find a way not to cause Maria any more worry than she already has."

"It seems to be working."

"So far—if I stay out of her way. She's a long way from forgiving me."

It was Kate's opinion that forgiveness in this situation would be Eleanor's prerogative, but she didn't say so.

"I...take it you've had no answer to your letter," he said without warning, watching her closely as he said it.

Kate shook her head. "I should have heard by now— if John takes what I've said seriously."

"He will."

"You can't know that."

"I know you well enough. And so does he. *I* would take you seriously."

She felt the sudden sting of tears and looked away.

After a long moment she took a deep breath and asked the question she'd been wondering about.

"Did Warrie tell you where Eleanor has gone?"

"No. She thinks I'm not fit to know."

"I'm sorry."

"I think…"

"What?" Kate asked when he didn't continue.

"If Eleanor lets Warrie know where she is, then Warrie will likely tell her I'm here. I just have to…wait and then take it from there."

She gave a quiet sigh. That was exactly what she herself was doing—waiting for something to happen, and then she would take it from there. But the waiting was so *hard,* and most days it was all she could do not to fall back into hiding to solve her problems, hiding so she would have the privacy to weep.

Kate looked at him. "Will you pray with me?" she asked. "For Harrison."

As he had before, he moved his chair to face hers and held out his hands.

"Are you going to tell me what's on your mind or are you going to keep staring at me?" Robert asked, because Maria clearly hadn't insisted on coming to the summer kitchen to join him for breakfast without some—as yet unknown—purpose.

"Nothing is on my mind," she said in a way that would cause any man who had grown up with a sister to realize immediately that such a statement was far and away from the actual truth.

"If you say so," he said, going back to eating the eggs and bacon she had prepared but didn't care to eat herself.

"More coffee?" she asked him after a moment, and when he looked up she was grinning from ear to ear.

"Yes, thank you," he said, ignoring her obvious mirth.

When she'd poured the coffee, she moved the cup back in his direction—and she was smiling again.

"I'm wondering when I got to be so entertaining," he said.

"I'm wondering when you got to be a preacher—despite what you said in church that Sunday."

"I'm not a preacher—yet."

"But you intend to be."

He looked at her. "I… Yes."

"And you're pining over Eleanor."

"No, Maria. I am not pining over her, though I freely admit that I would like to know that she's all right. I will always care about her. She and I were engaged to be married."

"Feeling guilty, then?"

"For what specifically?"

"For 'dying,' of course."

"I'll always feel guilty about that. I hurt the people I loved. But Eleanor wouldn't deliberately ruin her own reputation because she thought I died. Eleanor would come to my memorial service in a red dress."

"I did think it was something like that at first— that whatever scandalous thing she did or didn't do was because she was angry with you—for dying and leaving her."

"But you changed your mind."

"Well, I still think it has something to do with you. I just don't know what it is."

"And neither do I, until I can ask her."

"Aha!" she said, as if she'd uncovered some dark secret he'd been carrying.

"Now what does that mean?"

"You actually don't know, do you?" she said, leaning toward him, smiling still.

"I wouldn't ask if I did."

"What do you think of Kate?"

"What do I think of her?" he said, startled because she had veered off in a completely different direction.

"Don't ask what I ask. Answer."

"I like her," he said easily—because it was true.

"She likes you, too."

"Does she?" he said, surprised by the remark.

"Well, so she said."

"When did she say that?"

"Weeks ago—before she got to know you."

Robert glanced at her. She was teasing him now.

"Right after you came back and disrupted all our lives," she said to qualify her remark. "And you can frown all you like. It doesn't change a thing."

"Maria, you do know I haven't the slightest idea what we're talking about here—"

"Then, dear brother, I will tell you," Maria said, getting up from her chair.

"I wish you would," he said. "And soon."

"You want to be a preacher."

"I do," he said agreeably.

"And you like Kate."

"Yes."

"And she's been…helpful to you when you have your prayer meetings."

"And Mrs. Justice, as well—" he began.

"It's perfectly clear then," Maria said, interrupting.

"What is?"

"Preachers need wives, Robert, and you—my

dear, *dear* brother—are grooming her to become one. Yours."

"No, I'm not," he said as soon as he'd recovered enough from Maria's assertion to respond. "'Grooming,' as you put it, is not the reason I'm—"

"Oh, I know you think that," Maria said, dismissing the idea with a wave of her hand. "Max told me Kate is worried about Harrison, and I can see you're trying to help her by keeping her occupied—which is an excellent idea. But you should realize that that isn't the *only* reason. I've seen the way you look at her—and believe me it's not the way you looked at Eleanor. Kate Woodard is important to you. You would have had a much harder time being home again if she weren't here, now wouldn't you?"

She didn't wait for an answer. She smiled prettily and went out the door.

Kate stood outside the door for a moment, not wanting to cause Maria to lose her place with her knitting.

"There you are," Maria said when she realized Kate was there. "I've been waiting for you."

"Why?" Kate asked, but Maria was counting stitches and didn't answer. Kate glanced around the sitting room. No Robert. In fact she hadn't seen him all day.

"I should learn to knit," Kate said, more to herself than to Maria.

Warrie was putting the boys to bed in the nursery wing. She could hear her singing the song that was, as far as Warrie was concerned, a lullaby, her voice slightly brittle and off-key:

Go tell Aunt Rosie,
Go tell Aunt Rosie,
Go tell Aunt Rosie
The old gray goose is dead.

"I could teach you sometime," Maria said. "Right now I need some company. Come sit down. Mrs. Justice has gone to Mrs. Kinnard's house."

"On a visit or was she summoned?"

"I'm not sure," Maria said. "Whichever it is, the refreshments will be worth it."

Kate sat down in the nearest rocking chair, clutching the book she'd brought with her, the one she had no intention of reading, the one that always held Harrison's photograph. She was so restless. The more time that passed since she'd written that letter to John, the less she was able to sleep. The truth of the matter was that she couldn't remember quite what she'd said. Had she sounded legitimately concerned or completely overwrought?

"Has the mail pouch arrived?" Maria asked, looking up from her knitting.

"Not yet," Kate said. "There must not be any personal mail today."

"No," Maria said. She was clearly disappointed that she wouldn't have a letter from Max to read when she retired. And it wasn't only letters he sent. Kate was more than a little surprised by the romantic gestures her brother made via military postal delivery. Just last week he'd sent Maria some violets he'd dug up from a riverbank along the Neuse and potted in a tin can with a garish yellow Pie Meat label. The can had been wrapped in several layers of wet muslin and placed in a small wooden box before it left New Bern on the train. Incredibly the violets had arrived still fresh and beautiful.

"Is Robert not coming to visit this evening?" Kate suddenly asked, not caring how it sounded. She wanted to know, and if Maria thought the inquiry inappropriately forward, then so be it.

"I'm glad of your friendship with my brother," Maria said instead of answering Kate's bold question.

Kate made no comment, mostly because she didn't know what to think of the remark.

"Did you…know Max had spoken to him?" Maria said next.

"Yes," Kate answered.

"You did?"

"Yes. Robert told me."

"Robert *told* you?" Maria said, clearly surprised, if not out-and-out astounded.

"It's natural that Max would be worried about you—" Kate hesitated because of the expression on Maria's face.

"Natural?" Maria asked.

"Max wanted Robert to know about the baby—so he would understand what his responsibilities were while Max was gone—or that's how Robert put it."

"But that's not what I meant at all."

"What did you mean, then?"

"I meant that Max talked to Robert about a complaint he'd had from one of his officers."

"What officer?"

"I don't know what officer. Max didn't tell me his name. The complaint had to do with you."

Kate looked at her blankly. "I don't understand."

"This officer felt Robert was being much too familiar where you are concerned, and he thought Max should know about it."

"Max never mentioned anything like that to— Oh. I just realized. One of Max's officers cornered me in the downstairs hallway. He'd been drinking. He kept insisting that he would come here to visit me while Max was away. He was sure I needed the company of 'my own kind.' I couldn't get away from him, and Robert intervened. I'm afraid I let the man think that I might mention his behavior to Max. I suppose he wanted to give Max his version of what happened before I did. This is so aggravating," Kate added.

"What is?"

"My brother—and yours. I don't like being in the middle of some…incident, and not know anything about it. And I'm sure Robert didn't like being put in the wrong for something he didn't do. They didn't come to blows or anything, did they?"

"No. Or if they did, Max didn't tell me."

"Didn't Robert say anything to you about it?"

"No, nothing. According to Max, Robert said that your friendship was very important to him and he had the utmost respect for you and would never do anything to jeopardize it—and Max was satisfied."

Very important? Utmost respect?

Kate had no idea what either of those terms actually meant.

"Kate," Maria said, and she looked at her sister-in-law. "I think I should tell you what I think about this… friendship."

"All right," Kate said.

But Maria hesitated. Warrie had stopped singing,

and neither Private Castine nor Sergeant Major Perkins seemed to be wandering about on the ground floor. The house was quiet for a change. Too quiet.

"Maria, what is it?"

"I know my brother very well. I think I even understand why he didn't come home until now. But he's—" Maria stopped and began gathering up her knitting and putting it carefully into her yarn basket. "I've already been an overzealous busybody once today. It's not very becoming."

"For heaven's sake, tell me!"

"All right, I will. Kate, what is 'friendship' to one person may not be friendship to another."

"What do you mean? I have no designs on Robert." Because Robert is *safe,* she nearly said—safe for her to have as a friend, just as she was safe for him—because of Eleanor Hansen.

"I don't mean you. I mean him. I think he has deeper feelings than even he realizes. For you," she added.

"He loves Eleanor," Kate said quietly.

"Yes. But that has nothing to do with this."

Kate opened her mouth to say something, then closed it again.

"I just don't want either of you to be hurt," Maria said. "Men can be so unobservant sometimes. I think you will see where the situation is heading before he will. If you're privy to what I already suspect and it turns out that I'm right, then you'll be…prepared to handle it. As you said, it's aggravating being in the middle of a situation you know nothing about."

Maria stood.

"I truly am glad of your friendship with Robert,

Kate, whatever 'friendship' turns out to be. Think about what I've said. Good night. Pleasant dreams."

Think about it? How could she *not* think about it?

Kate stayed in the sitting room, her mind darting from Robert to Harrison and back again, until she couldn't sit still any longer. She got up from the chair and walked to the window. The summer kitchen windows were dark. Either Robert was not there or he was already asleep.

Very important.

Utmost respect.

Friendship.

Friendship was all that she'd wanted.

But even as that thought formed, she knew it wasn't true. Friendship was the only thing she could allow.

She sighed and went downstairs. Perkins had moved Max's campaign table from the sitting room to a corner of the foyer the day Max departed for New Bern. It was where Perkins left the private mail pouch when there was one. Kate glanced in that direction out of habit, expecting nothing to be there this late in the day, and she was not disappointed. The conversation with Maria had left her too agitated to even think of sleeping, so she wandered toward the kitchen. Mrs. Justice was sitting at the worktable, apparently just returned from her visit, because her bonnet was hanging by its ribbons on the back of one chair and her cloak was draped over another.

"Would you like some tea, my dear," Mrs. Justice asked kindly—a little too kindly, Kate thought.

"Yes, please," she said. She sat down in the only remaining chair and rested her elbows on the table, something her mother would have taken great exception to if she'd seen her.

There was already an extra cup and saucer on the table—which made Kate even more suspicious that offering her tea hadn't been accidental. She gave a heavy sigh as Mrs. Justice poured some and handed the cup and saucer to her.

"You mustn't be upset, my dear," Mrs. Justice said. "The effort he's been making—the grooming—is a compliment, really. It shows he has confidence in your potential."

Kate looked at her. "What grooming?"

"Oh," Mrs. Justice said, somewhat taken aback. "The…um…grooming Maria mentioned?" She looked so hopeful that no further questions would be forthcoming that Kate was almost tempted to let the matter drop.

Almost.

"Maria didn't say anything about grooming. Have I not been presentable enough for Mrs. Kinnard? Surely that's not what she wanted to see you about. I have all my dresses now—in fact I was thinking of having Mrs. Russell's sister make me one or two more."

"No, no, not your dresses. It's—Robbie."

"You mean the…friendship?" Kate asked, making a wild guess even though she couldn't see any kind of connection at all between "grooming" and "friendship."

"I wasn't talking about a friendship, my dear. I don't know anything about that. I only know that Maria and I agree—about the grooming."

"I must ask you again, Mrs. Justice. What grooming?"

"The grooming Robbie is doing—and having me do. The grooming to make you a suitable preacher's wife."

Kate stared at her. "You—and Robert Markham— are grooming me to be a preacher's wife," she stated carefully to make sure she'd heard right. She tried— and failed—to keep the incredulity out of her voice.

"Yes," Mrs. Justice said happily. "And you're making wonderful progress."

"And who is this preacher I'm being groomed for?" Kate asked.

"Why, Robbie, of course."

"He's looking for a *wife?*"

"Oh, he says not—according to Maria."

"Well, he should know."

Mrs. Justice leaned toward her as if she didn't want anyone to overhear. "We think he hasn't realized it yet."

"Has everybody forgotten he's going to marry Eleanor Hansen?"

"Oh, no. We haven't forgotten. We've decided that isn't going to work out."

"I see," Kate said. "Well—" She took a sip of her tea. "This has certainly been an evening for interesting…conversations."

Chapter Twelve

Kate came downstairs early to see if there would be a mail pouch on the campaign table after all. The table was bare, except for the small polished brass oil lamp Sergeant Major Perkins had added since the last time she'd looked. It, like the table, seemed lost in the all but empty foyer.

She stood for a moment, making a concerted effort to shore up the courage to face another anxious day. She tried not to worry, but she couldn't seem to help herself. Were other mothers—real mothers—able to let go of the apprehension they felt regarding their children's happiness and safety, or was she merely too excitable because she had always been on the fringes of Harrison's life?

She suddenly remembered Mrs. Justice's prayer. *Thy will.*

"Thy will," she whispered. "Not mine." And she turned around just in time to see Robert disappearing into the kitchen—backtracking, unless she was very mistaken.

Is he avoiding me?

She had been avoiding him, of course, since all that talk of "grooming" with Mrs. Justice, but it hadn't occurred to her until this moment that he might be doing the same. She waited, trying to determine which way he was going to go, then she hurried out the front door and around the house to the back. When Robert came outside, she was standing on the slate path, planted firmly between him and the summer kitchen.

"Good morning," she said pointedly.

"Good morning," he replied—once he got over his astonishment at finding her there when she'd only just been in the foyer. He seemed not to want to look at her at first, and then he seemed not to want to stop.

She looked back.

"Mrs. Justice said you were grooming me to be a preacher's wife," she said bluntly, and then she waited.

And waited.

He stood there, not exactly surprised by her comment, she thought, but not exactly...*not* surprised, either.

"Did she?" he said finally.

"No," Kate said. "She *said* you were grooming me to be *your* wife."

He took a quiet breath and then another one. Then, after much too long an interval, he nodded. "Good," he said. And he stepped around her and walked away.

Good?

She pursed her lips to say something, but there was no longer anyone around to talk to. He had disappeared into the summer kitchen and closed the door. She wasn't about to follow him, though it was clear that she would have to if she wanted him to elaborate. Follow him. And corner him.

She looked around at the arrival of a horse and rider—a soldier bringing the mail pouch. She went back inside, hurrying through the kitchen and into the hallway. The soldier was already leaving as she reached the foyer; the private mail pouch lay on the campaign table.

Kate opened the pouch, knowing she was usurping Maria's authority. This was her household and it was her duty to see to the mail. Even so, she dumped everything out, searching through a number of envelopes for a letter with a Philadelphia return address. There was none. She gave a sharp sigh of disappointment, then picked up one of the other pieces, a telegram. Her name was on it.

Her pulse pounded in her ears as she tore the envelope open. It was from John.

She read the message quickly, and then again:

H gone when we arrived. Looking for him here.
Advise Max he may come south.
John

"Gone?" Kate said aloud. She read the telegram again, more slowly this time. "Who is 'we'?"

Not Mrs. Howe. She had been ill. Her illness was the reason he'd stayed in Philadelphia. It must be Amanda, his wife, she decided. He wouldn't take his mother with him to the school if he could help it, even if she were well now—unless she'd read Kate's letter and insisted. Mrs. Howe was very good at that—insisting.

She abruptly crumpled the telegram in both hands

and stood there, eyes closed, trying not to cry. She had believed all along that something was wrong, and what a bitter thing it was to be proved right.

"Did you say something, Miss Kate?" Perkins said behind her.

"No. Nothing," she said in a rush, turning away so he couldn't see her face. She walked quickly down the hallway toward the back of the house, leaving the sergeant major to think whatever he liked.

Her abrupt entry into the kitchen startled one of the soldier-cooks who hadn't been there on her first pass through, but she made no apology. She was all but running now, and she didn't stop until she was a short distance from the summer kitchen.

I can't do this. I can't go running to Robert.

But even as the thought came into her mind, she knew she was going to do just that.

Robert caught a glimpse of Kate as she rushed headlong from the house. He immediately opened the door for her, but she had stopped dead.

"What's wrong?" he asked, alarmed by the distress he could see on her face. "Kate?"

She came closer but she didn't say anything. She handed him a crumpled telegram. He had to smooth it out to read it.

"Did you tell Perkins about this?" he asked, looking up at her. It was likely that Perkins would read all the incoming telegrams, but if he hadn't, Robert understood enough about the way the occupation worked to know that the sergeant major would need to be informed immediately.

She shook her head.

"Then that's the first thing you have to do—"

"No," she said.

"He already suspects something. Look," Robert said, nodding toward the house. Perkins was standing at the back door. "He's guessed something is wrong. Harrison's brother wanted Max notified, and he's not here. Perkins will have to handle it. Better him than any of the officers I've seen."

Kate looked toward the house again. Sergeant Major Perkins was on the verge of coming down the slate path. "Yes, all right," she said, trying to force herself to think clearly. Of course Perkins would have to be involved; nobody knew that better than she did.

"Mrs. Howe lives in Philadelphia," Kate said.

"Mrs. Howe?"

"Harrison's mother. If he's run away, I don't think he'll go there. She's a very...exacting woman. He'll think he's let her down and he'd be too ashamed. I think he's more likely to come here. To Max."

"And you," Robert said. "Perkins is coming, Give him the telegram." He handed it back to her.

"He may have already read it."

"Even if he has, that's not the face of a man who understands the situation he's found himself in."

"His sack and burn face," Kate said quietly. She took a deep breath and waited for the inevitable.

"Miss Kate," Perkins said as soon as he was close enough. "You know what I told you the night *he* showed up." He nodded in Robert's direction. "My duty is to the Colonel. I need to know what's going on. Now, if you please."

Kate hesitated, then handed him the telegram.

He read it quickly and looked up at her. "Is that Captain Howe's little brother he's talking about?"

"Yes," Kate said, not at all surprised that he had already discerned who "H" might be.

"The telegram doesn't say much. I reckon he's run off from wherever he was."

"Boarding school," Kate said. "He wasn't happy there."

"Well, if he's coming in this direction, how far he gets will depend on how much money he's got and more on whether or not he can hang on to it. There will be all kinds of riffraff wanting to relieve him of whatever he's carrying. If he runs out, he'll be stuck wherever the train stopped. Best thing is to backtrack from here—check with the conductors and with the people who make a living hanging around the whistle-stops." He looked at Robert. "Soldiers looking for him aren't going to find out much from the locals."

"I'll go," Robert said.

"I'm going with you," Kate said.

"No," both men said in unison.

"You'll slow me down, Kate," Robert said, looking into her eyes. "The places I may need to go, I can't take you. It would be better if you stayed here with Maria. There's no point in having her worry about both of us. If he's stuck somewhere along the line, I can find him, and as soon as I do, I'll get word to the sergeant major. Can you send somebody to find the chaplain?" he said to Perkins.

"What, again?"

"If he's sober enough, he can help."

It was clear to Kate that Perkins didn't see how,

but he apparently decided to trust Robert's judgment in the matter.

"Castine!" Perkins suddenly yelled over his shoulder, and the well-trained young soldier burst from the back door of the house as if he'd been alert and waiting for just such a summons.

"I need the chaplain here *now*," Perkins told him. "Take two soldiers with you in case he can't walk."

"Yes, Sergeant Major!" Castine said and hurried away.

"Can you get me some paper, Kate?" Robert said. "Drawing paper if you have any or some sheets of stationery. And pencils, or a pen and ink. Or charcoal sticks—and bring Harrison's photograph. The chaplain is an excellent artist—Reverend Lewis showed me some of his work. Maybe he can do some sketches of the photograph, and Perkins can make sure the soldiers who patrol the wagon roads see them."

Kate looked at him doubtfully. Man of the cloth or not, she'd never gotten the impression that the chaplain was an obliging man, drunk or sober.

"I may need to give him with some of Max's whiskey or brandy. I need you to bring the best he's got out here."

Kate's mind was reeling. She felt better that both Robert and Sergeant Major Perkins were so willing to help, but at the same time, it only made the situation seem all too real. And dire.

"Now, Kate," Robert said, putting his hand briefly on her shoulder.

"Yes, all right," she said, and she hurried back to the house. She had drawing paper. There were a number of sheets she'd never used in the writing box Grey had given her. She had to dodge Maria and Mrs. Justice to get upstairs without having to give some kind of explanation for dashing around the house and yard, and once there, she found everything Robert had said he wanted, including a bottle of Max's best cognac. She had no faith whatsoever that the chaplain wouldn't need it, regardless of the state Castine found him in.

When she returned to the summer kitchen, both Robert and Perkins had gone. She waited by the door for a moment, then went inside. She put everything she was carrying on the table and sat down by the fire. She realized that she didn't have the telegram; Perkins must still have it. She supposed that he would be sending the precise wording of the telegram to Max. In fact, that may be where he was now. She couldn't begin to guess where Robert might be.

She looked around the large kitchen. She couldn't tell where Robert slept—a bedroll on the floor perhaps, one that was kept out of sight during the day in case someone who needed to talk to him arrived. There were a few personal touches—books on the mantel, to be precise. The cookstove sat on the stone floor next to the hearth, sharing the chimney via a secondary flue constructed just for that purpose. She hadn't learned to build a fire in a cookstove yet, and looking at it now, the assorted doors and dampers were nothing if not intimidating.

Groomed.

She had never felt less groomed in her life.

The door rattled; Robert had returned, just ahead of Castine and the chaplain, who didn't seem to need any help. Kate supposed that was a good sign—until she saw him. The chaplain was sober, but he was unsteady on his feet. He sat down immediately in a chair at the table. Kate couldn't smell any whiskey on him, but she saw him look at the bottle of cognac. He glanced at her and then at the bottle again. He was about to be bribed, and he knew it, but he made no mention of that or of the bottle of spirits.

"Am I to know why I've been hurried here?" he asked. "Private Castine was less than forthcoming with his explanations…" He glanced in Kate's direction. "Other than his supposition that Colonel Woodard's sister urgently required my presence."

"We do need your help, Chaplain," Robert said, his voice respectful. "Kate, do you have the photograph?"

"Yes," she said, her voice breaking with emotion when she didn't expect it to. She knew her distress was very close to the surface, but she had thought she had it under better control. She took a deep breath and handed the photograph to him.

"It's very important that we find this boy," Robert said. "It would help us if you would make several sketches of him. Reverend Lewis showed me some of your very fine work," he added, causing the chaplain to look at him in surprise.

"A long time ago, I'm afraid," the chaplain said, but he took the photograph, then held it up and looked at it, squinting as he did so. "My eyes—" he began, but his voice was hoarse sounding now. He cleared his throat. "My eyes aren't what they used to be—I need more light."

Robert and Castine slid the table into a patch of sunlight close to the window. The chaplain picked up his chair and placed it in the location he considered the best for what he needed and sat down again. Once again he looked at the photograph, but not without looking at the bottle of cognac first. He licked his lips and took a deep breath.

"Yes," he said after a moment. "You'll only need sketches of the face, and I can do that well enough to give at least some idea of what this young man looks like."

Kate reached for the paper and pencils she'd brought and placed them in front of him.

"No," he said, holding up his hand when she was about to give him the pen and ink, as well. "Is that charcoal? Charcoal will do nicely."

She handed the charcoal sticks to him, and she watched him closely, moving out of his line of sight so as not to distract him. But he seemed a different man now and completely oblivious to her or anything else around him. He concentrated on the photograph of Harrison and began to work, sketching and smudging as he went. It took him no time at all to make several nearly identical drawings of Harrison's face. Kate stared at them. He had caught the boy's wistful sadness with such accuracy that it was all she could do not to weep.

The chaplain rose from his chair. "I take it I'm free to go now?" he said. He glanced at Castine, who did his best—and rightfully so—to look as if none of this had anything whatsoever to do with him.

"Yes," Kate said quickly, because she thought she understood the difficulty the man must be having, being so close to the cognac and its temptation. "I thank you, sir. I won't forget your kindness."

"You are welcome, Miss Woodard," he said. "Robert, I will see you later. I have some things I'd like to discuss. I wish you Godspeed in your search."

Robert picked up the sketches as soon as the chaplain and Castine had gone.

"I'd like to carry the photograph with me," he said. "I'll leave a sketch with Perkins and the rest I'll distribute to the stationmasters along the line. Kate?" he said, apparently because he realized she wasn't listening.

Kate took one more look at Harrison's face, then handed him the photograph.

"Tell me a passage from the Bible that will help me," she said.

"'Cast thy burden upon the Lord, and He shall sustain thee. He shall never suffer the righteous to be moved,'" he said without hesitation.

And if I'm not righteous? What then? she nearly said. She bowed her head.

"Don't waste time worrying, Kate. Pray."

"I'll…try to do that," she said, looking up at him.

"I'll send word when I find him," he said.

"You will find him, won't you?" she asked, her mouth trembling despite all she could do.

He rested his hands on her shoulders. "Kate—"

They both looked around because Perkins was outside, and Kate stepped away. Perkins opened the door and stuck his head in.

"Train'll be here in about thirty minutes," he said. He tossed Robert a small leather wallet. "Military authorization so you can ride any train, anywhere you need to. There are some signed chits in there, too. You can use them to pay for whatever the boy needs—Colonel Woodard's orders. Miss Kate, Mrs. Colonel Woodard and Mrs. Justice are looking for you."

Kate had no doubt that they were, and likely at his

behest. She looked at Robert. "Thank you," she said, her voice barely a whisper.

He nodded.

She took a few steps toward the door, then looked back at him. "God bless you, Robert," she said.

"I'm going to give you some advice, Mr. Markham," she heard Perkins say as she was walking away. She stopped on the pathway to listen.

"Given our violent history, I'm not sure that would be wise," Robert said.

"Maybe not, but you're going to hear it, anyway. Colonel Woodard left his most precious possessions in my care—his family—and that includes Miss Kate. There's not much that goes on in this town that I haven't heard about, and that includes *you*.

"It would be very good sense on your part if you settled things with one lady before you go starting something up with another one—especially if the second lady happens to be my commanding officer's sister. Are you understanding me?"

"I am, Sergeant Major," Robert said. "I've already had this conversation with the colonel."

"Good. We ought not have a problem then. You just do what you said. You find that boy for Miss Kate."

Chapter Thirteen

When, Kate kept thinking after Robert had gone. *When,* not *if.*

Robert meant to find Harrison; she was certain of that. But whether or not he could do it was another matter entirely. She had been spared having to tell Maria and Mrs. Justice what had happened. Sergeant Major Perkins had taken care of that detail, and she was grateful that she would not have to try to manufacture an acceptable degree of distress at having "a young friend of the family" go missing.

Kate sat at the dining room table now, pushing the cake Maria had served around with her fork rather than actually eating it—while Maria, Mrs. Justice, Mrs. Russell *and* Mrs. Kinnard discussed something pertaining to some aspect of an upcoming Lenten service. It was all she could do to stay seated.

"Well, we'll just have to go right now and see how much space there is," Mrs. Kinnard said.

"This doesn't have to be done until the last Lenten Sunday. We have *weeks* yet," Mrs. Russell said.

"There is no point in leaving everything to the last minute," Mrs. Kinnard insisted, and Kate suddenly realized that they were all getting up from the table. Mrs. Kinnard had spoken—but about what precisely, Kate had no idea.

"It will be dark soon," Maria said.

"I have my carriage. It will only take a few minutes to get there—Miss Woodard, I don't believe we will require *your* presence."

Good, Kate nearly said and her thoughts went immediately to Robert.

She said you were grooming me to be your wife.

Good.

Oh, Robert. What did you mean?

"Kate?" Maria said.

"I'm sorry, what did you say?"

"I said we'll be right back. Will you help Warrie with the boys if she needs it?"

"Of course," Kate said, but both of them knew that Warrie wouldn't ask for help, and she most particularly wouldn't ask for Kate's. Kate wondered if she somehow knew about the "grooming."

She was still sitting at the table when one of the soldiers came in to clear away the plates and put the dining room back in order.

"Sorry, miss," he said, turning to go.

"No, it's all right," Kate said. She went out into the hallway, glancing toward the campaign table as she always did before she went upstairs.

Nothing.

She climbed the stairs quickly, but she didn't go to her room. Instead she went out onto the second-story veranda and stood by the banister, breathing in the cool, fresh air.

Spring was coming. She could feel it, and any other time she would be heartened by it. Jonquils and pink thrift were already in full bloom in nearly every yard, and—according to Sergeant Major Perkins—the trees would be budding soon. On the surface, everything was as it should be. Life went on around her, just as it had after Grey was killed.

She looked up at the late afternoon sky. Four days. Robert had been gone four days.

"Harrison, where are you?" she whispered.

Please, please, Lord. Let Robert find him and let me help him. Please. Whatever he's running from—it doesn't matter. If he needs respite, then let him find it here.

She stood for a long time—until she could see Mrs. Kinnard's carriage returning. She went back inside, and she came downstairs despite the smothering presence of the others. She had to be where she could hear the delivery of the mail pouch if one came.

"Did you find enough space for…whatever it was?" Kate asked no one in particular as she reached the foyer.

"Yes," Mrs. Justice and Mrs. Russell said.

"No," Mrs. Kinnard said. "Two benches will have to be moved."

"There will be extra people there, Acacia. They will need a place to sit," Mrs. Russell said. "Church attendance is always higher during Lent."

"Only because they don't bother to show up the rest of the year. When one's presence at church is so lackadaisical, then one must expect consequences."

"I don't know why I don't have a headache," Maria whispered at Kate's elbow.

"You can have mine," Kate said, and Maria had to stifle a laugh.

"I'm so glad you're here," Maria whispered. "I don't think I could manage them without you."

"You'd still have Sergeant Major Perkins."

"Ladies, I think we've spent enough time on this," Mrs. Justice said, and the remark apparently had a direct effect on Mrs. Kinnard's eyebrows.

"I would like for us to have a prayer circle," Mrs. Justice said quietly. "In Bud's sitting room. Now." She looked at Perkins, who had come in from the back of the house. "Are the chairs ready, Sergeant Major?"

"They are, ma'am," he said, and she smiled.

"Then we shall go," she said.

For once Mrs. Kinnard didn't have a more urgent and appropriate alternative. She followed Mrs. Justice up the stairs, giving Kate and the rest of the women a look over her shoulder that suggested she was on the verge of finding all of them recalcitrant for just standing there.

Kate followed along quickly. It was what she needed at the moment, one of Mrs. Justice's quiet and comforting prayers.

Seven chairs had been brought into the sitting room.

"I was expecting that Reverend Lewis would join us," Mrs. Justice said, apparently to explain the seating. "Do please sit down, my dears. Do you remember the last time all of us were gathered like this—here—in Bud's house?"

"I remember," Mrs. Russell said, and it was clear that she didn't appreciate having been reminded.

"When was it?" Kate asked. No one seemed to want to answer.

"It was the night we all sat up waiting for General Stoneman and his horse soldiers to raid the town," Maria said finally.

"I'm reminding you of this for a reason," Mrs. Justice said. "We had that dreadful prison here, and we were all of us certain that the town would be burned to the ground like Atlanta and Columbia. But we prayed for God's mercy and for strength and courage no matter what happened. I would like us to do that again tonight, this time for Robbie and for the young man he has gone to find—" She stopped because someone was coming up the back stairs.

Kate looked at the doorway, expecting to see Reverend Lewis, but it was the army chaplain, Bible in hand. It suddenly occurred to her that she didn't know his name, and clearly, everyone was as surprised to see him as she was—except Mrs. Justice.

"Chaplain Gilford, welcome," Mrs. Justice said. "We are very pleased that you are willing to come out tonight—"

"I hardly think—" Mrs. Kinnard began.

"—*in* Reverend Lewis's stead," Mrs. Justice continued firmly. "It's his gout," she added to the group. "Very painful, I understand. Now. Do let me introduce you to the ladies you have not met."

To their credit Mrs. Kinnard and Mrs. Russell participated in the social amenities because—as Mrs. Justice had pointed out on a previous occasion—their mothers' teaching dictated it, especially in someone else's home. But it was clear to Kate that neither of them wanted to—and for very different reasons, she thought. For Mrs. Russell, the chaplain would be a vivid reminder of how her son had died. For Mrs. Kinnard, he would represent a situation where she had unwillingly experienced a certain loss of control.

But Chaplain Gilford handled both women with courtesy and skillful authority, perhaps the kind he hadn't exhibited in a long time. He clearly wasn't drinking, and he seemed confident and...peaceful. He acknowledged Maria and Kate and then took his seat.

Mrs. Justice kept looking at the doorway, likely for a reason.

Chaplain Gilford looked at each of them and then recited from memory. "'For where two or three are gathered together in my name, there am I in the midst of them.' And so we are here this evening—gathered in *His* name, seeking His help and His comfort. For the boy Robert Markham has gone to find, for Robert and for all of us here who want only to help them both, but have not yet found a way..." He stopped.

Warrie Hansen stood in the doorway.

"Warrie, come in," Maria said. "There's a chair for you."

Warrie stood awkwardly for a moment, then came into the room. "The boys is all asleep," she said. "I reckoned I'd come up here to the prayer circle." She sat down in the empty chair, and Kate wondered if she knew that the prayers tonight would be for Robert.

The chaplain waited until she was situated, then looked at Mrs. Kinnard before he began again. "We are grateful, Lord, that we have this opportunity to offer up our prayers to You. We have come with our troubled hearts and our worry, believing that we may lay our burdens before You. Your word tells us to ask and it shall be given us. Seek, and we will find. Knock and it will be opened unto us. I sought the Lord, and He heard me, and delivered me from all my fears—"

"Excuse me, Chaplain," Perkins said from the doorway. "Miss Kate, you need to come downstairs."

Kate got up immediately and followed him down the wide hallway.

"What is it?" she asked, but he didn't answer her until they had reached the foyer. The mail pouch had come; a stack of letters lay on the campaign table. He picked up one of them.

"Telegram," he said. "For you. It's from Robert Markham."

Kate took it from him, her fingers trembling.

"You've already read it?" she asked as she opened the envelope.

"I have. I thought it couldn't wait."

She struggled to get the telegram free and then began to read:

H found. Come as soon as possible. Perkins has details.
Robert

"What's happened? What details?" Kate cried.

"The boy is sick, Miss Kate, and it's bad. He's in some little whistle-stop in Virginia. Markham says he needs some medical supplies. I'm working on getting him what he wants. You need to go pack a trunk. The night train will be here before long, and I've got some more things to figure out."

"What kind of things?"

"Go pack, Miss Kate. Let me do what I need to do."

She stood for a moment, then nodded and hurried up the stairs. She could hear the chaplain praying when she reached the second floor. She went into her room and opened her smallest trunk, her mind in complete turmoil. She had to force herself to *think,* to concentrate on what she might need to take with her.

The boy is sick...

She suddenly realized that she had a good idea of what might be needed—thanks to her constant clashes with Mrs. Kinnard. She wouldn't fill the trunk with her belongings. She would take only the barest minimum for herself and reserve the rest of the space for things that might be necessary to care for someone who was ill.

She hurried downstairs to the kitchen and went into the pantry. The flannel Mrs. Kinnard had asked for—demanded—the night Robert had come home she knew was on the top shelf, and she climbed up on a box to get it. They could be used for heated brick or as washcloths.

She found a bar of soap, some candles and an unopened pack of matches to light them with, and some lumps of sugar wrapped in brown paper. As an afterthought she took down a bag of coffee and some apples, dumping all of it into an empty basket. She took the basket with her through the kitchen to the airing room to get several sheets and two blankets and two pillowcases from the linen cupboard. She put everything that was in the basket into one of them. A stack of clean aprons had been left on one of the ironing tables, and she took one of those, as well. When she came back through the house, Mrs. Kinnard was leaving by the front door.

Kate didn't see Perkins anywhere, and she didn't waste time looking for him. She went upstairs again and changed into her traveling dress with the open side pocket that allowed her to reach the underskirt, which had a pocket where she could hide most of the money she had set aside for traveling. The coins she left in her reticule. She packed the cotton calico dress, along with some clean undergarments, into the trunk. Thanks to recent events she had no qualms about having only two dresses, and with some rearranging, she managed to get everything into the trunk and the lid closed and locked.

When she came out into the hallway, she could no longer hear the chaplain. No doubt Perkins had advised everyone about Robert's telegram by now and had likely given every person in the house some kind of assignment.

Robert.

He had said he would find Harrison. When she had first met him, she had wondered if he were not the Southern version of a knight in shining armor. She didn't have to wonder any longer.

She hurried toward the stairs, not knowing how long it would be before the train came, and then she suddenly stopped.

"Thank you, Lord," she whispered. She had asked for the opportunity to help her son, and she realized suddenly that this was it. The realization brought with it a kind of calmness she hadn't anticipated.

"Help me to do this the best I can," she said. She took a deep breath, and continued down the stairs.

This time Perkins was in the foyer.

"You know you can't go on the train alone—" he began.

"I'm going!" Kate said, alarmed. He was *not* going to stop her. She didn't care how it looked, and she most certainly didn't care how her doing so would affect the smooth running of the occupation.

Perkins held up his hand. "Yes," he said. "*With* a chaperone."

"I don't need a chaperone," Kate said.

"Well, you won't get out of this town without one," he assured her. "Mrs. Colonel Woodard can't do it. Mrs. Justice needs to stay here so she won't wear herself out trying to help Mrs. Hansen with those boys."

"What are you telling me?" Kate asked.

"I'm telling you I got you a chaperone."

"Who?" Kate asked.

He didn't answer her, and because he didn't, Kate knew immediately that there was only one possibility.

"Oh, no," Kate said.

"She's the only one who will do, Miss Kate," Perkins said. "And she is happy to have the job."

"Why?"

"Having authority over the Colonel's sister *and* being able to order people around in another state? Nothing could suit that woman better. Besides that, if anybody else goes, all in this world Mrs. Kinnard would have to do is raise an eyebrow, and she'd cast all kinds of suspicion that things weren't proper and that the Colonel had no regard for the women in his family. And you know—"

"All right! I understand. We have to preserve my brother's standing as well as mine."

"Exactly."

"Does he know about this?"

Perkins hesitated. "I sent him a telegram."

"*Everything* about this?" She was asking if he knew Robert Markham's part in it, but she couldn't quite bring herself to say it.

"Most of it." Perkins was looking at her so directly, and it was all she could do not to avoid his gaze.

"I...thought it best not to tell him Markham sent for you," he said. "If he gave me an order contrary to what Markham is asking, I'd have to carry it out."

"And I'd end up in the stockade."

"Well, I don't think we'd have to go that far—Castine!" he suddenly barked. "What are you doing?"

"Helping Mrs. Justice and Mrs. Colonel Woodard pack a basket for Miss Kate to take with her."

"Well, hurry it along."

"I don't think I know how to hurry ladies, Sergeant Major," he called.

"I don't know how to hurry ladies, either," Perkins said, "but we're not going to tell him that."

Kate gave a brief smile. "Thank you, Sergeant Major Perkins," she said quietly. Perkins hadn't missed her intense worry about Harrison, and regardless of his duty to her brother, he was going out of his way to make it possible for her to go to the boy.

"For what?" he asked innocently.

"You know what," she answered, and surprisingly, he actually smiled in return. She was much more accustomed to his "sack and burn" face.

"Castine's going, too," he said.

Kate looked at him. She didn't know whether this was good news or not—for Castine. Ever since he had escorted her and Valentina to army headquarters and she had seen him being so helpful with the boys, she had found his presence…comforting, but he was even more disconcerted by Mrs. Kinnard than she was.

She heard a long, drawn out train whistle in the distance. Castine came hurrying down the hallway carrying the same basket she was to have taken with her on her last train trip.

"I'll carry the basket," Kate said, because he was juggling a haversack, a knapsack and a repeating rifle as well.

"Yes, miss," he said, handing it over.

"Kate!" Maria called, hurrying from the kitchen with Mrs. Justice in tow. When they reached her, they both embraced her, putting the basket in jeopardy of ending up on the parquet floor.

"Keep praying for him," Kate whispered. "Please."

"Don't you worry about that, my dear," Mrs. Justice said. "We will keep a prayer vigil for him, you can rest assured."

"We've put everything Mrs. Justice and I could think of in the basket. Take care of yourself," Maria said. "And send us word as soon as you know something. If he can be moved, you must bring him here to us."

Kate nodded and hugged them both again. She looked around because Castine was coming down the stairs with her trunk.

"Mrs. Kinnard's carriage is here," Perkins said. "You got everything, Miss Kate?"

"Yes," she said, because she was nearly certain that she had.

"All right then," he said, and he opened the front door.

Chapter Fourteen

Kate stood on the platform watching as the train slowed and lurched and finally stopped. Her mind had gone numb as the terrible significance of having to make this trip finally sank in. Harrison was seriously ill, and she had no idea how long this journey would take. All she knew was that she wanted to board the train as soon as possible and that—please, Lord—she didn't arrive too late.

The passenger car filled rapidly, intensifying the smell of dust and sweat and baskets packed with food. And underneath it all the distinct smell of whiskey and tobacco and babies whose diapers needed changing. She half expected Valentina to show up; this would surely meet her criteria for an "adventure."

Kate had to immediately change seats with Mrs. Kinnard, who couldn't abide being next to the aisle and having people she didn't know—and more importantly, who didn't know *her*—brush and jostle past her. Kate wondered if Mrs. Kinnard had even been on a train before. If she hadn't, this would be an eye-opening experience even under the best of circumstances.

Kate sat with the basket firmly in her lap, clutching the handle tightly as if that would help the situation somehow. She didn't dare let it out of her sight with all these people around. The train car grew more and more crowded, much too crowded for Mrs. Kinnard. She kept giving sharp sighs and holding her perfume-laden handkerchief to her nose, which Kate assumed would continue until they reached wherever they were going. There apparently was no name for the whistle-stop where Harrison was supposed to be, but Perkins, ever efficient, had advised the conductor at what point Colonel Woodard's sister and her party would need to detrain.

Castine, who was standing nearby, suddenly cleared his throat, and Kate looked up just as a man stepped into her line of vision.

"Miss Woodard," the man said, bending low enough for Kate to smell the clover-scented pomade on his hair. "Do forgive me, but I've only just heard that Colonel Woodard's sister was on the train. Might I persuade you to join me in my private car? You will travel much more comfortably there—my cook will prepare us a fine dinner. It would be an honor to offer some assistance to you—and your brother."

"I'm afraid I don't know who you are, sir," she said, despite the fact that Mrs. Kinnard perked up immediately at hearing the words, *private* and *car.* Kate caught a glimpse of Castine, who was clearly trying to tell her something with his eyes. Unfortunately she had no idea what.

"Well, that is easily remedied," the man said. "I'm

Welles Burnham." He said his name as if that should
explain everything.

Castine seemed to be writing something on a piece
of paper.

"Excuse me, sir," Castine said, pushing his way forward. "Miss Woodard, I have a—this message for you."

Kate took it, puzzled but intending to read it later,
without this strange man hovering over her.

"You need to look at it now, Miss Woodard," Castine said pointedly.

"Yes. Thank you, Private Castine."

"You're welcome, Miss Woodard," he said as she
opened the slip of paper.

She didn't open it far; there was only one word written on it: *carpetbagger*.

Castine had apparently realized immediately that
this was a situation that might cause his commanding
officer some difficulty. Max could not be seen as a
military commander who accepted favors from someone who was profiting from the local residents' plight.
Sergeant Major Perkins had taught Castine well.

Kate smiled slightly and handed the note to Mrs.
Kinnard, who looked at it much longer than was required to read one word.

"Mr. Welles—" Mrs. Kinnard began when she was
ready.

"Burnham," the man corrected.

Mrs. Kinnard made no attempt to backtrack and
use his correct name. "I'm sure Miss Woodard—*and
I*—would be more comfortable in your private car,
however, that is quite impossible. There have been no
formal introductions from people we both know. I have

no notion of how things are done where *you* come from, but *here*—as Colonel Woodard would certainly tell you—it would be most inappropriate to accept such an invitation. As Miss Woodard's chaperone, I must decline your offer. Now. If you would take your leave."

The man stood for a moment as if he didn't believe Mrs. Kinnard could possibly be serious.

"Surely, an exception—"

"No exceptions. Goodbye, Mr. Welles," Mrs. Kinnard added to underline what he was supposed to do next.

"Mrs. Kinnard," Kate said when he had gone. "I do believe you enjoyed that."

For a moment she thought Acacia Kinnard, the one who had stolen cookies on horseback, might actually smile.

But she didn't.

"Private Castine," she said abruptly, startling the young soldier once again. He looked in her direction. "That was…" She stopped, and Kate could see him bracing himself for yet another of her broadsides.

"Quite…adequately done," Mrs. Kinnard decided, making his ears turn as red as Valentina's indirect compliment had. "If you don't do anything too uncouth for the rest of the journey, I shall be certain to advise Mr. Perkins of your handling of the situation."

"Thank you, Mrs. Kinnard," he said quietly. But clearly he knew enough not to presume when a compliment was in as much danger of being withdrawn as that one was. "I was following orders, ma'am," he said. "The sergeant major intends for you and Miss Woodard to have a safe journey."

He glanced at Kate, and she gave him a small nod of approval.

All the seats were taken now, even the makeshift ones on bundles and baskets in the aisle. The train lurched and then began to move forward as the conductor passed through the car, asking for everyone's ticket except Kate's, Mrs. Kinnard's and Castine's, something that didn't go unnoticed among the other passengers.

Kate closed her eyes as the train gained speed and moved away from the station into the dark countryside. An oil lamp had been lit at each end of the car, and when Kate looked across Mrs. Kinnard toward the window, she could only see their reflections in it. There was nothing to occupy her mind now. No overly familiar carpetbagger, no trip preparations, no handling of Mrs. Kinnard. There was only the worry and the longing to see her son again that suddenly threatened to overwhelm her.

Don't worry—pray.

"Cast thy burden upon the Lord, and He shall sustain thee: He shall never suffer the righteous to be moved," she whispered, not caring if Mrs. Kinnard heard her. But even as she said the words, there was still that nagging truth. She was not righteous. She had shamed her family, and she didn't deserve God's favor. She had thought she might when she'd promised to marry Grey, but after he was killed, she had never been able to convince herself that she could dare to be happy again.

John.

She knew how much he loved Harrison and she knew how distressed he must be now.

Help us both, Lord, she thought. *And please—please—help our son.*

She gave herself up to the constant swaying of the car, and she managed to doze at times. So did Mrs. Kinnard. Castine, on the other hand, seemed to be alert and standing nearby whenever some slowing or accelerating of the train caused her to wake. She lost count of how many times the train actually stopped, but it seemed to her at one point that more people were getting off than were boarding. She kept thinking that there was but one comfort in all of this—Robert was with Harrison. She had no doubt that he would do everything he could for the boy, but all the while she knew she would have to guard against relying on him too much, regardless of what he had *almost* said.

Good.

In retrospect, "good" could have meant anything. She had heard him say Eleanor's name. That alone could leave no doubt that Eleanor Hansen had his heart.

She gave a heavy sigh and dozed again.

Robert stood waiting on the station platform. He kept staring down the tracks for some sign that the train was approaching, but he couldn't hear anything or see the billowing plume of smoke from an engine. All he had was the indifferent stationmaster's best guess as to when the northbound train would get here, and there were any number of events that could alter his estimation.

He walked to the end of the platform and back again—several times. The station itself was unlike any he'd ever encountered in his travels or during the war. It was a three-story wooden structure with a huge wraparound front porch. It didn't look like a train station, and yet it wasn't quite house or hotel, either, but something in between that had evolved as some architectural need arose and was subsequently met. It had seen some rough treatment during the war; there were numerous bullet holes in the wood on one side of the building, as if it had stood in the way of a heavy onslaught of musket fire.

He looked up at the increasingly overcast sky. He expected it to rain before sundown.

Weather prognostication.

He wondered at what point he'd learned to do that—read the sky and air around him and presume to know what the weather would be. He didn't remember having acquired the ability at all, but it had to have been before Gettysburg—he'd been in no shape to learn anything after that. It must have come from being—living—fighting—outdoors for so many months. It occurred to him that he might have come away from the war with a useful skill besides the killing of his fellow man—if he had decided to become a farmer.

His thoughts went to Harrison Howe. He'd hired the stationmaster's wife to keep watch over him while he came down to meet the train. He both dreaded Kate's arrival and longed for it. By the time she got here, she would have been on the train all night and most of the day. She would be upset and exhausted, and what could he tell her except the truth?

He had managed to locate a country doctor and bring him here to see the boy, but the man had offered no diagnosis beyond the obvious, a fever likely brought on by the beating he'd taken at the hands of a person or persons unknown. Whether it had happened at school and that was the reason the boy had run away, or whether it was the result of a robbery attempt when he'd gotten off the train, Robert didn't know. All he knew was that he could have come to the doctor's conclusion about the boy's condition all on his own. And he didn't need anyone to tell him that young Harrison Howe was not likely to survive. Robert had done the only thing he could. He had sent for Kate.

He looked around sharply at the sound of a train whistle in the distance. The waiting area of the train station began to empty out as more and more people began to crowd onto the platform. He stood back to let them pass, and as he did so, he felt the first drops of rain begin to fall. Clearly his weather prediction had been off by a few hours.

From his vantage point he could see all of the passenger cars, but it was some time before he finally saw Castine helping Mrs. Kinnard down the train car steps to the platform.

Mrs. Kinnard.

He couldn't begin to guess how that had come about, and he braced himself to have to deal with her unexpected presence. She spotted him immediately and came marching across the platform in his direction. He still didn't see Kate.

"Robert Markham," Mrs. Kinnard said as soon as she was close enough. "What is happening with this boy everyone is so concerned about?"

"Where is Kate?" he asked, sidestepping her question. Surely she hadn't sent Acacia Kinnard in her stead.

"She is giving away most of the contents of our food basket to a woman with three hungry children," Mrs. Kinnard said. "As she should. Now, about—"

"Excuse me, Mrs. Kinnard," he said, pushing his way through the crowd again to get closer to the train, because he could see someone he thought must be Kate making her way down the aisle toward the train car exit.

He stood waiting on the platform, watching her progress all the way until she finally appeared. She was so…beautiful to him and had been since the first time he saw her in the downstairs hallway of his father's house.

Maria was right. He did want Kate to be a preacher's wife—*his* wife—and he didn't see how their situation could be any more impossible.

Perkins had been right as well—as far as it went. Robert was not bound to Eleanor, and yet he was, and he would continue to be until he saw her, talked with her, understood what had happened between them and knew she was all right. In the meantime, he could do nothing, say nothing to Kate about the way he felt.

I love her, Lord.

He didn't know when it had happened, or how. All he knew was that it was so, that she was in his mind night and day—and now he was only moments away from breaking her heart.

"Robert!" she cried in obvious relief when she saw him. "How is he? Tell me!"

He helped her down before he answered. "He knows you're coming," he said. "But he's sleeping most of the time now."

She looked at him.

"Sleeping," she repeated as if she thought that he didn't mean "sleeping" at all, that he meant something much more ominous.

"This way," Robert said. "Let's get you and Mrs. Kinnard out of the rain."

"Robert—"

"You need to see him for yourself, Kate."

"He's here, then?"

"Yes. Mrs. Kinnard!" he called. "This way!"

Mrs. Kinnard came in her own good time, unmindful of the rain. "What kind of place *is* this?" she asked when she reached them. "I see no one about to offer a traveler any assistance whatsoever. You have lightened the basket, I take it, Miss Woodard?"

"Yes," Kate said. "Where is he, Robert?"

"That way. Go through those double doors," he said, pointing out the station entrance.

They crossed the wide porch, stepping around sleeping men who sprawled everywhere—salesmen, by the looks of them, "drummers" who preyed upon the unsuspecting traveling public with their "snake oil" cure-alls, as well as the ones who sold legitimate merchandise to the small town and the middle-of-nowhere general stores. Mrs. Kinnard went inside first. It was as chaotic around the ticket window as it was on the platform.

"Show me to the stationmaster's office," Mrs. Kinnard said to the nearest person she took to be some kind of railroad employee. "I must speak to the man about the way this facility is run," she said to Kate.

A baby began to cry loudly.

"Harrison's on the third floor, Kate," Robert said,

leaning down so she could hear him. "Let me have the basket." He had to take it from her hands.

"This isn't what I expected."

"I know. You need to see him now, Kate. Then I'll tell you what I know and you can decide what you want to do."

Kate heard the urgency in Robert's voice. She heard it, and she was afraid. The stairs were steep and difficult to climb. She felt light-headed and unsteady by the time they reached the third-floor landing. She stumbled, and Robert took her by the arm to steady her.

"Which way?" she managed to ask.

He led her to the door and opened it. The room was unoccupied.

"They must have moved him," Robert said. He walked down the hallway, trying one door after another until one of them opened.

"In here," he called to Kate and she hurried in that direction. He said something to someone inside the room but she couldn't hear him clearly or the response.

"The stationmaster apparently took it upon himself to move him in here," he said.

Kate glanced at his face then back again. He was clearly angry.

The room was so dark. There was only one small slit of a window near the ceiling, and the light from it, combined with that of an oil lamp burning on a nearby table, did little to illuminate her surroundings.

She stepped forward and made her way to the bedside, nodding to a woman who stood nearby.

"This is the stationmaster's wife," Robert said. "I'll leave you now. I need to find Castine."

"All right," Kate said, but she was barely listening. *Harrison!*

He appeared to be clean and the sheets on the bed were fresh, but the room was so damp and close and oppressive.

"Thank you for sitting with him," she said to the woman after a moment, her voice quiet so as not to disturb the boy who lay on the bed, his hair wet with perspiration, his eyes closed.

"I'm supposed to get paid for it," the woman said bluntly. She stopped short of holding her hand out for the money, but Kate wouldn't have been surprised if she had.

Kate touched Harrison's arm, then took his hand. It was cold and clammy.

"Harrison," she said softly. "Can you hear me? It's Kate."

She looked at the woman, who was fidgeting with her apron. "How long has he been like this?" she asked, her mouth trembling despite all she could do. She bit down on her lower lip.

"I reckon since sometime last night. Before that, he'd kind of come and go."

"What does the doctor say?"

"I don't know. He didn't talk to me."

Kate leaned forward to see Harrison better. "His face is bruised. Why is his face bruised?" She knew her voice was rising, but she couldn't help it. "What happened to him?"

"We—my old man—found him like this at the back of the station four...no, five days ago," the woman said. "It ain't hard to figure how he got there."

"What do you mean?"

"The boy had money and he didn't have enough sense to hide it. I reckon he got beat up and robbed and he laid out in the rain all night that night. It ain't our fault he got into trouble, if that's what you're thinking. We've been looking after him as best we could. Then Mr. Markham came and showed us the picture. We knowed it was him the minute we seen it. Mr. Markham, he said we'd get paid for—"

"This room won't do," Kate interrupted, because the rain she could hear beating on the roof was beginning to drip from the ceiling. "I want him moved to someplace with more air and light. Someplace *dry*."

"The roof don't leak unless there's been a couple days of rain," the woman said as if that somehow negated the leaks.

"I said I want him moved," Kate said.

"Well, there ain't no call to be so—"

"Tell the stationmaster I want to see him. *Now!*" Kate said.

They stared at each other, then the woman gave a sharp sigh and left, returning in a few minutes with a short, rotund man wearing spectacles.

"You're the stationmaster?" Kate asked ahead of whatever excuses he was about to make.

"I am—"

"Then you have the authority to appropriate any room on these premises, is that not correct?"

"That's right—"

"Then I want him moved out of here to a bigger room—one with windows and a ceiling that doesn't leak."

"I done told Markham I ain't got no other place to put him in—ain't no ex-Reb telling me how to run my station. Anyway I don't see how what room he's in can matter now," the man made the mistake of saying.

Kate turned to face him. It took everything she had to sound calm. "As you can see, *I* am not an 'ex-Reb,' as you put it. You will show me the rooms in this place—all of them."

He took a moment, apparently to decide who Kate might be and what would be his most profitable response. He glanced at his wife once before he answered. "If I do," he said finally, "how do I know I'll get paid?"

"You don't," Kate said. "But I can promise you this, you won't get any money at all unless you do as I say. I understand you expect this boy's family to reimburse you for his care before Mr. Markham arrived. Any claims you have will not be honored unless *I* approve them. Do we understand each other?"

The stationmaster didn't say whether he did or didn't; he merely threw up his hands and headed for the door. "The big room," he said to his wife on his way out.

"But we might need that room if there's any rich people coming in on the—"

"You heard what I said!" He shoved past Mrs. Kinnard, who walked up just as he was exiting the doorway.

"What's happening?" Mrs. Kinnard asked. "Who is that rude man?"

"Mrs. Kinnard," Kate said. "Will you kindly go with this woman? We're moving Harrison to another room. I need your opinion as to which one will be the most suitable." Kate looked at the stationmaster's wife. "Mrs. Kinnard ran a wayside hospital during the war, so don't suppose for a minute that she won't know what a gravely ill young man will need to aid his recovery. If she is happy with what you show her, then I will be, as well."

Kate turned her attention back to Harrison, not knowing whether either woman would comply, and she took his hand again. He hadn't stirred during the exchange, not once.

"I'll...tell somebody to bring you some fresh water," the stationmaster's wife said after a moment. "He's fevering again. I reckon he needs sponging."

"Yes. Thank you," Kate said, accepting the woman's token change of attitude—for the moment, at least. She took off her hat and jacket and rolled up her sleeves. She needed her trunk, but she wouldn't worry about that now. She pulled the one chair in the room near the bedside and sat down heavily.

The memory of Warrie Hansen singing to Jake and Joe and Robbie suddenly filled her mind.

Go tell Aunt Rosie,
Go tell Aunt Rosie...

Did anyone ever sing to you? she thought. Mrs. Howe? A nanny hired to make sure you were rarely seen or heard?

God relies on mothers. The midwife who had delivered him had told her that.

And how little help she had been thus far.

"Harrison—Harrison," she said softly to him, covering his hand with hers. "Listen to me, now. You're going to be all right. I'm here—and Mrs. Kinnard. You may have met Mrs. Kinnard when you came to visit

John last summer. If you did, then you know she'll get things done for you. We're going to find you a better room so you won't have to be here in the dark and—" Her voice broke and she barely smothered a sob.

She looked around at a small noise. She hadn't realized that Robert was in the room. He came to stand on the other side of the bed, and she looked up at him, shaking her head in despair.

"It's good to talk to him," Robert said. "Sometimes I could hear—understand—what people said. I heard you the night I came home—and I heard soldiers and the people who took care of me after Gettysburg. Talk to him, Kate. Give him hope."

She looked at him, still very close to tears, and he nodded his encouragement.

Hope.

And how could she do that when she herself had none? Even someone so inexperienced in these kinds of things as she, could see how very ill Harrison was. She heard Robert leave, and she sat there trying to think of what to say. Any mention of Mrs. Howe would likely take him right back to whatever had happened at school that had caused him to run away.

"You would be very surprised at the change in me," she said finally, leaning close again. "I can bake cornbread now. Can you believe it? Max and John don't know about that yet. Can you imagine what *they* will say? When you're better, I'll make us some—we'll have cornbread and tea with lots of sugar, just the way you like it, and we'll sit on the upstairs veranda at Max's house. We'll have the tea in tin cups—you know how we both break things.

"And I have some new books. I bought them at that

little bookshop—you know the one. We found it when we were supposed to be visiting the museum, but we went looking for Charles Dickens instead. Remember that? Mr. Howe's English friend sent you a bundle of old newspapers—he knew how much you liked to read the London papers, only he didn't know what you really enjoyed were the chapters they published of Mr. Dickens's books. You were missing so many chapters from *David Copperfield*—and nothing would do but we find the whole book—" She stopped again, thinking that the stationmaster's wife had come back.

But it was Castine who brought the fresh water and some hemmed pieces of clean flannel. Robert followed him into the room, and he took the ewer from Castine so he could set the basin on the table near the bed.

"Anything else you need me to do, Mr. Markham?"

"No. Thank you, Castine. Just keep an eye on the vermin in this place."

"Yes, sir. My pleasure, sir."

Robert wet a piece of flannel and handed it to Kate. They began to work together, sponging Harrison's feverish body. Robert showed her how to fan the wet flannel in the air to make it feel colder before she used it to wipe the perspiration away. And all the while Harrison didn't open his eyes, didn't move. There was only the sound of the rain and his labored breaths.

In.

Out.

Mrs. Kinnard returned. She had changed clothes and had put her elaborately dressed hair into a snood. At the moment she looked like someone who might work in the Kinnard household rather than its mistress.

"It took some doing, but the room is ready," she said.

Kate stood back as Robert and Castine—and two men she didn't know—lifted Harrison up, mattress and all and carried him out into the hallway. She gathered up her belongings and followed down the dark passageway to a room on the other side of the building. It was a large and airy corner room with whitewashed walls and double two-over-two windows. Rivulets of rain ran down the windowpanes rather than dripping from the ceiling.

The room didn't look as if it had been recently occupied, but more like one that had been held in reserve for a more important traveler than the gravely ill boy who was being carried into it now.

She waited outside until Harrison had been put to bed.

"Your room is there across the hall," Mrs. Kinnard said. "It's small but I expect you won't want to spend much time in it. Private Castine has brought up your trunk. If you have a dress more suitable for attending the sick, it—"

"I do," Kate said, interrupting. "And I brought sheets and some blankets and some other things I thought we might need as well—apples if you're hungry. I'll go get them."

"Excellent," Mrs. Kinnard said. "I've told those mercenary station people to move a cot and two more chairs in here. I believe we will likely need to take turns sleeping."

"Thank you, Mrs. Kinnard," Kate said, but Mrs. Kinnard had no intention of being thanked for what she considered should be obvious.

"I see what needs to be done and I do it, Miss Woodard. I always have, and with God's help, I always will. There is no need to thank me. It is simply the way I am."

Kate left and went to the small room across from Harrison's and closed the door behind her. She stood waiting for the rush of emotion she knew would come, but she was determined not to waste time weeping. She wiped at her eyes and gathered her strength and set to work unpacking the trunk.

Don't worry—pray.

Don't weep—do.

She closed her eyes, her mind a jumble.

Harrison—the Lord bless thee, and keep thee... thank You for letting me see him again... Thy will, not mine.

Thy will. Thy will!

She changed clothes and put on the apron, making sure she had her money tucked into one of the pockets. She didn't trust the stationmaster or his wife not to harvest whatever they could from her belongings.

When she returned with the sheets and a blanket, and the candles and matches, Mrs. Kinnard had taken over the job of sponging Harrison in an effort to bring his fever down. From time to time she moistened his lips as well, and she filled a quill with water from a glass and fed it to him.

"He can still swallow," she said when she realized Kate was there. "That is a good sign."

Kate believed her without question. How strange it was that she could be so glad, so grateful for this vexing woman's presence.

Thank You, Lord. For Mrs. Kinnard. For Robert. Thank You for them both, and for the others, as well.

Max and Maria and Mrs. Justice. Perkins and Castine.
I'm not alone... I'll try to remember that...

"Now," Mrs. Kinnard said. "I believe this boy should be allowed to rest for a time before we try to bring down his fever again. He's been bothered enough."

Kate nodded, still willing to accept Mrs. Kinnard's opinion. She sat down in one of the chairs.

"It would be more helpful if you went to find Robert," Mrs. Kinnard said. "We should know everything we can about this situation—even if it isn't much. And you, you're looking...pinched. Go get some air. Eat something—"

"I'm fine."

"You are clearly *not* fine, Miss Woodard, and I would prefer not to have two collapsed people on my hands, if you don't mind. I will stay by the boy until you get back."

Kate stood, trying not to look as "pinched," as Mrs. Kinnard seemed to think she did,

"His name is Harrison," Kate said as she walked toward the door.

She couldn't see Robert in the hallway at first, but she could hear his voice, and she continued in that direction. He was in a small alcove off to the side talking to Castine. She stood and waited until he was finished

"What did the doctor tell you?" she asked immediately.

"He thinks Harrison has a 'morbid fever.' He doesn't know if it's the result of the..."

"The stationmaster's wife told me he was robbed and beaten," Kate said when he didn't go on. "She hinted that it was his own fault, because he didn't know to hide the fact that he had money. She said he lay out in the rain all night."

Robert was watching her so closely. Propriety dictated that she should avoid such an intense gaze, but she didn't. She was so glad that he was here with her and it was all she could do not to tell him so.

"The doctor didn't know if the beating has caused the fever or if it's something else," he said finally. "He didn't offer anything in the way of treatment other than purging. I said no to that. I've seen too many men die from the weakness that comes with it. They're always worse afterward. The doctor didn't know of anything else to try. Perkins sent a field medicine chest—quinine for ague and laudanum for pain are about the only useful things in it. I don't think Harrison is in pain, despite the bruising."

"Or is he past feeling it?" Kate asked bluntly.

Robert didn't try to avoid the question. "That may be the case, but I don't know for sure. It's good that Mrs. Kinnard has come. I think she probably has more experience in this kind of thing than the doctor here does."

"We have to take him home, Robert."

"It's a long way to Philadelphia."

"Not Philadelphia—Salisbury."

"He's very weak, Kate."

"I know. Maria told me to bring him there if I could. I'm going to try to do that. I don't see him getting better in this place. But I don't know what it will take to get him space on the train."

"The authorizations Perkins gave me should take care of that."

"Yes," Kate said in relief. "The authorizations. I'd

forgotten about those. I thought I'd have to find another carpetbagger."

"Carpetbagger?"

"There was one on the train. He had a private car, and he knew who I was. He tried to use it to get into Max's good graces."

"I don't think we can count on a private car, a carpetbagger's or otherwise. Most likely Harrison will have to travel the way wounded soldiers traveled—a stretcher placed across the aisle—"

"Miss Woodard!" Mrs. Kinnard called loudly, and Kate ran down the hallway to Harrison's room. Incredibly Harrison was sitting up in bed and struggling with Mrs. Kinnard, who was trying to keep him from falling. But then Kate saw the boy's face, his wild, fever-bright eyes. This was not an improvement in his condition; this was something much worse.

Robert stepped around her to help Mrs. Kinnard. "Find the laudanum in the medicine case, Kate."

"Where is it? It was here on the table—"

Kate looked frantically around the room. There was no medicine case.

She stepped out into the hallway. "Castine!"

He came at a run.

"The medicine case is missing. We need laudanum."

He gave her a sharp nod of acknowledgment—as if that was all he needed to know. He whirled around and disappeared down the hall. He wasn't gone long, and when he returned he had one of the drummers by his collar, and he shoved him into the room. The man looked around wildly, then seemed to be satisfied that he had nothing to worry about—except Castine.

"This man rattled when he walked past me a little while ago," Castine said. "I'm wondering why."

Kate didn't hesitate. She stepped up to him and immediately began going through his pockets—while he leered. She found a number of bottles from the medicine case. The laudanum was in the last pocket she searched.

"Do you know what to do with him, Private Castine?" Robert asked over his shoulder.

"I do, sir."

"Then carry on."

"How much laudanum?" Kate asked Mrs. Kinnard.

"Five drops in water," Mrs. Kinnard said without hesitation. "Put some water in a tin cup—not much— just a swallow or two. Carry it over to the window so you can see the laudanum drops fall into it."

Kate got a tin cup and poured the water. She kept looking over her shoulder as Harrison tried to get free of the hands that held him fast. He was in torment, struggling to get away from something only he could see.

She dropped five drops of laudanum into the cup and handed it to Robert, who administered it quickly despite Harrison's resistance, and with as much skill as she had seen the hospital orderly use when he'd poured brandy into Robert the night he'd collapsed in the hallway. She wondered if it was something men in the war had to learn to keep each other alive.

Harrison continued to try to get free, but with less and less forcefulness, until at last he stopped fighting altogether and Mrs. Kinnard and Robert laid him back on the bed.

He was quiet now, but he wasn't asleep as he had

been before. He was still agitated, only he no longer had the physical strength to respond to it. His eyelids fluttered, and he mumbled unintelligible words. His fingertips plucked at the sheet covering him.

Kate took his hand and held it for a moment. He felt much hotter than he had earlier.

Mrs. Kinnard handed Kate a piece of flannel, and together they began wetting him down until his skin was noticeably cooler. They stopped and waited until it grew hot again and then they started all over. They changed the wet sheets. Castine brought more water, and Robert took over for Mrs. Kinnard. Kate lost all track of time. All her attention was focused on Harrison.

She realized at one point that the windows had grown dark and she thought that Mrs. Kinnard was no longer in the room. But Mrs. Kinnard was sleeping heavily on the cot in the corner, and it was all right. Kate was no longer as helpless at the bedside as she had been when Robert had needed water to drink. She had mastered feeding Harrison with a quill. She mixed some of the sugar she'd brought in water and gave it to him repeatedly with the quill—barely a swallow—and then she let him rest. Then another swallow of sugar water, again and again.

Was it helping? Kate didn't know, but at least she was doing something.

"Kate?"

She looked around, wondering why Robert sounded so insistent.

"Come with me," he said, taking the quill out of her hand.

She shook her head. "No. I can't leave him—"

"Mrs. Kinnard is here. You need to come with me."

She wanted to resist, but he had her firmly by her shoulders, and he walked her out of the room and down the hallway to some kind of storage room she hadn't been in before. There was a cot in the far corner, and it occurred to her that this must be where he slept—if he slept at all.

"Sit," he said, making her sit down on one of several tall stools, the kind she'd seen the clerks sitting on when she'd once gone along with her father to his Philadelphia bank, not because he had business he needed to attend to, but more that he wanted to make it known that he had a daughter of marriageable age. The rows of clerks, the reason for her being there—it was all so… Dickensian somehow.

Oh, Harrison!

She sat there on the stool, her head bowed.

"Look up at me," Robert said, and when she did, he placed a cold and wet piece of flannel over her face. "Let it be for a minute. It will make you feel better."

"How do you know?" she asked wearily, feeling both impatient and overwhelmed.

"Because I was a boxer. Just bear with me. You'll see."

He pressed the flannel gently against her cheeks and forehead, her eyes, then flipped it over, fanned it in the air a few times and reapplied it. The renewed cold against her face felt…wonderful.

"I can do it," she said, not knowing whether she could or not.

"I know. Just sit still."

But she took the flannel away and caught his hand.

"I have to go back. I can't leave him, Robert. You don't understand—"

"I think I do," he said.

She shook her head. "No—"

"I can see you in him, Kate. And you keep his photograph with you always. If this situation weren't so dire, you would never have handed it over to me."

"No, that's not—" She wanted to deny it, but tears suddenly welled up in her eyes instead. They spilled over, streaming down her face, years and years of unshed tears. She couldn't stop them no matter how hard she tried. Robert knew the truth, and she was glad.

"Drink this," Robert said.

Kate had cried for a long time, and he had stayed with her while she did it, wiping her face from time to time, but not intruding—until now. It was as if he knew she needed to let go at last.

"Drink it," he said, pressing the tin cup into her hands. "I mean it."

She very nearly smiled. She had no doubt that he could make her do it if he wanted to.

"What is it?" she asked, looking into the cup.

"I'm not sure—some kind of soup. It's good, though. Castine made it. I think he's going to turn into another Perkins."

She did smile this time. "Thank you," she said, looking up at him.

He pulled up another stool and sat down in front of her, she thought to make sure she ate the soup. She tasted it, then took a long swallow. Something with onions and potatoes. It was quite good.

She drank a little more, and she felt the effects of

finally having some nourishment almost immediately. She had no idea how long it had been since she'd eaten. She concentrated on holding the tin cup, knowing that Robert was waiting for her to look at him. But she kept sipping until she'd finished the last of Castine's soup, then she sat the tin cup on the nearest stool. She took a deep breath, knowing she was going to tell Robert everything.

"I was very...young," she said quietly.

"Kate—"

"He was born in Italy," she said firmly, looking into his eyes. "I was sent to a place there—for rich young women who needed to hide until their babies were born—I've always been good at hiding, you see.

"*Bambina povera.* That's what the midwife kept saying. 'Poor little girl.' I thought she meant the baby I'd just borne, but she meant me. 'Poor little girl...'"

She wiped at her eyes again. "I was his mother for six hours. The midwife gave him to me and told me to hold him as long as I could. So I did—until someone came and took him away. I don't think she was supposed to let me do that, but I was so..." She stopped.

"You don't have to talk about this, Kate," Robert said.

"No, I want to. I told her I wished I had died, and she said no. It was wrong to think that, because I was a mother now and God relied on mothers. Six hours. I always thought it wasn't long enough to count, but it was. It *is*. He is my child, and this is breaking my heart."

"How did...?" Robert began, then stopped.

"Go ahead," she said. "What were you going to say?"

"I don't understand how people so close to your family raised him."

"It was all part of the plan. Not *my* plan. I had no say about anything. The Howes and my parents were close friends. Their son—John—is Harrison's father. He didn't abandon me," she said quickly because of the look on Robert's face. "When he knew about the child, he wanted to marry me, but my father wouldn't agree to it. He thought I was too young and John was too…wild. And John's father—he wasn't about to let a grandchild of his be given over to strangers. So they did the only thing they could do. The Howes took Harrison. Mrs. Howe came to Italy, too—she was young enough to pass my baby off as her own. It wasn't that difficult. He may look like me in some ways, but he looks more like John. He and John were brought up as brothers."

"And you've always been close by."

"As close as I dared. I knew I couldn't get too close to him. If I did that, I wouldn't be allowed to see him at all. It's still hard—for me. Not so hard for John, I think. He has a firm place in Harrison's life," she said. "It's true that John was wild when he was young—so was Max. It's something young men do, apparently."

"Yes," Robert said.

"Some of them, anyway. I don't think Grey was ever like that."

"Grey?"

"Lieutenant Grey Jamison—I was going to marry Grey." She sighed. "But perhaps he was wild, too. He was a horse soldier in Kilpatrick's cavalry. Isn't that what they say about cavalrymen? That they're reckless and wild?"

"It's what the walkers—infantrymen—say about them."

"He was killed at Bentonville."

"I'm sorry," Robert said.

"When I said yes to his marriage proposal, I thought I could live with the lie of Harrison's birth and never need to tell the man I cared about who Harrison really was. *Now* I know I couldn't have done that. Those kinds of secrets only... It's..."

She sighed. "It happened so... John was... I always thought he was very...lonely, despite his fearlessness when it came to breaking the rules and flaunting authority. He was like an orphan in the storm, and I was—I don't know what I was. He'd come to the house to see Max that night—something had happened—something that upset him terribly. But Max wasn't there. No one was except me and the servants, and they'd all gone to bed. He wouldn't say what was wrong and he was in such...despair. I wanted to...comfort him, but I didn't know how—" She paused to look directly into Robert's eyes. "And then I...did know. I can't blame John for what happened. I could have stopped it, but I didn't. It was all—oh, I'm not making any sense."

She suddenly straightened and wiped her eyes. "So you see, I'm not someone who ought to be groomed." She looked at him.

"I love you, Kate," he said when she did.

It was the wrong thing to say and the wrong time to say it. Kate knew that, and so, she thought, did he. It was so simple and honest, and she believed him.

"I'm not bound to Eleanor—not in the way you think—" Robert said.

Kate shook her head sadly. "Bound is bound, Robert. I'm no more free from my past than you are." She took his hand and held it to her cheek. He rested his head against hers.

Just for a moment, she thought. *I love you, Robert!*

"I have to go back," she said. "Whatever happens, I have to be there."

Chapter Fifteen

There was no carpetbagger with an inappropriate invitation this time. If there had been, Kate thought, it was very likely she would have accepted it. She would have sacrificed Max's reputation for Harrison's comfort without a second thought.

As it was, six seats had been designated for transporting Harrison back down the line to Salisbury. A stretcher had been placed across the aisle with either end resting on a seat. The other four were for Kate and Mrs. Kinnard and items necessary to take care of Harrison for the duration of the trip. A straight chair had been placed close to the stretcher, because the lurching of the train made it too difficult to tend to him standing up. Robert and Castine were located two seats away, primarily to keep any curious passengers from trying to see what was happening. All of them took turns, even Castine, sponging away the fever, feeding Harrison water or a very thin broth.

When it grew dark, a lamp was lit. It hung from a hook in the ceiling, and the constant sway of the train made the shadows sweep back and forth across the car. Despite her exhaustion, Kate was aware of Robert's presence all the time, but never once did he intrude. He quietly made sure she had whatever she needed. She was free to concentrate on her son, and she loved him all the more for it.

She loved him. He loved her. And nothing would ever come of it.

Kate was dozing in one of the seats when Robert lightly touched her arm, startling her awake.

"There's been a change," he whispered, and Kate's heart fell.

"What—?"

"Shhh," Mrs. Kinnard said behind them. "I believe his fever has broken," she whispered. "I think he is sleeping naturally."

Kate immediately maneuvered to where she could see. Because of the moving shadows, it took a moment for her to decide. She reached out to touch Harrison's hand, and when she did, he clasped her fingers.

"Oh—"

"Shhh!" Mrs. Kinnard insisted again. "It would be premature to rejoice. Whatever emotion you're feeling, feel it quietly. Natural sleep is the best healer."

Kate nodded. She realized suddenly that she was crying, and she wiped at her eyes.

"I assume you want to sit by him," Mrs. Kinnard said, still whispering.

"Yes."

"Then do so. But do *not* wake him." She moved the chair so that Kate could sit down without letting go of Harrison's hand.

Kate sat there, trying not to rejoice—but it was so hard not to. At last she had a glimmer of hope.

Thank You for that, Lord.

She looked down the aisle to where Robert sat watching, and she managed to give him the barest of smiles.

She dozed off just as the sun was coming up. When she opened her eyes again, Harrison was looking at her.

"I knew…it was you…" he said.

Kate smiled. "Did you? How?"

"You're the…only one who calls…me 'Harrison.' You…and Mother."

"It's not going away," Robert said.

Kate looked up sharply. She had come outdoors to finish a letter to Max—her latest update regarding Harrison's progress. She had seen Robert at a distance. Surprisingly, he had been talking to Warrie earlier, but Kate hadn't realized he was nearby. He came closer.

"I…don't think I know what you mean," she said, avoiding looking at him directly when that was all in this world she wanted to do. Look at him. Sit with him. Talk to him. But it seemed that they had reached some kind of tacit agreement not to call attention to the change in their friendship, the kind Maria had been so worried about. They were still friends, and both of them knew it would have to stay that way.

"I mean Harrison is getting stronger every day," he said.

Kate glanced at the upstairs veranda where Harrison was sitting in an invalid chair, playing checkers with Castine. They were a quieter but no less intense version of Joe and Jake, who at the moment chased each other around and around the backyard—with two hound pups nipping at their heels.

She knew that Robert expected some kind of response to his remark, but she didn't say anything.

"Do you not see God's plan in all this?" he asked after a moment.

"I'm afraid to see God's plan," she said truthfully.

"Maria told me once that you thought you were brought up useless," he said, and she frowned. "Harrison and I both are proof that that is not the case."

She shook her head. "Robert—"

"You've come a long way from the young woman who missed her train," he said.

She looked at him then, and in a way she hadn't in the days since they had brought Harrison back here to recover. She had *missed* him, even though he was never far away. It was still there. All the feelings—the love— she had for him, and when she looked into his eyes...

"Come walk with me," he said, holding out his hand.

"I don't think that's a good idea—"

"Don't worry. We have more things to discuss than my willingness to die for you. Or live for you—whichever you happen to need."

He was teasing her, and she couldn't help but smile.

"I never know what you're going to say," she said.

"Neither do I," Robert assured her. "Are we walking?"

"All right," she said, putting the letter into her writing box and setting it aside. She took his hand. "Which way?" she asked as he pulled her to her feet.

"That way. I need to see Reverend Lewis."

She took his arm and they began walking down the path to the street that would take them to the church and the church parsonage. As they passed the front of the house, she turned and waved to Harrison.

"He's what I wanted to talk to you about," Robert said.

"Why?"

"Are you going to tell him?" he asked instead of answering her question, and Kate knew exactly what he meant. Robert knew everything about her and Harrison. It wouldn't be difficult for him to guess what was troubling her so.

"I want to," Kate said truthfully. "Are you going to try to talk me out of it?"

"No."

"Are you going to tell me what you think?"

"No," he said again.

"But you think something."

"I do."

"Then tell me."

"I think the same thing you do."

"And what is that?"

"You want whatever is best for your boy. And now you've reached the point where you have to decide what that is."

She stopped walking. They were standing in the shade of an apple tree that grew on the other side of a picket fence. The tree was covered in blossoms, and dozens of insects bobbed from flower to flower. "I want to tell him, Robert."

"Yes," he said.

Yes?

But he was merely acknowledging her desire. He was by no means condoning it.

"He's a lot like you," Robert said as they began walking again.

"Is he? In what way?"

"He's very…forthright. I like that boy quite a lot," Robert said. "He has a very practical way of looking at things."

"What do the two of you talk about?"

"The war. Religion. The benefits of a good education. Samuel."

He stopped walking. "I thought maybe you'd like to wait for me here while I go see the Reverend," he said. The church was only a few yards away.

"I don't—"

"Your lamp is lit late into the night, Kate," he said. "I think there's only one way to find the answer to the question that's keeping you awake."

Kate gave a soft sigh. It was true that she hadn't been sleeping. She was so grateful that Harrison was recovering, and she could manage all the prayers necessary to express her gratitude. What she couldn't manage was asking God what she should do now.

"I'm…afraid, Robert."

"All the more reason to talk to Him. He already knows what's in your heart. *Talk* to Him."

She hesitated, then turned and walked toward the church doors, looking up at the thuya tree as she passed. It was as serene and stately as ever.

It's to show, in God's house, everyone is welcome…

She went into the sanctuary and made her way down the aisle to the front and sat in the same place she had when Robert had spoken so eloquently to the congregation. She didn't think he realized how powerful his message had been.

She could hear the sparrows singing outside the windows, a carriage passing, children playing somewhere. She closed her eyes.

"I'm afraid," she whispered. "Too afraid to say what I want so desperately." She took a quiet breath. "Robert says You already know. Will You show me what to do? Please show me. Help me to understand Your will."

She bowed her head, and she sat there quietly for a long time. But she felt nothing. Neither better nor worse. When she came out of the church, Robert was waiting. He didn't ask her anything. He merely offered her his arm.

She didn't look at him until they had reached the house.

"Don't give up," he said when she did. "You *are* strong, Kate. Remember that."

"Kate!" Harrison called from the upstairs veranda. "Come on up!"

"I'll see you later," Robert said, and he left her standing in the yard.

"Kate!" Harrison called again, and she walked swiftly into the house.

"How is he?" she asked Castine as she passed him in the upstairs hallway.

"He's happy today—got a letter from Philadelphia."
Philadelphia.

If he was happy, then it must have been from John, she decided. Mrs. Howe hadn't written to him personally as yet; there were only a few sentences included in the letters John wrote. Kate could only imagine how displeased the woman must be that he ran away from school. Kate still didn't know the reason. She hoped he had written to John about it because he hadn't said anything to her.

"Kate!" he said as soon as he saw her. "I have something to tell you!"

"I have something to tell you, too," she said, because she knew at that very instant what she was going to do. Harrison was her son. *Her* son. He was part of her, and she was going to tell him the truth.

"You first, then," he said, smiling up at her.

"I can wait. Tell me what has you so excited."

"Well," he said, moving his spectacles up on his nose. There are two things actually. I'll tell you the best first—or maybe I should tell you the other one, I don't know."

"The best one," Kate said.

"All right. I got a letter from Mother today—a *long* letter. She isn't angry with me at all. She wants me home—there's a private railroad car coming to get me—if Max's army doctors say I'm well enough. If they do, I'm to send a telegram right away. I can't wait to see her—she'll know what to do about everything. She'll know how I can make amends—"

"Do you…need to make amends?" Kate asked. It was all she could do to keep her voice steady.

"Yes, of course," he said earnestly. "Robert told me a gentleman always makes amends when he's in the wrong—especially with the people he loves. I ran away and worried everybody. I shouldn't have. Mother will help me to do the right thing. She's very wise—she's the wisest person I know. We're going to have a lot to talk about. She says I'm to thank you for sending Robert to find me."

"Does she?" Kate said, fighting back the tears. She'd

hid her true feelings for years and years. She could do it again now—for his sake.

He wants to go home!

"Yes, and she says thank you for taking such good care of me. And for keeping me company when I felt so low. That part is from me—she doesn't know you kept me company. Now I need to tell you something."

"All right."

He was looking at her so intently, and she forced a smile.

"Well, it's this. I think Robert is too shy for his own good. He's like…that Pilgrim—Miles Standish. I think he likes you a lot, and since you're not shy at all and you're not getting any younger, maybe you should ask him if he wants to marry you."

"What?" Kate said, startled because she'd only been half listening. Her mind was filled with but one thought. Mrs. Howe was his mother in every way that mattered, not her. Never her. Regardless of how it began, that was the truth of his life and hers.

I can't tell him. Not ever.

If she did, it would be for her happiness, not his. He loved Mrs. Howe, relied on her, *missed* her. Somehow she hadn't taken that into consideration at all.

"Ask Robert if he wants to marry you," Harrison said.

"I…don't think that's the way it's done," Kate said.

"I don't see why not," he said. "You'd get a good answer. I know you would. Then you wouldn't be alone like you are now and he wouldn't, either. Can you just…think about it? It's a good idea."

"Yes," Kate said. "I'll think about it."

"Good. What were you going to tell me?"

"Oh, nothing important—with all this talk of marriage, I think I've forgotten."

"Then I'm ready for my afternoon nap now—you can tell me later. Would you find Castine? Mrs. Kinnard will be coming by soon, and I don't want to have to explain to her why I'm awake. Unless you'd like to do that for me," he added with a mischievous grin.

"I think not," Kate assured him, and his grin broadened. "I'll see you later."

"Don't forget what I said."

"No. I won't."

Kate left the veranda and went blindly down the stairs. Castine was in the foyer, talking—listening—to Perkins.

"He's ready to be wheeled in," she said. "Do you know where Mr. Markham is?"

"He's outside, Miss Kate," Perkins said, and she nodded.

She needed to find him. The question she'd been so afraid to ask had been answered—Harrison himself had answered it—and Robert was the only person who would understand.

"Wait, Miss Kate," Perkins said when she headed down the hallway. "I don't think you ought to go out there right now," he called.

But she kept going. She saw Robert standing in the yard, and she walked quickly in that direction.

"I was wrong," she said as she approached him. "I was *wrong*."

"Kate, what—?" He held out his arms and she walked into them.

"I was going to tell him," she said into his shirtfront. "I was going to do it, but then I couldn't. I didn't realize how much he loves his—mother. Not me. Oh, it hurt so much listening to him talk about her. I can't take her place—ever. If I told him, I would leave him with nothing but people who had lied to him." She leaned back and looked up at him.

"It's going to be all right," Robert said gently.

"Is it?"

"Yes."

She gave a heavy sigh. All these years she'd had some misguided idea of what Harrison's life had been like, but his sincere words about Mrs. Howe—his mother—had changed everything.

I was blind, but now I see...

She pressed her face into his shirt again, even knowing Mrs. Kinnard was due. "I love you, Robert," she whispered.

"I don't think I heard that," he said, and she looked up at him.

"Yes, you did," she said, and he smiled.

"Rob?" someone said behind them, and they both looked around.

A woman and a man stood at the edge of the yard. They were both smiling.

"I'm sorry to interrupt, but we have to catch the train. This must be Kate," she said, stepping forward.

"Yes," Kate said, looking to Robert for some guidance.

"This is Eleanor," Robert said to her. "And her fiancé, Dan Ingram."

Eleanor?

No wonder Perkins hadn't wanted her to come outside.

"Pleased to meet you, miss," the man said.

"Kate, do you mind if I have a word with Rob?" Eleanor asked.

"No," Kate said. "Of course not."

She stood there completely bewildered as they walked a short distance away. She suddenly turned her attention to Dan Ingram. He didn't seem to find this situation awkward at all.

"You're catching the train?" she said just to have something to say.

"We're heading back to Wyoming. I was afraid I'd be going home by myself, but Eleanor said yes."

"I…didn't know she was here."

"Nobody did except her mother and Mrs. Woodard. And then Rob. He told us about you—well, he told Eleanor, and she told me."

Kate stared back at him. Clearly a lot had been going on while she was lost in her own troubles.

"If you don't mind my saying so, you're looking like you ought to sit down. How about we walk over there to the porch steps?"

"I— Yes," she decided. Her mind was reeling. Sitting down was definitely a good idea.

When they reached the porch, she sat down on the top step and, surprisingly, so did Dan Ingram.

"It must have been a shock for her—finding out Robert was alive," Kate said. She could see Robert and Eleanor from this vantage point, but she couldn't tell anything about their conversation.

"At first. But then she remembered I'd done about the same thing after the war—run off from everything I knew. Only I went to Wyoming. You love him?" he asked bluntly.

"I— Yes."

"Thought so. It'll help him—if you tell him about it, that is, and you don't go trying to do what you think is best for him. 'Best' is having the woman you care about say she'll take a chance on you—however it turns out." He stood. "Here they come."

He offered Kate his hand, and she stood to meet them. Eleanor Hansen had no reticence whatsoever about calling Kate aside, clearly intending to say something she didn't want Dan or Robert to hear. It occurred to Kate, as she and Eleanor stood looking at each other, that both of them were thinking of the same person.

Robert Markham.

"Yes," Eleanor said after a moment.

"Pardon?"

"I thought you might be wondering if the things you'd heard about me were true. The answer is yes." Eleanor smiled a wry smile. "It's in the past, though. I know that now. Dan came all the way from Wyoming to make sure I know it. And Robert—he helped me to understand…some things. I never thought I'd ever hear myself say something like this, but I believe he's going to make a fine minister."

"So do I," Kate said.

They stared at each other for a moment longer, the conversation clearly ended.

"Dan!" Eleanor suddenly called, holding out her hand to the man she was going to marry. As he approached, she gave Kate an abrupt goodbye hug.

"Be good to him," she whispered in Kate's ear. "He's going to need someone like you. And don't waste time worrying about what people will think." Then she was gone, walking away on Dan Ingram's arm to catch a train to a new life.

Kate walked back to the porch and sat down on the top step again as Robert joined her.

"What did you mean—when you said you weren't bound to Eleanor in the way I thought?" she asked after a moment.

Robert looked at her. A slight breeze ruffled his hair. "She broke our engagement—before Gettysburg—but I still needed to find out if she was all right."

"And is she?"

"Yes. Dan Ingram is a good man."

"What about Warrie? Does she know Eleanor broke your engagement?"

"Eleanor told her. She would never have believed it if it had come from me."

"This has been the most—" She stopped because she had no words for the events of this day.

"Are you all right?" he asked, his eyes searching hers.

"I will be—as soon as I take Harrison's advice. And Eleanor's."

"And what would that be?"

She moved closer so their shoulders touched. "It would be this—Robert Brian Markham, will you marry me? If you think I'm groomed enough, that is."

He smiled. "This is their advice?"

"Harrison's. Eleanor told me not to worry about what people thought. And, since I'm not getting any younger—to quote Harrison—and both things seem reasonable, given our situation, I want to know—"

"Robert Markham! What would your mother say! Sitting out here like this where everyone can see you—"

"Mrs. Kinnard is here," he advised Kate. "I'm…not sure," he said to Mrs. Kinnard.

"And you, Miss Woodard. What do you think you're doing?"

"I'm asking Robert for his hand in marriage—but he hasn't given me his answer yet. Robert Markham, will you marry me or not?"

"I will, Miss Woodard," he said. "The sooner, the better."

"Good," she said, using his own word for the situation.

He suddenly reached out and took Mrs. Kinnard by the arm. "Come sit with us, Mrs. Kinnard."

"Robert Brian Markham—!" she protested, but he was relentless. She sat, and he put an arm around both of them.

"The very idea!" she said, but she stopped trying to get away.

"I know," Robert said. "But you're the only mother I have—you and Mrs. Justice. I'm happy, Mrs. Kinnard. I want you to be happy, too."

"Well, this is *not* the way."

Perkins came out the front door, took one look at the three of them and went back inside again.

"I love Robert with all my heart, Mrs. Kinnard," Kate said. "And you've just heard him say yes to my bold proposal. Now. Would you be so kind as to arrange my wedding?"

Epilogue

At first Kate had been afraid Mrs. Kinnard would plan something with so much pomp and circumstance it would rival a coronation, but she hadn't. An entirely different Mrs. Kinnard had seemed to be in charge this time, one who understood exactly what Kate and Robert wanted—a wedding that was warm and intimate and joyous all at the same time. And practical.

"We will want an evening wedding," Mrs. Kinnard had said. "So you and Robert can slip away sometime during the reception. And if we schedule it a few days before Christmas, the church will already be decorated."

Which had left Kate free to concentrate on her attendants. Having Maria as her matron of honor had been out of the question, because the wedding date would be too soon after the baby's birth for her to assume the duties required of her—nearly two weeks of her lying-in period would still remain, Kate smiled suddenly, thinking of the beautiful little girl who had been welcomed into Max's family—and hers.

Ann Maria Katherine Woodard.

Max and the boys were absolutely captivated by her mere presence, and what a job she would have later—keeping *all* of them in line.

And that had left the bridesmaid.

There had been only one other possible bridesmaid who met the age requirement that she be younger than the bride, only one who would see the position as both an honor and an "adventure."

"Kate!" Valentina said now. "Hurry! It's almost time!"

Kate took a deep breath. She could hear the swelling of the first chords from the organ.

"How do I look?" she asked Valentina as she smoothed the flounce on the underskirt of her dress.

"Beautiful," Valentina said earnestly. "And wait till you see Robert. Thanks to Sergeant Major Perkins and Private Castine, he's been polished to within an inch of his *life*."

Kate smiled and followed her into the vestibule. She had no doubt that that was true. And how beautiful the church looked, all candlelit and filled with the scent of Christmas greenery and the boxes of oranges that would be given to the children on Christmas Eve and to the poor. And there were so many people—Mrs. Kinnard hadn't quite accomplished the "intimate" part.

"Here I go!" Valentina said as the organist began playing her musical cue.

Kate could hear the creaking of the pews as people turned to see Valentina make her entrance.

"They're playing the charge," Max said mischievously as he offered Kate his arm. She smiled up at him. Clearly Perkins and Castine had done some work on him, as well.

"Max—"

"He's a good man, Kate. Even I can see that, but if—"

"I don't want to change my mind, Max."

"All right then. I'm ready if you are."

She stood on tiptoe and kissed his cheek. "Thank you, Max. For everything."

She could see Robert and his best man standing at the altar now. Harrison was grinning from ear to ear, and he poked Robert with his elbow as the music changed and she came into view.

She walked with Max down the aisle past a sea of faces, some smiling—Mrs. Justice and Robert's former comrades—and some not—Mrs. Russell and her forlorn daughter.

"Dearly Beloved," Chaplain Gilford began, his voice steady and full of authority. He was doing well now—thanks to Robert's help—and she was so glad they had chosen him to perform the ceremony.

Kate barely heard the rest of it because she was looking into Robert's eyes. It was as if all the many tributaries of her life had been flowing from some unknown source, colliding, joining, carrying her along to this very moment. It was so clear to her now. She could see it—in all that had happened to her and to him. She could see it in her finally understanding her place in Harrison's life and in the remarkable way she and Robert had met. She could see it in his pain and sorrow over Samuel's death and his coming home again. She loved Robert Markham with all her heart, and it was there, too. All of it—*all* of it, was God's plan.

For I know the thoughts that I think toward you, saith the Lord, thoughts of peace, and not of evil, to give you an expected end...

When the wedding was over, she would tell Robert. She would tell her husband how new and joyous she felt.

She smiled suddenly, still looking into his eyes, her heart soaring. She said her vows firmly and with love, and she listened to Robert do the same.

My husband.

She would live with him and grow old with him, and they would do their best to remember that no matter what happened, He would always be there.

* * * * *

After twenty-five years as a high school English teacher and independent-school administrator, **Laura Abbot** turned to writing the kinds of stories she'd always loved to read. She sold her first book to Harlequin Superromance, followed by fourteen more. Her other professional credentials include serving as an educational consultant and speaker, and as a licensed lay preacher. But her greatest pride is her children and eleven grandchildren.

Books by Laura Abbot

Love Inspired Historical

Into the Wilderness
The Gift of a Child
A Family Found

Visit the Author Profile page
at Harlequin.com for more titles.

INTO THE WILDERNESS

Laura Abbot

I am about to do a new thing; now it springs forth, do you not perceive it? I will make a way in the wilderness and rivers in the desert.
—*Isaiah* 43:19

To Paula Eykelhof, editor extraordinaire,
with gratitude for her encouragement, guidance
and enduring belief in me.

Chapter One

Fort Larned, Kansas
March, 1869

Lily Kellogg stood before her mother's small grave marker, oblivious to the raw spring chill. *Mathilda Louise Kellogg, b. 1820, d. 1868. Beloved wife and mother.* From these few words, who would discern the bravery and compassion of the woman buried there? Or how quickly she had succumbed to the influenza that swept through the fort a few short months ago, despite the heroic efforts of Lily's father, the post surgeon.

Once again Lily asked the familiar questions. *Is this ultimately what we amount to? A few facts etched in cold stone? Do we rest for eternity beneath a blanket of grass battered by wind, sleet and snow, subject to infestation by creatures both crawling and flying?* Standing there motherless, she struggled to believe in a merciful God.

Too late she thought of the questions she should have asked her mother, but hadn't, and the family stories she should remember, but couldn't. Yet she knew her mother had loved her, as she had loved her father, brother and sister. In part, she blamed this isolated place for her mother's death. If only they had remained in Iowa, living with her maternal grandparents as they had while her father served in the Union Army. When the conflict ended and her father elected to remain in the military, her mother, not without misgivings, had insisted that she, Lily and Lily's older sister, Rose, accompany him to this remote fort on the Kansas plains. Her mother had loved fine things and had assumed she would always live in the familiarity of the town where she grew up and in comfortable proximity to her well-to-do parents.

Since her death, Lily had harbored a painful question: Would Mama still be alive if the family had stayed in Iowa? She cast a baleful glance at the headstone. It all came down to choices, and her mother, a faithful wife, had chosen to follow her husband. Now that Mathilda was gone, Lily knew her father depended even more upon his daughters and worried whether Fort Larned was a suitable home for two unmarried women, one twenty-one and the other twenty-four.

Gazing at the gray clouds scudding overhead, Lily permitted herself a moment of self-pity. She tried not to complain and to trust in God's plan for her. But surely her destiny lay someplace else—in a city lively with creativity and dedicated to progress. Blinking back tears, she laid her hand gently on the grave marker.

The clatter of mounted horses interrupted her reverie. The arrival of new troops was no novelty, and, like others before them, these soldiers deserved a welcome. Gathering her cloak around her, she waved.

Their leader glanced in her direction, smiled and lifted his hat.

Whether it was his erect posture astride the black horse, his light brown curls blowing in the wind or his engaging smile that caused her heart to skip a beat, she couldn't say. Perhaps it was his air of confidence, the hint of mischief in his smile or his fleeting resemblance to the brother she had lost in the war that moved her. She turned away. *He is just another officer,* she reminded herself. Just another officer.

Dismayed by her spontaneous reaction to the man, Lily hurried toward home. No good could come from idle speculation about the new captain, handsome or not, and no such man could ever derail the exciting future she planned for herself.

When Lily returned to their quarters attached to the hospital, her sister met her at the door. "You look chilled. Come warm yourself by the fire." Rose gathered Lily's cloak and hung it on the hook in the entryway. "I've brewed some tea." She bustled to the stove to fetch it while Lily settled in the rocker in front of the hearth, grateful for her sister's solicitude. Rose, always a steadying influence, had moved effortlessly into her mother's homemaking role.

Her ample body swathed in an apron, Rose handed Lily her tea and sat on the bench across from her. "Did you see the new troops arrive?"

"Yes. They're fortunate to be assigned to this modern post, rather than one of the more primitive ones."

"And we are fortunate to have received an invitation from Major and Mrs. Hurlburt to dine with them and the newly arrived captain."

"How thoughtful." Ordinarily Lily would have been

delighted by such a welcome invitation from the fort's commander and his wife. Yet she was suddenly overcome with uncharacteristic shyness. The possibility of acquaintance with the new captain should not so unnerve her.

Rose leaned forward. "I'm wearing my apple-green. What will you choose?" They smiled in concert, knowing full well that aside from their few everyday dresses and recently discarded mourning clothes, they had only two Sunday gowns. "You look best in the lilac," Rose ventured. "Do wear it."

"Why are you so bent on how I look?"

Rose took a sip of tea. "You know I will not leave Papa. I am a homebody. But you? It's time to consider romance. Past time. If a dashing cavalryman is to sweep anyone off her feet, it is you, dear Lily."

"Such a prospect! To follow some man from post to post, never having a true home of one's own."

"That's what Mama did," Rose gently reminded her.

"Yes, but though she never complained to us, I always thought Mama acted more from loyalty than from enthusiasm. Remember when we first arrived here? How she would purse her lips and shake her head with resignation?" Lily squared her shoulders. "I have bigger dreams than living at assorted military establishments."

"Ah, yes. Your dreams." Rose's sigh spoke volumes.

"You just wait. I am determined to seek another path. Mother always planned for one or both of us to visit Aunt Lavinia in St. Louis if she offered to take us under her wing. Think what we could learn there! What we could see! Libraries, museums, theaters—all just waiting for us." She glowed with the possibilities.

"As for courtship, surely there are plenty of men of intellect and substance in the city." She glanced around the room. "Whatever happens, my future is not in an isolated place like this."

"Lily, if leaving is truly what you desire, I hope it happens even if I would sorely miss you. Mama recognized our different talents and temperaments. She knew you, not I, would thrive in a more sophisticated environment than rural Iowa or this fort. If Aunt Lavinia's invitation comes, you are the one to go."

Lily set down her cup and stretched her feet toward the fire. "Imagine," she said breathlessly. "St. Louis."

Lavinia, her mother's only sister, had married well. Henry Dupree had made a fortune in commerce and doted upon his wife, whose only apparent regret was that she was childless. She had begged Mathilda not to marry Ezra Kellogg, appalled that her sister would settle for being the wife of a small-town doctor. Then the war changed even that, and Lavinia had made no secret of her disappointment at finding Mathilda doomed to the itinerant life of an army surgeon's wife. Lavinia's letters following their mother's death had even intimated that she blamed Ezra for the influenza that had cruelly taken her sister.

Through the years, Lavinia had corresponded regularly, delighting her nieces with the wonders of St. Louis and the gaiety of her social calendar. Lily pored over the back issues of *Godey's Lady's Book* their aunt sent them. Transfixed by illustrations of the latest styles, she could picture herself dancing in the arms of a sophisticated city man at some fashionable soiree. Although she realized she was indulging in romantic fantasy, such daydreams alleviated the loneliness of her existence on the prairie.

Living among men of all ages and stations was not easy. Some ogled, some were crude and others were helpful, going out of their way to assist the surgeon and his household. Tonight she would meet another in a long string of officers, most of whom were either too forward or disdainful of women. Few viewed females as intellectual beings or appreciated a well-read woman. Why should this newly arrived captain be an exception?

Rose gathered their teacups. "We are due at the Hurlburts' home at six o'clock."

"Will Papa join us?"

"No, a serious case at the hospital requires his attention."

Lily seized on the excuse. She often served as her father's nurse. "Perhaps I am needed there."

"Papa said to assure you this was a delicate matter best handled by men."

Later as she and Rose walked toward officers' row, Lily wished her father's case had required her assistance. Then she could have avoided testing the giddy feelings of anticipation occasioned by the thought of meeting the new captain.

Captain Caleb Montgomery held up his arm to halt the cavalry troops behind him. From his vantage point on a small rise, he surveyed the endless expanse of Kansas prairie, barren except for cottonwood trees bordering a sluggish stream, which he took to be the Pawnee Fork of the Arkansas River. In the distance, neatly laid out in a rectangle, were the buildings of

Fort Larned, his final duty post before mustering out of the army.

Behind him lay the wagon ruts of the Santa Fe Trail. Protecting it from Indians and renegades was a far cry from the havoc of clashing Union and Reb forces, but that war was over. However, it never left the minds of those who had fought it as he had. Nor would he ever forget the recent heartless attack on Black Kettle and his people at the Washita River in Indian Territory. Both his innocence and the lure of adventure had been lost long ago, obliterated by the bloodshed he had witnessed. Only twenty-seven, he felt much older, seasoned by the harsh reality of "man's inhumanity to man," as the poet Robert Burns so aptly put it. Duty and honor remained, but did little to compensate for recurring nightmares. Pushing aside such grim thoughts, he spurred his horse and men toward the fort.

Approaching the compound, he spotted the figure of a woman standing in silhouette against the weak March sun. Tall and slender, she seemed oblivious to their approach. Only as they rode closer did he notice she stood in a cemetery, her eyes fixed on a small headstone. Caleb wondered whose grave she visited and what heartache might be represented by that solitary marker. He had seen many such markers, and, alas, too many comrades buried in nameless graves amid the confusion of battle. At the sound of the troops' approach, the woman faced them, then lifted her hand in greeting.

Doffing his hat, Caleb turned in his saddle to observe her more closely. She was fair-skinned, and tendrils of honey-hued hair escaped her bonnet. He was seized by an impulse to make her smile, to ease her burden of grief. He grunted. A foolish thought.

Entering the fort, Caleb was struck by the breadth of the parade ground and the height of the flagpole in its center. He drew his men into file for the approach of the commanding officer, Major Robert Hurlburt, who strode toward them. Caleb dismounted and saluted. "Captain Montgomery reporting for duty, sir."

The post commander returned the salute, then smiled broadly as he extended a hand. "Welcome to Fort Larned." He nodded at the soldier standing at his elbow. "Sergeant Major, show the men to the stables and then get them settled in the barracks." He clapped a hand on Caleb's shoulder. "Officers' quarters are over there." He pointed to a row of new houses on the west edge of the parade ground. "My wife and I would be pleased to have you dine with us this evening."

"It would be an honor, sir."

Before relinquishing the reins of his horse to a hostler, Caleb stepped forward and stroked the animal's nose. "Good job, Bucephalus."

The major regarded the horse. "Bucephalus? A noble enough steed for Alexander the Great. I hope his namesake has served you well."

"He's one of the finest, sir," Caleb said without going into detail about his affection for the horse, which had been with him through many fearsome engagements.

Following the major across the parade ground, Caleb commented on the fort's modern buildings, which had recently replaced more temporary structures.

Hurlburt nodded. "It is a fine facility. Better than most we've both seen, no doubt."

The major left him at the bachelor officers' quarters to get settled. Caleb was weary, not just from his travels but from military life, as well. Since enlisting at eighteen after the attack on Fort Sumter, he'd known nothing else. He mentally counted his few remaining months of service, eager to begin the next chapter in his life.

He unpacked quickly, ambivalent—thanks to his exhaustion—about dining at the major's home, but duty called and he would welcome a home-cooked meal. After washing up, he lathered his face then picked up his razor. Some of his fellow officers prided themselves on luxuriant beards and drooping mustaches. Caleb regarded such practices as peacockery and preferred to be clean shaven. Scraping the blade over his three-days' growth, he pondered the end of his military career. There were things he would miss—the physical challenges, the sense of accomplishment when missions went well and the camaraderie of his fellow soldiers; but he would never miss the thunder of cannons, the tumult of gunfire or the otherworldly, agonizing cries as bullet or ball ended a life. It was time to settle in one place, to put down roots.

Donning his best uniform, he made his way next door to the post commander's home, an impressive dwelling with a wide front porch overlooking the parade ground. Major Hurlburt greeted him and drew him into the parlor. "Captain, may I present my wife, Effie."

Caleb bowed slightly. "An honor, ma'am."

Mrs. Hurlburt was a plump, middle-aged woman with rosy cheeks, frizzy red hair and mischievous eyes. "Hurly and I are delighted to meet you."

Hurly? Her use of a pet name for her husband defied the customary formality of such occasions.

Noting the surprise he had been unsuccessful in concealing, she laughed. "I know, I know. We're supposed to observe stiff conventions. So silly. We are all in a strange place, thrust together by circumstance. Within my home, I will do as I please. Hurly can follow protocol elsewhere." She laid a hand on Caleb's sleeve. "I hope I haven't shocked you."

Caleb glanced at the major, whose eyes were fixed fondly on his wife. "No, indeed. I shall happily abide by the rules of this house."

Major Hurlburt moved to a sideboard. "Brandy, Captain? Tea?"

"I'd prefer tea, sir." While the major prepared his own drink and poured the tea, Caleb studied the room, furnished with a Persian rug, two settees, an armchair, a library table and a small piano. Several watercolor landscapes and embroidered samplers adorned the walls. The decor was tasteful but confining after his months in the field.

The major handed Caleb his cup, but before he could sit down, a knock sounded at the door. While Hurlburt went to answer, Effie said delightedly, "This will be the Misses Kellogg. Regrettably their father, our post surgeon, has duties which prevent him from joining us."

Feminine chatter filled the entry hall as the major took the ladies' cloaks. A sturdily built young woman with pale skin and freckles entered the parlor first. "Permit me to introduce Miss Rose Kellogg," the major said before turning to the second woman. "And her sister, Lily."

From her erect posture and demeanor, Caleb recognized Lily immediately—the woman in the cemetery. Close up, her flawless skin, the thick blond hair coiled on her head and her wide blue eyes rendered him tongue-tied. When had he last seen such a lovely female? Then, recovering his voice, he said, "Miss Rose, Miss Lily, the pleasure is mine."

Was it his imagination, or did a faint blush suffuse the latter's face? Before he could make that determination, the major seated the ladies and offered them tea.

Effie motioned for Caleb to sit beside her while the major served the Kellogg sisters. "Tell us, Captain, what brings you to Fort Larned?"

Although Caleb was certain she already knew, he briefly recounted his experience subduing marauding Indian tribes.

Rose leaned forward. "Did you also see service in the recent war?"

"I did, miss." He had no desire to elaborate.

Lily, apparently sensing his discomfort, deftly changed the subject. "That's history. I am interested in your opinion of Fort Larned."

Until they adjourned to the dining room, he offered his initial impressions of the place and then listened as the others told him about the recent rebuilding. Effie, in particular, put everyone at ease with her gently humorous comments and informality. Clearly the major was satisfied to let her hold sway at home, just as he controlled the fort.

At dinner, Caleb had the good fortune to be seated directly across from Lily Kellogg. He hoped his perusal of her wasn't too obvious, but it was difficult to keep his eyes averted. The delicacy of her features was at odds with the self-composed figure he'd seen in the cemetery. She was both dazzling and enigmatic.

Effie seemed determined to direct questions to him,

but he noticed her slyly studying Lily while he answered. He had a familiar sinking sensation. He was in the hands of a skillful matchmaker. If he wasn't bound by social niceties, he could save Effie Hurlburt the trouble. Looking at Lily Kellogg was one thing; entanglement, quite another. He had learned that lesson from bitter experience.

Buttering a slice of bread, the major commented that he was sorry about Ezra Kellogg's absence from the table. "A fine doctor he is. During the outbreak of typhus late last fall, he performed valiantly, keeping our mortality rate low."

"He's very skilled," Effie agreed. "As is his most proficient nurse." She smiled at Lily, who bowed her head modestly.

"I do what I can."

"Sister, you are a marvel," Rose said. "Few of us could do what you do."

Lily looked up. "When you find something interesting and fulfilling, it isn't work." Caleb watched her eyes light up. "Learning about the human body and how to control and treat disease is fascinating. If only…" Her voice trailed off.

Caleb suspected she'd been about to say "If only women could be doctors," but no one else picked up on the thought. To spare her the awkward moment, Caleb said, "May I ask how you began nursing?"

The young woman set down her fork. "Before she died, my mother attended women in childbirth. I was curious, and she began to teach me. Then when she was ill, we—" she nodded at her sister "—helped nurse her, and I discovered I had a gift. Our father is often shorthanded or in the process of training inexperienced enlisted men, so I assist him as I can."

"A regular Florence Nightingale she is," Effie said, beaming approval.

"Miss Nightingale is an idol of mine, but I would never venture to compare myself to her."

"The nurses I observed during the war performed invaluable services," Caleb said, recalling painfully the field hospitals he had visited. "It is important work, and I commend you."

The conversation then turned to the latest rumors about a railroad to be built to replace the Santa Fe Trail. "The railroad is only the beginning of a new era, I suspect," the major observed. "With such progress, we will no doubt experience many changes."

"Not the least of which is moving to the parlor for coffee." The major's wife rose to her feet. "And perhaps Miss Lily will honor us with a selection on the pianoforte."

Caleb smiled inwardly. Miss Lily Kellogg seemed to be a woman of myriad and contradictory talents. He didn't want to be intrigued by her, but even fatigued as he was, the prospect of learning more about her kept him alert. A half hour later, after further conversation and two pleasing piano pieces, the major asked him to escort the Kellogg sisters home.

Outside, clouds played tag with a nearly full moon. The light-colored stones of the buildings shifted and glowed as shadows came and went. From the enlisted men's barracks came sounds of revelry. It was nearly time for taps, so as they proceeded across the parade ground, the noises gradually subsided. At the door of the small house adjoining the hospital, Caleb took each of the ladies' hands by turn. "Miss Rose, Miss Lily. Good night." His gaze caught Lily's. "Thank you for an evening I will long remember."

"Good night, Captain," the women said in unison before disappearing inside.

Caleb strolled back across the parade ground, reaching his quarters just as the bugler sounded taps. As they often did, the haunting notes recalled other nights, other encampments. Deeply moved, he lingered on the porch, taking in the fort, the surrounding countryside, the limitless sky. Feelings he hadn't experienced in a long time, if ever, came over him. Part longing, part mystery, part promise—all centered in the disturbing sense that it wasn't by accident God had put Lily Kellogg in his path.

Sighing wearily, he regained control of his thoughts. He would need to be on his guard. A woman had hurt him once, and he never wanted to feel that vulnerable again. No matter the provocation.

Chapter Two

Sunlight filtering through the windows of the post hospital the next morning brought an illusion of cheer to the convalescing patients. Lily moved among the beds, changing a bandage here and wiping a fevered brow there. Only after she had checked all the patients did she pause at the bedside of a young man who had been kicked by a horse, suffering painful bruises and a concussion. Taking his hand, she gently called his name.

The man stirred, then groaned. Lily spoke louder. "Benjamin, tell me where you are."

His eyes fluttered before focusing on her. "In heaven?"

"Try again. Where are you?"

The hint of a smile teased his lips. "Just joshin,' Miss Lily. Hospital. I'm in the hospital." Then just before he fell back to sleep, he mumbled, "Clumsy nag of a horse."

Across the room lay a cook, scalded by a pot of boiling soup, his hands mittened in gauze. She made her way to him. "I have time now, Timothy, to write that letter for you."

She retrieved paper, pen and the lap board and listened as he dictated his message. "Tell me mum I am dandy. Say I had a bit of an accident, but that I'll be cooking again before she even gets this letter. Ask her to write."

Lily had seen the burns on his hands and doubted he'd be cooking anytime soon. She prayed he would be spared infection, so common with burns. "I will post your letter this afternoon."

"Thank you, miss," he whispered, tears flooding his eyes. She turned away to spare him embarrassment.

When she had finished her duties, she stepped into the small surgeon's office where her father was working on his weekly medical report. "Do you need me further, Papa?"

Ezra Kellogg looked up, his blue eyes gentle behind his spectacles. "You're a godsend, daughter, but we'll manage for the rest of the day."

Lily studied his pale face and stooped shoulders. There was an air of resignation or…a lack of vigor… something that had diminished him. It was as if when his wife's life drained away, his spirit had ebbed, as well. She and Rose did what they could to lighten his heart, but, in truth, all of them sorely missed Mathilda. Only after her death had Lily realized the extent to which her mother had been the family's anchor.

Not quite six years before, a similar shadow had passed over the family and forever changed them. During the war she, Rose and her mother had prayed unceasingly for the safety of her father and brother, David. Lily's chest tightened, as if a claw gripped her heart. David. So amiable and strong. It had been natural to idolize the big brother whose hearty laugh had charmed them all. In her innocence, she had thought him invincible. Until that awful news. The telegram from the War Department had stated in cold, impersonal terms that their beloved David had been killed in the Battle of Lookout Mountain.

She remembered the sickening feeling she'd experienced with the realization that he had been dead for many days before they received word. Days when he had still lived in her imagination—eating, laughing, singing and…fighting. That blow had been especially cruel since they had no efficient way to communicate with Ezra. Their father's return following the war, though a cause for celebration, was a somber occasion, the four of them grieving for the son and brother who would never again grace their family circle. Recalling past family dinners where there was always one empty place at the table, she was reminded of last night's meal.

"Papa, we missed you at the Hurlburts' dinner."

"I hope you and Rose enjoyed it."

"We did. The new captain dined with us."

"What did you make of him?"

"He seemed pleasant enough."

Her father rose to his feet and laid a hand on her shoulder. "I worry about you girls being in this place. There are good men here, but others…" He grimaced. "Others you shouldn't even have to see, much less come into contact with."

"Captain Montgomery is no cause for alarm."

He kissed her forehead. "I probably shouldn't have brought you here with me, but we had been so long apart during the conflict that I—" his voice cracked "—needed you."

"And we needed you, *do* need you." She patted his arm. "Never blame yourself for our circumstances. Rose and I are fine, and, after all, we are a military family. Women do their duty, too, you know." Then, to emphasize her point, she saluted airily and took her leave.

As Lily made her customary way from the hospital to the cemetery, the breeze carried a tantalizing hint of spring. Full sun warmed her back as she stood before her mother's grave, pondering the exchange she'd had with her father. Finally she spoke. "Mama, we miss you so. Papa is lost without you." She closed her eyes, picturing her parents embracing. "How he must have loved you. And you? How sad to die in a harsh place like this so far from the home you loved."

Turning to leave, she glanced in the direction where yesterday she'd seen the new cavalry troops arrive, led by Caleb Montgomery. He had none of the arrogance of George Custer, who had been stationed at Fort Larned a few months ago, nor the affected dandyism of some of the others. Montgomery seemed...was *solid* the word for which she searched? Yes, that, but more. *Dependable? Trustworthy?*

She chided herself for attempting to pigeonhole the dashing captain. His essence would not be captured, even as she ruefully admitted thoughts of him had captured her, despite her best efforts to will them away.

Although it had been a week since his arrival at Fort Larned, Caleb had slept poorly, troubled by disturbing dreams. Awake before reveille, he dressed quickly and stepped onto the front porch to watch the sunrise. Smoke rose from the mess hall kitchen, and in the distance a horse whinnied. After a few minutes, he made out the form of the bugler, who sounded notes that brought the fort from quiet to bustling activity. Lantern light flared in the barracks, and he heard the raucous shouts of prompt risers rousing the slugabeds.

From inside, the lieutenant with whom he shared quarters grunted and coughed. Will Creekmore, a fellow from Wisconsin, began every day with prayer. While Caleb found the practice laudable, he wondered how it had served the man on the battlefield. He himself had struggled to find God in the chaos of armed conflict, finally latching onto the instinct for sacrifice, even love, that he observed in the way men in extremity cared for their brothers in arms. He had concluded that just as evil existed and tempted men to war, so was mercy present in the myriad selfless acts he'd witnessed. That thought was all that made his duties bearable. Yet his uneasy truce with God had suffered a significant setback at the Washita River.

He would go to his grave with the horrors of November 27, 1868. On that wintry dawn, he had led his troop to a rendezvous point above the Washita River where they waited in hushed darkness for Lt. Col. George Custer's command to attack the camp of Chief Black Kettle and roughly two-hundred-fifty vulnerable Cheyenne. A survivor of the infamous 1864 Sand Creek Massacre, Black Kettle had negotiated for peace, but had been unable to control younger, more belligerent warriors, engaging in raids against white settlers.

Swallowing sourly with the memory, Caleb saw it once again in his mind's eye. Their orders were to take woman and children hostage, but to kill anyone who fired on them and destroy the enemy's horses. When the first rays of the sun illumined the horizon, the command came, bugles blew and the cavalry charged down on the sleeping village. It took only one shot from a single hapless Cheyenne to incite a frenzy of fighting. Screaming women clutching their children ran for the river, old people fell in their tracks, and bodies littered the snow.

In his nightmares he would forever see the little girl holding a cornhusk doll, a bullet hole through her chest and the lifeless body of a woman cradling beneath her a piteously mewling infant.

He had experienced horrific combat in the War between the States; however, that cause was justified and didn't involve women and children on the battlefield. But the engagement on the Washita? That was different. It was a massacre. To his eternal shame, he had been unable to prevent it. No wonder he had lost his zest for soldiering. It was even difficult to believe himself worthy as a man.

The orange ball of the sun brought light into his dark thoughts. "God," he whispered, "help me to understand. Why? Why?" Scraping a hand across his beard, he paused as if waiting for an answer, and then went back into his quarters to shave.

After breakfast, Major Hurlburt gathered the officers for a briefing. Spring wagon trains setting out for Santa Fe would soon be passing their way along with the usual supply wagons. Roving bands of Kiowas, Pawnees and Arapahos, angered by the white man's usurpation of their tribal lands and hungry after a long winter of deprivation, were on the prowl. Scouts had already located Kiowas camped along the Pawnee Fork. Caleb and his sergeant were ordered to accompany a seasoned troop the following day to deal with the situation and familiarize themselves with the immediate territory.

That evening, keyed up in anticipation of action, Caleb sought the quiet of the post library. Before the war, he had entertained thoughts of studying at university, but now that was a distant dream. However, he reckoned the lack of formal education needn't keep him from learning.

In a somber mood, he pulled a volume of Tennyson's poems from the shelves. The book fell open to "The Charge of the Light Brigade," and Caleb was transported instantly to the suicidal attack in the Crimean War. "Into the valley of Death / Rode the six hundred." He looked up from the page, grimacing at the image of men riding to certain doom. Did mankind ever learn? Such atrocities were no different from what his own army had inflicted on the peace-seeking Indians massacred at Sand Creek and the shameful Battle of the Washita.

He closed the book, rubbing his eyes, gritty with the need for sleep. Crimea. Unwittingly, Florence Nightingale came to mind, her lantern bringing hope to the wounded and dying there. How incongruous that the lovely Lily Kellogg could also be engaged in such grisly hospital work. Yet her name had surfaced again and again in the conversations of men at Fort Larned. Although she brooked no nonsense, they said, she had a fearless and compassionate heart, and sometimes their healing had depended as much on that as on any medicines or procedures.

As if he had conjured her, the door opened and Lily entered, her attention fixed on the stack of books she carried. When she saw him, she uttered a startled "Oh" and dropped her armload on the floor. He hastened to her side, where they both knelt to gather the volumes.

"I didn't mean to alarm you," he assured her.

At that same moment she was saying, "I wasn't looking where I was going."

In the lantern light, her hair cast a golden glow, and he found himself at a loss for words, finally managing, "Do you come here often?"

"It's my favorite place," she murmured.

He assisted her to her feet and then gathered the books and laid them on a shelf. "Mine, too. No matter the post to which I'm assigned."

Looking over his shoulder, she noted his book, abandoned on the chair. "What were you reading when I disturbed you?"

"First of all, you didn't disturb me. Besides, Tennyson's 'The Charge of the Light Brigade' is rather gloomy. In truth, I was daydreaming rather than reading."

She crossed the room, picked up the poetry collection and skimmed it. "I do so admire his work. 'Flower in the Crannied Wall' is one of my favorites." She closed her eyes and recited, "'Little flower—but *if* I could understand / What you are, root and all, and all in all, / I should know what God and man is.'"

"A big *if.* Can we ever know about God and man? Would we even want to? Man has a habit of mucking up things."

She smiled, a glint of humor in her eyes. "Not only 'man.' In rare instances, 'woman' can also create problems."

Rather than going to the unhappy place where a

woman had created a problem for him, he chose to respond to her lightheartedness. "In *rare instances?* My dear miss, have you forgotten Eve?"

She laughed, a delightfully musical sound. "I fear, sir, that any discussion of serpents and apples might take an unpleasant turn."

"Perhaps, instead, we should both pledge to re-read Milton's *Paradise Lost* and compare our reactions later."

"He is a marvelous poet, isn't he? Such descriptions of the Garden of Eden. Why, I myself might have bitten into the forbidden fruit."

He had a sudden image of her rosy lips grazing a red-ripe apple. He mentally erased the charming picture. "Did you come for a particular title?"

She moved to the bookshelf, where she hesitated. "No, I'm browsing." She laughed again. "That's not exactly true. I've read nearly everything here."

"Then I shall look forward to hearing your recommendations." He was pleasantly surprised. From his brief exposure to her at the Hurlburts', he hadn't figured her for a bookworm. Discussing literature with her would provide at least one antidote for the boredom that was part of military life.

"I favor Mr. Dickens and the Romantic poets," she said.

"My, quite a divergence of taste."

"And why not? Fiction, poetry, biography, essays— we don't have sufficient time to read everything, but I try."

He inclined his head in an abbreviated bow. "Permit me, then, to take my leave so you may find the hidden gem that you have not read."

She bestowed a smile that banished any thought of the Crimea. "Good night, Captain."

"Good night, Miss Kellogg." Then as an afterthought, he added, "I shall look forward to sharing our opinions concerning *Paradise Lost.*"

"As shall I," she said.

Walking toward the officers' quarters, Caleb pondered the *if* in Tennyson's poem. To understand God and man. He longed to understand God, to find answers to his questions. As for "man," they were a mixed lot. As he had to admit women were, too. Even on short acquaintance it was clear that Lily bore no resemblance to Rebecca, the faithless woman who had broken his heart.

"In like a lion, out like a lamb," Rose announced on the last day of March as she and Lily made their way to the sutler's to buy provisions and collect the mail.

The day was warm, and wagon wheels and horses' hooves had churned the ground into dust that clung to their boots and the hems of their dresses.

"We'd best enjoy days like this," Lily observed. "Remember last summer? I swear equatorial Africa couldn't be any hotter. In mid-July, we will look back on this weather with gratitude."

Rose linked her arm with Lily's. "Enjoy the day, this day. God's day."

Lily squeezed Rose's hand. Their mother had often uttered those very words when her impatient daughters peppered her with questions: "When is Papa coming home from the war?" "How long until my birthday?" And more recently, "How are you feeling this morning, Mama?"

When they entered the store, enlisted men buying tobacco and assorted medicinal items made way for them. Several tipped their caps, a few ventured mumbled hellos and one insolent corporal winked leeringly. Jake Lavery, the proprietor, beamed as they approached. "Ladies, what can I do for you?

After placing their grocery order, Lily ushered her sister to a corner where yard goods and sewing notions were displayed. Thus removed from the prying eyes of men, the sisters studied some newly arrived bolts of cloth.

Rose stroked a brown calico covered with sprigs of tiny yellow flowers. "I rather fancy this for my summer dress."

Each summer and winter, their father provided them with money to make one serviceable gown apiece. Lily always had difficulty making up her mind, and today was no exception. She draped a navy blue muslin across her shoulders.

Rose shook her head. "Too drab. Try the gingham. It reminds me of the ocean. That is, if I'd ever seen it."

Lily unrolled a couple of yards and carrying the bolt to the small mirror on the wall, held the gingham to her face. The color did something magical for her eyes, tinting the usual blue with a hint of sea-green. She turned to Rose. "I like it."

"That was easy. I do, too. Have we need of patterns?"

Lily shook her head. "I have some ideas about adapting ones we already have."

"I trust you. You're the expert seamstress."

Mr. Lavery's wife measured and cut the material, then wrapped it in brown paper and tied it with string.

"Come show me when you've finished the gowns." A wistful expression crossed her leathery face. Observing the woman's worn gray dress, Lily ached for her. Frippery was hard to come by on the prairie where simplicity and practicality were both necessary and valued.

Lily tucked their purchases in the mesh bag they had brought with them. Their last stop was the mail counter. "Kellogg. Anything for us?" Rose inquired of the red-bearded postal agent, recently arrived at the fort.

"I know who you are," the man said, as if offended that they would identify themselves to someone with such a brilliant memory. "You're those girls the men are always talking about."

Rose bristled. "I hardly think so."

The man leaned on the counter and folded his gnarled hands, peering at them with beady eyes. "Bet on it, miss. It's just as well your papa don't hear some of what they say."

Lily drew herself up to her full height. "Sir, our mail, if you please."

He grinned wolfishly, then took his time moving to the mail slots.

"I declare," Lily whispered to her sister. "The nerve."

Rose took the letters from the man, uttered a huffy "thank you" and led Lily out of the place.

"That was demeaning," Lily said when they were out of earshot.

"Yes, but, Lily, I imagine the men do talk of us… *you*. Think about it. They're far from home, missing their wives and sweethearts. And some of them are so young. Bachelors." She trudged on deep in thought, then added, "Don't you see how they look at you?"

"Me?" Lily blushed.

"Oh, there's some that might settle for me, but you're the beauty."

"Hush, Rose. Don't you go tempting fate with that talk. 'Pride goeth before a fall,' and I don't want to be prideful."

"You can't pretend you don't notice their interest. For example, that new captain couldn't keep his eyes off you at the Hurlburts' dinner." She stopped in her tracks and studied her sister. "You could do a lot worse," she said gently.

"I'm not husband hunting." Lily grinned coquettishly. "At least not until St. Louis, if that time ever comes."

"St. Louis. A den of iniquity, if you ask me."

"I didn't."

With a shrug, Rose held up the mail. "I suppose then that you'll be wanting to look over the letter that came today from Aunt Lavinia."

"Oh, do let's hurry." So eager was Lily to read the letter, she didn't notice how Rose lagged behind. Nor did she see the concern in her sister's eyes.

At home, scanning Aunt Lavinia's letter before sharing it with Rose, Lily sighed in disappointment. There was no invitation for either of them. Just a description of Lavinia's new Easter bonnet, the menu of a sumptuous dinner at the home of a local politician and a recipe for an elegant presentation of tenderloin of pork, as if they often had such a cut of meat available.

Bent over her crocheting, Rose looked up as Lily read the final paragraph.

"I shudder to think of you girls subjected to the cold winds and extreme weather of the prairie.

Not to mention living in a forsaken army post, surrounded by who knows what sort of individuals. For the life of me, I cannot understand why Ezra took you to such a place. Would that your mother had persuaded him to abandon his army career. Well, water over the dam. I pray for your safety and hope conditions will permit us once again to meet. Perhaps after the miasma that is summer here along the Mississippi.

Your devoted aunt,

Lavinia"

Lily put the letter aside and sought composure by going to the sewing cabinet to locate the pattern for Rose's new dress. Only now in light of Lavinia's vague promise could she admit how much she had counted on deliverance from this wilderness outpost. She tried to take each day as it came, but the fierce, unpredictable spring winds tried her soul and increased her longing to escape. At times she wanted to scream from sheer frustration.

Rose had said something, but lost in her thoughts, Lily had to ask her to repeat it.

"Dear sister, patience." Rose wasn't trying to irritate her, and, yes, patience was needed, but right now the advice rankled.

"What's the matter with me, Rose?"

Her sister set aside her crocheting. "You really do want to leave. It's more than a dream, isn't it?"

Lily sank back into her chair. "I'm so restless. Every day is like every other day. Rose, there's a whole world out there, and I want to be part of it. If only I were a man, I could choose my lot and go wherever my fancy took me."

"I would miss you."

Chastened, Lily hung her head. "And I you." She had thoughtlessly hurt her sister. The tug to home and to Rose and Papa was strong, but so was the pull of the exciting world beyond the prairie. Why couldn't she lay aside these dreams that only grew more compelling with each passing day?

"Are you very disappointed? Had you thought Aunt Lavinia's invitation would come this soon?"

Lily looked helplessly at her sister, unable to confess the degree to which she had counted on Aunt Lavinia to save her. "Mama wouldn't like me to act like this. She would say everything happens in God's time, not mine."

Rose nodded as if her suspicions were confirmed. "Then leave it to God." She began crocheting again. "Meanwhile, I so love having you here for company. And take heart. Aunt Lavinia didn't rule out a visit later in the year."

Lily unfolded the pattern, but, disappointed by the letter and consumed by guilt over how her departure would affect Rose, she couldn't concentrate on dressmaking.

Several nights later, Caleb stretched out by the campfire, wearily resting his head on his saddle. This morning the cavalry had caught up with a band of Kiowas secluded in a small grove of trees. The soldiers had mounted a charge. Outmanned, the Indians had fired a few warning shots and then, to Caleb's relief, had fled on horseback. Since the Washita, he had no stomach for engagement.

He understood there was no stopping the westward migration of his own people, but at the same time he grudgingly admired the Indians, both those who came in peace and those risking their lives for their tribal lands and honor. Perhaps the Indians weren't that different from the emancipated slaves with whom he had fought in the war. Rarely had he been in battle with more dedicated or able fighters. Yet so many of his fellows treated these so-called "buffalo soldiers" as inferiors and made known their prejudice both with their abusive words and their fists.

Gazing up at the infinity of stars, Caleb wondered what God thought of the arrogant human beings He had created, so anxious to lord it over their fellow creatures whom they deemed ignorant or savage. Were the Indians and the former slaves that much different from himself? He suspected all any man wanted was dignity. Yet he knew firsthand that any one of them was capable of barbarity.

Tired of his gloomy thoughts, he withdrew a worn letter from his pocket. Slowly he unfolded it and squinted to make out the words, although he had already practically memorized them.

Dear brother,
Sister Sophie, Pa and I are continuing to purchase additional acreage near Cottonwood Falls for the Montgomery cattle operation. As I've told you, grazing land is lush and water is plentiful. The other settlers are welcoming and enthusiastic for

the prospects in this sparsely populated part of southeastern Kansas.

Thank you for the monies you have sent us. Your share of the ranch will be waiting for you when you muster out. We are all thankful that time is fast approaching. We are adding to the herd, so with hard work, this fall when we go to market, pray God we will see the realization of our hopes.

We likewise pray for your safety as we await the day of our reunion.

Your affectionate brother,

Seth

Their ranch—a dream come true. Joining his father and brother in the exciting enterprise would finally anchor him in one place. His place. A place where money could be made. Where a family could grow and prosper. A peaceful place.

Once before he had thought to establish a home. To live in harmony with a woman he loved. To plan a future together. That dream, interrupted by the outbreak of war, had sustained him through long marches and frenzied battles. Until Rebecca's letter, creased and soiled from its long journey, made its way to him in the winter of 1864. It was painful, even now, to recall her flowery words, made no less harsh by their embellishment.

It is with profound and heartfelt regret that I rue causing you any disappointment or loss of marital expectations. It has been my greatest endeavor to pass these uncertain days in the hope of your deliverance by a beneficent providence. But we are all, in the end, human beings—human beings with a need for love and companionship. So I beg your understanding and forgiveness for informing you that on Saturday last your friend Abner and I published the banns for our upcoming marriage.

Rebecca had, with a single blow, severed their relationship, one he had entered into wholeheartedly and purposefully. Beyond that, Abner's betrayal of their boyhood friendship had cut deep. Caleb closed his eyes, the lullaby of coyotes baying on a distant hill doing little to induce sleep. The Garden of Eden. The tempted Eve. Caleb snorted under his breath. Rebecca had certainly succumbed to temptation and, in the process, taught him a bitter lesson concerning trust.

And what of Miss Lily Kellogg, the first woman since Rebecca to interest him? Was she made of sterner, truer stuff? Did he dare acknowledge how appealing he found her? Even for an intrepid cavalryman that was a daunting thought. One he should not entertain, not when his hands were tainted with the blood of innocents.

Chapter Three

Caleb joined his fellow officers Saturday night at the tavern just a short walk from the fort. It was a rough frontier establishment, crudely built and redolent of sweat and beer. Loud, harsh voices assaulted his ears. A bar covered one wall, and in the back were several tables of serious card players. Two women, no longer young, their faces caked in makeup, sashayed among the men. Caleb didn't drink liquor, but neither did he want to appear standoffish. Through the years, he had learned a great deal about those under his command by observing their off-duty activities. Yet such places made him uncomfortable.

"Cap!" Maloney, a cavalryman who had been with him during several engagements, waved him over. Maloney was always good for a few stories. Caleb settled into a chair at the man's table and didn't have long to wait for the opening line. "Did you hear the one abut the general who saw a ghost?"

While the storyteller waxed eloquent, Caleb studied the crowd. Some gambled, some ogled the ladies, others, their eyes glazed over, threw back whiskey, undoubtedly searching for oblivion. He, too, sometimes longed for oblivion, but had long ago made the decision not to drink or gamble. He'd seen firsthand what such indulgences could cost a man—in some instances, not only his dignity but his soul.

When Maloney's story came to its hilarious conclusion, Caleb rose and headed toward the door. Passing by a table of enlisted men, he overheard the tail end of a conversation and recognized Corporal Adams as the speaker.

"...and that one's ripe for the pickin' and I might just be the one to harvest her."

"In a pig's eye," his fellow cackled. "She's too good for the likes of you, Miss Lily is."

"They's all the same beneath that flouncin' and finery. You just wait. I've got my eye on her. Some dark night—"

Caleb jerked the man to his feet. "You'll do no such thing, Adams, or I'll have you on report so fast it will seem like a cyclone hit you." It took all of Caleb's will to refrain from hitting the man in his obscene mouth.

Sniveling, Adams looked up at him through bleary eyes, his mouth stained with chewing tobacco. "'Twas just talk."

"You make sure of that or you'll deal with me." Caleb thrust the man back in his seat and glared at him to be sure he understood.

"Mighty protective, aren't you?" the corporal mumbled.

"What was that?"

"Nothin'." Then he added, "Sir," as if that would vindicate him.

"Change the subject, then," Caleb said before striding out into the night, fists clenched at his side. This wasn't the first man Caleb had heard talking about Lily, but most were respectful. Adams was a sneak, and Caleb hoped he was all talk, but based on his history with the corporal, he wasn't so sure.

Walking back to his quarters, he wondered if he would have reacted so strongly had it been just any woman under discussion. He hoped so. But the mere suggestion of such a creature touching Lily Kellogg made his blood boil.

The much-anticipated spring band concert was a break from the monotony of life at the fort. This particular evening featured two fiddlers, a banjo player and a wizened harmonica player. Benches had been set up in the commissary, and the officers' wives and daughters had prepared cookies and tea for a social following the musicale.

Major and Mrs. Hurlburt sat in the front row. Effie gestured to Ezra to bring Rose and Lily and join them. There was a stir of anticipation as the musicians took their places. The band performed old folk tunes as well as more recent camp songs. Early on, some of the enlisted men began clapping in time to the beat, and for an hour, all thoughts of danger and homesickness were suspended.

Lily was aware of the bachelor officers sitting in the row behind her, their buttons brightly polished, their gloved hands resting on their knees. Since the arrival of Aunt Lavinia's letter a couple of weeks ago, Lily had been pondering her future. Was it unrealistic to consider another world—one of sophistication, in-

telligent discourse and high fashion? Rose had urged
her to encourage Captain Montgomery, yet it would be
hypocritical to lead him on. Attractive as he was, her
favorable impressions of the man were surely skewed
by the limited world of Fort Larned.

At the conclusion of the concert, the musicians
bowed to enthusiastic applause and then asked the audience to join them in singing "Aura Lee." Behind her,
Lily heard a rich baritone voice and discovered when
she stood to leave that the singer who had pierced her
heart was Captain Montgomery.

Effie shoved her way between Rose and Lily and
grabbed the captain by the arm. "Rose and I are helping serve the tea, but perhaps you could get some refreshments for this young lady." She nodded at Lily.

"My pleasure," the captain said, following the major's wife to the food table to comply with her request.
Before Rose moved off to join Effie, she poked Lily
in the ribs and whispered, "It won't hurt you to flirt a
bit." When Lily glared at her, Rose affected wide-eyed
innocence and added, "Consider it a rehearsal for your
assault on St. Louis beaux."

Juggling two cups and a plate of cookies, Captain
Montgomery returned to Lily. Most of the crowd had
gone outside to eat, but he set the refreshments on a
bench. "Shall we stay here?"

She looked around, flustered to see how few con-
cert-goers remained. "This is fine," she said, sinking
onto the bench.

He handed her a cup, then made a toasting gesture
with his own. "To you," he said quietly.

"Whatever for?"

He smiled. "For gracing this place with beauty and

gentleness. Most of us have lived with men for far too long. You are a breath of fresh air."

The compliment both flattered and disturbed her. "Sir, I think you give me too much credit. I would suggest it is easy to say such things when, by your own admission, you have been long deprived of feminine companionship."

"Do you think me so devoid of discernment that I am drawn to just any woman?"

Drawn? He was drawn? How to answer such a question? "Forgive me, Captain. Of course, you must know your own mind."

"As I believe you must know yours. From what the men tell me, you are a fair, but demanding taskmistress—is there such a word?—among your patients."

"A hospital is not the place for indecisiveness or the encouragement of malingerers."

"Although one might not blame them for preferring your company to that of a drill sergeant."

"I assure you there are times in that environment when I bear a closer resemblance to a drill sergeant than a docile maid."

"From what I've seen of you, *docile* isn't a word that comes readily to mind."

She couldn't help herself. She chuckled. "What word *does* come to mind?"

He leaned back as if to study her. "Perhaps *curious.* Or maybe *determined.*"

"And what led you to such conclusions?"

"Your interest in medicine, your passion for that which interests you, whether it is nursing or literature. I suspect there is more going on in that head of yours than meets the eye."

"You, sir, are a keen observer. I shall have to watch my *p's* and *q's*."

He set down his cup. "Would it be presumptuous to ask you to call me by my Christian name?"

Lily was flustered. This conversation was moving beyond her powers to control it. "You have me at a disadvantage, Captain. Are we to become friends, then?"

"That is my intent, especially as we are both book lovers."

"Then, as friends—" she leaned forward by way of emphasis "—in informal situations, I will call you Caleb."

"Good." He hesitated as if hearing his name echo. "Would you object to saying it again?"

She looked at him quizzically, then softly repeated, "Caleb."

"Thank you. It has been many months since I have heard my name uttered by a lovely woman. And, then, only by my sister, Sophie."

Unaccountably, Lily felt her eyes moisten. She had never considered how a soldier might miss simple feminine interactions or long for a soft, endearing voice. Casting about for a safer topic, she said, "Tell me about your sister."

He stood. "Perhaps we could take a turn around the parade ground while I relate some Sophie stories." He held out his hand to assist her to rise.

Tucking her arm through his, she was startled by a sensation very like happiness. Surely, she told herself, it was the beauty of the spring night rather than her companion that provoked such an emotion.

On their walk, she discovered that he was a gifted raconteur. His mother had died giving birth to Sophie, and he obviously doted on his younger sister, a tomboy of the first magnitude. His tales of her cutting off her long hair when she was ten in order to look more like a boy and wading into the river to noodle for catfish were both humorous and poignant. He painted a vivid picture of his sister's flyaway curly red hair and ended by saying, "Sophie possesses a mind of her own, but she has a generous heart."

"I think I'd like her," Lily said, full of admiration for the independent young woman who dared to live beyond the conventional.

Caleb faced her. "She would like you." He clasped her hand between his own. "*I* like you."

"Captain—"

"Caleb, please."

"Caleb, I don't know what to say."

He snugged her hand beneath his arm and started walking slowly toward her home. "You don't need to say anything."

She decided silence was the best course lest she offer any more encouragement than, inadvertently, she may have already given. As they walked, an awkwardness seemed to develop where earlier there had been camaraderie. She could ask him about the mother he had lost, but they were nearing the hospital. Perhaps another time. *Did she want another time?*

At her door, he gently disengaged his arm and faced her. "Miss Lily, I pray I have not overstepped my bounds."

Again, she was at a loss for words. "It's late, Captain. It's best to say good-night." When his eyes clouded, she took pity on him. "Until we meet again, Caleb." She liked saying his strong, masculine name.

"Good night, Miss Lily." As if remembering his manners, he added stiffly, "Thank you for a pleasant evening."

Inside the house, she leaned against the closed door, bewildered. He had shown signs of his interest in her, but in the past few minutes had seemed to retreat into formality. She had enjoyed his company more than she cared to admit. That concerned her. She would need to steel herself and not let her fickle emotions side-track her plans.

When Lily entered the bedroom she shared with Rose, her sister was just finishing plaiting her long reddish-blond hair. The light from the candle on the bedside table cast an intimate glow. Lily loosened her buttons, plucked her nightgown from its hook and pre-pared for bed. Rose watched her, a smug smile playing about her lips. "Well?" she finally said. "How did you find your Captain Montgomery?"

"He's not mine," Lily said decisively, taking the pins out of her hair and beginning her ritual one-hundred brush strokes. Knowing that those three words would not satisfy her sister, she went on. "Like many of our officers, he is lonely. I provided a temporary diver-sion, no doubt."

Rose hooted. "Are you blind? The way he looked at you was special."

"He can look all he wants, but I will not encourage him. He would only be a distraction in my life."

"The life that's taking you to St. Louis?"

Lily set down her brush and put her hands on Rose's shoulders. "I'm sorry it's difficult for you to under-stand, but I have to be true to myself."

Rose reached up and clasped Lily's hands. "I know.

Papa and I have realized for some time that this place is too confining for your spirit." She bowed her head, whispering so quietly Lily had to bend closer to hear her. "But it is so hard to let you go." Rose looked straight into Lily's eyes. "I suppose I had hoped that if you married an army officer, our paths would cross now and again. And of the lot, Captain Montgomery seems a good man—a man who would cherish you or whomever else he chose."

"It is a fine thing to be cherished. Pray that I may find such a suitor in the city."

"I cannot honor your request. I will pray for you, of course, but for your well-being, happiness and the fulfillment of God's purpose for you, wherever you may be."

Lily embraced her sister, so good and true. Then she blew out the candle, and they curled into the depths of the feather bed they had shared since childhood. Soon she could hear her sister's gentle exhalations, but sleep eluded Lily. She lay awake for some time, not thinking so much about St. Louis as remembering the name *Caleb* and how he had needed to hear it spoken.

She turned on her side and shortly before falling asleep whispered to the shadows, "Dear God, why can't life be simple?"

When Caleb entered his quarters, Will Creekmore was sitting at the desk writing a letter by lantern light. "Did you enjoy the concert?"

Caleb stripped off his gloves and jacket and tossed them on a chair. "It was a welcome morale boost. Routine drills get mighty boring for the men."

"And for us."

Caleb noticed a daguerreotype sitting on the desk. He pointed to it. "Your family?"

The lieutenant picked it up and gazed at it fondly. "No. Fannie, my sweetheart back in Wisconsin." He hesitated and then added, "She's been waiting a long time. I'm asking her to come here. To be married. But it's far from her home. I don't know if…" He sighed. "All I can do is ask, though I do hate to inflict such a long journey on her."

"It's a lonely life out here. For your sake, I hope she says yes."

"Speaking of the ladies, how was your evening with Miss Kellogg? I couldn't help noticing how you favored her."

In the confusion of his feelings, Caleb didn't want to discuss Lily, but neither did he want to be rude. "She is a delightful young woman."

His fellow officer speared him with a look. "Whose company you enjoy."

Caleb shrugged helplessly, wishing he had done a better job of resisting Miss Kellogg's charms.

Will stood and clapped a hand on Caleb's shoulder. "Heaven help us, then. We can fight the rebel and the savage, but one look from a pretty woman and we're goners." He gathered up his ink, pen and paper. "I'm turning in. Good night, Montgomery."

"Good night. Leave the lantern. I want to read for a while."

After the man departed, Caleb picked up the book he'd left on the shelf and settled in a chair. But the book remained unopened, forgotten in the swirl of his thoughts. Lily Kellogg was a puzzlement. At the same time she had seemed interested in their conversation, he'd sensed a reserve on her part, as if she was unwilling to commit fully to their dialogue. Perhaps he had been too forward and she was merely being proper. Given his lack of recent experience with women, he was at a loss. He fingered the leather-bound volume in his lap. If only there were a treatise to teach him how to read women. How to court them without the fumbling awkwardness he had felt when he left Lily at her doorstep.

Courtship? Where had that idiotic notion come from? But even as the idea formed, the specter of Rebecca rose in his mind, and his spirit curled in on itself. He was too near his goal of joining his family in the cattle business to be waylaid by a woman.

He closed his eyes, picturing the verdant hills of the Montgomery Ranch, the beauty of the blooming redbuds his brother had described and the panorama of orange-pink sunsets stretching across the horizon. It was there he would ultimately build a home and father children. Someday he would have a wife. But why, lately, did the "someday" wife of his imagination look like Lily? Could she—or any woman—endure his nightmares? Accept his role in the Washita battle, especially when he couldn't?

The unseasonably warm April afternoon was made even more unpleasant by wild winds rattling windows and blowing dust high into the air. Lily moved among the beds of men laid low by spring fevers, following her father as he stopped to recommend treatment or offer encouragement. After their rounds, Lily prepared medications and folded clean laundry.

She consciously tried to appear busy to avoid the

unpleasant stares of one of the enlisted men recently assigned to hospital duty rotation. He had a weasellike appearance and followed instructions to the bare minimum a chore might require. It seemed every time she moved around the ward, he was lurking nearby with the same insolent look on his face. She was probably overreacting, but something about Corporal Adams made her distinctly uncomfortable. She shuddered before resuming her work.

Late that afternoon her father asked her to go to the post office to check on a package he was expecting, a medical book about the treatment of snake and insect bites. She welcomed her escape.

However, when she stepped outside, strong winds buffeted her, whipping her skirt around her legs. She tightened the sash on her bonnet and struggled toward the sutler's. Once there, she checked with the officious postal agent. "Have you a parcel for the surgeon?"

"Nasty day, what?" he said, his eyes roaming over her in an unseemly manner.

"Indeed."

He waited another beat before withdrawing a package from under the counter. "Wouldn't do to get it wet. Best hasten home, missy. Clouds are comin'."

"I'll hurry." She grabbed the package and turned to leave, stunned to see Corporal Adams slouched against the door, hands in his pockets. When she tried to slip past him, he fell in beside her. "Doc sent me to help you."

She eyed him with suspicion. Her father had never before sent anyone in such a situation. "I'm fine, thank you, Corporal."

Despite her dismissal, he followed her outside. Suddenly the fierce winds died, and a humid, pea-green canopy fell over the fort. Looking to the west, Lily saw thunderhead upon thunderhead mounting to the heavens and rolling toward them. She picked up her pace, leaning protectively over the package as the first pellets of rain fell. Then before she had gone more than a few yards, the sky went black, a gust of wind hit her and the heavens opened up.

"Here, miss." Adams seized her by the arm and pulled her into a darkened storehouse. "We'll be right cozy in here." His eyes glinted dangerously, and his grip on her arm hurt.

She struggled against him. "I'm going home."

The soldier moved closer. "You'll get wet. Now don't be a spoilsport. Besides, ole Adams just wants to have a bit o' fun."

He grabbed her around the waist, and she smelled his foul breath on her face. She could hardly breathe. "Get your hands off me!"

In the dim light, his mocking look said it all. He had no intention of letting her go. Fear such as she had never known buckled her knees. It was then that he pulled her to him, pinching her cheeks between his callused fingers. "You ain't goin' anywhere, missy."

Outside the wind roared among the buildings, zinging with power. In some corner of her brain, Lily registered the torrents drumming against the roof.

Adams's tone changed to sinister cajoling. "Now calm yourself, and give us a kiss."

Drawing on all her strength, Lily reared back, raised her arms and hit him over the head with the book, then raced into the storm, praying she could outrun him.

Blinded by the rain and slowed by her soaked dress,

she sprinted toward the headquarters building, visible in the lightning flashes that briefly illumined the parade ground. Behind her, she heard the corporal's howled oaths, but as she neared headquarters, he fell back and gave up the chase.

Breathless, she kept on running until she had nearly reached the wooden boardwalk outside headquarters. Then, somehow, she felt herself being lifted into strong arms and held in a protective embrace. When she looked up and saw Caleb, so great was her relief that she was racked with trembling. "Shh," he murmured in her ear. "You're safe now." Then he stared out over her head. "Was that Adams I saw?"

Bile filled her throat and all she could do was nod.

Caleb's voice was steely. "He won't be bothering you any more. I'll see to that."

Weak as a kitten, Lily laid her head on Caleb's broad shoulder, drawing from him warmth and security and reminding herself over and over, "I am safe."

Afterward she had no idea how long she had remained sheltered in the comfort of his arms. All she knew was that she had found peace in the storm.

Chapter Four

Scarcely daring to breathe, Caleb held Lily, moved by both her trembling and her floral-scented hair brushing his chin. Conflicting emotions tore through him— the unexpected joy of the embrace set against his rage at Corporal Adams. He itched to get at the man. First, though, he needed to see Lily safely to her family. Reluctantly, he stepped away. "I'm sorry, Miss Kellogg. This man should never have accosted you. I assure you he will be punished."

She straightened to her full height, adjusted her collar, then smoothed flyaway tresses back from her face. "I will count on that, Captain."

"Are you steady enough for me to escort you home?"

"I think so. It was all so sudden…and shocking."

"I'm glad I could be of assistance." He was aware of the forced formality of their conversation. Had she been offended by his embrace? Yet she had lingered there contentedly as she recovered from her panic.

"Please give me a moment," she said, turning away from him as if to study the storm, now diminishing in strength. She held herself purposefully, like a shattered vessel that had been glued back together. She seemed to be composing herself by sheer effort of will. "All's well that ends well," she finally said.

His pent-up anger threatened to explode. It hadn't ended well. That cad Adams had terrified her.

With a deep sigh, Lily faced him. "When we see my sister and father, I would ask you not to dramatize the situation. Rose doesn't need undue worry. As for Papa, he already suffers guilt for bringing us here with him. I fear he might never forgive himself."

"Eventually the facts must be told and Adams held accountable. But I will permit you the telling of the tale."

"Thank you, Captain."

"Caleb?" he asked hopefully.

For the first time in their conversation, she mustered a half smile. "Caleb. You were more than a friend today. You were my rescuer."

"I'm thankful I was here to help."

They stood a foot apart, their gazes locked, until a clap of thunder caused them to start. Caleb took Lily's arm and they dashed through raindrops to the Kellogg home.

Rose must've seen them coming. She flung open the door and hugged her sister. "We've been worried about you. Were you caught in the storm?"

Ezra Kellogg stood behind Rose, his eyebrows knit with concern. Never taking his eyes off Lily, he acknowledged Caleb with a curt "Captain."

Caleb squeezed Lily's arm gently before relinquishing his grasp. "Your daughter had a bit of a fright—"

"But I'm quite fine now, thanks to Captain Montgomery."

"Please come in, Captain." Rose took Lily's damp cloak and stood aside. "We all need a cup of tea. Lily, sit down and collect yourself and then do tell us what has happened."

Ezra directed Caleb to a chair by the fire and settled Lily on a small sofa. While Rose brought in the tea, Ezra wrapped Lily in a wool afghan, then sat down beside her, pulling her close. She rested her head on his shoulder. "Now," he said, "what's this all about?"

When Lily didn't respond, Ezra turned to Caleb. "You, sir. We're awaiting an explanation."

"Papa, there is little to explain." Lily raised her head and looked at them one by one. "I had started home when the storm broke. When it raged all about me, I sought temporary refuge in a storeroom and then made a dash for headquarters. There Captain Montgomery was kind enough to ease my fears."

Caleb sent her a questioning glance. She couldn't let it go at that. "Lily?" he said by way of encouragement, then inwardly reproached himself for taking the liberty of using her first name in this setting.

She glared at him, defying him to correct her version of events. While he hoped the matter of Adams could be taken care of discreetly, Ezra Kellogg deserved a fuller answer. Caleb suspected in a more intimate setting with her sister, Lily would confide the truth, but perhaps the incident was still too raw for her to discuss with her father.

Ezra turned to Lily. "Daughter, I recommend you take a tonic when you finish your tea. Then after supper it would be best for you to retire for the evening.

You have had a trying experience, but rest should restore you." He leaned over to kiss her forehead. "You are safe now, for which I thank God."

She touched her father's cheek. "And Captain Montgomery."

"Ah, yes."

Rose stepped forward and gathered Lily, afghan and all, and led her from the room.

After the women had departed, Caleb stood and prepared to leave. The surgeon crossed to him and laid a hand on his shoulder. "Sir, might I have a word with you in private?" Ezra Kellogg was no fool. The look on his face revealed his suspicion that Lily had withheld information. "Follow me."

The surgeon ushered Caleb to his office in the hospital, closed the door behind him and leaned against his desk, arms folded across his chest. "There is more to the story, am I correct, Captain?"

"Yes, sir." Although Caleb felt uncomfortable telling the part of the tale that Lily had chosen to omit, her father needed to know.

Ezra gestured to the wooden chair against the wall. "I'm listening."

Caleb lowered himself into the seat, then fixed his eyes on the doctor. "One of our enlisted men attempted to assault Lily."

Ezra raked his fingers through his graying hair. "I've been afraid of something like this."

"Fortunately Lily was able to escape his grasp and run away from him before anything more serious happened. When I first saw her from headquarters, she was running lickety-split across the parade ground, pursued by the cad, who fell back when I stepped outside. I did what I could to calm her and assure her she was safe."

Ezra spoke in a steely tone. "Do we know the identity of this scoundrel?"

"I do. Corporal Adams. I will be ordering him held in the stockade as soon as I leave here."

Ezra rounded his desk and slumped into the chair, burying his face in his hands. "I should never have brought my family here. I knew what rough-and-tumble places military forts are. I permitted my own needs and desires to override my common sense."

"With all due respect, sir, I think you're being too hard on yourself. Most of the men are good souls who respect women."

As if he hadn't heard, Ezra said, "I'll never forgive myself. What have I done to my daughter?"

Caleb realized he needed to get the man's attention. "Sir, listen to me. This was not your fault. It was the result of one man's actions, a man who needs to be drummed out of the army in disgrace." He paused to gather his thoughts. "Lily begged me not to tell you about this. I think she was afraid you'd react just as you have. In no way does she regard any of this as your fault. Furthermore, she seemed to recover well. She is brave and resilient. She will worry about you if she thinks she has been a cause of your increased concern."

"Have you ever had a child, Captain?"

"No."

"Then you cannot know how strong is a father's instinct to protect his children. It is a grave responsibility, which I have failed."

"Even the best father cannot foresee and prevent all

circumstances. Let Lily guide you. She loves you very much and wanted only to spare you pain."

Ezra scraped his hands across his face, then looked at Caleb. "I fear I have forgotten myself. My daughter called you her rescuer, and for that I am most grateful. I know that for every scoundrel and hooligan, there are fine, conscientious men like you, Captain." He stood then and offered his hand across the desk. "Thank you, sir. I am in your debt for your service to Lily."

Caleb grasped the man's hand and said, "Rest assured justice will be done in this matter, sooner than later. I will attend to it directly."

"I would expect no less."

Exiting the hospital, Caleb strode across the parade ground to the enlisted men's barracks. Inside, some men were playing cards or writing letters, but in the back corner a tight group clustered around a dice game, Adams among them, the visor of his cap pulled low as if to make himself invisible. The minute the duty sergeant saw Caleb, he shouted, "Attention!" The men rose to their feet, braced for what might follow and saluted.

Caleb let his eyes rove over the assembly, before closing in on Corporal Adams. Then he called him out. "Adams, front and center. You are summarily ordered to the stockade, pending investigation of a charge of assault."

No one looked at the culprit as he slunk through the stony silence toward Caleb, his shifty eyes darting about as if soliciting sympathy. Caleb waited until the man stood in front of him. "Do you understand the charge?"

"I didn't do nothin'," Corporal Adams whined.

"That is for your superior officers to determine.

Thank your lucky stars it isn't solely up to me. Consider yourself officially on report. Come along."

Caleb saluted the sergeant and, accompanied by the unrepentant corporal, strode from the room, holding on to his temper by only the shortest tether.

In the days that followed, Lily tried to forget the afternoon of the storm. She couldn't bear to think what might have happened had she not escaped the leering corporal, nor did she want to remember how protected she had felt in Caleb's arms. It had been bewildering to go from the clutches of one man to the welcome embrace of another. Rather than dwell on either sensation, she threw herself into her work at the hospital, even though her father had expressed reservations. "Are you sure this isn't too much for you?"

From Ezra's obvious concern, Lily suspected that Caleb had told her father exactly what had happened. The captain had sought her out the day after the attack to assure her that Corporal Adams was locked in the stockade awaiting a hearing.

Even so, Lily was now more cautious as she moved among the men, no longer innocent concerning the occasional one who eyed her just a trifle too long or smirked when he thought she wasn't looking. But mostly the soldiers were embarrassingly solicitous of her. Whatever hopes she had entertained of keeping the affair quiet had been disappointed. A military hearing could hardly be kept secret, but thankfully justice had been swift. Adams would remain under guard pending transfer to Fort Riley.

Rose had been tender with her the night of the incident, finally coaxing the story out of her. Lily had confessed to the fear that had clotted her throat when the corporal dragged her into the storeroom and laid his hands on her. Even now the rasp of his coarse fingers on her skin and the smell of his sour tobacco breath lingered in her memory. Rose had wiped away her tears and rocked her in an embrace. "There, there," she had said. "Try to concentrate instead on your good fortune that Captain Montgomery saw Adams and protected you."

Every day since, warm spring winds howled and dust flew in the air and choked the throat. Restlessness unlike any Lily had ever known surged within her. No place—not the hospital, the library or the cemetery— brought her peace. Even thinking about St. Louis made her dejected—it seemed a distant goal. She felt as if the flame of her soul had been snuffed out.

Near the end of April a few wagon trains appeared. Camped near the fort to avail themselves of both protection and the opportunity to restock provisions, the settlers brought with them stories of previous hardships as well as their idealized hopes for the future. The women, in particular, gazed fondly at the fort, perhaps wishing they could stay rather than launch into the dangerous, unknown sea of prairie grass.

Lily had seen Caleb going about his duties, and once or twice they'd been together in the library. However, others were present so no further literary discussions had ensued. Lily fretted in a limbo of frustration.

Late one night a few days later, she was awakened by frantic knocking on their door, followed by her father's commanding voice. "Take her into the hospital and I will get my daughters to assist."

Closing the door, he called to them. "Girls, are you

awake? Come quickly to the hospital to assist with a delivery. Bring plenty of towels."

Rose, dressed first, fetched clean towels. Lily slipped into a shift, and both donned clean white aprons before extinguishing the candles and hurrying next door.

Behind the curtain drawn around one bed came the sound of a woman bawling in pain. Lily moved to the head of the bed where the woman lay, her skin ashen, her cracked lips caked with the salt of her tears. Rose had gone to boil water, and her father stood at his patient's side palpating her abdomen, his face grave. "She has been in labor since yesterday evening," he said quietly. "I fear both she and the child are in distress. Daughter, can you determine how the baby is presenting?"

Lily dipped her hands in hot water, scrubbed them with soap and moved to the foot of the bed. What she saw upon examination was not reassuring. When her father raised his eyebrows in question, Lily shook her head in the negative.

As another contraction racked the whimpering woman, the surgeon made his decision. "I fear mother will not last long. We must take the infant."

While he went to inform the father, Lily and Rose prepared the instruments and changed the bed linens. The woman watched them with large, sad eyes. "Save my baby," she whispered. Then she added in the howl of a wounded animal, "I told Jacob I never wanted to come west." Her tone hardened. "Never."

Lily knew that many women died in childbirth on the trail. That, along with cholera and typhus, posed an enormous threat, not to mention possible attacks by hostile Indians. Yet so many of these wives had no choice; they were tied to their husbands and lacked alternatives. Lily vowed under her breath that she would never submit to such grim realities. If only she could wait in God's time for deliverance from this wilderness.

Ezra reentered the room, and after that, all extraneous thoughts fled in the intensity of the procedure. Her father's deft movements were swift, and soon he had extracted a tiny, wrinkled infant who, with Rose's ministrations, finally managed a feeble cry. While Rose cleaned and swaddled the baby, Lily and her father worked frantically to stem the woman's bleeding and close the incision. Lily sutured while her father listened to the mother's heartbeat and took her pulse. "Thready" was all he said. A knowing glance passed between the two. They had done what they could, but the mother's life hung in precarious balance.

Lily's nimble fingers tied the last knot and she stood back, flexing her hands. Ezra seemed preoccupied. "We've done all we can," he finally said. "I'll fetch her husband."

In her father's absence, Lily gave the woman a drink of water and gently wiped her feverish face with a cool cloth. The woman's eyes fluttered briefly. "My baby?"

"A boy."

The woman's features relaxed and she closed her eyes, her breath now coming in irregular rasps.

After a few moments, Ezra led the father into the room, followed by Rose carrying the newborn. The father rushed to his wife's side. "Good news, Patience. We have a son."

Rose placed the baby in his mother's arms. She opened her eyes and gazed at the child, her limp fingers caressing his face, his hair, his tiny hands. A tear traced its way down her sunken cheek. "Beautiful," she murmured.

Lily turned away.

The husband knelt at his wife's side, cradling her and his son. His body language conveyed knowledge of the end, but his words spoke denial. "My love, our boy will grow into a fine young man." He kissed her forehead.

Once more the mother examined the baby. As her son studied her in return, his little hand curled around her finger. "Alas." The word came with an effort. "I shall not see that day, Jacob."

His expression wild with questions, the husband looked around the room, seeking reassurance. In honesty, neither Lily, nor Rose nor Ezra could offer any. Then a strangled "No!" rose from his chest. When he looked back down at the bed, the baby kicked weakly against the lifeless body of his mother.

Lily bowed her head, struck, as always, by the random quality of death, whether it claimed her brother, her mother or this hapless woman. *God, in Your mercy, bless this dear soul, her motherless baby and her grieving husband.* She bit her lip and then added, *And help me to accept what is so difficult to understand.*

After Ezra led the father away, Lily washed and prepared the corpse while Rose went in search of a wet nurse among the women of the wagon train. This poor soul! One more poignant example of the risks women took in the isolated country they traversed.

When Lily finally left the hospital, the eastern sky was streaked with pale light. Too disturbed to go home, she instead sought refuge in the cemetery. Better than anyone, her mother would understand her tears of help-lessness.

As she crossed the parade ground near the officers' quarters, she noticed a man sitting in the shadows of the porch. Caleb. She couldn't think about him right now. Yet standing beside her mother's grave a few moments later, he was the person she thought of.

He, too, was a son whose mother had died in child-birth. How had that loss affected the young boy and influenced the man he had become?

Tonight's was the first birth she'd attended that didn't have a happy outcome, and she could not have foreseen how deeply it would affect her. She wept for the mother and father and for their baby. She wept for herself. And she wept for the motherless eight-year-old Caleb.

Caleb stood at the edge of the cemetery, not daring to interrupt what seemed to be a sacred moment. In recent days, he had rarely spoken to Lily privately. When she had emerged so early from the hospital and walked toward the cemetery, lost in her thoughts, some impulse that she not be alone seized him and he'd followed her at a distance. Yet drawn to her as he was, he hesitated, trapped in self-doubt.

He watched as she touched the headstone, much as one might dip fingers into holy water, and then, head down, walked toward him. Fearful of startling her, he spoke softly. "Miss Kellogg?"

She looked up and upon recognizing him, halted. In her piteous glance he read both exhaustion and sorrow. "Captain?"

He hastened to answer her unasked question. "I saw

you walking across the parade ground at this unusually early hour. You looked sad, and I wanted to be of assistance…comfort…" He struggled to find the right note. "It is not my intent to intrude, but…"

She laid a hand on his shoulder. "No harm. You are right, I am overwhelmed with grief, frustration—and questions."

Confused by her answer, he tucked her hand in both of his. "Pray what has happened to cause you such distress?"

She shook her head as if dispersing cobwebs. "I shall not burden you with my concerns."

"Let us walk together." He took her elbow and they started slowly toward the hospital. "You could never burden me. If you want to speak of whatever has happened, I will gladly listen."

Then, more to herself than in dialogue with him, she told of the senseless death of the settler's wife despite efforts to save her. She bit her lip in the effort, he guessed, to keep from crying when she told him about the precious little boy, now motherless. As if coming out of reverie into the harsh light of reality, she vented. "I can't bear thinking about the travails of women, subject to the whims or ambitions of their husbands, who risk their lives and the lives of their children, for what? For some distant paradise gained only by crossing vast miles of unknown land where death waits at every turn of the trail?" She stopped again, sweeping one arm in a gesture encompassing the empty horizon. "Who leads them? God or ruthless ambition?"

Caleb knew he should be shocked by her outburst, which went beyond the accepted standards for polite conversation. Instead, he was moved by her passion and grateful that she could speak so openly.

"Last night had to be a wrenching ordeal. I have known that same kind of powerlessness to stop the inevitable." His jaw worked as he recalled his inability to alter the unconscionable massacre at the Washita, over in a matter of minutes but horrific for its victims. "Sometimes there are no answers to the question 'Why?'"

"God may know, but at times like this, that is little comfort." She cocked her head to one side, studying him intently. "Tell me about your mother. How did you go on without her?"

He rarely spoke about that time before his mother died when she filled the house with laughter and song. About her cinnamon rolls which had spoiled him forever from savoring any others. About the way she cuddled him and his brother at bedtime and made Bible stories come to life.

He must've gone to another place, because Lily's voice returned him to the present. "Forgive me, Caleb. That is an overly personal question."

"Not between friends," he said, swallowing hard. They resumed strolling. "As a little boy, I thought I was the luckiest child in the world to have a mother who looked like a princess. Ours was a happy family. My older brother, Seth, and I never tired of her songs and stories. But she also didn't put up with too much mischief from us. As hard as I try, though, there are some things I can never remember. But I always knew she loved me." He was silent for several minutes. "After she died, Father, Seth and I had difficulty speaking of her. It was too painful. Besides, boys don't cry. It was easier to let baby Sophie divert us."

"Your mother would be proud of the man you've become."

"I hope so." Yet even in that breath, guilt washed over him. His mother, who had revered each living creature God had put on the earth, would have been appalled by what happened with Black Kettle and his band and, no doubt, ashamed of her son's role. And even though it was a necessary cause, could she have countenanced his behavior in the heat of battle in the War between the States when his very survival depended upon killing the enemy? He sighed as he thought about the dubious acts he had committed when following orders. Perhaps it was best that he would never know what his mother might have thought of his soldiering, nor was he eager for Lily's opinion.

The two of them were approaching the hospital when she said, "Thank you for your concern on my account and for sharing memories of your mother. Death is hard, but perhaps it shapes us in ways known only to God. We must believe something good ultimately comes from such experiences."

He prayed it could be so, but nightmares and insomnia argued to the contrary. "Your outlook is more sanguine than mine."

She looked up at him. "It would appear we are both searching for answers."

To lighten the dark mood, he said, "Perhaps we should turn to the poets. John Donne would say, 'Death, be not proud.'"

She smiled sadly. "Indeed."

They had reached her door. "Thank you for coming

to my side this morning," she said, her eyes glistening with unshed tears, the blue-gray cast to the skin beneath her eyes an indication of her exhaustion.

He gave a short bow. "Miss Kellogg, we seem to have traveled some similar roads. It is a comfort to know I am not alone."

Now the smile relaxed and her eyes deepened into pools of blue. "Lily. My name is Lily. Your friendship is most welcome."

He exhaled in relief. "Lily." The name was melodic on his tongue. "Until we meet once more."

He waited until she was safely inside and then ambled toward his quarters. The sun was full now on the horizon, and morning activity buzzed all around him. But he was ignorant of it, lost in the memories of his mother, the horrors of battle and of the one person who might either understand it all or condemn him. Lily.

Chapter Five

On an afternoon in late April, Rose, Lily and two lieutenants' wives, Carrie Smythe and Virginia Brown, gathered around Effie Hurlburt's dining room table to sew bandages for the hospital. Talk ranged from the gardens they planned to variations on bean recipes. Effie, ever cheerful, laughed when they complained of the upcoming heat of summer. "You cannot stop the seasons in their turn. Just as the cold winds blew in January, so July will become an oven. Best not to let either overwhelm your spirit."

Lily acknowledged Effie's sound advice even as she felt weighed down by the prospects of boiling temperatures. "I wish I shared your optimistic nature," she said.

"Bother. It's all in what you decide—life is either a pleasure and an opportunity or a dismal ordeal to be endured."

Carrie shrugged. "You are undoubtedly right, but there are days it is hard to keep positive."

"I think what Mrs. Hurlburt is trying to say," Rose interjected, "is that it serves no purpose to let conditions we can't control alter our natures."

Lily lowered her eyes to her sewing. Was her sister criticizing her desire to escape the frontier? In fairness, each single day was bearable, made sweeter by proximity to her family. But taken in total, day after day of this existence with no end in sight ravaged her soul. Boredom was the greatest enemy. Perhaps she should be grateful for her work at the hospital, the occasional conversations with people like Effie and Caleb and the solace of a good book.

Effie's warm voice intruded into her thoughts. "What we need is to create diversions to occupy us and help pass the time."

"What do you have in mind?" Virginia inquired.

Effie laid down her sewing. "Now that the weather is better, the men are starting to play baseball again. Perhaps we could organize a pie supper after a few Saturday games. Not just pies, but cakes, too."

Rose warmed to the idea. "The men enjoy home-cooked food. It would occupy us and please them. Sometimes we forget that they are far from home, just as we are."

"Excellent point, Rose." Effie looked around the table. "What else?"

A thought occurred to Lily. "We could organize a monthly reading—poetry, biographies, travel books. I've seen several of the men in the library, so I'm confident we could engage their participation."

"I like that idea," Carrie said. "Some of the troops cannot read well, if at all, so they might enjoy listening to others."

"You see?" Effie beamed in satisfaction. "We can be the authors of our own entertainment."

She rose from the table, gesturing to the rest to remain seated. "I shall fetch the pound cake and tea from the kitchen. Then we can celebrate our brilliant ideas."

After she left the room, Rose began folding the completed bandages for laundering. "We are blessed to have such an accommodating commander's wife."

"I've been told some are cold and condescending," Carrie ventured.

"True enough," Virginia confirmed. "At our last post, I lived in fear of an invitation to the commander's home."

Lily nodded. "Our mother always said to count our blessings. And surely Effie Hurlburt is one."

As they were eating the delicious cake, talk turned to marriage and the balance between supporting one's soldier husband in his duties and, at the same time, attending to a marriage.

"I confess impatience with my husband when he is away on a mission," Carrie said, "or even when he is right here, drilling, but still unavailable to me."

"We're always at the whim of the regiment," Virginia complained. "Sometimes I feel as if I have no influence on our lives whatsoever."

Lily was surprised. Usually the junior officers' wives were more circumspect with a commander's wife, but Effie seemed not to mind. Lily thought of her as a mentor and protector of the women stationed at the fort, and they certainly needed one.

"Marriage is a challenge, especially in military life," Effie agreed.

Overcome by sudden curiosity, Lily laid down her fork. "What is your secret? How do you and the major make it all work?"

Effie brushed a crumb from her lips. "There is no

mysterious formula. Commitment to one another and to overcoming any challenges is foremost. Honesty is the other."

"What exactly do you mean—*honesty?*" Lily asked.

"My husband and I promised at the beginning that there would be no secrets between us. Regardless of the subject and its pleasantness or unpleasantness, we would share our thoughts and feelings."

"Not all men are good at that," Carrie mumbled.

"No, they are bred to be brave and to withhold their emotions. This is especially true of soldiers. But—" she grinned conspiratorially "—they can be trained. The point is not to overreact when they say something you might prefer not to hear or which is initially painful to you. With practice, husbands can become more comfortable with confidences."

"What you call 'training' could be difficult," Rose said.

"I'm not denying that, but consider the results. I'm happy, and I believe the major is, as well."

A morsel of cake lodged in Lily's throat. She longed for the kind of relationship Effie described, but she had already experienced one man's reluctance to confide. Caleb had finally—and only briefly—talked about his mother, but had never said a word about his war experiences, which surely formed a large part of his identity. Lily admired the bond Effie had with her husband, one characterized by freedom and openness. Was such a thing possible? Not for most people, she imagined. Subservience was the more accepted practice for wives.

She wondered whether her parents had shared everything. For instance, could her mother have expressed her reluctance to leave Iowa? Or had both husband and wife held back, fearful of offense or hurt?

As if realizing the conversation had grown overly intimate, Effie changed the subject. "Now then. The first baseball game is this coming Saturday. Let's talk about the desserts we will prepare."

Rose agreed to make three raisin pies while Lily volunteered a chiffon cake. She wished a pie supper or a series of readings would change her attitude about being here, but she doubted it. When she returned home today, she would write a letter reminding Aunt Lavinia of her hopes for a St. Louis visit.

"Caleb!" Buried in darkness, Caleb heard a voice, felt himself being roughly shaken. "Wake up, man!"

Indians screaming war whoops hounded him from all sides, bullets hailed down upon him and the earth trembled with the reverberations of cannon fire. Moaning, he clawed his way to consciousness. Will Creekmore stood over him, his face illuminated by the moonlight filtering through the window of the officers' barracks. "Montgomery, can you wake up?"

Caleb tried to focus, then sat gingerly on the edge of the bed, groggy and disoriented. "The dream," he croaked.

"Again?"

All Caleb could do was nod in disgust and humiliation. The ghosts of combat refused to relinquish him. He had come to dread sleep because of the horrific night visitors. He wiped beads of sweat from his brow even as he shivered in the cool night air. Mustering strength, he stood and clapped Will on the back. "Sorry to have disturbed you."

Will smiled ruefully. "You're not alone. We all have our battle scars."

That was true, and Caleb understood each man's struggle was personal. "Go back to bed, friend." He drew on his trousers. "I'll be fine. I just want to clear my head."

He stepped out on the front porch, needing to purge from his body and soul the terrors that sat upon him like lead weights. Would this torment ever abate? Could anything or anyone cleanse his poisonous memories? He leaned on the railing, gazing over the encampment. Others were sleeping, most, peacefully, he surmised. But on nights such as this, sleep was a luxury he could not afford to indulge, not when it might invite again such troubled dreams.

He looked up at the sky, brilliant with moonglow and starlight. If there was a God, was He up there? Amid the countless stars, why would He concern himself with one tortured cavalryman? And yet... "His eye is on the sparrow..."

He reminded himself of the good in the world. His family. His loyal troops, some risking their lives to carry wounded mates to safety. Lily—a lovely young woman acquainted with grief. He must not, however, come to depend upon her to be the light in his darkness. Rather he should spare her his demons.

Such wisdom, though, was at odds with his instincts toward friendship. What could friendship hurt? Her frequent visits to her mother's grave confirmed that a military outpost could be a lonely place for a woman, too. As he remained on the porch, surrounded by night sounds, gradually an image of Lily replaced that of his nightmares. He fixed on it, grateful for his clearing mind and slowing respiration.

He didn't know how long he stood there, but finally he went back inside, lighted the lantern and tried to lose himself in Charles Dickens's *David Copperfield*. Unable to concentrate, he set the book aside and picked up a piece of paper and a pen. He held the pen in the air, gathering his thoughts. Finally he dipped it in the ink and began writing. With each succeeding stroke, he felt his torment subside.

May 1 dawned with the cheery songs of birds and the tantalizing aroma of hotcakes. Lily patted the empty space on the mattress beside her. Rose was already up and cooking. Cocooning herself in the covers, Lily lay listening to the avian reveille, soon joined by the bugle version. She found something predictably reassuring about military schedules, which, like clocks, remained constant.

She had posted her letter to Aunt Lavinia and hoped she had been subtle but effective in saying how much she anticipated reuniting with her aunt and being introduced to the wonders of St. Louis. She knew such a trip would be expensive and that her father could not afford the entire cost. Months ago, Lavinia had offered to underwrite the expense. Had she forgotten? Or was the delay merely about timing? Lily appreciated that summer was not the season to go, but if she was to travel in the fall, plans had to be made.

She sighed, then reluctantly left the warmth of the bed and moved to the pitcher and basin on the nightstand to make her morning ablutions. She chose her rose-colored dress, which seemed a fitting way to greet the new month.

Her father was already sitting at the kitchen table, a cup of coffee cradled in his hands. Rose bustled at the stove, pouring more batter into the sizzling iron skillet. "Good morning, everyone," Lily said.

Her father smiled. "Top of the morning, daughter."

"I didn't mean to dawdle, but it was so cozy." She moved to Rose's side. "How can I help?"

"Put the butter and honey on the table and I'll bring the hotcakes."

When they were all seated, Ezra said grace. Lily had just picked up her first forkful of food when she thought she heard a light tap on the door. Rose, too, cocked her head toward the sound. "Did you hear that?" Lily asked.

Her father looked up. "What?"

"Perhaps a knock," Rose said. "I'll go."

When she didn't return right away, Ezra called, "Was anyone there?"

"Not exactly," Rose said, a hint of laughter in her voice. When she came back into the kitchen, she concealed something behind her back. Ezra regarded her expectantly. "You look like the cat that ate the canary."

"A surprise was left on our doorstep." Then she produced a small bouquet of wildflowers wrapped in a newspaper secured with twine. "Happy May Day, Lily." Rose beamed, handing the bouquet to her sister and winking at her father.

A blush rose to Lily's cheeks as she studied the flowers. Nestled among the wild violets, primroses and sprigs of fern was an envelope inscribed with her name.

"It would seem you have an admirer," her father

said. "I remember well the times I left a May Day bouquet at your mother's door when I was courting."

Lily set the bouquet on the table and pulled a note from the envelope. Scanning it for a signature, she murmured, "Not an admirer, Papa. A friend."

Then engrossed in the message, she failed to see a knowing look pass between her father and sister.

In strong masculine handwriting, the words blurred in her vision as she recalled her last conversation with Caleb at her mother's grave.

If when thy thoughts to gloom do fly
And sorrow seeks thy soul to cloy,
Mayhap these blooms may still thy sigh
And serve as harbingers of joy.
A friend

"Well?" her father studied her inquiringly.

Rose, as usual in sympathy with her sister, deflected his question. "I think, Papa, that such a gift is not meant to be immediately shared." She picked up the platter and handed it to Ezra. "Have another hotcake."

Lily, overcome with confusing emotions, silently blessed her sister for her tact. And blessed Caleb, whose poetic bent and sensitivity to her mother's loss belied a soldier's stoicism.

The Saturday of the baseball game was especially hot for May. By late morning, the flag hung motionless from the pole and open windows did little to cool interiors. Lily pulled her cake from the oven, lamenting the slightly burned top. Rose's pies were perfect, so, as usual, Lily's baking paled by comparison. No matter. The soldiers would not be picky.

By one o'clock Rose and Lily were at the make-shift ball field where, under Effie Hurlburt's direction, some enlisted men were assembling trestle tables for the baked goods and others were erecting plank benches along the baselines for the spectators.

As soon as all the desserts were laid out on the tables, Effie covered them with cheesecloth to protect them from dust and insects. Most of the ladies wore summer-weight dresses and sported sunbonnets for protection. Lily's blue-and-white-sprigged muslin was last year's dress, but showed off her tiny waist and fair complexion. When everything was done to Effie's satisfaction, she herded the women to the benches set aside for them. Only then did the nonplayers fill in, jostling for position. Lieutenant Creekmore's troop was opposing Captain Montgomery's, and there was much good-natured joshing and more than a few wagers placed.

When the teams ran onto the field, the crowd clapped and hooted. Major Hurlburt, the umpire, stepped up to the team captains and appeared to be reminding them of the rules. Before the game began, the players stripped off their jackets and rolled up their sleeves. Lily noticed that Benjamin, her former concussion patient, was playing in the outfield while Caleb took the pitcher's position. Although she couldn't follow all the fine points of the game, she understood that Caleb's skill was frustrating those attempting to strike the ball. Just as she was feeling sorry for Caleb's opponent, he connected with the ball and sent it soaring into the outfield beyond any of the players to the great delight of that team's boosters.

When it was Caleb's team's turn at bat, Rose poked her in the ribs. "I imagine you're partial to this nine."

Had Rose noticed her eyes following Caleb's every move? "You should be, too, sister. We know Captain Montgomery better than we know Lieutenant Creekmore."

Despite Lily's determination not to play favorites, she couldn't help noticing Caleb's broad shoulders and muscled forearms. Before he pitched again, he came over to the nearby water bucket and ladled out a drink. She lowered her gaze lest he discover her staring at him. He was one fine-looking man.

As the game wore on and the high jinks in the stands grew louder and more partisan, Lily reflected that events like this benefitted morale. From the beginning, the score seesawed. Finally in the last inning, Caleb's team eked out the winning run. Amid whooping and huzzahing, the teams left the field, many heading out to wash up before the pie supper.

Lily and Rose hurried to the dessert tables to slice cakes and pies and set out plates and cutlery. Major Hurlburt, his face red from the exertion of umpiring, approached them. "Mighty nice of you women to provide such a treat," he said with an approving smile.

As the men reassembled, the major made a short speech. "A fine sporting event, gentlemen. Played fair and square. To the victor belong the spoils. Captain Montgomery, lead your team to the desserts."

Caleb, his thumbs hooked in his suspenders, grinned. "We'll try to leave some food for the others."

Amid good-natured catcalls from the opposing team, the men descended on the dessert tables.

Carrie and Virginia dispensed lemonade while Rose and Lily helped Effie dish up servings of pie and cake.

Caleb eyed the selections. "Which one is yours?" he asked Lily.

"Oh, don't try mine," she said. "You'd prefer Rose's pie."

As other men moved past him, he looked her in the eye. "Why wouldn't I want yours?"

"Let's just say I'm a better nurse than I am a cook."

"I'll be the judge of that." He studied the table. "Which one?"

Reluctantly she pointed out the less-than-perfect chiffon cake.

"Cut me a big slice."

She had no choice but to serve him what he wanted, but she added a sliver of raisin pie to his plate. "I'll be sitting over there." He nodded in the direction of the first base bench. "Would you do me the honor of joining me when you're finished here?"

Heads bobbed up all around and curious stares settled on the two of them. She felt trapped. "You may be finished with your food before I have completed my duty."

His quirked eyebrow told her he knew she was procrastinating. "I'll wait," he said, moving off to the field.

Lily bent over the food, avoiding anyone's gaze. It was one thing to take a companionable stroll from the cemetery or to be escorted home from a band concert. This meeting would be all too public. Already she felt the pressure of the I-told-you-so looks passing among the troops.

Rose sidled up to her. "You can't be rude," she murmured.

Lily wasn't worried about rudeness, more about the erroneous perception she felt growing all around her. "We're just friends," she said to her sister. "Don't go thinking anything else."

Rose smiled innocently. "Of course you are."

One of the sergeants in Caleb's troop insisted on carrying her lemonade and cake to the bench. "Here, ma'am," he said, setting them down. "Take good care of this little lady, Captain."

"My pleasure, Sergeant." Caleb shoved his empty plate aside and turned to Lily. "Now what was the matter with that cake? As you can see, I had no trouble disposing of it."

Lily held up her dish. "This is Effie Hurlburt's perfect apple cake, so much better than my burned one."

"Burned? I didn't notice."

"You're just being polite," she said, spearing a piece of Effie's dessert.

"When you know me better, you'll find I don't say much of anything I don't mean. Your cake was delicious."

Lily feared they were not talking merely about cake. She continued eating while he stretched out his legs. The informality of his attire and the sight of his hair, tousled from the ball game, made him seem unfamiliar, more…she couldn't find the word. *Manly?*

"It was thoughtful of you ladies to feed us. The men were really looking forward to today." Then he turned toward her. "So was I."

"Speaking of thoughtful—" she hung her head, overcome with sudden shyness "—thank you for the

May Day bouquet and poem. The sentiments were timely and so well expressed." She gazed up at him, sensing that he, too, was suddenly bashful. "I'm in awe of your poetic powers, sir."

His rich, hazel eyes swept her face. "If my words in any way could be described as poetic, it is because I had a most insistent and lovely muse."

Again feeling put on the spot, she took a hasty sip of the lemonade, willing herself not to blush. She desperately needed to change the subject. "I understand from my father that there is trouble brewing with the Indians."

His lips thinned and his expression grew more serious. "It's the time of year. The winter has been harsh, so when the wagon trains start through here in earnest, the Indians seize upon that opportunity both to protect their lands and to replenish their supplies. We will be setting out at the end of next week."

"Will you be gone long?"

"It depends on how widespread the threat is and how successful we are in quelling disturbances."

Despite her vow not to make this encounter personal, she felt a frisson of alarm on his behalf. "Please, be safe."

"I will do my duty, but I assure you I will also exercise care for my men and for myself."

"I will pray for all of you."

"That can do no harm."

She eyed him speculatively. "Do you doubt the efficacy of prayer?"

"I cannot say. At times I have felt abandoned by God, but at other times only His grace has saved me." He stared up at the clouds, now gathering on the horizon. "You could say I'm still searching for answers to such questions."

"Perhaps we are not supposed to know the mind of The Eternal."

He picked up her hand. "We're getting mighty serious here." He glanced again at the sky. "It's cooling a bit. Would you favor me with a walk down to the river?"

She should say no, but the hopeful look in his eyes was compelling. Besides, the day was too glorious to go home. "That would be just the thing after indulging in dessert."

They picked up their plates and returned them to the table where the other women had succeeded in clearing nearly everything away.

"Rose, Effie, I'm so sorry. I should've been helping."

Effie waved her on. "Nonsense, we were all enjoying seeing you and the captain together."

Lily's heart sank. Why must a simple conversation be taken for more than it was. She wished now that she hadn't agreed to the walk.

Caleb moved to thread her arm through his. He nodded to Rose and Effie. "Ladies, may I borrow Miss Lily for a stroll?"

"Enjoy yourselves," Effie said, nudging Rose in the ribs.

Lily was caught. On the one hand she couldn't wait to move away from the women and their approving glances. On the other, she wondered why she had ever agreed to the walk.

By now, most of the men had dispersed to their barracks or the taverns beyond the fort. As Lily and Caleb moved into the shade of the trees bordering the river, it felt as if they were entering a private bower. She stooped to finger a tiny white flower. "It's a joy to see blooms again after such a long winter."

"In the same way after months of cold weather, it's great for the men to let off steam with events like this afternoon's game."

"Baseball seems a fine, though complicated, game."

"Perhaps one day I can give you a tutorial on the rules."

"Perhaps," she repeated, not wanting to commit to any further meetings. Yet, in the same breath, she knew she didn't want this day to end.

They came to a place where a fallen log formed a kind of bench. "Shall we sit?" he asked.

She gathered her skirts and sank onto the log, which presented a peaceful view of the stream, overhung with leafy branches.

He joined her. "Sitting here, it's hard to believe that the world can be in such turmoil."

"All the more reason, as my mother was wont to say, to live in the day, this day."

His voice grew husky. "I am pleased to be living this one with you."

She looked up. The need in his eyes rendered her breathless. Several seconds passed before she could look away. "I treasure our friendship," she said softly.

For the second time that afternoon, he took her hand in his. "As do I. Perhaps this is a way God has blessed us."

She was suddenly curious. "What is it that causes us to be friends?"

He ran his thumb over the top of her hand before replying. "You provide a sympathetic ear. We have both experienced loss. We share an interest in literature. We have profound questions about the nature of God."

Everything he said was true. "I, too, feel as if there are few subjects we cannot discuss."

He did not relinquish her hand. They sat in companionable silence, listening to birds chirping and watching a squirrel jump from branch to branch in a nearby oak tree. She relaxed into the sheer pleasure of the moment.

Finally she pulled away, leaning back on her hands to study the blue sky, crisscrossed with trails of cloud. "Do you ever miss home?"

"I've been in the army so long, home seems like a distant memory."

"We've talked about your mother and sister, but I've never known where you grew up." It suddenly seemed important to fill in the gaps of her knowledge about Caleb.

"I was born in Jefferson City, Missouri. We lived on a small farm just outside of town along the river. My grandfather owned a grist mill. After he died my father took it over, but he was never really happy being confined at the mill. Like him, we kids loved the farm and the freedom to roam. Summertime was the best. We could be gone from dawn until dusk." He picked up a small twig and twirled it between his palms. "That all seems a long time ago in another time and place. My family relocated to southeastern Kansas a couple of years ago."

"The war changed a great deal for all of us." There was no need to elaborate. How could one ever gauge its impact on individual lives? "Papa couldn't return to Iowa as a doctor. Another man had already taken his place. He'd been so long away that continuing in the military seemed the best alternative."

"But it uprooted you."

"I didn't want to leave. But as my mother said, 'Sometimes you have do what you'd rather not.'"

Caleb laid aside the twig. "She supported your father, then?"

"Always, at least outwardly." Now that she thought about it, Lily had even greater appreciation for her mother's sacrifice—and for her love of her husband. "Wives often have little choice, I suppose." All the more reason Lily intended to chart her own course.

The drowsy hum of bees and the slow-moving current lulled them both into silence. After an interval, Caleb turned to look at her and said, "I'm growing quite fond of you, Lily Kellogg. If ever I doubted womanhood, you and Sophie have set me straight."

Lily smiled. "That's quite a compliment. I know I'm in good company when you mention your sister."

The lightening of the mood led to a resumption of their stroll. They started back along the riverbank and then moved into the sunlit grassland. On a small hillock slightly off the path, Lily spotted a delicate purple blossom she'd never seen before. With a delighted "Oh," she scampered on ahead and knelt in the grass. She had just reached out to cup the petals in her hand, when she froze, her heart catapulting in her chest.

At her feet, concealed in the grass near a hole, was a nest of copperheads. One of the larger snakes slithered directly toward her. Paralyzed with fear, she screamed hysterically, "Moses, Moses!"

Chapter Six

Moses? Caleb couldn't fathom why Lily had called out that name, but no matter. He reacted instantly to her urgent cry, running to her and pulling her back from the nest of vipers. She trembled in his arms and her eyes had a distant, glazed expression.

"Oh, oh," she repeated tremulously. He picked her up, cradling her against his chest and carried her quickly toward the fort.

As they neared the cemetery, she asked him to stop. He headed for a stone bench under a huge sycamore tree and then gently set her down, still encircling her with his arm. Waiting patiently for her to stop shaking, he murmured an occasional "There, there."

He picked up her hands, noticing how icy they seemed to his warm flesh. Finally, she sighed deeply and relaxed a bit.

"Thank you, Caleb. I'm sorry." Her eyes glistened with unshed tears. "I'm terrified of snakes."

"You've had a bad experience in the past?"

She nodded, then stood up and paced in front of him, as if that effort could dispel her fears.

"And Moses? Was he part of that experience?"

She stopped in front of him, wringing her hands in the effort to calm herself. "Without him, I doubt I'd be here."

Caleb waited, knowing he could not rush her story.

Lily glanced around as if assuring herself of their privacy, then settled back on the bench. She began quietly, but in the telling of the tale, her voice grew gradually louder.

"Last summer a troop of buffalo soldiers was stationed here."

"I have fought with them," Caleb said, remembering the valiant emancipated slaves who had found a home in the army. "Committed soldiers and generally fine human beings."

"Alas, not everyone here thought so. Some of the white soldiers treated them shamefully. They were good hospital workers and were more orderly than most of the men."

That had been Caleb's experience, as well. He nodded, encouraging her to go on with her tale.

"One August day, I went out on the prairie behind the officers' quarters to collect sunflowers, growing wild there, for a bouquet to put on the table for my father's birthday." She hesitated as if not wanting to face her memory. "Moses, along with a few other buffalo soldiers, was in a nearby field, hoeing weeds. I had gathered an armful of sunflowers when I heard an unmistakable, spine-tingling sound."

"Rattles?"

She shivered. "Yes. I froze. Tears ran down my cheeks, and I clutched the flowers as if they would somehow protect me. Then I spotted the snake, coiled not six feet from me. So great was my terror that it seemed as if all sound but that of the rattling had vanished.

"Then as if from a great distance, I heard myself screaming. Moses raced past me, his hoe raised over his shoulder, and then with one mighty swing, he chopped the snake in half. I could neither look away from the severed reptile's gyrating body, nor could I move.

"Before I could scream again, Moses came to my side, not daring, of course, to touch me. 'Whoa, easy, missy,' he said in a deep, gentle voice. 'You be all right. Mister Rattler gone to his maker. Moses saw to that. You can be breathing again. He won't hurt you no more.'"

Caleb silently thanked God for Moses. "No wonder you were so frightened today."

"If it hadn't been for Moses..." She shuddered. "From then on, we had a special bond. I would slip him pastries and help him write letters home. I was sad when he left Fort Larned, but proud of him. He had made corporal. I still correspond with him occasionally."

"I hold the buffalo soldiers in highest regard and, along with you, regret the abuse and harsh treatment they often receive. They, too, are God's creatures with the same needs and hopes as the rest of us."

She looked up at him as if with newfound interest. "Except to my family, I've never dared speak of my friendship—that's the only accurate word—with Moses, nor my gratitude to him. He not only saved my life, but taught me a great deal about tolerance."

"Then perhaps your scare with the snake served God's purpose."

For the first time in many minutes, she smiled. "Perhaps, sir. But I still do…not…like…snakes." She drew out each word by way of emphasis. "And there won't always be a Moses or a Caleb to rescue me."

He recognized the truth of her words. They sat quietly for a time, resting. It was as if the effort to tell the story had exhausted her. Finally he said, "Are you ready for home?"

Nodding, she stood, then faced him. "I'm not usually such a frail flower. Thank you for saving me for the second time."

In her eyes he read such vulnerability and affection that without stopping to think, he drew her into his arms and laid her head against his chest. "I will do everything in my power to keep you safe," he murmured.

She remained in his arms while time seemed to stand still, then drew a deep breath and stood back, searching his face as if seeking some impenetrable answer. "You do me great honor, Captain."

With a racing heart, he sought to regain a semblance of normalcy. The woman had a dangerous way of making him forget caution. "Caleb?"

She ran a hand up and down his sleeve, as if appreciating their customary name game. "Oh, yes," she agreed. "Caleb."

Then she took his arm and together they walked toward her home.

On the way, they passed the barren ground and charred timbers standing in mute testimony to the fire that had destroyed the buffalo soldiers' stable the previous January. A fire, she told him, believed to have been set by some bigoted person objecting to the buffalo soldiers' presence at the fort.

As they skirted the scene, Caleb heard Lily whisper the poet's words he had often muttered himself, "'Man's inhumanity to man.'"

Caleb walked slowly across the parade ground toward his quarters, thinking about Lily. He didn't often find someone with whom he could share his views about emancipation. Many of his comrades from the North had shared his revulsion over the concept of slavery, but others were openly hostile about giving freedmen the right to vote. As for the buffalo soldiers, Caleb had found most of them to be decent fellows. One sergeant with whom he had fought had been a house slave in Virginia whose master had treated him so humanely that the soldier was at least as literate as Caleb himself. Reaching the porch, Caleb reflected how interesting it was that Lily's experiences with the buffalo soldiers mirrored his own.

When he entered his quarters, Will was seated at the table, writing a letter. He looked up and grinned at Caleb. "Out sparking, were you?"

"Sparking?"

"That is surely what it looked like to me. Sitting with that pretty Miss Lily fawning over her dessert and then taking a bit of a stroll. Reminds me of how I courted Fannie."

Caleb was still trying to understand. "Sparking? Courting? Is that what you think I was doing?"

"The signs are all there, Cap'n."

Caleb collapsed onto a wooden bench. "We're just friends."

"Are you convinced that's all?"

"Friendship. That's all I've ever intended."

Will laid down the pen and faced him. "That, my friend, is how it always starts, at least if the relationship has any future. Think about Fannie and me. If she says yes to my proposal, and I pray she will, then I'll be marrying not only my sweetheart, but my best friend."

"Marrying? Why, that's the furthest thing from my mind."

Will shot him a knowing look and before turning back to his letter, he simply said, "We'll see. But if I was a wagering man..." He let the sentence die.

Suddenly feeling confined by the four walls of the room, Caleb headed for the door, grateful for the cooler evening air. He stood on the porch, his thoughts aboil, Will's words flustering him. Courting? Was that what others thought he was doing? Worse yet, could that be Lily's interpretation of his behavior, even though they both kept emphasizing friendship as the basis for their relationship?

If he was brutally honest, Caleb had to admit to flights of fancy where he'd imagined himself in the future with a wife like Lily. But that was a long ways down the road. Not now. Not here.

He shut his eyes against unwelcome memories of Rebecca. He had courted her once. He had loved her and, more fool he, had believed his affection was returned. He grunted in disgust. Not only was she faithless, but she had betrayed him with a man he had considered his friend. Will Creekmore's insinuations about Lily had struck fear in his heart. No man walks twice into the same trap.

He sank down on the top step of the porch, his elbows on his knees, hands dangling. Had he given Lily a false impression? Truth be told, he had come close to kissing her on a couple of occasions and had enjoyed holding her in his arms, but any fellow would be likewise tempted. He tried replaying their encounters in his mind. Surely he'd never been less than gentlemanly.

The problem was, he would now have to be more guarded around her, lest he mislead her. Anyway, how could he possibly fall in love when his future was uncertain and his past was a cautionary lesson? Beyond that, how could he inflict his nightmares on Lily or any woman? What kind of a man could expect a wife to share his demons? Or exorcise them?

For a moment, he wished he was like Will Creekmore, so sure of his love and confident about his future. Caleb assumed he would one day find a suitable mate, but the timing was all wrong now. In some ways it was a pity because it would be difficult to ever find someone as intelligent and compassionate as Lily.

Following the snake scare, Lily had experienced even greater difficulty abiding life on the prairie with all its hidden dangers. Despite the lack of an enclosed note, the latest package from Aunt Lavinia, containing new issues of *Peterson's Magazine* and programmes from concerts, had only whetted her desire to escape. Her sole refuges were the hospital, where work kept dissatisfaction at bay, and the library, where she could lose herself in a book.

With Effie Hurlburt's help, she was recruiting a group to offer a poetry reading during the first week in June. One of the Scots in the cavalry had volunteered to read Robert Burns's "To a Mouse," and Colonel Hurlburt had agreed to render Longfellow's "The Wreck of the Hesperus." Lily hoped Caleb would consent to read from *Paradise Lost,* but his troop was still out on a foray to root out small bands of Pawnees intent on preying upon the wagon trains.

One afternoon she and Effie found themselves alone in the quiet of the library as they searched for possible poems to include in the reading. Effie pulled out a slim volume including Elizabeth Barrett Browning's sonnet "How Do I Love Thee?" and handed the book to Lily. "This is a moving poem. Amid all the rough-and-tumble of the men's lives, they need an occasional sentimental touch. This might even bring a tear to the eye."

Lily scanned the familiar poem cataloging the forms of true love. For an unknown reason, she found herself profoundly moved. Such a love as that described by the poetess was rare.

"Well?" Effie asked. "Would you be willing to read it?"

"Me?"

"Yes. The words lend themselves to a gentle female voice. I know you could do it justice."

"You have more experience of love than I."

"Experience? Yes. But there is nothing like the first tender beginnings of a romance."

"I know nothing of that, either."

Effie responded with an affectionate smile. "Are you so sure, my dear? The way you and Captain Montgomery look at one another is enough to remind me of those heady first days with Hurly."

Lily was appalled. How could Effie jump to such a conclusion? "I don't mean to be rude, but you are mistaken if you think there is aught but friendship between the captain and me." She felt a compelling need to set the record straight. "In fact, I plan within a matter of months to be on my way to St. Louis to visit my aunt Lavinia. It is there I hope to establish my future."

If she had thought to sidetrack Effie, she was mistaken. "Be that as it may, Lily, I know a love match when I see one." Effie turned and replaced the book of poetry on the shelf. "Time will tell," she murmured.

Later that evening when a serious case of malaria required her presence in the hospital, Lily welcomed the distraction. As the patients fell asleep one by one, she found herself sitting quietly through the early hours of the morning with only her thoughts for company. Surely Effie was wrong. Caleb had always made it clear that theirs was a friendship, nothing more. Surely it was her *friend* she was missing while his troop was out in the field, because she had to admit, she often wondered about Caleb and prayed for his safety and that of his men. Any friend would do likewise.

Love was something altogether different. As Elizabeth Barrett Browning had put it, "I love thee to the depth and breadth and height / My soul can reach…" Could a person ever achieve that degree of affection with another? Why Effie would think her capable of such feeling for Caleb, she couldn't imagine.

Irritated by that line of thinking, Lily rose from her chair and walked slowly through the ward, checking on the men. She could not explain why she was terrified of snakes, but able to deal calmly with unpleasant illnesses and ugly wounds, even finding in her nursing a kind of fulfillment. Perhaps the answer lay in the fact that she felt useful and skillful.

She settled back in her chair and was nodding off when she felt a gentle touch on her shoulder. She opened her eyes to find her father looking at her with concern. "Are you all right, daughter?"

"I'm fine, Papa. The men have been quite peaceful."

"Why don't you slip on home and get some rest now that I'm here?"

She stood and kissed him on the cheek. "Thank you." She paused and then went on. "And thank you for giving me this training and the opportunity to be of use."

"Lily, you are a highly qualified nurse, and I am proud of your dedication and skill."

Later as Lily slipped into bed beside Rose, she glowed. That was high praise from her father. Just before falling asleep she mused that it had been a strange day. First Effie's misconceptions about her relationship with Captain Montgomery, the thoughts about love the poem had raised for her and now her father's rare and heartfelt compliment. Yet a niggling concern persisted. How would she use her skills in St. Louis? She doubted the crowd Lavinia moved among thought it fitting for a young woman to minister to the needs of the ailing or maimed.

Her eyes were heavy, but she managed brief prayers. The last word on her lips before she fell asleep was *Caleb*.

The ride had been long and hot. Columns of dust billowed behind the hooves of their many horses. Early on in the mission, Caleb had felt reinvigorated. Action was welcome after weeks of routine drilling, but the constant glare of the sun and the wind cutting across their faces had made parts of their trek unrelieved misery. Maddeningly, the marauding Indians had been canny in their efforts to elude the troops. Even when the army scouts located them, often by the time the column of riders arrived at the rendezvous point, the enemy had vanished into the endless rolling prairie. The high point, thus far, had been searching for and finding a five-year-old boy who had wandered away from his wagon train encampment.

Despite the heat and the lack of success in fighting the Indians, it was a comfort to be back in the saddle, performing familiar functions and sleeping under the stars. The final night's bivouac was a scant ten miles from Fort Larned. After making a routine sweep among his men, most of whom were already asleep, he bedded down shortly before midnight.

He had barely closed his eyes when he was awakened by a sentry. "Horse thieves," he muttered. Caleb struggled into his boots, grabbed his rifle and took off at a lope toward the perimeter where the horses were tethered.

The sentry whispered hoarsely, "Indians. They're hiding among the horses."

Caleb whistled for Bucephalus, then fired a warning shot in the air. Several more troops staggered toward them. "Rout them out before they steal our horses."

Led by Caleb, several of the men plunged into the mass of horseflesh. With only a sliver of a moon for light, it was difficult to distinguish between horses and Indians, especially when they were adept at straddling an animal, clinging to the mane and dropping over the side so as to be undetectable.

Caleb leaped on Bucephalus, clutched his mane with one hand and prodded him forward. In the distance he could barely make out a group of eight horses slowly detaching from the herd. He galloped after them as they began moving more swiftly toward a nearby hill. To his right he noticed one of his cavalrymen. "Follow me!" he shouted. They charged into the open prairie fifty yards or so from the group of stolen horses. The Indians, slowed by the horses they were leading, tried to escape. By then a few more mounted cavalrymen had joined the hunt. When they narrowed the gap, Caleb yelled, "Spare the horses, but fire on the riders."

In the ensuing fray, three cavalry horses broke loose and galloped off, but five still remained in enemy hands. Every time Caleb thought he had a clear aim, the Indians changed direction. Finally he drew a bead on the leader. With one shot, he succeeded in bringing him down. Almost simultaneously, other deafening shots rang out, felling two more thieves. One pinto tore for the hills, its rider bent low.

The remaining horses were rounded up by morning. Thankfully, no cavalry mounts had been lost. The three dead Indians would either teach their fellows a lesson or incite them to retribution. Yet Caleb took no satisfaction in killing. This was a war without rules and little way to distinguish peaceable Indians from their more hostile numbers.

After burying the dead and packing their gear, the troop made its way toward the fort. Even considering the excitement and danger of the night, Caleb, instead of feeling spent, was energized. They had foiled the horse thieves and were headed home at last. The steady rhythm of horses' hooves and the creak-crack of saddle leather provided accompaniment for the mental exercise of preparing his report for the colonel. Before he knew it, they had crested the rise just beyond the fort.

Something clenched within him, and he knew, despite Will Creekmore's remarks about courting, he had been counting the hours until he would see Lily again. As they trotted into the fort, it was all he could do to keep his eyes forward instead of sweeping the scene for her slight figure.

After securing the horses and checking in at headquarters, he and Will headed for their home and the welcome bath that awaited them. Will unpacked quickly, bathed first and then strode toward the sutler's to collect their mail.

Caleb had just finished shaving when Will burst through the door with a loud huzzah, waving a letter over his head. "She's coming! My Fannie's coming!" He danced a jig before stopping in his tracks, a large smile wreathing his face. "Cap'n," he said in a wondering tone, "my Fannie is going to marry me."

"You're a lucky man, Will."

"A blessed man," the lieutenant corrected him. "Blessed beyond all measure." He stared at the letter before slowly folding it and stowing it in his pocket. As if speaking only to himself, he said, "I am half a man without my Fannie."

Caleb turned away, lest he reveal too much of himself. Thanks to Rebecca, he knew that feeling of being half a man. Yet he, too, had a restless urge to complete himself, to know the kind of love Will celebrated.

That evening after supper, he sat rocking on the porch with Will, who smoked a cigar, its pungent aroma perfuming the night air. Mourning doves cooed in the distance. From the enlisted men's barracks came the sound of singing, the rich harmonies a plaintive reminder of so many nights around campfires.

Suddenly, his breath quickened. Lily came out of the library and stood for a moment, a small book clutched in her hand, scanning the officers' quarters. She must have seen him then, for she raised her hand in greeting.

He nodded, incapable of speech even if it had been called for.

Then she picked up her skirt and walked toward her home.

Caleb leaned back in the rocker, the sounds and the smells of the fort a comfort to him amid his questions. Had Lily been looking for him as he had been looking for her? And why, despite the need to exercise reason, had the sight of her filled him with such spontaneous joy?

Chapter Seven

Not for the first time Caleb wondered why he had agreed to take part in the poetry reading. It was one thing to find personal enjoyment in the genre, but quite another to expose himself to possible ridicule by his men. At least his selection—Milton's description of Satan's fall from Heaven—had teeth in it. He stood at the back of the commissary, listening to the others rehearse. Major Hurlburt did a fine Longfellow, but the wife of a junior officer massacred her assigned Shakespearean sonnet.

Effie Hurlburt, self-appointed director of the production, positioned the readers on the makeshift stage, then hurried to the back of the room to be certain each could be heard.

Caleb was surprised by Lily's absence. With her love of poetry, she, of all people, should be involved. As if anticipating his unvoiced question, Effie returned to the front and reviewed the program. "You will begin, Sergeant." She nodded at a barrel-chested man with oratorical skill who had selected "No More Words," a

Civil War poem. "Then we will follow in the order by which we practiced, ending with Miss Kellogg's reading. Alas, duties at the hospital prevented her from joining us for rehearsal, but I assure you she will provide a fitting conclusion for our evening's entertainment." She paused, eyeing them in the manner of a strict schoolmarm. "Now then, are there any questions?"

"Do you think anyone will come?" asked a jittery company clerk.

"If I have anything to say about it." Effie glanced smugly at the major. "And if I have to pull rank, I will." She smiled encouragingly at the clerk. "Listen to me, son. This is fine entertainment. Afterward, the others will all wish they could so commandingly declaim poetry."

Caleb mentally rolled his eyes. It would take more than that to impress some of the more jaded fellows, but even poetry trumped boredom.

As the group dispersed, Effie Hurlburt approached him. "Captain, would you kindly help me hang streamers from the walls? A bit of bunting will add a festive air to the proceedings."

As they went about their work, Effie chattered about the weather and offered tidbits of fort gossip. Caleb couldn't help wondering why she had selected him, rather than an enlisted man for this duty, but the answer soon came. When they finished, she turned to him. "For your labors, you deserve a reward. Escort me home for tea cakes and a spot of lemonade." From the brisk way she began walking toward her house, he had little choice but to follow.

At her door, she led him in and urged him to sit in what was clearly the major's armchair. When Caleb raised his eyebrows in question, she anticipated his concern. "You stay right there. Hurly's in his office working on a dispatch, so we won't be disturbed. Now, if you'll excuse me, I will see to our refreshments." She bustled from the room, leaving him to study the lacy antimacassars on the sofa and the Chinese vase on the fringed scarf atop the piano. It was almost as if Mrs. Hurlburt had lured him to her parlor for some purpose.

"Here we are." She set a tray on a nearby table. After she had served him his lemonade, she took her own drink and sat on the sofa facing him. Without preliminary, she said, "I understand you will be leaving the army late this summer."

"Yes, ma'am."

"It's just the two of us, dear. You don't need to 'ma'am' me. I'm Effie. Besides, we're just two friends having a cozy tête-à-tête." She paused to sip from her lemonade. "What are your plans after you muster out?"

He told her about working with his father and brother on the ranch.

"Then you should not be too far from here."

"About one hundred-fifty miles as the crow flies."

"Do you plan to marry and start a family?"

"Eventually, but that's down the road a long ways."

"Why?"

Her bluntness set him back. "I'm not ready yet. I need to get settled."

"Forgive an old woman's candor, but I think you're fooling yourself."

A trickle of perspiration worked its way down the small of his back. This was more inquisition than polite chat. "I'm sorry, but I don't understand."

"It's simple. Why are you waiting when golden opportunity is knocking at your door? You'll be hard-pressed to find the likes of Lily Kellogg again."

The light dawned. Just as he'd originally deduced, Effie Hurlburt delighted in matchmaking. "I do not dispute that she is a fine young woman. I value our friendship, but a friendship it must remain."

"Poppycock!" Effie pursed her lips. "I do not understand why you are deluding yourself when you are so clearly in love with Lily."

He couldn't have been more shocked if she'd suddenly turned into a lioness. He sputtered, searching for a response. "With all due respect, wouldn't I know that better than you?"

"Not at all. You young people can be oblivious to what's right under your nose." She fixed her eyes on him. "Are you going to sit there and tell me you've never thought of Lily as a potential wife?"

There was no satisfactory answer to that question. "No matter, because she would never regard me in that light."

Ellie's tinkling laughter unnerved him. "Are you daft, boy? She is crazy about you. She just hasn't admitted it to herself yet." She stifled a giggle. "And you? You big galoot. Whatever nonsense you tell yourself, you are in love with Lily Kellogg as all the world can clearly see."

In love? He couldn't be. He wouldn't be. Not after Rebecca's betrayal. "You mock me, ma'am."

"On the contrary, I'm trying to knock some sense into that thick head of yours. If you let Lily Kellogg get away, you'll regret it the rest of your life." She sat back, leaving the idea suspended in the silence. Then in a gentler tone, she said, "Now then, young man. Something is holding you back. What is it?"

He swallowed against the bitterness rising in his chest. "Love? It's not all poetry and moonlight." He bit off the words threatening to pour out of him. He'd already said too much.

"I see." Effie's expression softened. "So you've been hurt." She nodded in apparent sympathy, gazing at him with such affection that he felt embarrassed. "I understand you don't want to put yourself in that position again. And, yes, love involves risk. But are you convinced you want to let the woman who hurt you control your destiny?"

He looked at her quizzically. "What do you mean?"

"As long as you fail to act when love presents itself, you permit what she did to you to determine how you respond to new women in your life. Women like Lily. Tell me this. Was it Lily who hurt you? Lily who rejected you? No, so why do you make her the scapegoat for your past disappointments?"

Dumbfounded, he could scarcely take it all in. Effie Hurlburt had spared nothing in trying to open his eyes. "I hardly know what to say."

"No need to say anything. You could, of course, call me a romantic meddler, but I'd prefer you think of me simply as one holding up a mirror to what is already in your heart."

Desperate to avoid her penetrating gaze, he rose to his feet. "I appreciate your interest, but if you will excuse me, I really must take my leave." As she stood to usher him out, he relented and took her hand. "I have no mother, but if she were still alive, I know she would like you."

"That's a fine compliment, Captain." She squeezed his hand. "I'd like to think that she would say to you exactly what I've just said."

Over the next hours, he vacillated between irritation at Effie Hurlburt's interference and an attempt to probe the nature of his feelings for Lily. Could it be that others were seeing what he could not? Certainly Will Creekmore had come to the conclusion he was courting. Every time Caleb saw Lily it was as if his heart outpaced his brain. He was a soldier. Discipline was his stock-in-trade. Where Lily was concerned, though, he'd failed at governing himself. Even admitting his affection for her, could she ever accept a man flawed by the violence of battle? Yes, he had some serious thinking to do. He must face his reservations and come to a conclusion. Either court Lily or break off their friendship. While he would hate to end the latter, perhaps that was best. She could go her way, and he could leave the fort with a clear conscience and no encumbrances.

Once he'd decided that courting was out of the question, he spent the next day filled with relief. He'd made a decision. Now he merely had to act upon it.

That good intention prevailed only until the poetry reading. About half the troops turned out and were generally more attentive than he'd predicted. Some relished the poetry while others listened in bored stupefaction. Caleb had been well received, but he attributed that more to Milton's magnificent words than his own elocution.

As soon as the readers had presented their offerings, they took their seats in the audience. After a dull rendition of "The Destruction of Sennacherib," Lily came to the center of the stage for the finale. Lantern light cast an aura around her, creating a halo of her hair. She wore a misty sea-green dress, which made her resemble the beautiful lily for which she was named. Quiet settled over the audience. Then she began.

"How do I love thee? Let me count the ways.
I love thee to the depth and breadth and height
My soul can reach, when feeling out of sight
For the ends of Being and ideal Grace.
I love thee to the level of every day's
Most quiet need, by sun and candle-light."

Caleb clenched his hands. He was unmanned by her words. By her. Then in a voice that spoke to his soul, she continued.

"I love thee freely, as men strive for Right;
I love thee purely, as they turn from Praise.
I love thee with the passion put to use
In my old griefs, and with my childhood's faith.
I love thee with a love I seemed to lose
With my lost saints—I love thee with the breath,
Smiles, tears, of all my life!—and, if God choose,
I shall but love thee better after death."

Caleb heard neither the hushed silence when she finished, nor the thunderous applause which followed. Stunned, he choked back the sobs threatening to tear from his throat. Pain. Promise. Where did one end and the other begin? He had no answer. All he knew was that, come what may, for good or for ill, he was desperately in love with Lily Kellogg.

* * *

After the poetry reading, Lily was surrounded by well-wishers, eager to comment on her emotional delivery of Elizabeth Barrett Browning's sonnet. She caught a glimpse of Caleb across the room and hoped to find him later to congratulate him on his masterful reading of Milton. Given the fiery nature of the lines he read, she doubted even the most insensitive of his fellows would ever mock him.

"Miss Kellogg?" She'd noticed the private, barely out of his teens, waiting to speak with her and yielding his place to officers and their wives. Finally, the others had dispersed and he approached. "You don't know me, but I'm Private Sydney Long. I, well…" He ducked his head. "I wanted to tell you how moved I was by your poem."

"Private—may I call you Sydney?—I'm grateful for the compliment." The lad looked up, and she was astonished to see tears pooling in his eyes. "Dear me, are you all right?"

He pulled a handkerchief from his coat, turned aside and blew his nose. "I'm sorry, it's just that—"

"So you have a sweetheart, Sydney? Is that it?"

"*Had,* miss. *Had.* She died of the diphtheria."

"Mercy, I'm so sorry. Is there anything I can do for you?"

"You already did it, ma'am." Then, in a mournful tone, he recited, "'and, if God choose, / I shall but love thee better after death.'"

When he finished, Lily touched him gently on the shoulder. "Your young woman was lucky to have you, even for so short a time."

When the private moved toward the door, Lily studied the nearly empty room. She caught a glimpse of Caleb in the company of Lieutenant Creekmore. She considered hurrying after him to compliment him, but she didn't want to make a spectacle of herself or give rise to rumors. Just before Caleb left, he turned in her direction, but without raising a hand in greeting or otherwise acknowledging her. On his face was the strangest look—serious, yet detached, and more puzzled than welcoming. Almost as if he were a man she didn't know.

Thinking about it that night and most of the next day, she felt a prickly sense of uncertainty. Theirs had been an open and pleasant friendship, but that impression had been sorely compromised by his distancing stance at the reading. Had she done something wrong? Had something changed? And why did she permit such questions to plague her throughout the day?

Arriving home from her work at the hospital, the distraction of a letter from Aunt Lavinia pushed all thought of Caleb to the back of her mind.

Rose handed her the envelope, then stood wadding her apron in her hands. "Open it, Lily, or I shall die of curiosity."

"I'm almost afraid. What if she thinks I've been presumptuous to write her and practically invite myself? Maybe I've offended her."

Rose, ever practical, harrumphed. "Quit stalling. No amount of fretting will change by one whit what's in that letter."

With a silent plea heavenward, Lily slit the envelope and extracted the letter, written on heavy stationery embossed with Lavinia's monogram.

My dearest niece,

I received your recent letter and am gratified by your interest in our fair city and your eagerness to visit Mr. Dupree and me. My understanding is that it is only you and, alas, not also your sister, Rose, who entertains the notion of traveling to St. Louis for what I hope can be an extended stay.

At this time, it is impossible for me to offer you firm plans for your trip. For a month this summer we will be traveling to New York City where Mr. Dupree has business and then on to stay with friends in Newport, Rhode Island, a welcome respite from a Missouri summer.

When we return from that trip, I shall have my husband's secretary investigate suitable means of transportation and establish a travel schedule for you. I regret the uncertainty of my response, but you may tentatively plan to leave Fort Larned sometime in August. It will be my pleasure to attend to the financial arrangements for your trip. We may anticipate September for your possible arrival, which will thankfully give us sufficient time to work with the dressmaker to sew you up a new wardrobe more suitable to the demands of the social events you will attend.

A shiver went down Lily's spine. Now that her dream was on the verge of being realized, she was overcome with trepidation. The fantasy of lovely gowns and sophisticated soirees had always been blessedly in the future; the genuine possibility now seemed daunting. What did she know of high society? Of ball gowns and coiffures? Caught up in the moment, she had nearly forgotten Rose, rooted to the spot, her face pale, her freckles prominent. "I can't believe it," Lily whispered. "It may actually happen."

"I want to be happy for you, I really do." Sniffling, Rose reached in her apron pocket and withdrew a handkerchief.

Lily wrapped her sister in her arms, and they clung to one another for several moments. Then Lily patted Rose's back. "Nothing has been decided," she said. "I won't count on anything until I have the tickets in my hand. We will simply wait to see what God has in store for me."

"Yes, that is best." Rose stifled a half giggle, half sob. "I am not about to question the Almighty, even though His ways can be mysterious."

A new thought struck Lily. "What shall we tell Father?" She worried about leaving him, especially since he'd already lost David and her mother.

"The truth. If and when it happens, your departure will trouble him sorely, even as he will understand it's the right course for you. Perhaps the longer he has to anticipate your leaving, the less painful will be the actual fact of it."

"Or will it just give him more time to fret?"

"There is no easy answer, Lily, but honesty is best."

Later as Lily sat darning her father's socks, she pondered the question of honesty. Of course, she wanted the adventure she'd always longed for, but leaving her father and sister was painful to contemplate. She had always blithely assumed they would flourish without her, but Private Sydney Long's loss had reminded her that nothing could be taken for granted or wished away.

* * *

Keyed up, Caleb repeatedly tapped the toe of his boot against the fence post. In the corral, horses milled, snorting and pawing as if sensing the onset of action. Behind him, men checked saddles and harnesses, while in the armory, weapons were being cleaned and oiled and ammunition stacked for transport. The anticipation of their upcoming mission coupled with the need for careful preparation set his nerves on heightened alert. This would be no ordinary foray into the prairie. Instead, they would be marching over fifty miles to engage a massing force of hostile Indians intent on protecting their tribal lands.

Although a small contingent would remain at the fort for protection, most of the troops would be leaving at sunrise the next day. Caleb wished he could share in the elation and bravado of his men, itching for a fight. Instead, he was experiencing nightmarish reservations about the looming engagement with a motivated and desperate band of Indians.

He shut his eyes against the remembered stench of the horses and smell of blood. He prayed this would be his final assault before leaving the army. August couldn't come soon enough. He had done his duty— and would do it the upcoming days—but his soldier's heart had deserted him. He knew that spelled trouble. He could ill afford to become overly careful or protective. A leader carries the charge to his men—skilled and fearless, an example of courage under fire.

He turned away from the corral. When had cynicism replaced idealism? Sadly, he knew, almost to the minute. On a winter's day at the Washita River. Determined to rid his mind of such grim phantoms, he walked briskly toward the officers' briefing with Major Hurlburt, resolving to focus on business.

Passing by the hospital, he flushed. All his best intentions of bravery in battle were one thing. Confronting his feelings for Lily was something else, strangely akin to cowardice. Effie Hurlburt had shot an arrow squarely into his heart. Listening to Lily read Elizabeth Barrett Browning's sonnet had opened the wound. How was it possible for him to be in love? How could he again expose himself to rejection? But with the swiftness of an eagle came his next thought. How could he leave Lily? Or imagine a life without her?

He had deliberately avoided her over the past week, knowing that until he could master his feelings, it would be unwise to see her, even as he longed to do that very thing.

Nearing headquarters, he paused, glancing up at the flag atop the pole. He had sworn loyalty to his country. How could he deny his feelings for either country or Lily and still regard himself as honorable? In that moment, he made up his mind. When he returned from this mission, he would declare his love for her. After he spoke with her, he would know one way or the other— either she returned his feelings or she didn't.

All day the atmosphere at the fort had been bustling, the troops purposeful as they made preparations for their departure the next morning. In the hospital, Lily heard much grousing among the men confined there. "I can't believe I'm missing this" and "My fellows need me, and here I am, laid up with a bum leg." Privately she was appalled by their appetite for warfare, but she supposed battle was part of their culture.

In the late afternoon, a young corporal suffering from a serious case of poison ivy tugged at her sleeve. "Miss, please, talk to the doctor."

"Pray tell, what for?"

"I can go with my men. I know I can." The urgency of his plea was a tribute to his sense of duty.

"Corporal, Dr. Kellogg has told you how dangerous it would be for you to leave and risk further infection."

"But it's cowardly to remain here."

"Never. The cowardice would lie in your possibly endangering others during the mission. The honorable course is for you to remain here, heal and be fit for the next call to duty."

He covered his eyes with his forearm. "You're right, but 'tis hard to be a slacker."

"No one will accuse you of that. If they do, they will have to deal with my displeasure."

He uncovered his eyes and managed a wan grin. "None of them boys would want to face the wrath of Miss Lily."

"Very well, then. Lie still and get some rest."

As she finished her duties and headed toward the cemetery, she felt a sense of accomplishment. She was not only a nurse, but, at times, a kind of counselor. She was often touched by the confidences her patients shared with her and, as with the corporal, their disappointments. Although she never forgot the specter of the terrible day of the storm and the leering Adams, thankfully now removed to Fort Riley, by and large she found the men to be both forthcoming and, ironically, vulnerable.

The late sun sent shafts of light sparkling through the leafy trees. After the high temperatures of the day, the shade gave at least an illusion of cool. Lily sank down on the grass beside her mother's grave and removed her bonnet. Not for the first time it occurred to her that if she went to St. Louis, she would leave not only her father and sister, but this sacred place where she communed with her mother's spirit. Only here did she feel a peace which often eluded her at the fort.

Engrossed in her thoughts, she only belatedly became aware of a figure standing several feet behind her. Looking around, she saw Caleb. He stood silent, erect, his expression unfathomable.

"I thought I would find you here," he said, extending a hand to help her to her feet.

"'Tis my custom," she said, avoiding his eyes. She had been halfway irritated with him ever since he so obviously ignored her at the poetry reading for reasons she could not imagine. Why had he bothered to approach her now?

"I know." Silence hung awkwardly between them.

"Well?" She clasped her hands in front of her and waited for some explanation of his presence.

"I ride out tomorrow."

"I wish you and your men a safe journey." Their conversation was perfunctory and stilted, and she chafed under the clumsiness of this meeting.

"Before leaving, I wanted to apologize for failing to compliment you on your poetry reading."

"I, likewise, would have complimented you, but, alas, you made a hurried retreat before I could do so." She cringed at the sarcasm in her tone.

"There was a reason for that."

"Ours is not to wonder why," she said.

He moved closer, staring at her so intently, she had to avert her eyes. "I was avoiding you."

Surprised, she looked up. "Whatever for? I thought we were friends."

"And so we are." He lifted a hand and gently caressed her hair.

Dwarfed by his broad shoulders and the sudden warmth in his voice, she felt herself grow breathless in response.

She struggled for the words that would still her racing heart. "I am glad of it," she finally said.

He tilted her chin, so that she was helpless to avoid his honey-brown eyes, swimming with affection. "Friends we are, but, Lily, is there a possibility we could be more than friends?"

Thunderstruck, she stared at him, trying to fathom the implications of his words. More than friends? Yes, she admired him. And, yes, in her bed in the dark hours of the night, she had admitted to an attraction to him. But…more than friends?

He gently cupped her face in his hands, preventing her from looking away, or even breathing. "Please, Lily. While I'm gone, say you'll think about us."

Us? Rioting emotions rendered her incapable of speech.

"Will you?" he asked in a low, insistent voice.

She would say anything to subdue the tingling she felt in every nerve. "Yes."

"Thank you, dear Lily," he murmured, just before leaning forward and kissing her.

Nothing had prepared her for the riot of emotions sweeping through her, for the undeniable need she had to feel his lips on hers or for her new, topsy-turvy sense of self.

He stepped back and held her hands in his. "We will talk when I return. I have much to tell you." He paused, then added with a rueful shake of his head, "And much to confess." He leaned down and picked up her bonnet, holding it tenderly against his chest before handing it to her. "I will miss you, Lily."

She couldn't help herself. The words popped out, uncensored. "And I you."

Then he was gone, leaving her standing in the twilight of the cemetery, warmth suffusing her body. What had she just promised? Whatever it was, it was profound. She turned and faced her mother's headstone. *Oh, Mama. What is happening to me?*

Chapter Eight

Along with the other women, Lily waited in the dawn watching the cavalrymen assemble on the parade ground, their postures erect, their eyes fixed on Major Hurlburt, mounted on a white steed. Other than the occasional nicker of a horse, it was eerily quiet. Rose stood on one side of her and Effie on the other. Walking his steed back and forth in front of his troops, the major began to speak.

"Duty calls us to restore order and peace to Kansas and the Indian Territory. We cannot afford to let the native peoples pose additional threats to the settlers moving through the frontier. Obey your officers, fight with valor and bring honor to these United States of America. Let us go with God and return safely." Then with a flourish, he wheeled his horse and led them from the fort.

Beside her, Effie drew a ragged breath, belying the usual calm she projected as the commander's wife. Stifling a sigh, Lily wondered into what dangers the men were advancing. They made a grand sight trotting in formation. The sound of hoofbeats and the clouds of dust made talking difficult, a relief to Lily. What words were there for such an expedition? She supposed that any being uttered were in the form of prayer.

What irony lay in the major's words to "go with God." Was it presumed God was partisan and would protect the soldiers while the enemy was killed? She wondered to whom the Indians prayed. She suspected both sides were capable of bloodlust and both of humanity.

From the first massing of the troops to the now diminishing line crossing the prairie, she had focused on Caleb, sitting erect in the saddle, his jaw set with purpose. Even after Rose and Effie wandered off, Lily remained, an arm around a post, watching as Caleb became nothing more than a speck on the horizon.

Tossing and turning in the night, she had examined and reexamined her encounter with Caleb in the cemetery. She had imagined the many different ways their conversation might have played out. She could have reacted angrily to his admission he had been ignoring her. She might have brushed his hand away when he touched her hair. And most certainly she could have rejected the surprising kiss. And what had ever possessed her to agree to "think about" something beyond friendship? Yet even in this recital of possible alternatives, she could never bring herself to renounce her final statement to him, because it was true. She would, indeed, miss him.

Yet she was disturbed by what he might tell her when he returned. He had used the word *confess*. He must carry some burden unknown to her. She had already observed that he was tight-lipped about his past, especially his war experiences. Most soldiers had their individual stories. Some shared their adventures with gusto; others remained steadfastly silent. She suspected Caleb was in the latter group. She wondered how a "confession" might change him and the nature of their relationship.

When the last of the horses disappeared over a hill, she glanced around the fort—too empty, too quiet, the life seemingly having gone out of it with the departure of the soldiers.

She walked slowly toward the house, caught up in the one memory she couldn't dismiss, no matter how she rationalized it. The kiss. Surprisingly sweet, it had aroused emotions in her with which she had no experience. Why, she had practically swooned at the delicious sensation of his lips warm and soft on hers. If she was honest, as Rose reminded her they always should be, she was attracted to Caleb in ways it was no longer possible for her to deny. Perhaps their *friendship* was a mere code word for feelings they both had been fighting—feelings they would need to confront when he returned.

Lost in thought, she didn't see Effie standing on her front porch. "Lily, could you spare me a minute? I am in need of a friend."

Grateful for the intrusion upon her disturbing thoughts, Lily climbed the steps to the porch. "Happily. I am not yet due at the hospital."

"Sit with me, then," Effie said, gesturing to the wooden rockers. "I find the void after Hurly leaves difficult to bear."

A flash of empathy stirred Lily. "The fort has lost vibrancy, that's for certain."

"It never changes, this leave-taking. You would think I might have grown accustomed to it by now." Effie rocked awhile in silence before going on. "Hurly and I are a true love match, and I simply cannot contemplate a life without him."

"We must continue, as always, to pray for the safety of our men."

"And to busy ourselves so that the time will seem to elapse more quickly."

"Is that ever really possible?"

The older woman smiled at the absurdity of it. "Never."

"Effie, thank you for setting such an example for us. We would all be blessed by a relationship like the one you and the major share."

Effie eyed her shrewdly. "Do you think such a match is possible for you?"

"Perhaps. When I meet the right man."

"And when might that be?"

"I am hoping to meet someone when I go to St. Louis to visit my aunt."

"Ah, I see." Effie slowed her rocking. "The perfectly handsome, sophisticated, successful man-about-town. Am I correct?"

For reasons Lily couldn't grasp, the image Effie had created sounded downright distasteful. She felt her cheeks redden. "Something like that."

"Posh. Why hold out for a fantasy man when you have a flesh-and-blood man right here who loves you with all his heart?"

Caught off guard, Lily could only stammer. "Ef-effie? You're quite mistaken."

The older woman hooted. "Oh, child, I know you're

doing your best to discourage Caleb Montgomery
and stifle your feelings, but mark my words. God has
brought you two together for a purpose. You can fight
it if you want, but in the end, you'll remember this
conversation and allow as how Effie Hurlburt knew a
thing or two about love."

"It is true I am fond of the captain, but—"

"Stop right there. No *but*'s. For now, being fond of
him will do."

Lily had the distinct impression that based on some
innate, superior knowledge, Effie was inwardly laughing at her—that she knew Lily's feelings went beyond
fondness. How she had stumbled into this awkward
conversation she had no idea, but she knew she needed
an escape. She consulted the watch suspended from
a chain around her neck. "Dear me, I must fly to the
hospital." She rose then, and as she prepared to leave,
laid a hand on Effie's shoulder. "We will all help you
pass the time until the men are safely home. I know
the major will make haste to return to you."

Effie smiled. "Thank you, dear. May that day come
in God's good time."

Walking toward the hospital, Lily was struck by
the message she continued to receive from so many
sides—everything in God's good time. That included
her upcoming conversation with Caleb.

That night Lily was awakened by a ferocious wind
howling around the house and rattling the panes of
window glass. In the intermittent flashes of lightning,
she could see clouds of airborne dust swirling through
the air. A clap of thunder seemed to split the house in

two. Somehow Rose continued sleeping, oblivious to the maelstrom outside.

Lily stepped out of bed and pulled her robe over her gown before tiptoeing downstairs. She didn't like storms, especially since she'd arrived here and heard troubling stories about cyclones and the damage they could inflict. Despite telling herself she was safe, she trembled with fear each time the wind battered the walls. Entering the kitchen, she was surprised to find her father sitting at the table in the dark, a blanket pulled about him. "Papa, you couldn't sleep, either?"

"No, but then I've always enjoyed watching storms."

She knew there was more to it. Perhaps at times like this, his thoughts, like hers, turned to Mathilda's and David's absence. She sought to divert him. "And maybe you're standing watch over two young ladies and a few men in a hospital?"

In the illumination of lightning, she saw a grin crease his face. "That, too."

Just being in his company, she noticed that her shivering had ceased and the knots in her stomach had eased. They sat in companionable silence until her father spoke. "Lily, perhaps we should talk about Captain Montgomery."

She gripped the edge of the table. "Papa, whatever do you mean?"

"He has taken quite an interest in you."

"What is the harm? We are friends."

Ezra sighed. "These are the times when I wish your mother was still alive. I am hopeless at delicate conversations." He paused, as if marshaling his thoughts. "While there has been no unseemly talk, many of us have noticed that he seeks you out and enjoys your company. I have no doubt that thus far, your relationship with him has been within the bounds of propriety. But—"

Out of the blue came the image of Caleb's kiss and the forbidden thoughts it gave rise to. Lily hoped the dim light masked her blush.

"—it is a father's duty to caution that you must not encourage a man's attentions unless you have deep feelings for him."

"Papa, you know I cannot undertake a romantic relationship. You know Mother's dream and mine has been that I might one day go to St. Louis."

"Does *he* know that?"

She shrugged. "No, but it is of no consequence."

"My dear, I fear you are misreading the captain's intentions."

Was she? What exactly had Caleb meant about moving beyond mere friendship? So confused had she been by their conversation and the memorable kiss that she had avoided full consideration of his remarks. How naive she must appear. "Help me understand, Papa."

"The captain will one day be leaving the army. If he is like most, he will want to settle down, establish a home…marry. Has it occurred to you he may think of you in that regard? If so, you have the potential to hurt him. I would hate to see that happen for you or to such a good man."

She stiffened her back. "I am going to St. Louis. I will make that clear to him when he returns."

"You are decided, then?" When she nodded her head, he continued. "I confess I have entertained the hope that you might give up that dream and stay with Rose and me. Or perhaps marry an army man."

She knew he was referring to Caleb. But marriage? In a flash of insight, she realized she had not been forthcoming with Caleb. She vowed she would tell him of her St. Louis visit as soon as he returned. It would not do for him to think she was toying with his affections. Above all, she did not want to inflict any further pain upon him.

"Lily?" Her father succeeded in regaining her attention. "Regardless of what I think or want, you must follow your heart, both in matters of love and in self-fulfillment. Much as I would like, I can no longer protect you from the world nor be the arbiter of your behavior and decisions. Your mother and I always wanted the very best for you, but I see now it has to be *your* best, not ours."

Never had Lily loved him more than in that moment. She rounded the table, came up behind him and put her arms around his shoulders, resting her chin on his head. "Thank you, Papa. I will search for happiness, and when I find it, I will thank you."

A comfortable silence fell, punctuated only by the sound of raindrops on the roof.

Storms alternating with hot humid days had made conditions during the march challenging. Once the cavalry reached the area from which they would launch their attack, the rains disappeared, leaving only the unrelieved misery of sun and high temperatures. Caleb did his best to circulate among the encamped men and keep them motivated, but as time dragged on, the weather, bugs and winds took their toll. Mealy rations and the long wait did nothing to improve conditions. Lurking in all their minds was the upcoming task of subduing the Indian uprising. The veterans knew full well with what ferocity the tribes could fight and how fearlessly the warriors faced death.

Now with the attack set for the next day, the men grew increasingly quiet and restive. By midmorning Caleb felt perspiration dampen his undershirt. He ran a brush through his gritty hair and buttoned his jacket before heading out to Major Hurlburt's command tent for a briefing.

Along the way, he passed by a slightly built private sitting against a tree, scribbling on a piece of paper. "Sir?" The fellow stood up, then looked about as if fearing detection. "Would you deliver this message to Miss Lily? Well, you know—" he cleared his throat "—if something happens to me."

Caleb wondered how the young man was acquainted with Lily, but set that thought aside as he observed the fear in the private's eyes. He took the proffered note, then stepped closer so as not to be overheard. "Son, have you been in battle before?"

The soldier hung his head. "Just once, but that time the Indians ran away. I, uh, I don't think that'll happen this time."

"Nor do I." Caleb had seen it before—the terrifying projections made by raw soldiers. Any reasonable man would admit to some fear, but paralyzing fright ill-suited a soldier in the thick of an attack. "You will see action tomorrow, but remember that you will be surrounded by battle-hardened, well-trained comrades. We live as a unit and we fight as a unit. They will do their part, and you will do yours." He clapped a hand on the youth's shoulder and looked deep into his eyes.

"Rely on your training and instinct. We're counting on you, son."

"Yes, sir. Thank you, sir."

Caleb pocketed the note, then turned away, concerned for the untested soldier about to come under fire. From naive, idealistic boys playing fifes and drums to grown men deserting their fellows in the thick of an engagement, warfare took the measure of a man and cruelly destroyed illusions. He groaned inwardly. Only time would tell whether his talk with the private had stirred his fighting blood.

Inside the command tent, the officers huddled around a field map. Studying the terrain, they ultimately decided on a three-prong approach. Lieutenant Smythe would march on ahead to outflank the enemy from the west, Will Creekmore would lead his men on the east flank and Caleb, the most experienced of the officers, would direct the frontal charge from the south. The plan was to force the enemy back against a line of sand hills. While many of the Indians would be armed with lances and bows and arrows, a significant number also possessed rifles. The cavalry would set out at 3:00 a.m. to be in place for a sunrise attack.

Caleb spent the rest of the afternoon and early evening speaking with his men, checking their preparations and offering encouragement. After the sun set, he retreated to his tent, lit a lantern and pulled out the small, leather-bound volume of Tennyson's poems he always carried with him. However, between his nerves and the discomfort of his scratchy uniform, he couldn't concentrate. His thoughts were elsewhere. Could he acquit himself with honor one last time on the battlefield,

even though he had come to believe that his tolerance
for warfare had run its course?

Sitting there, watching darkness blot out light, he
closed his eyes and tried to picture the lush green grass
of spring in the Flint Hills where the Montgomery
Ranch's healthy herd grazed. There under vast blue
skies, he could build something permanent and pro-
ductive. Tomorrow, by contrast, would be characterized by bloodshed. He closed his eyes, formulating a
prayer. *Dear God, deliver us from danger, protect us
from our own worst selves and make us always aware
of Your ultimate goodness.* The words seemed inade-
quate, but he knew that somehow God understood the
yearnings of his heart.

One battle. One day. Then they would return to Fort
Larned. He would return to Lily. Until then he would
hold her in his heart in the full and surprising knowledge of his love for her. He drew in a sharp breath with
the realization that not for a long time had he personally had so much cause to desire his own deliverance
in armed conflict.

Lily awoke with a start, her damp gown wrapped
around her legs, her heart racing. Not one breeze fil-
tered through the open window to cool her feverish
skin. Beside her Rose gently snored. Lily tried to get
her bearings. What had so abruptly awakened her? She
heard nothing unusual. Creeping to the window, she
scanned the quiet, nearly deserted fort. All appeared
normal. Stars twinkled in the sky and the sliver of a
moon rested on the horizon.

Yet she was in a panic. Something was terribly
wrong. Had a nightmare thus upset her? Snippets of a

dream slowly came to her. Screams. Tortured screams. Suffocating dust. Then she remembered being part of a long line of mounted soldiers galloping off a cliff. "Into the valley of death." Tennyson's lines swirled alongside chaotic visions. No matter how she tried to orient herself to reality—to her bedroom and the quiet army post outside the house—she felt only the presence of doom.

How long had the cavalrymen been gone? She counted the days. Nearly two weeks. A long time. A sense of dread came over her. Were the men of Fort Larned in danger?

Under the cover of darkness, the mounted troops slowly advanced toward their attack position. Caleb could only imagine their thoughts. Anticipation was almost the worst part of battle. As they waited with drawn breaths astride quivering horses, each moment seeming at once an eternity and a flash, and they longed for action even as they prayed never to hear the order to advance.

Unbidden memories washed over Caleb—the adrenaline rush of the first charge, the cacophony of gunfire mingled with the screams of the wounded and dying, and the slippery earth, sodden with sweat and blood. He hated it. That realization took him by surprise. Never before had he so openly admitted his reservations about being a soldier. He squared himself in the saddle and stroked Bucephalus's neck. Pray God, he would use that hatred to fuel his courage.

Then came the strident bugle summons. Following Caleb's lead, his troop raced toward the Indian encampment, flags flying and weapons drawn. Then all rational thought was overwhelmed by a rain of gunfire and a long line of mounted braves charging toward them with frenzied battle cries. Caleb found himself surrounded in a sea of clashing forces, lances and arrows too often finding victims among his men. An Indian with startling war paint raced toward him, shrieking like a banshee. Only at the last minute did Caleb succeed in shooting him through the chest. The man fell from his horse as if in slow motion. Behind Caleb, another brave raised his rifle, and he avoided that shot only by ducking low over his mount's head. Wheeling around, he dropped his assailant. Out of the corner of his eye, he noticed several soldiers whose horses had gone down, leaving them relatively defenseless. He spurred to their side, handed his pistol to one and then rallied others to form a defensive position behind the horseless soldiers.

All up and down the line pandemonium raged. Several of his men lay on their backs, arrows still quivering from their chests. In the thick of it, Caleb could not tell whether Smythe and Creekmore had yet attacked from the flanks. He devoutly hoped so, or his men would become victims rather than victors.

The sun crested over the battlefield, illuminating downed bodies and soldiers locked in hand-to-hand combat with their nearly naked foe. Caleb could hardly take in the shattering violence of it all. What in God's name were they doing? With angry tears, he turned away from the sight, bent on going to the rear to urge his men forward to reinforce their fellows.

Kicking Bucephalus, he bellowed into the din. "Rally, boys, rally!" Reaching the reinforcements, he had just turned to urge them forward when the sky exploded in a blinding flash of color. His vision blurred and nausea clogged his throat. Sounds, as if wrapped in cotton batting, echoed far, far away. Why couldn't he hold on to the reins? Caleb's last conscious thought was how awkward and unsoldierly it was to slip from a horse and end up facedown in buffalo grass.

Chapter Nine

After supper a few nights following her nightmare, Lily sat on the porch with Rose, both of them fanning themselves. A pall had fallen over the fort. Even the usual racket of the cicadas sounded listless. No lively harmonica music issued from the barracks, and dogs lay motionless on doorsteps, panting. The sinking sun was a molten stone and nary a wisp of cloud adorned the sky.

Lily rested her head against the back of her rocker. In a strange way, her body felt as if she were constantly holding her breath. Indeed, the entire fort seemed to be suspended in time, waiting for something, anything, to happen.

"Remember last March when we talked about dreading summer?" Rose fanned herself more vigorously. "This is what we meant."

"Memory can't compare with the real thing." Given the heat, Lily was grateful that because of the cavalry's absence, they had few patients in the hospital. She had perfunctorily gone through the motions of reviewing the inventory, changing sheets and linens, and restocking the medicine chest. Yet even those duties failed to fill the time dragging by interminably.

"Do you suppose it's this hot in St. Louis?" Rose asked.

"Lavinia's letters suggest that summer is even worse there with the humidity from the river."

"Malaria." Rose sniffed in disapproval. "The newspapers are full of stories of how widespread the disease is in low-lying places."

"Are you trying to tell me something?"

Rose's expression softened. "I don't intend to borrow trouble, but I want you to be safe when you leave us."

"*If* I leave you." Lily gestured with an arm at the expanse of the fort. "Besides, there are plenty of dangers and diseases right here, and working in the hospital, I've already encountered most." She went through a mental catalog: typhus, diphtheria, snake bite, influenza and, even here, the occasional case of malaria. She winced against the memory of the ordeal of the woman who died in childbirth.

Rose grudgingly agreed. "I suppose."

Lily sensed that Rose had something she wanted to say. "You're a good sister to worry about me."

"I try not to, but I do. With our dear brother gone, I worry even more about you. How you will make the trip to St. Louis, what ruffians you might encounter and even how you'll be received by the elegant people you will meet there. It seems such a strange world to me."

Lily wouldn't admit that her sister had just voiced

some of her own concerns. "A different society, assuredly, but one I long to experience."

The two sat rocking, praying for the hint of a breeze to relieve the oven of the porch. Lily finally spoke. "We talk a great deal about my dreams, but, Rose, what about yours? What is it you want in life?"

"Oh, Lily, I'm a simple soul. For now, I'm content keeping house for Papa. I confess I've thought about marriage and a family someday, but I'm no beauty and most fellows look for that."

Lily interrupted. "But you have so much to offer."

"Even if that were true, most men don't view me as a potential mate."

"It will be a very special one, indeed, who recognizes your inner beauty as I do."

"I try not to dwell on the future," Rose said with a sad smile. "What will be, will be, according to God's plan."

Lily sat forward with a sense of urgency. "Promise me you won't compromise. You deserve a good man who will cherish you as Papa and I do."

"Just as you deserve such a one, sister." Rose rocked for a few moments before adding, "One like Captain Montgomery."

Lily sank back in her chair. First Effie, then her father and now Rose. Was the entire fort conspiring to engage in matchmaking? And was this pressure coming from a genuine sense that Caleb was right for her or a desire to keep her from going to St. Louis?

"You, too? Why is everyone pushing Caleb at me?"

"Now don't get touchy. Maybe we see something you don't want to acknowledge."

Lily felt suddenly suffocated, not just by the heat but

by others' expectations. She couldn't deny the attraction she felt to the handsome captain who shared her love of literature or the sense of safety and comfort she felt in his arms, but she had advanced too far with her dream of the city to jeopardize it for a summer fling.

Hearing footsteps, the two women simultaneously looked up. Their father, his shoulders drooping, approached from the direction of the cemetery. Lily knew he sometimes went there to seek peace just as she did.

Lily stood. "Papa, come rest a spell with us."

He raised his hand in greeting as he approached. "Gladly." He mounted the porch, pulled a vacant rocker nearer to them and sat down. "It's the calm before the storm," he said.

Rose examined the horizon. "I don't see any clouds."

"Not that kind of storm, child. The kind humans make." He folded his hands in his lap, but his thumbs circled each other in a nervous dance. "This is the period of inertia followed by the loosening of hell."

"What do you mean?" Lily asked.

"The war. Field hospitals. We would experience an unearthly calm before an attack followed immediately by the chaos of bodies upon bodies piling up around us." He seemed to choke back both his words and his memories. "I have that same sense tonight."

Despite the heat, Lily shivered. "About our troops?"

"Maybe it's just an old man's premonition."

Rose leaned toward him. "About what exactly?"

Ezra sighed forlornly. His words fell like stones into a deep well. "About the fact that Lily and I are soon to get very busy." He clutched Lily's hand. "My dear, I fear you have not yet seen battle wounds on the scale I am anticipating."

Early the next morning Lily was awakened by the bugle's alarm followed by the sound of a galloping horse. Hurrying to the bedroom window, she saw one of the scouts dismount and run toward the house. Her father must've heard him, too, for he stepped out on the porch before the soldier could knock. Through the open window she heard the man's breathless words.

"Prepare the hospital, Doctor. I regret to report that we have several casualties." He paused to catch his breath and then added with awful finality, "And deaths."

During the next few hours while the ambulance wagons were en route to the fort, Ezra Kellogg corralled the enlisted hospital aides, reviewed procedures, and exhorted them to stay calm and follow his orders. Meanwhile, Lily rounded up some of the women to serve as a soothing presence and assist with follow-up care. Rose busied herself at the stove preparing tisanes and broths. Lily prayed she could remain professional and bring her experience to bear for the benefit of the wounded. About the dying…she couldn't even contemplate. Nor could she let her mind assume the worst about those she knew. About Caleb. Sadly, there was no mistaking the cause of the hammer blows emanating from the carpentry shop. Coffins.

Just as the first wagon rolled into the fort, Ezra took Lily aside. Putting his arm around her as if to steady her, he said in a low voice, "Daughter, you are going to see things I had always hoped to spare you, but I need you today. The wounded need you. No one else has your skills." He pulled her closer and uttered a brief prayer that they might be instruments of God's healing.

Then the first wagon arrived at the hospital, and from that point on, the groans of the wounded and Ezra's barked orders filled the room along with the odors of alcohol, sweat and blood.

After the litters were unloaded from the wagon, Ezra moved swiftly from man to man assessing injuries. One he immediately sent to the operating table; another, already feverish, was taken by Effie and a stunned private to be stripped and bathed in cool water. A terrified-looking Carrie Smythe administered chloroform just before Ezra amputated the first soldier's left leg. Out of the corner of her eye, Lily watched Carrie nearly swoon before collecting herself, but Lily had no time to intervene. She was too busy cleansing the dirty head wound of a dazed sergeant. From him, she moved on to a lad whose makeshift bandage was coming loose.

Time lost all meaning as the hospital crew worked frantically to patch up those with minor wounds and deal with the pressing needs of the more grievously wounded. Lily wiped perspiration from her moist brow, willing perseverance in these difficult conditions. Two more ambulance wagons discharged soldiers in all stages of distress. Some had suffered arrow wounds; others, gunshot wounds. A few, as a result of losing their mounts in the thick of the conflict, had broken bones, including Lieutenant Creekmore. Aside from the calm orders of the surgeon, the grinding of his saw and the swish of skirts as the women moved from cot to cot, the only sounds were piteous groans and cries of "Mother" or "Help me."

Dear God, yes, help them and grant them relief from pain. Lily hoped her prayers and those of others would suffice, since unfortunately the fort had been without an assigned chaplain for some months.

Although she recognized several of the wounded, Lily was relieved that so far Caleb appeared to have been spared. That comfort deserted her when patients were unloaded from a late-arriving fourth wagon. She saw him immediately, his eyes closed, his face ashen, his breath coming in faint wheezes. Her legs started to go out from under her, and she had to grab the arm of a nearby soldier to keep from falling. The man shook his head regretfully. "We tried to get Cap out first, but he came to just long enough to order us to remove the others first."

Recovering herself, Lily ran to her father, who had just finished a second amputation. "Papa, come quickly. I fear Captain Montgomery is mortally wounded."

As her father examined the field-dressed shoulder wound which had stained Caleb's jacket a deep red, Lily steeled herself by concentrating her anger at an enemy who had inflicted harm on so fine a man and by praying, *Save him. Save him.*

Ezra beckoned both Lily and Caleb's litter bearers to follow him to the operating table, recently vacated by the amputee. "Lily, I need you to be strong. His only chance depends upon whether I can extract the bullet lodged so close to his heart. If I am successful, I will need you to bathe the wound and suture it closed."

Once more, Lily fought off light-headedness. "Yes, Papa." Her hands shook so that she could hardly imagine how she would be able to thread the needle, much less close the wound. Caleb lay so still, his arms resting at his sides. She picked up his nearer hand, cold to the touch, and held it in her own. She felt the calluses on his palm, saw embedded dirt beneath his fingernails and, to her relief, felt a pulse under her index finger. Her thoughts and emotions whirled. *Focus,* she reminded herself. *You've done this before.* An orderly bared Caleb's shoulder, revealing an ugly-looking open wound. Carrie, her eyes the size of small pancakes, poured chloroform onto a cloth, and Ezra reached for his instrument.

In that moment, a miraculous calm enveloped Lily, and her whole world reduced to the supine body on the table and the function she was to perform. Ezra's face screwed up with concentration. When his initial efforts to probe for the bullet were unsuccessful, his eyes met Lily's from across the table. "I don't know, daughter."

"Please, Papa. Try once more."

Ezra bent to his task and then, by changing his angle, found the bullet. "Aah," he breathed, pulling it from the wound.

Without conscious thought, Lily cleansed the wound and then carefully sutured it shut, thanking God that sewing was her talent. Throughout the procedure, Caleb's respiration remained shallow. She dared not ask her father about his chances. It was enough that Caleb had survived thus far.

The orderlies moved him to a cot near the window where several of his men already lay. Lily was shocked to see that night had fallen. Yet with that realization, she began to feel the wretched ache in the small of her back, the crick in her neck and the fog of exhaustion threatening her. The hospital was quieter now, and she saw the figures of men and women sitting beside the patients, cooling their faces with damp cloths or murmuring encouragement.

She gathered up Caleb's undershirt and jacket, holding them in her arms as a kind of perverse good luck charm. When her father nodded to her in dismissal, she couldn't leave. Instead, she sat on the chair beside Caleb, studying his pale face and willing his recovery. Sleep was necessary as a restorative, but how she wished just once he would open his eyes and whisper her name.

She began to fold his garments. In one pocket she felt a bulge and, inserting her fingers, came into contact with an envelope. Slowly she drew it out and stared at the name on the front—hers. Was it something Caleb had written? Curious, she slit the flap and pulled out a single sheet of paper. The signature took her by surprise. *Sydney Long*.

In the dim light she barely made out the scrawled words.

My dear Miss Lily,
I asked Cap'n Montgomery to give this to you in case I don't make it back. I'm a'scared of this battle, but not of dying. If I pass on, I'll dwell in eternity with my sweetheart, and you know I been a'grieving her sorely. The Almighty knows better than us'ns what we need. So if I'm supposed to be with my beloved now, please write my parents and tell them I've made my peace.
Your friend,
Sydney Long

Tears obscured the sad message. She dabbed at them, then reread the letter. Glancing down at Caleb, then around the room, she felt her heart break. What could possibly be the purpose of the human carnage she saw around her? Where was God in this?

She knew what she had to do next, whether she wanted to or not. Adjusting the sheet around Caleb's shoulders and placing a hand on his warm forehead in blessing, she stood, left instructions with an orderly and walked out of the hospital, across the parade ground toward the carpenter shop.

There, driven into a post by a nail, was a scrawled list she had hoped never to read. Steeling herself, she approached the post. In the dim light of a flickering lantern, she read the names of the five men killed in action. The fourth was *Long, Sydney, Pvt.*

Returning home, Lily saw through her tears the figures of Major and Mrs. Hurlburt sharing an embrace on their front porch. Relieved for Effie, Lily fell into her bed, not pausing to remove her clothes in case she was suddenly called to the hospital. She needed to sleep, but every time she closed her eyes, images of wounded soldiers, looking strangely like David and Caleb, jolted her awake. She was used to dealing with illnesses and the occasional accidental wound, but nothing had prepared her for the numbers and severity of battlefield injuries. Most would survive if they could avoid infection. But Caleb? She stuffed a fist in her mouth to avoid waking Rose with her outcry. Beyond the threat of infection was the specter of pneumonia. He would need constant monitoring.

She pictured him as she had seen him that day at the ball field—young, vigorous, even playful—and at the cemetery where he had listened and calmed her fears. The memory of a sweet baritone singing "Aura

Lee" filled her ears. She rolled over, away from her sister, lest Rose awaken and see her crying. *Is there a possibility we could be more than friends?* Caleb had asked before leaving on this mission. He had expected an answer when he returned, an answer now deferred by his precarious state and one for which she had, as yet, no clear response.

There was no question they were drawn to one another. On her part, could their bond be simply a result of gratitude for his twice saving her or of the ennui of post life? She wiped her tears with the edge of the sheet. All such issues were moot, pending the outcome of his injury. At heart, though, he was special to her.

She lay on her side, knees pulled up to her chest, listening to her sister's soft breathing. In the dark, she began whispering the Twenty-third Psalm. "'The Lord is my shepherd, I shall not want… Yea, though I walk through the valley of the shadow of death, I will fear no evil; for Thou art with me…'" Her heavy eyes fluttered closed and she felt herself drifting away to oblivion. "'…and I will dwell in the house of the Lord forever.'"

Something was fighting her. Fists pummeled her; she struggled but could not escape. Burrowing under a blanket, she resisted, but voices kept calling her. "Hurry!" "Come now!" Surfacing from a distant dream world, she realized no one was pummeling at all, just gently shaking her. Opening her eyes, she beheld Rose standing over her. "Wake up, Lily. Papa needs you in the hospital."

Groggy, Lily sprang from the bed. How long had she been asleep? Rubbing her eyes, she observed the faintest cracks of light seeping through the window. Dawn. She buttoned up the collar of her dress and tried to shake out the creases. Stepping to the mirror, she repaired her hair, all the while filled with alarm. "Tell Papa I'll be there momentarily," she told Rose, who was already hurrying down the stairs.

By the time she arrived at the hospital, some of the patients were stirring and occasional moans betrayed their discomfort. She scanned the room and quickly spotted her father bent over Caleb's cot. With a thudding heart, she hurried toward him. During the night, someone had put an extra pillow beneath his shoulders, so that he was semireclined. Even at a distance, she could see from his flushed face that he was feverish. His hair was matted with sweat, and as she approached, he flung one arm off the cot. "Papa?"

Her father looked up, and in his bloodshot eyes she read both exhaustion and deep sorrow. "The captain is delirious and needs to be kept still. He is fighting infection. You will need to bathe his face and chest with cool water and stay with him lest he begin thrashing about." He glanced around the room. "We have sufficient help for the others." He nodded at a young enlisted man carrying a basin toward them. "Private Nathan will assist you and fetch anything you need."

"The baby!"

Both Lily and her father started at Caleb's sudden harsh cry.

"Get the baby. The baby!" The word *baby* reverberated from the rafters.

Shaking his head, Ezra rose to his feet and handed Lily the damp cloth he'd been using. Lily's throat was paralyzed with fear. "Papa?"

He stood a moment or two without speaking, then pulled her into his arms. "It's in God's hands now."

With a heavy sigh, he released her. "Do what you can for him, Lily."

Lily crumpled into the bedside chair, knowing that no base Corporal Adams or vicious serpent had ever filled her with the terror now consuming her being.

Colors. Firebursts. Reds. Yellows. Flashes of white. Then blankets of black. He kicked his horse, spurring him on, but no matter how vigorously he urged the steed, the beast refused to move. *Help her! Help her, I say.* Dropping the reins, he leaned over, stretching out his arms for the doll. *The doll. I'll save it, little girl.* Then suddenly he was grasping not a doll, but a dry shuck of corn. Where was the little girl? The doll?

A mewling sound like that of a trapped kitten. Where? *The baby! Help the baby!*

A heavy weight crushed his lungs. A savagely painted warrior straddled his chest mouthing words he could neither hear nor understand. Flailing. Flailing. He could fight him off, couldn't he? Couldn't he? Then came the thunderous roar—a cannon blast throwing up blue-clad bodies and great clumps of earth. *Charge!*

Then he was thrashing in cold water, fighting the current, futilely grabbing at tree branches traveling past him in a green haze.

Breathing. Too hard. He couldn't find the word. The one he needed. The one that would make the difference. The cold river water filled his mouth, slithered down his windpipe and clogged his lungs. The word, the word. *Help!*

Every half hour throughout the day, Lily sent Private Nathan to fetch more cool well water. As she bathed

Caleb and smoothed his damp hair back from his fever-ish forehead, she hummed softly. Hymns. The familiar tunes eased her body and brought a kind of suspended peace to her soul. She couldn't explain it, but here in the midst of life and death, surrounded by those victim-ized by man's inhumanity to man, instead of the baf-fled anger at God she had often experienced, she found hope in the tender care being lavished upon the fallen.

Even Caleb's frenzied outbursts seemed God's way of helping him exorcise demons she could only guess at. Someday perhaps he would tell her about whatever baby had taken root in his heart and what doll had been so important to him. He repeated the word *Charge!* at intervals throughout the day, shuddering in the after-math of his order.

When he tossed about, Private Nathan would help her massage his limbs while she crooned lullabies she hoped were among those his mother had sung to him. Even when he slept, he slept fitfully, lashing out at her with his hands. Periodically her father came to check on Caleb, but he offered no encouragement beyond saying, "Keep doing what you're doing."

Toward nightfall, Lily stood and took in the scene. So focused had she been on Caleb that she was sur-prised to see that several of the men had apparently undergone treatment and returned to their barracks. The two amputees were receiving special care from Effie and Rose. Lily was numb with fatigue, but she would not leave her post. Sometimes she thought Ca-leb's fever was breaking, but then it would rage and he would become agitated again. More than anything, one pathetic word, repeated again and again, glued her to the spot. *Help!*

Just after seven, Lily overheard her father speaking with someone at the door. When she glanced around, her jaw dropped. A young woman, barely five feet tall, wearing a simple gray dress and bonnet, was saying clearly, "I am here to see Lieutenant Creekmore." Lily didn't recognize the dark-haired stranger, but couldn't mistake the determination in her voice.

When Ezra pointed toward the nearby bed where Will Creekmore lay, the woman uttered a hurried "Thank God" and made a beeline for his cot. She was only halfway across the room when Will, one arm in a sling, struggled to his feet, swaying with pain. "Oh, Fannie, is it you? Tell me it's you!"

The woman called Fannie arrived at Will's side just in time to hold him up in an embrace that seemed to have no end. "Will, my darling Will." At long last, she pulled back and helped him sit. Even from across the way, Lily could hear the man's sobs of relief. Fannie knelt in front of him, wiping his tears with her handkerchief. "Beloved Will."

He cradled her face in his hands. "I can't believe it's you. That you're not a dream."

"I'm no dream. I'm your betrothed." She brushed back a stray lock of his hair. "If you'll still have me." Lily heard the smile in her voice.

"*Have you?* I can't wait." Will looked around the room then. "Hey, folks. We're going to have a wedding here!"

Scattered applause and muffled laughter greeted his announcement. Beaming at Fannie, Will then said, "Thanks be to God for you, Fannie Jackson. I love you with all my heart."

Moved by the affectionate reunion, Lily turned

away, wondering what had induced a young woman to leave her home and family for life in an alien wilderness. She dipped the cloth in water, wrung it out and bathed Caleb's neck and shoulders. There was no accounting for Fannie's devotion.

Fuzzy. A face. Out there, just beyond his reach. Then light. Behind the face. He lifted his arm, but watched it fall back down. Now he was walking on a path. In the forest. Toward the sun. From the trees, a doe studied him, her limpid eyes full of...what? Love? Then he heard a voice. An angel's voice. He walked faster toward the sound. It was a song he knew. *Mother?*

Warm light bathed him, soothed him.

"Caleb!"

His legs were tired, so tired. He sat down on the path.

"Caleb, don't you dare give up!"

Not his mother, he thought. Then the face was close to his. A woman. Not his mother. An angel?

"Caleb, I want you to squeeze my hand."

Then he felt soft fingers on his hand, the pressure of a palm. Squeeze? He tried.

"Again!"

As he gripped the hand, it felt like a lifeline tugging him back from the forest, back from the sunlight.

With great effort, he opened his eyes and looked into the face. The beautiful face of a woman. He knew her. Like a balloon his heart inflated with ecstasy. Her name. He needed to remember her name. Then the strange, raspy sound of his own voice filled his ears. *Lily?*

In response, another voice thundered. "Caleb, this is

Ezra Kellogg. Keep fighting, lad. I think you're going to make it."

The pretty woman was there again, and something wet was falling from her eyes onto his skin.

Chapter Ten

Throughout the long night, Lily refused to leave Caleb's side except when Rose took her place. His fever had broken, but he was so weak that only by scant teaspoonfuls were they able to force him to sip water or broth. When he opened his eyes, Lily was unsure whether he recognized her. His only words—*angel* and *baby*—were uttered in a hoarse whisper. Rose had brought a small jar of bacon fat to rub on his dry, cracked lips, and every few hours Ezra appeared to change his dressing and examine the wound.

In the wee hours of the morning, Lily, exhausted, rested her weary head on his bed. She was instantly lost in the white gauze of sleep until she was roused by a gentle voice calling her name. With the greatest effort, she sat up, squinting dazedly at the woman standing by her side. Coming into awareness of her surroundings, Lily panicked. "Dear God, Caleb?"

"Your man is asleep. That will hasten his healing more than anything."

Your man? Lily shook her head, trying to reorient herself to the situation. Running a hand through her disheveled hair, she studied the diminutive young woman whose brown eyes were seas of calm.

"Let me introduce myself. I am Fannie Jackson, come to wed Will Creekmore."

Events of the previous night washed over Lily—Fannie's arrival, her romantic reunion with Will and Lily's admiration for the young woman's devotion to the lieutenant. Lily extended her hand. "Welcome to Fort Larned. I'm Lily Kellogg."

Fannie held Lily's hand in both of hers. "I know who you are. Will has told me wonderful things about you, and I am so eager to make your acquaintance. I shall be so in need of a friend here."

Lily reacted with both spontaneous affection and guilt. Even in these few minutes, it was obvious Fannie could, indeed, become a special friend; but if she went to St. Louis, she would disappoint Fannie by leaving Fort Larned.

She paused to gather the sheet around Caleb and adjust his pillow before continuing the conversation. "We are impressed that you would make such a long trip. Was it difficult?"

Fannie smiled. "It had its moments, but nothing could have kept me from coming. I concentrated on Will and God's plan for us to be together."

Lily envied Fannie her certainty. She had thought she knew her destiny: to go to St. Louis and live a cosmopolitan existence. Yet, so great had been her fear for Caleb's life that all thought of the city had been knocked out of her awareness until just this minute. How difficult it had suddenly become to distinguish her own plan from God's. "I envy you, Fannie."

"How so?"

"You seem so certain of your direction."

"God planted love in my heart, and I have never doubted His purpose for me."

"But how do you *know?*"

Fannie began massaging the coiled muscles in Lily's neck. "It just feels right in a way nothing else ever has."

It just feels right. How Lily wished she knew what might "feel right" for her. At this moment, though, questions were all she had. What if she never saw Caleb again? What if she never experienced life at Aunt Lavinia's? What if she was following her own stubborn will, rather than God's? In resignation, she bent her head and for several minutes gave in to the ministrations of Fannie's soothing hands.

Finally Fannie stopped, but not before wrapping Lily's shoulders in a warm embrace. "Why don't you go get some breakfast and take a nap?"

It dawned on Lily that she was ravenous. "Perhaps I will."

"Please do not fret. I will be tending to your man."

There it was again. *Your man.* Lily had neither the energy nor the will to correct her new friend. Ever since the kiss in the cemetery, she had avoided speculation concerning her relationship with Caleb. Was there any way at all by which he could be considered *her* man? If so, she was simply too tired to ponder the implications.

Rather than commenting further, Lily simply said, "Thank you."

"How're you doing, son?"

Caleb pried his eyes open and saw Major Hurlburt standing at his bedside. "I'll make it, sir."

"If determination plays a part in your recovery, I have no doubt of that."

Caleb felt disoriented. "How long have I been here?"

"Nearly a week."

Painfully, Caleb pulled up on one elbow and glanced around the hospital. "The others?"

The major settled in the bedside chair. "We took some casualties."

Caleb closed his eyes against a question he didn't want to ask. "How many?"

"Twelve wounded. Five dead."

He was glad the major hadn't minced words. The toll had been high. "Who?"

"There will be time enough for that, son. Right now, your duty is to get well."

Caleb wasn't sure he would ever be well again, not with the scars of so many comrades lost, not just in the recent battle, but in every conflict in which he'd participated. "I'll do my best." With sudden urgency, another question filled him with dread. "Bucephalus?"

"Your mount is safely home."

Caleb closed his eyes, limp with relief.

After a few moments, the major spoke again. "You've had mighty attentive nursing."

"Lily." Caleb looked away so his commander wouldn't see the emotions threatening to unman him. In the midst of his horrific memories, her name itself was a balm.

"Yes, Lily, but also Rose Kellogg and Fannie Jackson, Creekmore's fiancée."

Caleb racked his fuzzy brain for the information he knew he should be seeking. "The mission? Was it a success?"

The major rubbed a finger under his nose. "From a strategic point of view, yes, but those Indians fought to the death."

Exhausted, Caleb sank back on the pillow. He had so many questions, some that only God could answer. "Thank you for coming, sir," he managed weakly.

The major stood. "No problem, Captain. You work on getting better. I need men like you."

Caleb closed his eyes. The army might need men *like* him, but not *him*. He was leaving this all behind and for the promised "greener pastures" of the Flint Hills. A place of tranquility and peace where he could become a different man.

Eight days after the battle, a chaplain arrived from Fort Riley to conduct the service to honor the dead. The mood at the fort was subdued. It was almost as if the men had too much time to think…and remember. Effie Hurlburt assembled a makeshift choir for the event, and in her spare time after working at the hospital, Lily played the piano for their rehearsals. The entire fort gathered at the cemetery on a hot July morning. The soldiers stood in ranks and the women clustered together.

Lily listened to the singers. Every chorus of "Abide with Me" threatened to undo her, and the final, piteous notes of taps hushed even the birds. The service was more personal for her as a result of her own brother's death at Lookout Mountain and her brief, but poignant encounter with Sydney Long. The young soldier had already known tragedy, but for his life to be cut off so soon…unthinkable. Following the ceremony, she fulfilled the difficult task of writing his parents. She had delayed so that she could describe the service. Yet she knew that mere words, no matter how heartfelt or eloquent, would be of little comfort.

Caleb, still weak and chafing about the slow pace of his recovery, had wanted to attend the service, but Ezra Kellogg would not permit it. Lily knew Caleb felt it was his duty to be with his men to bid farewell to their comrades. "They were good soldiers," he had told her. "It was an honor to fight side by side. I just wish…" He had clamped his mouth shut, unable to continue.

Because the chaplain planned to stay at Fort Larned for several weeks, Will and Fannie took advantage of his presence to plan their wedding. Fannie was living temporarily with the Hurlburts, and she and Effie were thriving on making arrangements. Lily continued to be in awe of Fannie's equanimity. "Naturally, I miss my parents and sister," she confided one evening to Lily. "I would've liked them to be at my wedding, but it was more important that I be with Will."

The officers' wives had pitched in to purchase a rich, amber-colored material for a wedding dress. Lily had agreed to make the gown, and deep in a chest containing her mother's clothes, she had found some antique lace with which to trim the collar and cuffs. She was humbled and pleased when Fannie asked her to stand up with her and Will. If Caleb was sufficiently recovered, Will hoped he would serve as his best man. Ezra was pleased with how well Will's bones were mending, but the eager bridegroom had said whether his arm was healed or not, nothing would postpone the wedding.

Working on Fannie's gown was therapy for Lily. She could lose herself in darts and hems and briefly forget the sad events of recent days. Watching Fannie and Will was a tonic in itself. Their obvious love spread a kind of magic wherever they went and occasioned many a smile.

One evening as Lily was leaving the hospital, Caleb detained her. "I'd like to go outdoors."

"You are too weak to walk that far."

"Not by myself. But if you helped…?" He hoisted himself to his feet, pausing to get his legs under him. "If you put your arm around my waist, like so—" he guided her arm "—and I rested my hand on your shoulder, we could make it."

She staggered slightly when he shifted his weight onto her and wrapped his arm around her shoulder. Apprehensive, she braced for their first step. "I'm not sure this is a good idea."

Sounding more like the old Caleb than he had since his injury, he said, "To the contrary, it's a fine idea."

Was it her imagination or had he squeezed her shoulder? "We must proceed slowly," she said primly.

"Slow is good." They advanced toward the door. "I am so weary of confinement."

"You've been very ill. Healing takes time."

Just outside the door was a row of benches, and Caleb, supported by Lily, slowly eased himself onto a seat. His breath came in gasps. Even that small amount of exertion had cost him dearly. "Here." He patted the seat beside him. "Sit with me."

Lily could no more refuse than fly. Besides, if she didn't stay at his side, who would help him back to bed?

"'Healing takes time,'" he repeated, expelling a long sigh. "There will never be enough time."

The resignation in his voice caused Lily to study

him carefully. His hands clenched his knees and his jaw was rigid. "Are you talking about your wound… or something more?"

"Oh, the injury will heal," he said dismissively, "but any man who has seen battle will tell you that though scars may form, there are some wounds that are with you until Gabriel's trumpet blows."

This was the moment for which she had waited, but would he risk confiding in her? What she said next would make all the difference. "Caleb, you would honor me with your trust. Perhaps you could begin by telling me about the baby."

"The baby?" His expression went blank, and Lily immediately regretted making an assumption.

"When you were delirious, there were two memories that recurred over and over in your speech. One was something about a little girl and a doll. The other was the word *baby*. You kept repeating it with great agitation."

"Washita."

"I beg your pardon?"

"The Battle of the Washita River. More even than my experiences in the War between the States, it haunts my dreams." He seemed to go into another world, one inaccessible to her.

After a few moments, she prompted him. "The baby?"

He shrugged. "I couldn't save it."

"I don't understand."

"It isn't a pretty story."

"If it affects you, I want to hear it." Lily sensed they were on the verge of passing into strange new territory.

Briefly he recounted the nature of the mission they

were to undertake with Black Kettle and his encampment. "But something went horribly wrong. To this day, I don't understand what. One minute we were poised to disperse the Indians there, and in the next, we were thrust into horrific confusion. They fired on us, and our men began slaughtering them—men, women and children." He paused with a ragged hiccup. "I tried to stop them, but there was confusion on every side. I could not believe the evidence of my eyes and it plagues me still."

He paused, and Lily knew better than to interrupt the memories now spewing from a place deep within him. When he resumed the story, it was as if to leave out any detail would dishonor the victims.

"There was bloodshed all around, but two images seared themselves into my brain. The first is of a little girl, not more than seven I wager, who still clutched a sad little cornhusk doll with a blue dress. The poor child lay on her back, eyes vacant, shot through the chest."

With economy of motion, Lily laid her hand atop one of his, now busy kneading the fabric of his trousers.

"Nearby was a woman lying facedown, her long braid blood-soaked. She must've been shot protecting her baby. I could hear the baby crying, oh, so weakly, but when I attempted to dismount to save the child, I myself was attacked. By the time the gunfire ceased and I returned to the scene, the infant had suffocated." His tortured eyes sought hers. "I have killed men in battle, both in the recent war and now fighting Indians, but I never signed on to be part of a massacre. And that's what the Battle of the Washita was. As God is my witness, I never would have gunned down a woman or child. But I was there. I am guilty." He swiped a sleeve across his eyes. "I can't do this anymore, Lily," he said, his voice shaking.

Lily had no notion how to respond. She had wanted him to be more forthcoming, to share himself with her. Well, her wish had been fulfilled, but in no way had she been prepared for the anguish of his nightmarish memories. Healing? She realized she didn't know the first thing about this kind of wound.

"So there. Now you know what kind of man I am. Damaged."

Reaching up, she turned his ashen face toward her and gazed purposefully into his desolate eyes. "Here's what I know. You are a man who has seen what no one should ever have to witness, a man who grieves for innocent souls caught up in violence, a man who cares deeply about human life." She hesitated before adding, "A man who will always have my utmost respect."

"Those are fine words, but you may change your mind after you think about what I've told you. Until the end of my days, I will live with what I've done. That is not a burden to put upon another."

She wanted to say she would gladly accept that burden, yet how might such a sentiment be interpreted? Would she be committing to a deepening of their relationship? Her mind blocked further contemplation of that question. Now was not the time. Instead, she offered what solace she could. "Caleb, God has forgiven you. I have forgiven you. Can you forgive yourself?"

"I despair. Where was God that day? Where is He now?"

"God was present in your compassion, with the mother who so fiercely protected her child and with every man who ministered to another on that battle-field. In the same way, He is here holding our hands and healing our broken hearts." Lily had no idea where her answer had come from. Perhaps divine inspiration?

"I'd like to believe that." He straightened up and his voice grew stronger. "I will try to believe that."

"We can pray for such understanding." She studied his pale face and trembling hands. "I fear our conversation has tired you. Let me help you back to your bed."

On the return trip, his body hunched with exhaustion and pain, and she took the full brunt of his weight. He seemed too tired to utter a single word. She eased him onto his bed and poured him a drink of water.

Finally he spoke. "You must think me a coward."

She guided the cup to his mouth. "Quite the contrary. To have confessed what you just did is an ultimate form of bravery. It took courage to reveal yourself to another."

He swallowed, then waved the cup aside and fell back on the pillow. "I shouldn't have told you such a gruesome story. It is not fit for a woman's ears."

"Caleb, your trust in me is a gift."

"Trust. Yes, that must be it." He sighed again and closed his eyes.

Lily tiptoed from his side, knowing that after such an ordeal, he needed his sleep.

Caleb lay still, his eyes shut, listening to Lily's skirt brush the floor as she moved away. *Trust?* What had he been thinking? How had she wormed that story out of him? Lily was the woman he loved, yet he had undoubtedly shocked her. From boyhood, he had been taught to honor and protect women, to treat them with gentleness, but what had he done? Spit out the venom built up within him during his years in the army and revealed his own dark nature. The weird thing was that, despite his shame, he also felt so great a relief it was scary. Like when he was a child and held his emotions in check until, finally, at night he loosed tears upon his pillow.

His lungs ached now with the breath he held. He didn't know if he would ever breathe easily again until he next saw Lily. He didn't want her pity, nor would he welcome any attempts she might make to heal his past. He threw an arm over his face. What did he want? He knew. He'd spent much of his recuperation thinking about it. Especially after today, though, he had little prayer of receiving it. He wanted her to look at him with unconditional love, to accept him with all his flaws and promise to be his forever.

He rolled onto his side, away from prying eyes, and, at last, asked God for forgiveness…and another chance with Lily.

When he awoke from a deep sleep a few hours later, the hospital was dimly lit. Only a few of those wounded in the recent engagement were still there, joined by one or two others with seasonal maladies. He roused himself, sat up and threw his legs over the side of the bed. One thing had become clear to him in the night. Self-pity would ill serve him; it was the resort of a coward. What had happened to him in the past was unchangeable, but perhaps the future was still in his hands. His immediate goal was to recover his strength. Then to pursue Lily with all his heart. That was a battle too important to contemplate losing.

* * *

The next afternoon Lily was surprised and pleased to find Caleb sitting at a small table reading and looking rested. She had fretted through the night about the physical and emotional strain to which he had subjected himself, both walking outside and then sharing his horrific memories. Unspeakable as his descriptions were, she knew there were many more wrenching details he could have shared, more than any woman could possibly imagine. The self-control it took for most of these battle-scarred soldiers to function as well as they did was admirable. Beneath that veneer, Lily suspected that what they most needed was understanding and tenderness.

She approached Caleb and stood over him. "What are you reading?"

When he looked up at her, she saw none of the fatigue of the previous afternoon. "I'm boning up on *Paradise Lost.* Remember, you promised me a discussion of Milton's version of Eve's fall."

"Be that as it may, I've had quite enough of serpents lately."

"But the one in the poem talks."

"He talks, yes, but as a tempter. Oily he is. Can you really blame Eve for biting into the apple?"

"You women always fall for a glib tongue."

She was about to whack him with her handkerchief when she noticed the mischievous grin on his face. "Sir, I think you are teasing me, and, in truth, that is welcome. You must be on the mend."

"I hope so. I've lost too much time here."

"Your body needed that time," Lily reminded him. He sobered. "As did my soul."

It was his only reference to their conversation of the previous afternoon. She could pursue that train of thought, but that choice was best left to him. "Healing can't be rushed."

"I've heard you say that before, Miss Kellogg."

She smiled. "It's sound advice."

"And I will heed it, though with a strong dose of impatience." He pointed to the vacant chair across the table. "Do you have time to sit for a spell or is duty calling you?"

She glanced around the room to satisfy herself that there were no pressing needs among the patients. "I would like that." She sat down. "Especially because I have received a letter that might interest you." She reached in her apron pocket and pulled out a piece of paper. "This is from Moses."

"Please, read."

"'Miss Lily, you bin good I hope. Ole Massa snake bin keepin' in his hole?'"

Caleb winked at her. "If only Moses knew. Those snakes follow you like bees to honey."

"Let's not talk about it." Lily smoothed the wrinkled page and continued.

"My post is Fort Sill in Injun Territory. It's hot, missy. Like burning coal cinders. Officers keep us busy, but they a good lot, by and large. I hope you safe. I don't forget how nice you be to me."

Lily folded the letter and returned it to her pocket. "It's signed 'Your true friend, Moses.'"

"Your kindness and generosity of spirit obviously meant a lot to him."

"As his bravery and selflessness did to me." She shook her head sadly. "If God created all of us in His image, why can't we get along?"

"I pray unity is God's ultimate plan. Until then, we fight the devil within us, I guess."

Rather than continue with so deep a subject, she attempted to lighten the mood. "Clever, Captain. Now you've brought us right back to *Paradise Lost* and Satan's starring role." She rose and in a mock maternal tone said, "No more, sir, of serpents. This Eve has duties to perform, and they don't include apples."

When she turned to leave, he grasped her by the wrist. "Before you go… Milton also said that we can make a hell of Heaven or a heaven of Hell." His eyes sought hers. "Lily, you have helped make a heaven of my hell." He dropped her wrist, yet she remained rooted to the spot, speechless. "You have restored my trust."

The remainder of the day, she replayed their final exchange, reveling in his compliment, yet feeling both the full weight of the responsibility he had placed in her and her anxiety about fulfilling whatever it was he wanted from her. What had started as friendship and simple attraction had escalated into something else, something she wasn't sure she could handle, at least not without hurting Caleb, who was already so vulnerable. Or was she fooling herself?

A week later, Fannie stood admiring herself in Effie's full-length mirror while Lily, on hands and knees, measured the hem of the wedding dress. "You are a wiggle worm. Hold still."

"I'm so excited. Lily, I never dared dream of such a splendid gown."

Effie bustled into the room, bearing a small notebook and pencil. "I am off to the sutler's to buy ingredients for the cake. I pray the man has vanilla in stock."

Fannie laughed. "No matter. The wedding will be perfect regardless of what happens."

"How can you say that?" Lily mumbled with pins in her mouth.

"Because I am marrying my Will. All the rest is just, oh, dear, I'm afraid I'm about to make a joke, icing on the cake." Effie hooted and Lily spat pins all over the floor, reflecting that since Fannie's arrival she'd laughed more than she had in a great long while.

After Effie departed, Lily helped Fannie out of the nearly completed gown and folded it carefully. While Fannie dressed, Lily poured two glasses of the lemonade Effie had left for them. They carried the drinks onto the porch where, thankfully, a breeze made the heat bearable. Fannie turned her big brown eyes on Lily. "I know we haven't been acquainted long, but I am so very fond of you. Do you mind if I ask you a personal question?"

"There are no secrets between true friends. Please."

"How do you feel about Captain Montgomery?"

"Caleb?" Lily blushed. "He is a fine man and a good friend."

"That's the way Will feels about him, too. He says he's never had a better comrade." Fannie pursed her lips as if weighing her words, then went on. "He's in love with you, you know."

Lily gaped. "Love?" Yet even as she expressed

doubt, she was overcome by a certainty she had avoided acknowledging. "Surely you are mistaken."

"I think not. Will came to that conclusion even before I arrived. I, too, have seen how the captain looks at you, the way his eyes follow you as you move around the hospital." She shook her head decisively. "If Will and I are any judge of such matters, the man is totally besotted."

Lily set the cold glass of lemonade on the porch railing and then wrapped her arms around her waist in a futile attempt to contain her emotions. "No, no."

Fannie quirked an eyebrow. "Come now, my friend. Surely you have noticed something."

"I fear I have no experience with matters of the heart."

"Well, you better be getting some, because, my dear, I think that horse has already left the barn."

Lily rocked back and forth nervously, trying to recapture her moments with Caleb. Any single one of them could be considered innocent. But taken as a whole? And then…the kiss. "What do I do?"

Fannie smiled as if at a wayward child. "What do you want to do?"

Lily had never felt so at sea. "I don't know."

"But you admit it is possible that Caleb could be in love with you."

Helplessly, Lily nodded.

"What about you? Are you in love with him?"

The thought was preposterous. Granted, she had enjoyed the fluttery feelings of attraction and admiration. But love? No serpent of Milton's had ever planted such seeds of confusion as Fannie just had. "I… I can't be."

"Why ever not?"

"Because I'm leaving soon." Lily rushed on to avoid thinking about the shocked look on Fannie's face. "I'm visiting my aunt in St. Louis. It's my dream come true."

Fannie folded her hands in her lap and didn't speak for some time. "Only you know what's best for you. I could tell you not to go, not to turn your back on love, but I won't."

"Perhaps I will find love in St. Louis."

"Perhaps," Fannie said unconvincingly. "May I ask a favor? Please consider your future carefully. Caleb is a fine man whose like you may not find again." She rose from the chair then and came to kneel at Lily's side. "Whatever happens, I am your friend, Lily, and I want only what makes you happy. Forgive me for upsetting you."

"In speaking your mind, you have only done what true friends do."

"I, too, had an important choice to make about whether to come here and marry Will. In my confusion, I learned that all I could do was turn that decision over to God."

"You truly believe God knows what is best for us, that He will provide an answer?"

"I wouldn't be here if I didn't."

Just then Effie came striding toward them, a huge grin on her face. "Vanilla," she shouted triumphantly. "I have it!"

The day then became so busy that it was only that evening in bed that Lily could permit herself to consider the huge questions Fannie had raised. The more she thought about Caleb, the more wide-awake she became. Could it be? She couldn't deny that he often had sought out her company. Protected her from danger. Offered gestures of affection. Was that love?

And what of her feelings? Others could have attended to Caleb after his wounding. The truth was that not only had she stayed by his side to nurse him, but no force, however powerful, could've dragged her away.

All of that aside, he had opened his soul to her, an act of such vulnerability that it had brought tears to her eyes. Yes, there was no doubt. He trusted her.

She lay awake until dawn, her conscience stabbed by the biggest question of all. Was she capable of shattering the trust of a man whom she, indeed, might love in return?

Chapter Eleven

Over the next few days, Lily found it difficult to act natural around Caleb. Ever since her conversation with Fannie, she was self-consciously aware of his eyes upon her, and she found herself overanalyzing everything he said to her. Her friend seemed so sure of her observations, but, then, Fannie knew about love—what it looked and sounded like. Lily, on the other hand, had no experience to guide her. She would like to believe Fannie was embellishing the situation, but deep down, Lily knew something was different about her present relationship with Caleb, and that knowledge both thrilled and troubled her.

Fortunately, as of the day before, Lily didn't have to interact with him at the hospital. Her father had dismissed him to his quarters and ordered his duties curtailed. Now she saw Caleb only by chance across the parade ground or among other people. It seemed to her that he, too, might be experiencing the new awkwardness between them. Perhaps he regretted confiding his battle stories.

Lily, blessedly, had other thoughts to occupy her mind. Fannie and Will's wedding was to be the next Saturday, and the women of the fort were in a frenzy of baking and decorating. The officers and their families plus the men of Will's troop were invited guests. Among those newly assigned to Fort Larned was a violinist who would provide the service music. Other musicians among the men would play for the dancing to follow the ceremony. Caleb had agreed to move in with a couple of bachelor officers so the newlyweds could have privacy. Fannie could hardly contain her excitement, and Will walked around grinning like a well-fed puppy.

The night before the wedding, a hard rain fell, bringing pleasant temperatures the following morning and renewing the drooping vegetation. By noon, all the ladies were dressed in their Sunday best while the soldiers had donned their least threadbare uniforms. The commissary was festooned with gaily colored ribbons collected from hope chests and sewing baskets, and two vases of wildflowers decorated the front of the room.

At precisely one-thirty, the chaplain, a gnomelike man with a cherubic smile, stepped up to face the congregation. Lily waited in the back with Fannie, radiant in her new gown, and Major Hurlburt, who would stand in for her father. Effie had arranged Fannie's hair in a ringleted upsweep, and from her sparkling eyes to the tip of her toes, the bride was, quite simply, breathtaking.

Lily smoothed her own full blue skirt, then handed Fannie the small white Bible she had chosen to carry.

Just as the violinist began "Sheep May Safely Graze," Fannie drew Lily close in an embrace. Lily had just time to say, "Much joy," before it was her turn to process toward the chaplain—and Caleb, who stood beside Will. Fans rustled and heads turned as she made her way down the aisle. Not daring to look at Caleb, she kept her eyes lowered until she took her place at the front.

Then Fannie made her entrance on the major's arm, and whispered exclamations filled the room. "What a beauty!" and "Lucky man, that." Effie beamed, as if she single-handedly had produced this vision of a bride. Will had eyes only for Fannie. As Lily pivoted to face the chaplain, Caleb caught her attention and smiled. Despite her efforts to remain calm, her trip-hammer heart betrayed her.

Will earnestly repeated his vows, clutching Fannie's hand as if he would never relinquish it. "For better for worse, in sickness and in health, to love and to cherish, until we are parted by death." What depths of love it would take to sustain such devotion. A sudden image of her parents surfaced. They had lived that promise. As her mother had known, life could be hard. How much more difficult would it have been without love?

Lost in such musing, Lily was deaf to the chaplain's words until she roused to hear, "I now pronounce you man and wife. Those whom God hath joined together, let no man put asunder."

Will traced a finger down Fannie's cheek, then turned and offered her his arm. Suddenly wistful, Lily bowed her head. "Lily?" Caleb materialized at her side. "Shall we?"

They followed the bride and groom out into the sunshine. Before others departed the building, Will enfolded Fannie in his arms and kissed her with enthusiasm. The bride's lilting laugh provided a grace note to the nuptials, Lily thought. As the newlyweds began greeting their guests, an aura of happiness enveloped them, and, looking on, Lily knew this was what Fannie's certainty looked like.

Caleb smiled down at Lily. "I doubt my friend could be any happier."

"Nor the bride any lovelier."

He lowered his voice. "No lovelier than her maid of honor."

Lily was loath to look up, afraid what his eyes might reveal…and hers. "You've just never seen me so dressed up." She disengaged her arm from his and twirled about, showing off her dress.

"Your gown is pretty," he conceded, "but I was talking about the woman wearing it."

She had thought to deflect his admiration, but he had countered her ploy. "You flatter me, sir."

"Whoa. I thought we had pledged honesty to one another. Flattery is not among my weapons of choice."

"Then I must do as my mother always taught me in the face of a compliment."

"And what is that?"

"Say, 'Thank you.' So, Captain Montgomery, thank you."

"You deserve compliments, Lily. For your beauty and for your character."

"Surely you are still ill, and it is your feverish brain talking."

He threw back his head and laughed. "No, I am

not ill, but I think I have found a way to get you flustered. That's an achievement. You're not usually so flappable."

"And you like getting me flustered?"

"Of course. I spent years teasing a younger sister. Surely I can't let all that experience go to waste."

She mustered a begrudging grin. "There will be food going to waste if we don't join the bride and groom at the table."

The post cooks had roasted a pig for the festivities. In addition to the tender pork, the serving table was laden with baked beans, potatoes, fresh vegetables, cole slaw, melon slices and a tempting assortment of desserts made by the women. Caleb, Lily and the Hurlburts sat at a table with the bride and groom. Dancing followed, and it was comical to watch some of the soldiers dancing with one another.

Lily had been concerned about Caleb's stamina, but he insisted on dancing both with Fannie and with her. When he took her in his arms, she couldn't look at him, but instead concentrated on the feel of his palm on her back, guiding her across the floor. Relaxing into his grip, she felt as light as a butterfly. The Hurlburts glided past, and Effie called out, "You two put the rest of us to shame."

Caleb spun Lily around and then whispered, "We are pretty good together, don't you think?"

Lily gazed up at him, but lost in his twinkling eyes, forgot what she had intended to say.

"I'll take that as a 'yes,'" he said.

Where had she lost utter control of the situation? In the romance of the wedding? The contagious joy of the celebration? Or something else altogether? The magnetism of the handsome captain?

When the music ended, Caleb escorted her to her seat, but soon relinquished her to others seeking a dance partner. Throughout the afternoon's festivities, Lily was aware of Caleb's beaming approval, as if they were a couple and he was merely indulging the other men.

By early evening, the party wound down, and accompanied by noise makers, applause and laughter, the guests escorted Fannie and Will to their quarters. Watching as Will lifted Fannie with his good arm and carried her over the threshold, Lily uttered a silent prayer for their happiness.

Beside her, Caleb sighed and Lily sensed melancholy come over him. She touched his arm. "Already missing your bunk mate?"

"Walk with me?" He tucked her arm in his and began strolling toward the cemetery. "Bunk mates come and go. No, I was just remembering." They walked a few more paces before he spoke again. "I was almost married once."

Curiosity won out over discretion. "What happened?"

He chuckled wryly. "It's not a very original story. Rebecca and I were young, we were engaged to be married, and then the war came."

Lily said nothing, waiting for him to continue.

"I marched off with my fellow soldiers, she promised to be true to me, and many, many months passed. More than either of us had imagined. The thought of her was part of what kept me going."

Lily dreaded hearing the rest, even as she knew he needed to tell it. "But something happened?"

He barked bitterly. "Oh, yes. My best friend happened. It seems while I was off fighting a war, Rebecca took a fancy to Abner. After all, he was right there at home with her. A heart condition prevented him from serving the Union."

"How hurt you must have been."

"Hurt. Angry. Ashamed." They had reached the cemetery bench. "Sit with me, Lily. I want to tell you something."

As she settled on the bench, she reflected that she had never seen Caleb so serious. He picked up her hand and held it tightly. "After I lost Rebecca, I swore off women. I threw all my strength and effort into being the best army officer I could be. I enjoyed the camaraderie of my fellows and satisfied myself that happiness did not depend upon having a sweetheart. That was a lie. There comes a time for most men, I believe, when they miss the companionship and love of a woman." He swallowed, then turned to look directly at her. "That time has come for me."

Lily desperately wanted him to stop with those words just as she equally desperately wanted to hear what he would say next. She sensed they were teetering on a precipice in their relationship, and she wished she could halt time.

"You, Lily," he said, "you have made the difference."

She knew he was waiting for her to comment, but for the life of her, she couldn't think. "I... I don't know what to say. I'm flattered, naturally, but—"

"You don't have to say anything now. But I couldn't

continue holding in my feelings. We pledged honesty." His voice fell to a whisper. "I'm in love with you, Lily Kellogg."

Her breath caught in her throat. This couldn't be happening. This was not the plan. Yet at the same time, as she gazed into his eyes, so full of both pain and love, she wanted only to make him complete. "Honesty..." She thought about the importance of what she said next. "You are dear to me, Caleb, and I am honored by your declaration. I know little of love. It would be premature for me to respond."

He raised her hand to his lips and tenderly kissed it. "You need time."

"I do. You have given me much to consider." She struggled to go on. "My fear is that I will hurt you."

He stood and pulled her to her feet. "That is a risk I am willing to take. I have said what I needed to say. Now then, may I escort you home?"

They walked in silence most of the way to her door. Never had Lily known such conflicting emotions. Worst of all, she had not been totally honest with him, and she hated herself for that. She had not told him about St. Louis.

The next day as Caleb went about his duties, he found himself second-guessing yesterday's conversation with Lily. He hadn't really expected her to swoon at his feet, yet he had hoped for something more promising than her careful response. While it had been a huge relief to unburden himself to her, he had been perturbed by her concern about hurting him. He didn't need more rejection, but why had she so immediately considered that possibility?

In fairness, perhaps he was rushing things, but with his army stint drawing to a close in a month, he had little time for courtship. He grinned at the irony of that word—exactly what Will had accused him of and now here he was, knee-deep in it. He wanted to paint for Lily the vision of their home amid the beauty and sweep of the Flint Hills, of children growing up with the freedom of wide-open spaces, of a lifetime of love and devotion. The challenge was having so little time to persuade her.

He drew up short in his thinking. He didn't want to have to persuade her of anything; he wanted her to embrace the future he hoped for them. Ultimately, however, her decision was out of his control. If they were meant to be together, then it would happen.

To that end, before supper, he made his way to the hospital. He had already observed Lily walking toward her mother's grave site and hoped to catch Ezra Kellogg alone. The surgeon was in his office, bent over a book. Caleb tapped on the door. "Could I have a word, sir?"

Ezra closed the book and took off his spectacles. "Of course. Are you having difficulties, son?"

"I fatigue more easily and still haven't full use of my shoulder, but that's not why I'm here."

Ezra pointed to a chair. "Have a seat. What can I do for you?"

Caleb sat down and considered how to phrase his request. "It surely has come to your attention that Lily and I have been spending considerable time together. She is a talented, compassionate nurse. Beyond that, I find her to be a woman of character and grace of whom I am quite fond." He felt beads of perspiration forming on his brow and decided to cut to the chase. "I have come seeking your permission to court Lily."

Ezra stared across the desk at him as if searching out his hidden flaws. "'Fond,' are you?" The word sounded somehow tainted in the surgeon's mouth.

Caleb rubbed his palms on his thighs. "That is not quite accurate." Lily's father was not making this easy. "I am in love with your daughter."

Caleb detected the suggestion of a smile in the man's gaze. "Then why didn't you say so in the first place?"

"What is in my heart didn't make it to my lips, but my feelings are no less genuine for my dissembling."

"Does she reciprocate your feelings?"

"I don't know. I certainly hope so. I have expressed my love for her, but I didn't feel it appropriate to ask for her hand until I spoke with you."

"Admirable."

Was the surgeon playing with him? Thus far Caleb had no sense of the man's reactions. "She asked for time."

"Time, yes. Never good to rush into these things."

"Ordinarily I would agree. However, I will be mustering out of the army sometime around mid-August."

"Does Lily know that?"

"Not yet. I respect her need for time. I don't want my leaving to pressure a response from her."

Ezra pulled out a handkerchief, picked up his eyeglasses and proceeded to clean them. Caleb waited, trying to conceal his discomfort. Finally, the surgeon spoke. "My daughters are dear to me, and I want them to be loved and cherished. You, Captain, are a worthy gentleman, but I will neither encourage nor discourage your suit. Like all girls, Lily has ambitions and dreams for herself on which may well depend her future happiness. If you fit into those plans, I would be pleased. Meanwhile, you have my permission to press your suit." The surgeon rose and extended his hand across the desk. "Best wishes, son."

Caleb thanked the man for his support and made as hasty an exit as was prudent. He hadn't achieved a ringing endorsement, but he admired the surgeon's commitment to his daughters' well-being.

Walking back to his quarters, Caleb was stunned to realize he lacked an important piece of the puzzle. Ezra Kellogg had referred to Lily's ambitions and dreams. The more he thought about that statement, the more Caleb realized he hadn't the least notion what Lily's ambitions and dreams were.

"I thought I'd find you here." Fannie plopped down on the ground beside Lily. "You come here often, don't you?"

"I hope it doesn't seem morbid, but I feel my mother's presence here." Lily patted the mown grass of the grave.

"You were close?"

"Very. Only now that she's gone do I realize how many lessons she taught me."

"Like?"

"Like doing for others. Like how the power of love helps get folks through hardships. Like the need to appreciate each and every day on this earth."

"A wise woman. I've certainly been appreciating the past two days since the wedding." Fannie's face lit up. "I have officially begun my life as Mrs. William Creekmore."

"And?" Lily leaned forward, as if to tease details from her friend.

"And… I am so blessed. Oh, Lily, you can't imagine how glorious it is to lie in the arms of your beloved and know it will ever be thus in this lifetime."

Lily shivered. Why couldn't she so readily identify her feelings for Caleb? Did Caleb feel about her the way Fannie did about Will? "I am happy for you."

"Thank you, dear friend. I would wish this same happiness for you." Fannie cocked her head inquiringly. "Do you have anything to tell me?"

Lily's blush gave her away.

"You do! I knew it!" Fannie scooted closer. "Tell me."

Lily felt sudden panic. She hadn't intended anyone to know about Caleb's profession of love. She could hardly find words. "I don't know where to begin."

Fannie covered Lily's hands with her own. "At the beginning, of course, but before you start, please know I will keep any confidences to myself." Then she sat back, permitting Lily time to gather her thoughts.

"Oh, Fannie, I'm so confused."

"Caleb?"

Lily nodded. "We had such a fine friendship."

"Had?"

"We could talk so easily, we both enjoy literature…"

"And he's handsome."

"Yes, that, too, but mainly I just enjoyed his company. Then when he was injured—"

"You could hardly leave his side. Did you think no one else could nurse him satisfactorily?"

Lily chewed her bottom lip. Why had she been so devoted a nurse to Caleb? "No, but—"

"It wasn't only about your patient. You needed to be with your man. That was obvious to all of us in the hospital."

"But he's not my man!" Lily's emotions were spiraling out of control. Why was everyone forcing her to deal with her feelings about Caleb?

"Perhaps not. He would like to be, though, wouldn't he?"

Lily hung her head, all the fight draining out of her. "Yes," she murmured. Figuring she might as well go on, she added, "He told me he is in love with me."

Rather than giving a hoot of triumph, Fannie squeezed her hands, then, relinquishing them, sat back. "Now what?"

"I wish I knew. I don't want to hurt him. I really don't, but—"

"You're leaving." Fannie sighed with resignation. "Be sure you know your own heart, Lily. Then follow it, as I did mine, wherever that may lead you."

Lily closed her eyes, wishing she could have Fannie's certitude. "I care a great deal for Caleb."

"But you also have your dream."

"Yes."

"Pray, Lily. God will guide you." Fannie gathered her skirt and stood. "Take some time here with your mother." Then she slipped away, leaving Lily no more certain of her feelings than she had been before talking with Fannie.

Later that evening while Rose was visiting with Virginia Brown, Ezra and Lily sought the cooler air of the front porch. They sat in companionable silence for some time, Lily playing and replaying events of the past two days, no nearer to reaching any conclusions.

"Are you still determined to go visit Lavinia?" The creak of Ezra's rocker filled the silence.

"She says she will send tickets."

"Daughter, that wasn't my question."

"I think I'll go."

"That doesn't sound definitive. What's the problem?"

How could she answer without giving away more than she cared to? She simply shrugged.

"Your mother would be able to get it out of you."

"I miss her."

"As do I." He rocked awhile. "Since Mathilda isn't here, I guess it's up to me to ferret out the cause of your lack of enthusiasm. Caleb Montgomery. Am I right?"

"Papa, I don't know what to do." Even to her own ears, her voice sounded strangled.

"One thing you mustn't do is toy with that fine young man's feelings. He has asked my permission to court you."

Lily's heart sank. She'd had no idea Caleb would take such a step so soon. "He mustn't."

"Too late, my dear. Do you care for him?"

"Yes, but—"

"There can be no *but*'s. Your mother and I knew that. A good marriage is based on unshakable commitment. No matter the challenges, there can be no looking back and asking 'What if?'"

Lily thought she might very well love Caleb. But did she love him enough?

Her father went on. "Would you live to regret giving up your St. Louis experience for a man? For Caleb?

Are you willing to risk losing him if you make the trip? These are hard questions, but ones you must answer, Lily. Your mother would ask them, too."

"I know." Even embraced by her father's concern and love, Lily still felt alone. All she could do was heed Fannie's advice. Pray for guidance.

Chapter Twelve

Caleb waited a couple of days, deferring a conversation he and Lily needed to have, one fraught with uncertainty. At the fort, it was difficult to find opportunities for privacy, but the cemetery was a place where few ventured—and one place he knew Lily frequented. As was her custom, after she finished her hospital duties, she ambled toward her mother's grave, seemingly preoccupied. He afforded her a few minutes before he approached her. "Lily?"

When she looked up, he noticed the stress lines creasing her forehead. "Caleb, what are you doing here?"

"Following you." She didn't seem overjoyed to see him. "I believe we have cause to talk more honestly with one another."

Lily glanced around, apparently satisfying herself that they were alone. "Could we walk in the cool shade by the river?"

He offered his arm, and they made their way in silence down the path. To be so near her and yet feel so distant was agony. "I've missed you," he said quietly.

She kept walking, head lowered.

"I hope my declaration has not offended you."

At last, she stopped and gazed up at him. "On the contrary, you honored me."

"I fear I took a great deal for granted. You may know I spoke with your father."

He received a nod of confirmation.

"My intentions are serious. Though it is difficult, I am giving you time. After speaking with your father, I realized I have not been as sensitive to your feelings as I should have been and perhaps have jumped to some conclusions."

"I don't understand...."

They reached the fallen log where they had rested the day of the baseball game. He helped her sit, then joined her, knowing that much depended on explaining himself clearly. "I have selfishly considered my own interests and plans, assuming you might share them. In thinking about it, I wondered if I had ever communicated my dreams or, more important, inquired about yours. I love you, but love can only sustain a relationship when two people have a common vision of their life together. Maybe it will assist your deliberations if we speak more openly about our hopes and expectations."

"You are right." Lily reached down and plucked up a blade of grass, worrying it in her fingers. "I have not intentionally withheld anything from you. I have little experience in matters of the heart and did not recognize the depth of your feelings. Before, there seemed little purpose to be served in baring one's soul. I do not want you to think me idly flirtatious. I enjoyed our times together without considering the consequences. Perhaps

I was naive. Now I see that you deserve to know what prevents me from encouraging you further."

As if cold hands had seized his throat, Caleb could hardly find his voice. Where he had sought that very encouragement, he was to be denied it. "I am reluctant to hear what you have to say, but our pledge of honesty compels me to ask you to continue."

"I have plans to leave Fort Larned soon."

She couldn't have said anything that would have shocked him more. "Leave? Why? Where?"

She discarded the blade of grass and laced her fingers together. "My mother's sister Lavinia lives in St. Louis. She is quite well off and moves in fine society. For much of our girlhood, Mother encouraged Rose and me someday to visit her and learn city customs and experience the many opportunities available there. Although that is not something Rose wants for herself, such a visit has been my longtime dream."

His heart sank. How could the Flint Hills compete with the sophistication of the city?

She went on. "You have come into my life when I am at a crossroads. I have every reason to believe that any day now I will receive tickets from Aunt Lavinia enabling me to go to St. Louis to spend a matter of months. Yet I did not reckon how difficult it would be to leave you."

Only then did she look up at him, her eyes muddy with concern. Part of him wanted to lash out, to plead his case; but another part recognized her anguish. Her decision was obviously difficult. No wonder she needed time, but was time on his side? "Is there still hope for us?"

"Honestly? I don't know." She turned away then. "St. Louis is everything I thought I wanted. Until you."

He cupped her head in his hands and with aching tenderness, lowered his lips and found the sweet nectar of hers. He caressed the silky smoothness of her cheek, inhaled the lilac fragrance of her neck and felt an overpowering need to claim her as his own. "Dear, dear, Lily. Above all, I want you to be happy."

"I desire that for you, too, Caleb."

"You are my happiness. I had hoped I could be yours." In the gloaming the hum of insects and the croak of frogs seemed joined in a lament. Neither of them said anything. At last, in a soft voice, Caleb intoned, "'How do I love thee? Let me count the ways. / I love thee to the depth and breadth and height / My soul can reach…'" He circled an arm around Lily's slender waist and drew her close. "When you recited those lines at the poetry reading, that was when I knew I loved you and wanted to spend my life with you. If you are determined to follow your dream, then I must let you go, but I cannot permit that to happen without asking you to listen to my dream and consider altering your own."

Knowing he had so much more to tell her about his plans yet wild with the need to assure himself she would be part of them, he slipped from the log and knelt in front of Lily. He hoped against hope that she would hear and respond to the urgent call of his heart. He picked up her hands and held them in his, seeking in her astonishing blue eyes the response he needed to hear. "Dearest Lily, I ask you before God to become my wife. I pledge you my undying love."

Her eyes filled with tears, Lily shook her head back and forth, gripping his hand as in a vise. She opened her mouth to speak, but no sound came. Adrift, Caleb could only stand, draw her to her feet and enfold her in his arms. Her slight body trembled in his embrace and muffled sobs gave evidence of her distress. How long they stood thus was measured by the cooing of doves and the arrival of the first fireflies of the evening. Finally she stepped away and gazed at him with such love he feared ever forgetting the moment. A glimmer of hope. That was all he needed. Then she spoke.

"If mere sentiment and emotion might be the basis of a decision, I would be moved to accept your proposal. But there is also reason, intellect and a lifetime of expectation to be considered. Caleb, dear, you have already been hurt by one who treated your heart lightly. I cannot, I will not, do that. So I beg of you once more, permit me time. Haste must not be a determining factor. May I have a week to consider your proposal?"

Caleb knew it had been unrealistic to expect an immediate answer, much as he craved an acceptance. Right now, a week seemed unendurable, yet if that week ultimately produced an engagement, the time would pass as a blink of an eye. "A man in love is an impatient creature, but you are worth it, Lily. Take the time you need."

Just when he opened his mouth to tell her he would soon be mustering out and to share his future expectations for the ranch, he heard a familiar voice calling his name. He and Lily drew farther apart and Caleb began to laugh. "It can't be." He yelled out, "Seth?"

Lily looked at him quizzically and then at the broad-shouldered, bewhiskered giant lumbering toward them, his arms extended. "They told me you might be here, brother." Then Caleb was enveloped in a bear hug.

Extricating himself, he turned to Lily. "I've told you about my big brother, Seth, and for some reason, here he is. May I present Miss Lily Kellogg."

Seth picked up Lily's hand and bent over it. "My pleasure, ma'am." Then he examined Caleb's expression, turned back to Lily and said, "My pleasure, indeed."

Caleb stared at his brother, dumbfounded at his presence here. "What brings you to Fort Larned?"

"First of all, Sophie, Pa and I have been sore worried since you were wounded, so I came to check on you. Beyond that, I have an important mission the family wants you to undertake after you muster out next month."

"Mus…muster out?"

Both brothers wheeled to Lily, whose eyes flicked from one man to the other. Seth found his voice first. "Why, yes, Miss Lily. Caleb's leaving the army."

"Lily, I'm sorry, I was just now getting ready to tell you."

"Woo-ee. Old Seth spoke out of turn, I reckon."

Lily dusted imaginary dirt from her skirt and, ignoring Caleb, spoke to Seth. "Welcome to Fort Larned, sir. If you'll excuse me, I'll see myself home. I imagine you two have much to discuss."

She turned and marched toward the fort. Caleb paused only a moment before trotting after her. When he reached her side, he took hold of her arm, which she promptly jerked away. "Please, Lily. I was on the brink of telling you all about my plans and about where I would take you if we married and—"

"So much for honesty" was all she said, but even without those words, her withering look doomed him.

* * *

Once out of sight of the brothers, Lily picked up her skirts and ran toward home, blinded by angry tears. How dare Caleb withhold such information, assuming she would just go along with any plan he had in mind? For a moment back there, all she had wanted was to fall into his arms, cover his face with kisses and swear her eternal love. To say, "yes," for pity's sake. To scuttle any plan for St. Louis. How could she have been so misguided and besotted?

She dashed through the front door and raced up the stairs, intent upon avoiding her father's startled look and Rose's well-intentioned inquisition. Throwing herself on the bed, she beat the pillows with her fists. Sweet talk, that's all it had been. She had actually believed she had fallen in love with the man—a man she had thought honorable. Yet all along, he had concealed any talk of his future, the very future he had the gall to invite her to share. Spent, she rolled over on her back, dried her tears and focused on calming her rapid breathing. Closing her eyes, she kept whispering her renewed mantra, "St. Louis, St. Louis, St. Louis."

Only when she heard the creak of the bedroom door did she look around. Rose and Fannie stood expectantly at the threshold. "Do you wish to be alone?" Rose asked.

Lily knew the story would have to come out eventually. Much as an incision needs to be made and poison purged, she saw no reason to postpone the inevitable. "It's all right. Come on in."

Fannie went to the washbasin, poured some water and dampened a cloth. "Here," she said, handing it to Lily. "Lay this on your forehead. You are overheated."

The contrast of the cool, damp towel made Lily aware of the oppressive heat in the tiny room. "Thank you."

Fannie perched on the side of the bed, and Rose pulled a chair close. "Sister, we are concerned for you. When I saw how upset you were, I summoned Fannie. We don't mean to intrude, but if we can share your burden, whatever it is, we want to do that."

Lily didn't know where to begin or how to express the conflicting emotions raging within her. "I feel like such a fool."

"How so?" Fannie asked.

"It is surely Captain Montgomery who has put you in such a state," Rose said.

"Caleb." Lily could hardly say his name for the huge lump in her throat. "I... I was falling in love with him." Even to her own ears, her voice sounded tinny.

"Was?" Fannie's eyebrows shot up with the question.

"This evening he asked me to marry him."

"Surely that didn't come as a surprise," Rose said.

Lily looked at her sister. "I know you like him, but I cannot marry him."

"Did you tell him that?"

Lily mentally reviewed the conversation. "Actually, no. I asked for a week to consider his proposal."

Fannie leaned forward. "But you've already made up your mind?"

"How could I not when I learned he has not been totally forthcoming with me? Rose, you remember when Effie talked about marriage and the importance of communication, of not keeping secrets?"

Rose nodded.

"You will understand, then, how surprised I was to learn this evening that Captain Montgomery is shortly to leave the army. And for what? That is also a piece of information he has not shared. How could he expect me to traipse off into the unknown like some beleaguered pioneer woman?" She shook her head vehemently. "No, I am not such a fool."

"Sister, you speak of openness. Does Caleb know about your desire to visit St. Louis or have you kept that to yourself?"

Lily shrugged. "I kept putting it off. I finally told him tonight."

"Dear, I believe communication works both ways." Rose shook her head sadly. "Do you love him?"

Lily groaned. Her sister *would* have to ask that question.

"I doubt you would be so upset," Fannie interjected, "if you had no feelings for Caleb. Perhaps there is a reasonable explanation for his withholding his plans. It could be the proposal just popped out of his mouth, or maybe his future is still somewhat indefinite, or—"

"Or he asked me to share my dream, but for unknown reasons failed to share his own. Whatever his vision, mine is firmly set. I am going to St. Louis."

Fannie picked up her hand and gently massaged it. "This is anger and disappointment talking, Lily. Caleb has given you a week to make your decision. I know you are hurt right now, but I urge you to use the next few days to consider what your life would be like without him. Whether the charms of St. Louis are strong enough to overcome your feelings for the man. There is nothing to be gained by an impulsive reaction. Take the time, dear friend. Take the time."

Rose nodded in agreement. "This decision is too important to hurry. Consider, too, that there may be things you don't know that Caleb has been trying to share."

Lily gritted her teeth against the memory of his words: *I was just now getting ready to tell you...* Was that true or merely his way of placating her? "I'm so angry."

Fannie smiled in understanding. "Of course you are. You're feeling betrayed. So often in relationships such schisms are a result of miscommunication. If there is any chance you love him, you will need to confront him with your concerns and hear him out."

Lily wilted under the sympathy and love of her sister and friend. "I don't know if I can do that."

"You must," Rose said in a big sisterly tone that left no room for argument.

Lily sighed. Much as she hated to admit it, Rose was correct. The nature of her relationship with Caleb needed to be settled once and for all. "All right," she said in capitulation. A knowing glance passed between Fannie and Rose, as if to say, "Mission accomplished."

Seth sat on the top step of the barrack porch watching Caleb pace. The brothers had not spoken on their way back from the river. Seth had draped an arm around Caleb as they walked, but seemed to be waiting for him to initiate the conversation that would explain the upsetting events of the past few minutes. What words were there to justify the botch he had made of everything? Or to find the sense in Lily's St. Louis plan? Whether through oversight or assumptions, neither he nor Lily had been as open with the other as they should have been. He didn't know much about love, but Rebecca had surely taught him that honesty was at the heart of any lasting relationship. Why, he hadn't even told Lily about the ranch and how he pictured their life together. No, he'd asked her to take him on faith. Dumb!

"You're wearing out the floor," Seth muttered at last. "I'm a pretty good listener, you know."

Heaving a deep sigh, Caleb collapsed onto the step beside his brother, head down, hands clasped between his knees. "How are Pa and Sophie?"

"Not so fast. They're fine, and there will be time enough to tell you about them. But I recognize a dodge when I see one. What is going on with you and Miss Lily Kellogg?"

Caleb shrugged helplessly.

"That bad, huh?" Seth stretched out his legs, then continued. "Spit it out, Captain."

"I thought I was on the verge of something wonderful. A man doesn't like to have the rug pulled out from under him twice."

"Forget Rebecca. She's not worth talking about. Has this Lily betrayed you, too?"

"Not like that."

"You're pretty sweet on her, then?"

"I asked her to marry me."

"Oh." Seth raked a hand through his curly hair. "Yep, that qualifies as 'pretty sweet.' What was her answer?"

"That's just it. She hasn't said no, yet, but she might as well have. She has plans to leave the fort for a long visit with an aunt in St. Louis. A rich aunt. More fool me, I proposed without knowing about that. Seems her dream has always been to go to the big city and hob-nob with the swells."

"Can you change her mind?"

"I'll try, but I'm not optimistic about my chances. Besides, what if I succeed and later on she resents me for interfering with that dream?"

Seth seemed to be considering Caleb's words. "That is a risk, all right. But if she's worth fighting for—"

"She is." A hole as big as the prairie opened in Caleb's heart. He dared not consider a life without Lily. "I will fight, but…"

"If the good Lord wants you two together, He'll figure a way."

"That's putting powerful pressure on Him."

Seth grinned. "He can handle it. His shoulders are broad. Cast yourself on Him."

"If only it were that easy."

"It is." Seth put an arm around him and drew him close. "Besides, you're going to St. Louis, too."

Caleb reared back. "What're you talking about?"

"When you leave the army, there's no sense you coming to the ranch right then, not when we need you in St. Louis to order supplies and make contacts with bankers and livestock dealers. What do you say?"

"I'll do what's needed for the ranch, though person-ally I fail to see how being in St. Louis will matter if Lily turns me down."

"Patience, brother. We none of us knows what the future holds. That's in God's hands."

Caleb wished he shared his brother's unwavering faith, but right now his future was in Lily's hands, and that didn't feel good at all.

* * *

Lily watched out the window two days after the debacle at the river as Caleb rode out with a small contingent of troops. She could tell he was still favoring the side of his wound. She had tried her best to stay mad at him, but now she worried whether it was too soon for him to be on active duty. Then her mere concern made her angry all over again—at herself for caring. In her hand she held a note delivered a few minutes ago by a young private. She had read it twice, shaking her head at the sheer folly that characterized her relationship with Caleb. Despite herself, she unfolded the page and scanned it once more.

My dear Lily,
I could not leave today without attempting to set things right between us. I should have told you I would soon be leaving the army, but truth to tell, after meeting you, I had not anticipated that severance with enthusiasm, since I knew it would remove me from your presence. In a very short time, you have endeared yourself to me in the ways of which I have already spoken. It was never my intent to be dishonest with you.

You were justified to accuse me of not sharing my dreams before asking you to be my wife. The urgency of my love for you overcame reason. Let me share those dreams with you now.

I have saved much of my army pay to join with my father and Seth in buying land for a cattle operation in southeast Kansas in an area called the Flint Hills. Sophie, Pa and Seth have been there for some months and have succeeded in getting the necessary fencing and buildings in place. Despite their labors to that end, my dream is still incomplete. I long for a family of my own. At the heart of that family is a woman to love and to cherish as my wife. That woman, dearest one, is you. However, all I can do now is ask for your forgiveness for my oversights and shortcomings and hope that you will give this letter prayerful consideration.

In humility and love,

Caleb

Stuffing the note in her pocket, she put on her bonnet and circled the parade ground, deep in thought. She couldn't deny her feelings for Caleb. He was everything she should want in a husband. He was a noble and ambitious young man, who shared her values, and a treasured companion. The fact that she melted when he held her hand or kissed her was a delicious bonus and a reason, out of all proportion to common sense, to visualize a happy life with him.

If only...

But the Flint Hills? Another wilderness just like the one she was fleeing? Full of the same heat, drought, prairie fires, wild winds and blizzards? Not to mention vermin and snakes? All of that coupled with her memory of the settler's wife who died in childbirth caused her stomach to clench.

More than ever she wished for some master puppeteer to pull the strings of her destiny. Anything but having to make decisions for herself.

So intent was she that she barely noticed a platoon of mounted soldiers nearly on top of her. Jumping aside, she watched them pass. The beasts towered above her, and she had a sudden sense of her own insignificance. Self-pity was unbecoming. She had to be prepared with a decision when Caleb returned.

Then as if Mathilda Kellogg was suddenly whispering in her ear, Lily remembered the familiar words with which her mother ended every prayer. *Thy will, not mine, be done.* She would open her heart to God and await His direction.

Chapter Thirteen

Wincing with every jolt of the trot, Caleb bit back a moan as the cavalry made its way over stony ground. He'd been medically cleared for duty, but this sortie had tested him. They had accompanied a wagon train safely through territory where scouts had earlier sighted small bands of Indians and were now on their way back to the fort. Each hoofbeat sent pain radiating across his chest and down his arm.

It hadn't helped that the night before his nightmares had recurred in full fury. Already agitated about Lily, the dream had left him exhausted and frustrated. What had seemed so simple and beautiful several days ago—declaring his love to Lily—had turned to disappointment, but more than that, to hurt and the sense he'd made a fool of himself by trusting a woman again. While he hoped his note to Lily would cause her to see their relationship and future in a clearer light, he wouldn't permit himself to hope.

Bucephalus clattered over a dry streambed, sending shocks through his system, but that was nothing compared to the emotional pain of potentially losing Lily.

Seth's arrival had been a tonic and had given Caleb a glimpse of his promising future. The basics for a working ranch were in place, and now it was a matter of establishing the herd and deciding on markets for the livestock. Caleb wished he could have responded to Seth's glowing plans for the ranch with equal enthusiasm. Although he would enjoy the change of pace from the army, he feared the most important element of his future might be missing. Lily.

Never having been married, Seth had given what encouragement he could to Caleb's suit, but had spent most of his visit going over the list of supplies and equipment he wanted Caleb to purchase in St. Louis. Rightfully so. The ranch was, after all, their primary focus.

Suddenly Bucephalus shied to avoid a huge anthill, and Caleb nearly lost his seat. Unsettled. That was him. In another day or two, his fate would be sealed, one way or the other. He couldn't remember ever feeling so helpless.

Late in the afternoon Lily stood in the door of the hospital watching the cavalrymen return to the fort, their faces shadowed with trail dust. At the front rode Caleb, his hat pulled low over his eyes, his features drawn as if in pain. Sighing, Lily put words to her concern—had this ride come too soon after his recovery from the shoulder wound? When he dismounted to salute the colonel, she noticed his fleeting grimace. Surely he would seek medical attention if needed.

She had other worries. Advice had rained down from all sides, including Seth. She had been surprised when he sought her out shortly after Caleb left. His had been a persuasive argument.

"Miss Lily," he had said turning his hat in his hands, "might I have a word?"

She had offered him a seat in one of the front porch rockers, then taken another for herself. Even though he was larger than Caleb, he had the same curly hair and warm hazel eyes. "How may I be of help?"

He cleared his throat nervously. "I reckon I shouldn't be interfering in your business, but Caleb is my business. We've been best friends since we were pups, especially after our mother died. He was always the smart one, his head forever stuck in books. I admire him mightily. If I could've, I'd have protected him from these past years in the army." He hesitated. "He's seen terrible things."

"I know. His are experiences no man should have to endure, but, alas, so many had no choice."

"Then you'll understand, ma'am, why his happiness is important to me and his pa and sister."

"Caleb has told me how close you all are."

"True, but it hasn't been the same without him. We're mighty pleased he'll soon be joining us in God's beautiful country."

"Your ranching enterprise sounds quite ambitious."

"We have big plans, and Caleb will play an important part in achieving success. He's a good man, you know."

Lily lowered her eyes. "Yes, he is." In that moment her heart swelled with affection for the brother so devoted to Caleb.

"I don't exactly know how to put this." He tugged

at his cuff as if buying time. "He's powerful in love with you, Miss Lily."

Lily blushed, unable to speak.

"I don't want my brother to get hurt. He would be a fine husband for any woman, but he doesn't want just any woman. I do believe if you turn him down, that'll be the end of courtship for him." He hurried on, as if racing to complete his spiel. "You would like our family. Why, you and Sophie? Shoot. You'd be sisters in less time than it takes to skin a rabbit. And Pa and me? Why, we have pined to have another woman about the place. Our ma was special. I think you are, too. With all respect, ma'am, please give Caleb a chance. He truly was trying to tell you all his plans when, like a big galoot, I interrupted." He stood and clapped the hat on his head. "I expect I've said all I came to say, and I'll be leaving for home tomorrow. I hope I haven't overstepped my bounds by speaking with you, but I love my brother and wanted to do all I could to reassure you that he is the finest man I know. There. That's all."

Lily would like to have put the man out of his misery with the answer he had come to solicit and he had certainly made some telling points, but she was still of two minds about her future. "Seth—may I call you Seth? You have done yourself and your brother proud. I promise to consider what you have said. You are absolutely correct—Caleb is a fine man who doesn't deserve further hurt. However, there are many factors at play, and I'm doing my utmost to consider what will be best for both of us."

"Thank you. That's all I can ask." He tipped his hat. "I hope to see you again someday."

Then, without a backward glance, he had lumbered off.

Watching now as the soldiers dispersed, Lily saw Major Hurlburt and Caleb walk toward headquarters, deep in conversation. Every now and then Caleb made a grab for his arm; it was then she knew that he was, indeed, in pain. Many men might have asked to be excused from duty for medical reasons. Not Caleb. It wasn't in his nature to shy away from a fight.

Her father had already gone home for dinner when Lily finally finished remaking the beds of two soldiers who had been dismissed to their barracks. Her back ached and the stifling heat rendered her clothing uncomfortable. Before leaving, she splashed cool water on her face and wrists. She knew she was delaying, finding distraction in her duties. Tonight she faced the difficult task of deciding once and for all where her heart lay.

She had prayed for guidance, even going so far as to ask God for a sign to help with her decision. However, she had not counted on His surprising efficiency. When she entered their home, her father stood near the kitchen table beside Rose. As Lily approached them, she was discomfited by their wary expressions.

Then she saw it. Lying on the table. A flat package. Addressed to her. Color flooded her cheeks. A package from Aunt Lavinia. She couldn't move.

Rose came to her side. "Aren't you going to open it?"

Her father eased himself into a chair and sat, hands folded in his lap, head bowed.

"Yes," Lily said, untying the string enclosing the parcel. She was all thumbs and the knots were proving difficult. Finally she succeeded in unwrapping the contents and spreading them across the surface of the table. An itinerary. Money for travel clothes and stagecoach fare to Independence. Tickets for passage on a riverboat down the Missouri. And a letter from Aunt Lavinia.

She crumpled into the chair beside her father. "I'm really going, aren't I?"

His Adam's apple worked and all he could do was nod. Looking up, Lily watched Rose turn toward the stove, but not before a tear ran down her face.

Lily knew she should be ecstatic. Lying before her were the means to achieve an ambition she had cherished since childhood, the fulfillment of years of daydreams and fantasies. Yet the hurrahs that should be bursting from her mouth were nothing more than sawdust. She had never been so confused in her entire life. Any decision would be the wrong one. *Thy will, not mine, be done.* How was she to know the difference?

After Rose went to bed and her father left for his nightly hospital rounds, Lily sat at the kitchen table, bent over two letters, one of which would seal her fate. The first from Aunt Lavinia, the other, Caleb's. She moved the lantern closer and read, for the fourth or fifth time, words that had etched themselves on her heart.

I long for a family of my own. At the heart of that family is a woman to love and to cherish as my wife. That woman, dearest one, is you.

She caressed the note with her fingertips before laying it aside and returning to her aunt's message, one replete with enticements she had long envisioned.

My darling niece,
We are back from Newport—a charming sum-

mer retreat among the most genteel families. How I wish you could have enjoyed our pastimes—sailing, lawn tennis and first-rate evening amusements. I am confident that day will come for you after you make a fine marriage. Already I have identified some up-and-coming young men for you to meet. What fun we shall have picking among them!

I have booked river passage for you on the *Mary McDonald,* due to arrive here in mid-September. The trip will be arduous, but with what a loving welcome we will greet you! It will be a joy to show you the sights and have you as my companion for the theater. Mr. Dupree has agreed to squire you to lectures by noted area intellectuals since that is not my cup of tea.

All of this, of course, will be preceded by dressmakers', milliners' and cobblers' appointments and a tutorial concerning the local social customs. By coming here, you will not only bring me much pleasure, but you will also honor your mother's fondest wish. From her letters, I know how Mathilda yearned for you to experience the opportunities and culture available here.
Awaiting your arrival with love,
Aunt Lavinia

Lily extinguished the lantern. She could no longer confront the words tugging at her as if she were a rag doll being contested by two children. But these were not children. They were two loving human beings, both committed to her happiness. Childless Aunt Lavinia, offering her a Cinderella transformation, a fairyland of diversions and fulfillment of both her own and her mother's aspirations. And Caleb...offering her the uncertainties and hardships of the prairie, the promise of a home and family and...his heart. No closer to a decision than she had been all evening, she buried her head in her arms, willing a lightning bolt to etch the answer across the night sky.

"Lily?"

She must have dozed, because when she looked up, her father was standing over her, his hand resting gently on her shoulder. "Papa...what time is it?"

"Just after eleven." He sat down at the table, reaching out to cover her hand with his own. "Can't sleep? What's fretting you?"

"I'm so confused."

He patted her hand. "Big decisions, daughter. Do you want to talk about it?"

She had talked with others until she was exhausted by the effort, but this was her father who had never done anything but love her. She nodded.

"Well, then, let's lay out both cases. What compels you to go to St. Louis?"

She ran through all the reasons she had amassed through the years, including her longing for intellectual stimulation and her antipathy for frontier living. She ended with what was, for her, the most binding emotional argument. "It was what Mama wanted."

"And young Captain Montgomery?"

"He would take me to the very prairie I mean to escape."

"One's environment can be important," her father said noncommittally. "What else?"

"He yearns for a wife and family. He is a hard worker and a good man."

"You make him sound like a paper cutout." In the moonlight, he studied her face. "What are you holding back, Lily?"

She looked away from her father's probing eyes, her chest constricted by what she couldn't bring herself to utter.

"Lily? No running away. Not when you have such an important decision to make." He withdrew his hand and leaned forward on his elbows, repeating his question. "What are you holding back?"

Finally she met his eyes. "He loves me and I don't want to hurt him."

"I agree that he is very much in love with you. What about you? Do you love him?"

There it was. *The* question. "I don't know."

"I think you do know." He paused to let his words penetrate. "What is holding you back?"

"Oh, Papa." She stood and began pacing the room. "I'm afraid. I'm afraid if I don't go to St. Louis, I will one day regret that I didn't and, worse yet, resent Caleb for frustrating my dream. I'm afraid of the harsh life I might lead as the wife of a cattle rancher. I'm afraid I will be disloyal to Mama. I'm afraid of making a mistake I can do nothing to rectify, not without involving too many other people."

"The best decisions never arise from fear, daughter. They result from love." He rose, rounded the table and held her in his arms. "Here is what I have learned. Love must be grounded in truth and in the desire to put another before oneself, but there are no certainties. Love is a huge risk. You must be sure you take it with the right man." He held her close and she could hear the steady beat of his heart. "One last thing. Your mama is no longer here, but I can tell you with certainty what she most wanted for you. Your happiness. She would approve whether you go to St. Louis or marry Caleb so long as you are happy."

Lily was overcome by the depth of her father's love for her and hers for him. No matter what she chose to do, leaving him and Rose would make any decision bittersweet.

"Now, child, let's retire for the evening." With a pat on her shoulder, he was gone, and shortly, she followed him upstairs.

Will Creekmore sidled up to Caleb after the morning briefing. "You all right, Montgomery? I notice you favoring your arm."

"Still feeling a bit rocky, but I'll be fine."

"I don't reckon the latest mission helped any."

Caleb laughed mirthlessly. "We army men do what we must."

"Not much longer for you. When do you leave?"

"Around the middle of August. It feels strange. This—" he gestured around the fort "—has been my entire adult life."

"You'll be a fine rancher. After a bit, you won't miss the army."

Caleb nodded, but knew he would never forget where he had been and what he had done in the line of duty.

"Maybe it's none of my business, but Fannie and I wonder how you plan to leave things with Lily."

"I've laid my cards on the table. Now it's up to her."

Will gave him a two-finger salute. "We're rooting for you, Cap." Will proceeded across the parade ground toward his home, leaving Caleb standing alone, staring up at the flag flapping in the breeze. Across the way he heard a hammer clanging on an anvil in the smithy's shop, the raucous shouts of the hostlers outside the stables and the playful whinnying of horses. Saw the line of peaceful Indians, settlers and soldiers coming and going from the sutler's. Smelled the aroma of fresh-baked bread from the baker's oven. All of it familiar and soon to be forever left behind.

Seth's visit had provided an incentive to prepare himself for the next chapter. His brother's excitement about the ranch was contagious, and being with Seth had made him long for his father and sister. In some ways he wished he were going straight to the Flint Hills, but being assigned the St. Louis trip on ranch business made him feel useful and needed.

His daydreaming came to an abrupt end when a sergeant approached, saluted and handed him an envelope with the single word *Caleb* inscribed on it. As he wandered toward the stables to check on Bucephalus, he opened the envelope and unfolded a small scrap of paper. "Please meet me tonight after supper in the cemetery. Lily." He stopped in his tracks. The barest of messages, couched in the most neutral of tones, saying nothing to give him hope. He had no means either to make time fly or to affect her answer. The day simply had to be endured.

Lily excused herself from supper, offering no explanation. Before she met with Caleb she wanted time with her mother. The earth was still warm when Lily sank to the ground beside the grave. When the time came, how difficult it would be to leave this sacred spot. Yet more enduring than this place were the memories of her vibrant, loving mother which would accompany her wherever she went.

"Mama," she murmured. "It's time for me to go— either to St. Louis or to marry Caleb. How I wish you were here to advise me. I think I know what I must do. Please help me to go forth with courage and hope and live each day fully, as you taught us to do." Her mother's *Amen* came in the rustle of wind through the grasses and the repetitive song of a whip-poor-will.

She stood, adjusted the skirt of her best dress and waited, hands patiently folded, for Caleb to arrive. She had not spoken to him during this long week, their only communication being the exchange of notes.

Then she spotted him, striding toward her, dressed in his official "best," his polished buttons, shiny boots and clean-shaven face a testimony to his care in preparing to meet her. He approached, stopping several feet from her. His was an arresting presence—so straight of posture, his broad shoulders a bulwark of strength. Nerves threatened to undo her. "Good evening, Caleb."

"Lily," was all he said, and on his lips her name sounded like a prayer.

"Shall we walk?"

He put an arm around her waist. "It's what we do, isn't it?"

Without a word, they made their way toward the river. Now that he was here by her side, her heart fluttered like a hummingbird's wing. Every thought, every argument, every emotion she'd experienced in the past seven days seemed centered in the sensation of being nestled against him. "I noticed you were favoring your shoulder when you returned from the last mission."

"Ever the nurse, aren't you?" His smile looked forced rather than teasing. "As you've pointed out, healing takes time."

"Lots of things take time."

He stopped walking and turned to face her, his expression solemn. "Like decisions?"

"Like decisions."

Neither of them spoke for a long while, their eyes locked in a communication beyond the power of words. Lily wished this moment would never end, because to end it would set a course from which there could be no return.

Caleb lifted his hand to her face, his fingers moving lightly as if memorizing her features. "Nothing has changed for me, Lily. I love you and pray you return that sentiment. These days of waiting have been agony."

Her lips trembled under the butterfly-wing touch of his thumb, and her body quivered, racked by a storm of indecision. But no. She had made up her mind. Inhaling deeply, she forced out the words. "You honor me with your love and with your proposal. I have considered both long and prayerfully."

"And...?" In his eyes she read the pain of one facing an executioner.

"Caleb, I cannot marry you." She watched him bite his lower lip, then stare over her head at some point on the far horizon.

"You're going to St. Louis to live in your aunt's world."

On his lips, the words sounded like a renunciation of all that she held dear. "I must. Please let me explain."

"What's there to explain? You have the chance to move in social circles I could never offer you, with opportunities beyond my power to provide. You have been clear with me that such an adventure is what you have always yearned to experience. I suppose I can understand that life on a ranch in the middle of nowhere can hardly compete."

Lily knotted her fingers in anguish. "It's not that. Your offer to share your dream, even if it is vastly different from mine, touched my heart. And I know you meant to tell me all about it before Seth arrived, but, Caleb, what if I gave up my dream for yours and ultimately came to resent you? I don't want a life where I'm constantly second-guessing my decisions."

"Nor do I. If you cannot give yourself to me unreservedly, as I do to you, then we are doomed." He kicked the toe of his boot into the dirt. "What kind of man would I be if I stood in the way of your dream?"

"What kind of man will you be, anyway?"

He shook his head, and she couldn't bear to meet his eyes. "A broken one without you." A tinge of bitterness crept into his tone. "But again, healing takes time and, somehow, I will heal."

"It isn't that I don't care about you." Even to her own ears, that sounded weak.

"I suppose there is no need to prolong this conversation. I would prefer we try to end as we began, as friends. Further talk might make that impossible. Please, though, permit me to satisfy myself by asking one more question."

"Of course."

Quite unexpectedly, he drew her to him, so close she could feel the heat rising from his body. "We've always pledged honesty. Now, Lily, tell me you don't love me."

Surely he must hear the crack of her heart and sense the anguish of her soul because, God help her, she could not utter those words.

Caleb never knew how he held himself together to escort Lily in silence to her home. Foolishly, he had believed that she had come to love him as he loved her. All his pipe dreams of making a home together and fathering her children had gone up in a puff of smoke. He knew he would never be the same, nor would he ever stop loving her. It had been one thing to lose Rebecca to another man, but to be rejected for himself was a hurt beyond describing. Yet, loving Lily, he could hardly stand in the way of her happiness. Reaching her porch, he took a deep breath and forced himself to say, "I shall love you till the day I die. I hope your dreams come true. I wish you only the best."

"Thank you, Caleb. Your understanding means a great deal." She laid the flat of her hand against his heart. "Honestly, I cannot say that I don't love you. I very well may. What I *do* know is that when I commit to a man, it will be unconditionally and forever."

"I appreciate your honesty." Before he turned to go, he captured her face between his hands and kissed her with all the regret and love warring within him. "Be happy, Lily." Then he walked swiftly away before she might hear the unmanly sobs gargling in his throat.

As he strode across the parade ground, a long-forgotten memory came to him. He and his mother in their garden, hunkering beside a bird, struggling to fly. "Oh, poor thing. Look, Caleb. Its wing is broken."

"Can we fix it? Please, Ma. It can't fly."

His mother had studied his crestfallen face and then scooped the tiny creature into her apron. "All right, son, we'll do our best, but you have to understand one thing."

Elated that they would try to save the bird, he had scarce heard what she had said next. "We can nurse the bird, but it will never be ours. We will fix the wing so the bird can enjoy what it was born to do. Fly. We cannot keep creatures unless we give them freedom."

Now her words came back to him like a clarion call, and he understood them as never before. Lily could never be his until she flew away to freedom. All he could do was let her go. And pray.

Chapter Fourteen

For Lily in the ensuing days, it was as if she was experiencing everything for the very first time—and the last. Why hadn't she paid more notice to the sheer gold of the sunflowers as they followed the sun across the sky or to the flutelike trills of the bold meadowlark perched on a nearby post? Never before had Rose's biscuits and honey tasted so satisfying, nor the chorus of male voices singing camp songs from the barracks sounded so hauntingly melodic. As departure approached, she gathered such memories into her heart. Bittersweet memories.

It pained her to observe Caleb going about his business, never glancing in her direction. However, there was nothing more to be said. She had hurt him, and for that she was regretful. Occasionally she succumbed to second thoughts, but then chastised herself. She had charted her course and was determined to take full advantage of the journey upon which she would soon embark. Another letter had arrived from Aunt Lavinia, enclosing a beautiful invitation to an early fall garden party at the home of a neighbor. The elegant engraving abraded Lily's finger, a tactile reminder of the wonders awaiting her.

She had been filling her days instructing Fannie concerning hospital procedures. Worried about Papa being shorthanded, she had been relieved when he solicited Fannie as her replacement. Fortunately, Fannie was proving an apt pupil.

The two sat in front of the apothecary's chest, Lily introducing Fannie to the properties and uses of the medicines stored there—from quinine for malaria to home remedies for coughs and catarrh. "Once you begin administering these, you will have no trouble remembering their uses," Lily reassured her friend.

Fannie looked up from the notebook in which she was inscribing Lily's instructions. "I'm excited to have this opportunity. Besides, it will help pass the time."

"It does do that. Daily fort life can be dull."

"With the help of this hospital work, I have not yet been bored."

"Spoken like a true newlywed."

Fannie turned to Lily, her eyes sparkling. "I pray it may always be so. With my Will, I am confident it will be."

Lily suppressed the flicker of envy that caused her to look down at the bottle of iodine she held in her hands. "You are truly blessed."

"Indeed."

Lily sensed Fannie had been about to speak of Caleb, but had censored herself. She stood to replace the iodine in the cabinet, but that action served for naught because the question tumbled out, anyway. "How is he?"

Fannie did not pretend ignorance. "Caleb goes through the motions of work, Will says, but mainly keeps to himself. I've often seen him entering the library in the evening. No doubt you would like me to say he is fine, but that would be an untruth. The man is pining." Fannie closed her notebook. "Perhaps you would prefer that he pine, since that offers strong proof of his affection for you."

"I need no proof of that," Lily whispered. "I know I am walking away from a wonderful man."

"It is not for me to judge. You are my friend, and I trust you to know what is best for yourself."

"Can one every really know that?"

"I know. Will is best for me." Lily saw the concern for her that Fannie could not conceal. "One day, you, too, will know beyond any doubt what makes you happy." She snapped the notebook open. "Now then, tell me about belladonna."

For the next hour, they applied themselves to the lesson. When they finished, Lily patted her friend on the shoulder. "Good work. I feel so much better about leaving Father."

"You worry about him."

"I can't help it. Ever since my brother and then Mama died, he has aged rapidly. I think he's tired."

"And grieving."

"That, too. Leaving him and Rose for so long will be hard."

"Try not to fret. I will write frequently, keeping you posted on things, including your father's well-being."

"Thank you, Fannie. I am blessed to have such a friend as you."

Fannie leaned over and hugged her. "Let us vow always to be close."

"I am counting on that," Lily said, suddenly envisioning the miles and miles she would soon put between herself and everyone she loved. She would need all the courage she could muster.

With only two weeks left of his army service, Caleb found himself slowly transitioning out of involvement in strategic planning. At loose ends, he often found refuge in the library, but not even *Moby Dick* with its vivid descriptions of whaling could capture his attention. More often than not, he simply sat in a chair holding his open book, wishing for the hours and days to pass until he would no longer be tortured by proximity to Lily. Yet, paradoxically, the thought of being separated from her was devastating.

Just before taps one evening, the library door opened, and he was surprised to see Ezra Kellogg. "I thought I'd find you here," the older man said.

Caleb remembered his last conversation with Ezra. How different he had felt on that occasion when he'd been given permission to court Lily. Now he couldn't imagine what they could possibly have to discuss. "I enjoy the quiet." Caleb pointed to a chair. "Please. Sit."

Ezra had the grace not to mince words. "I am sorry that Lily's decision has probably disappointed you."

"Thank you." Caleb didn't trust himself to say anything further.

"You must be wondering why I've sought you out."

Caleb shrugged.

The surgeon leaned forward in his chair, pinning

Caleb with his piercing blue eyes. "I have a favor to ask, one that I have no expectation you will want to fulfill. Yet please hear me out."

Caleb sat back and folded his hands. "I'm listening."

"If I had any other recourse, I would not presume upon your good will. From young Creekmore, am I correct in understanding that your brother has asked you to go to St. Louis on ranch business?"

Caleb had an uneasy suspicion where this conversation was headed. "Yes."

"Difficult as it might be, I am asking you to consider accompanying Lily on her trip there."

Caleb felt blood suffusing his cheeks. He wanted to slam his fist on a table or stalk out of the room. How dare the man suggest such a thing!

Ezra held up his hand. "Before you say anything, just listen."

Caleb waited. He figured silence was his most gentlemanly response.

"Lily has never traveled by herself. You and I both know the possible perils for a single woman in a stagecoach or on a riverboat. I am concerned for her safety. She is headstrong enough to think she can handle the exigencies of such a journey."

Caleb closed his eyes against images of foulmouthed frontiersmen and coarse, beefy sailors—all of whom would salivate over a beautiful young woman.

"I have no one else to ask. Lily is precious to me, and I'd like to believe to you, as well. There is no denying the awkwardness and, dare I say, the pain of such an arrangement." The man took off his glasses and swiped at his eyes. "It is difficult enough to let her do this thing without also wondering each hour if she is safe."

Caleb gritted his teeth. He couldn't imagine a worse torture than spending days on end with a woman he loved who could not return that sentiment.

"If you care about her, as I know you do, surely you see the wisdom of traveling together."

"I'm not sure I can make such arrangements at this late date." The minute the words came out of his mouth, Caleb knew he'd capitulated.

"I have telegraphed the steamboat line to secure your passage. Your river voyage will be at my expense, sir." He paused. "As for the stagecoach, perhaps the ranch can cover that cost. If you agree to help Lily, you might have to spend a few extra days here after you muster out."

"When is she leaving?"

"August 20." Caleb half listened as Ezra outlined the plans in more specific detail. Every fiber of his being cried, "No!" Why was he even contemplating such a masochistic endeavor?

Lily. The love of his life. That was why. "Against my better judgment but out of concern for your daughter, I will accompany her to the wharf in St. Louis."

Ezra slumped in relief. "I, sir, will be forever in your debt."

The morning before she was scheduled to leave, Lily sewed the final button on the jacket of her new traveling costume—a serviceable blue, matching her bonnet. Her trunk was packed, despite the fact Aunt Lavinia would probably cringe at her unfashionable wardrobe,

and she had made a list of the items she would carry
in her reticule. Snipping the final thread, she sat back,
running her hands over the bodice of the jacket. How
many days would she alternate between this and her
only other travel ensemble? Now that her departure was
imminent, she was filled with a cascade of emotions—
excitement, anxiety, nostalgia, homesickness—and a
number of questions. How difficult would it prove to
be on her own? To leave her beloved father and sister?
To say goodbye to her mother's grave site? She swallowed threatening tears. To travel for three or more
weeks with Caleb?

She stood, shook out the jacket and moved to the
ironing board. The iron heating on the stove hissed
when she tested it. Spreading the jacket on the board
and bending to the task, she remonstrated with herself. She had formulated her dream, and with Aunt
Lavinia's help, she was on the verge of realizing it.
Now was not the time for faintheartedness. Upset as
she had been when her father gave her the news that
Caleb would travel with her, she acknowledged grudgingly that his presence would help secure her safety
until she reached St. Louis. However, it would not en-
sure a relaxed trip.

The day passed in a whirl of last-minute details.
The Hurlburts were entertaining the family for her
final dinner at Fort Larned. Before dressing for that
occasion, she made a final visit to the cemetery. The
setting sun cast burnished rays of light upon the grave,
and the familiar cooing of doves produced a plaintive
requiem. Lily stood, rapt, staring at the chiseled name
on the stone. *Mathilda.* In a moment of clarity, she re-

alized that no matter how far from this place life took her, her mother's influence would accompany her. She placed a hand on top of the grave marker. "Mama, Papa told me all you ever wanted for me was to be happy. I intend to do that by taking full advantage of new opportunities. Thank you for your love and example." Then, oddly, she found herself smiling, as if her mother had touched her in blessing.

The dinner party was a time of forced gaiety, involving the major and his wife, Fannie and Will, Ezra and Rose...and Caleb. As a result of the cavorting butterflies in her stomach, Lily picked at her food, knowing full well she would think of this sumptuous spread many times as she sampled the fare at stagecoach way stations. Adding to her nervousness were the veiled looks passing between Effie, Fannie and Rose and then redirected to her, as if she were a patient who required observation for an undetermined illness. No clairvoyant, she nevertheless knew exactly what they were thinking. How could she launch into this adventure and turn down a man as fine as Caleb? She had ultimately given up trying to explain. She was moving on to the "beat of a different drum," as Mr. Thoreau had put it.

Before the party broke up, Effie pulled Lily aside and wrapped her in a motherly hug. "We will miss you more than you know," she whispered. Then she pulled away, held Lily by the shoulders and added, "Whenever you find a man suitable as a husband, remember the importance of honesty."

Lily nodded. "No secrets, right?"

"Open communication. Trust."

Lily embraced the older woman again. "Thank you. I shall miss your counsel."

"And I, your sunny, generous nature."

Later, snuggled under the light sheet next to Rose, Lily realized she would probably never again share a bed with her sister. Starting the very next night, she would find herself alone for the first time in her life. Her new reality came crashing down and she moaned softly.

"Lily?" Rose turned to face her. "You can't sleep, either?"

"No. So many thoughts are running through my mind."

"I can't believe the time is finally here."

"Nor can I. Before, such a trip was a fantasy."

"Papa and I will miss you so."

"And I you." Even on the eve of her trip, Lily found it difficult to imagine a life without her family.

"I've cried all the tears I have within me, but I want you to know that Papa and I will be fine. We will be praying for the fulfillment of your dreams."

"When we meet again, Rose, I shall have so much to tell you."

"I will count the days." Rose laced her hand through Lily's. "I love you, sister."

"I love you, too." Somehow in the silence, Lily managed to calm her racing heart and fall into a peaceful slumber, her fingers still entwined in Rose's.

Caleb had been part of too many leave-takings to watch Lily bid farewell to her family. Instead, he busied himself loading their trunks on the stagecoach. Insofar as possible, he planned to keep his distance from her, staying just close enough to protect her from unwelcome attentions. Surveying the fellow passengers, he saw only one other woman, a toothless crone headed for Council Grove, and four men, from their Western dress, obviously veterans of the trail. He would need to keep his eye on them, particularly the one ogling the assembled women, spitting tobacco indiscriminately and turning the air blue with oaths.

The driver bawled out the order to leave. Lily threw herself into her father's arms, her "Oh, Papa!" moistening every onlooker's eyes, including, to his chagrin, his own. With the halfhearted effort of a jaunty salute, he hauled himself onto the top of the coach. If he could maintain this seat for the trip to Independence, he could avoid all but the most cursory conversation with Lily. The passengers began taking their seats, but Lily lingered until she was the last one to climb into the coach. Then, with the crack of the driver's whip, the vehicle lumbered onto the trail, jostling passengers and careening from side to side as the horses picked up speed.

From his perch, Caleb watched the buildings of Fort Larned grow indistinct until the only landmark remaining was the towering flagpole with the colors flying in the stiff breeze. Unexpectedly he felt a lump rising in his throat with the reality that the painful first chapter of his adult life had closed. Too much conflict, too much blood, too much guilt. He had hoped to end his career with the promise of a new life with Lily. Now, somehow, he faced that next chapter even more alone than he had been when he had marched to war with his comrades from Jefferson City. He pulled the brim of his hat lower over his face, resigned to the long, challenging trip.

Lily had only thought she knew discomfort before. Miserable August heat, clouds of dust, mingled odors of unwashed bodies and the nausea-producing motion of the lurching coach caused her to pray constantly for deliverance even as she knew she faced more days on the trail. Alighting at night, she hoped for relief, but the inns along the way were primitive and the food so unappealing she could scarcely eat, even though she knew she must. It was only at meals that she saw Caleb, who hovered close by to spare her the conversation of trail-hardened men. Her fellow passengers were an odd lot—the old woman said nothing, one of the men hummed under his breath in a sleep-inducing monotone, two engaged in hotly contested card games and the fourth made her miserably uncomfortable by staring at her over the edge of the newspaper he pretended to read.

Arriving finally at an inn offering a bath, Lily could not wait to divest herself of her soiled clothing and cleanse away the grime of the trip. Afterward, she felt minimally refreshed and was pleased to find in her reticule a small vial of eau de cologne. Dabbing a drop behind each ear, she felt feminine for the first time since leaving home. She combed her newly washed hair into a chignon and went downstairs for a supper no better than the others along the route. For once, she beat Caleb to the table, but she was not without company. The unpleasant newspaper reader sidled up next to her and sat down. "How you doin', purty lady?"

She inched away from him, not daring to look into his lascivious face. "Middling."

"A lady such as yourself shouldn't be on the trail all by her lonesome." He bit into a hard biscuit and continued talking, spewing crumbs across the table. "Might need a man to escort you. I'd be just the fella. Wouldn't let nobody hurt ya."

Lily froze, her spoonful of beans halfway to her mouth. She'd heard another man talk like this once before. Ingratiating. Sly. Contemptible.

"Cat got yer tongue?" The man leaned forward and circled her neck with his rough hand, his foul breath hot on her face. "Yer not only sweet-smellin', yer purty, too."

Adams! Without even thinking, she sprang to her feet, spilling her meal across the table and onto the floor. "Stay away from me!" She ran for the door, only to be swooped into Caleb's arms as he entered the tavern.

"Go to your room, Lily. Lock the door." Caleb set her down and strode toward the offensive passenger. As she darted up the stairs, she heard scuffling and then Caleb's commanding voice. "If you ever touch that woman again, even look at her, I will do to you what I have not hesitated to do to my enemies in battle. Are we clear?"

Lily could not make out the man's answer, but she sank, trembling, onto the cornhusk mattress, grateful beyond words for Caleb's intervention. Again. Whatever their current relationship, he was still her knight in shining armor.

A light rap sounded on the closed door. She moved

cautiously and put her ear against the wood. "Lily? Are you all right?"

Relieved, she opened the door a crack. "I am fine, thanks to you. You seem to make a habit of saving me."

Caleb stood with his hands behind his back, worry etched on his face. "I'm glad I was here. I have put that man on notice. Furthermore, he and I will be trading places. Tomorrow he will ride topside, and I will join you in the coach."

Her heart gave a lilt before catapulting back down. She would be grateful for his protection, but having him by her side for the upcoming miles would pose challenges. She could not permit herself to get too comfortable with him or put too much reliance on his good will. "I shall welcome that change. He was a most disagreeable companion."

"That's putting it charitably," Caleb muttered. Then he seemed to draw himself up. "I bid you a good night."

"It is already good. You have been a source of great help. Thank you." She gazed up at him, at once wanting to prolong their conversation, but knowing she must end it. "Good night, Captain."

He nodded, then turned to walk away, but not before she heard him correct her under his breath. *"Caleb."*

The paddleboat *Mary McDonald* was a pleasant surprise to Lily, outfitted with the latest furnishings and amenities and carrying genteel passengers in the cabins near hers. The dining room sported crystal chandeliers, and the tables were covered with sparkling white linen and silver place settings. A string trio played in the background while the diners feasted on delicately prepared dishes, a far cry from the tasteless fare of her thirteen days on the trail. Still, the slow-moving boat, maneuvering the snags and shoals of the river with care, offered little relief from the heat. During the day she often sat on deck. She and Caleb had been seated at the same dinner table, so perforce, they were speaking often.

Three days before their docking in St. Louis, he sought her out on the deck. "May I sit?"

She waved vaguely at the vacant chair next to her. "Of course."

He settled beside her and pulled a book from his pocket. "I found this volume in Independence and thought you might like it."

He handed it to her. *"Little Women?"* She couldn't hold back her smile. "I've read about Miss Alcott's work."

"It gives a different view of the War between the States. It is a touching story about a mother and her four daughters and the challenges that faced the families of soldiers."

She cradled the novel to her chest. "I will begin posthaste in order to finish it before we dock."

"No need. It is yours." He studied the passing shoreline as if to avoid looking at her. "An appreciation for literature is one thing we have in common."

She remembered fondly their discussions of poetry. "Thank you. I shall look forward to the story."

He stretched out his legs and folded his hands across his middle, seemingly engaged by the passing scenery. A puff of black smoke snorted from the stack and the boat shuddered as the paddle wheel began turning faster. Lily opened the book and tried to read, but lack of concentration caused her to go over one sentence four times. What was the matter with her?

Then Caleb put it into words for her. "We have only three more days together." Lily waited for him to go on. "I long ago decided that there is no purpose to be served by taking one last opportunity to press my case, nor to upset you by an emotional plea." After a slight pause, he turned to her. "But, Lily, you are my friend. I hope I am that to you, as well. I confess to having avoided you for much of the trip. Frankly, being near you is, in some ways, painful. However, I would like to propose that we spend this remaining time enjoying each other's company so that we may part from one another with mutual affection."

It was as if Caleb had read her mind. Even though her life was soon to take off in a dizzying direction, she craved the reassurance of his company and his steadying influence. Truth to tell, the nearer the boat approached its destination, the more edgy and insecure she felt. She had not seen Aunt Lavinia since childhood, nor, despite letters from her through the intervening years, could Lily picture with accuracy the grand life she was about to enter. "I should like that very much."

"Perhaps we could revisit our unfinished yet lively debate about Milton's poetic vision of the Garden of Eden."

"Let's do. Pray tell, of what value was poor Adam to the curious Eve?"

Their animated conversation began, continued during a promenade around the deck and concluded only when the dinner table conversation involving other passengers shifted to the latest news about railroad expansion across the West and the very recent introduction of reliable passenger service to those parts.

Rocked in the easy motion of her berth later that night, Lily smiled with the recollection of their stimulating conversation and in anticipation of future such dialogues with learned St. Louisians. Caleb's dedication to educating himself made him a stimulating and humorous partner in discourse. She would concentrate on those qualities and not on his mischievous eyes or his hearty laugh. And certainly not on the quivery feeling she had in the pit of her stomach every time he looked at her.

The closer they churned toward the wharf, the more boats of all sizes crowded the two rivers joining forces in St. Louis. Smoke belched from stacks, bells sounded warnings and rivermen's raucous cries filled the air. Caleb stood at Lily's side on the rail, watching the beehive of human activity around them. Or in Caleb's case, pretending to watch. All of his senses were centered on the beautiful young woman beside him who so filled his every waking thought. Out of the corner of his eye, he tried mentally to capture the exact hue of her honey-spun hair, the apricot glow of her cheeks, the insouciant turn of her mouth, the expressiveness of her long fingers, knowing even as he did so, that the image would fade like an old tintype.

Beside him, he could sense her breath coming in short gasps as tension stiffened her body. Before them spread an incredible sight—wagons, carriages, omnibuses weaving through a crowd of pedestrians of every race and nation; men of color, their bodies gleaming with sweat, hauling thick hawsers or hoisting bales of goods on their shoulders; huge warehouses lining the docks alongside taverns spilling noisy men onto the streets. "This isn't Fort Larned," he said in wry understatement.

Lily clutched his arm, her eyes widened in surprise. "Caleb, what have I done?"

He wondered that himself, but his role was to smooth her transition. "This is no place for a lady. Your aunt will soon whisk you off to their lovely, quiet residence."

She continued to hang on to his arm while the paddleboat nudged the dock, the porters began offloading baggage and the first passengers disembarked. She spoke, but in the whistle from the stack, he hadn't understood her. He leaned forward to hear her repeat herself. "I don't want to go."

"Faint heart, my lady? That will never do. You are experiencing a momentary loss of courage. I know you better than that. You are setting forth on a mission, the culmination of your dreams. Now then, take my arm and we'll find your aunt." Never had such cheering words been spoken with less sincerity. All he wanted to do was pick her up and carry her off, to save her from... What? He sighed. He couldn't save her. He was setting her free.

They made their way through the crowds to a place where a stack of baggage from the *Mary McDonald* awaited claiming. He had just located her trunk, when he heard a shrill voice. "Lily? Lily Kellogg?"

Lily stood on tiptoe and waved her hand. "Here I am, Aunt Lavinia."

With the dignity and command of a general, a woman dressed in a full-skirted emerald gown of flounces and appliqués and crowned by a large feather-covered hat parted the proverbial seas to reach Lily. "Niece, at last." She enveloped Lily in an embrace, and then stood back to study her. "You are lovely, my dear. I shall enjoy choosing a wardrobe to put you à la mode. You will be the talk of St. Louis."

Caleb hung back. He could hardly imagine Lily would want such recognition, but perhaps he was mistaken.

"Aunt Lavinia, I would like to present my friend and escort Captain Caleb Montgomery."

The woman's eyes swept over him in both inspection and dismissal. "Your service to my niece is appreciated, sir." Then she turned to Lily and pointed at the ground. "Are these your things?"

"Yes."

"My driver will gather them." She looked around, turning up her nose in distaste. "Let us remove ourselves from this disgusting place and wait in the carriage." She encircled Lily's waist. "Come along, now, dear. You're almost home."

Before Caleb could gather his wits to tell Lily goodbye or once more let her know that he would always love her, the formidable aunt had ushered her through the crowd toward a handsome carriage. Caleb stood motionless as if the ground had collapsed beneath him, unaware of anything but Lily's fleeing back and the glint of her golden hair. Then, slowly, he made his way to a vantage point where he could watch her approach the vehicle that would carry her away from him forever. Lavinia Dupree had a death grip on her niece's arm, but he noticed Lily dragging her feet. Then just before she entered the carriage, she turned her head, somehow finding him in the crowd. Her eyes met his, and then she smiled—so wistfully that even from that awful moment, he mined a nugget of hope.

Chapter Fifteen

Lily dipped her pen in the inkwell and then set it down. The blank sheet of stationery on the desk stymied her. How would she ever be able to describe for Rose and her father the grandeur in which she found herself? Her fantasies had been one thing; the reality was quite another. From the moment she sank into the lush carriage cushions at the wharf until she cast eyes on the Italianate facade of her new home, she had entered a world beyond her imagining. Stately elm trees shaded the avenue, lined with other equally imposing residences set back from manicured lawns. A housemaid, dressed in a black uniform and starched white apron, had greeted them at the door to relieve Lily of her hat and reticule. In that first moment, she could hardly take in the furnishings—marble floors, Chinese vases, silk tapestries, gilded mirrors—and everywhere elegant tables and chairs, artfully arranged on thick Persian carpets. The air itself, fragrant with floral potpourri, seemed rarefied.

Glancing around her ornate bedroom, hung with

velvet drapes, she marveled at the poster bed, chiffonier and dressing table, all delicately painted in gilt and ivory. What would Rose make of this room? Even after two weeks, Lily was having difficulty falling asleep in the commodious bed. Fort Larned seemed very far away, indeed. Despite her sumptuous environment, the city was noisy and confusing, and she struggled to keep homesickness at bay.

Procrastination would get her nowhere. With a sigh, she adjusted the blotter under the stationery, picked up the pen again and began writing.

Dearest Rose and Papa,
By now you will have received my first, abbreviated message announcing my safe arrival in St. Louis and thanking you for taking the precaution of engaging Captain Montgomery to accompany me.

It is time for a more leisurely epistle in which I recount "Lily's Grand Adventure," not unlike that of Gulliver, who also entered strange, new lands. Aunt Lavinia has been most generous, transforming me from a rather drab personage into a belle (those are her words).

Once more Lily set aside the pen. Her family would be distressed to know the means of that transformation, beginning with consignment of most of her clothes to the rag bin. Since her arrival she had been prodded by corsetieres, measured by shoemakers, draped by dressmakers, coiffed by hairdressers, topped off by milliners and subjected to milk baths, hand creams and cucumber facials—all in the name of fashion. Her reading of *Godey's Lady's Book* had ill-prepared her for how exhausting the pursuit of style and beauty could be.

> You would not recognize your prairie flower, decked out in crinolines, satins, laces and dancing slippers. At last, Aunt Lavinia has pronounced me fit for polite company. Yet there is much I still must learn to prevent embarrassing myself in society. I hasten to assure you that every minute here has exceeded my expectations. Despite that, I miss you both more than I even imagined and pray nightly for your health and well-being.

She concluded with a cursory description of the house and a mention of the garden party which would serve as her introduction to the Duprees' coterie. Blowing on the page to dry the ink, she slipped it into the envelope she had already addressed and rose to deliver it to the mail stand in the front hall.

Reaching the bottom of the stairs and depositing the letter, she decided to go to the library in hopes of finding something to read. The room was dark, and high shelves laden with books dwarfed her. Crossing to the window, she pulled back the drapes to let in the sunshine. Studying the spines of the volumes nearest the light, she didn't hear Lavinia enter.

"Child, whatever are you doing in here?" Her aunt stood in the doorway, her brows elevated in surprise.

"I am hunting for a book to amuse or educate me."

"Amuse? Educate?" Lavinia made the words sound like blasphemy. "Libraries are for men. No point to fill your pretty head with tedious ideas, especially not on a lovely autumn day like this. Repair with me to the morning room, and I shall fill you with all the latest gossip, a better education for society than any treatise in that library. Then this afternoon, you may accompany me on my weekly social calls."

Wisely, Lily did not argue even though she longed to point out that many modern women were becoming more broadly educated. Caught up in Lavinia's wake from that moment on, it was only that night in the solitude of her bedroom that Lily had time to reflect on the strange episode in the library. Never in her life had she been discouraged from reading. Quite the contrary. Apparently, though, it was not an activity smiled upon for women in this milieu. Lily was dumbfounded. Were females supposed to park their brains at the door? Rely upon men for news and intellectual stimulation? For the first time she began to wonder what she had bartered away for her St. Louis adventure.

His business in St. Louis concluded after a couple of weeks, Caleb was set to embark upriver late in the afternoon for Independence and then on to the ranch by horseback. He had been able to negotiate some favorable terms and delivery dates and felt satisfied with the contacts he had made. After the relative quiet of Fort Larned, the hubbub of the city was a constant assault on the senses. Outside his hotel window, heavy conveyances rattled past at all hours, hawkers selling wares shouted their spiels and from the riverfront came the never-ending noise of gears grinding and whistles screaming. The heavy smoke settling over the town made him long for prairie breezes.

Yet desirable as leaving this place might be, the idea

set him on edge. Once he departed St. Louis, whatever chance he had to see Lily again departed with him. All morning as he set about packing his belongings, he fought with himself. He had seen Lily's aunt and her carriage. *Opulent* was the only word for the life Lily had entered two weeks ago, the life, he reminded himself, that was the fulfillment of her dream. Why couldn't he leave it at that? Walk away into his own new life?

Against all reason, he couldn't forget her farewell smile, rather like that of a home-loving waif being packed off to boarding school.

Finally, with no chores left to accomplish and several hours yet to kill before boarding the boat, he acted on an impulse that even he knew was the height of folly. He hired a horse-drawn cab and gave the driver the address Ezra had provided him.

"That's a posh part of town, sir. Old families with piles and piles of money. Some made honest, some on the sly."

"Drive on." Caleb didn't relish the man's opinions, which only confirmed his own.

Once they arrived in the "posh part of town," Caleb wondered what he'd been thinking. That he'd somehow spot Lily strolling down the street? That he would pound on the Duprees' door and demand an audience? Or did he simply need to torture himself with a glimpse of her fashionable world?

"We're here, sir." The driver slowed the horse to a walk, then gestured at a huge stone residence. "This be old man Dupree's. He's got more money than he can count."

"Stop." Caleb studied the place, the likes of which

he had seen only in travel books. The heart seemed to drain out of him. Lily had most definitely arrived. Just as he leaned forward to ask the driver to move on, the front door of the mansion opened. At that same moment, the Dupree carriage rounded the drive. Lavinia sailed forth and stood waiting imperiously. But following her…it couldn't be. A fashion plate in an elaborate full skirt topped by a crimson pleated jacket with wide sleeves stepped out, pulling on lacy gloves. Yet the tilt of her head and the spun gold of her hair left no doubt. His Lily. *No, no,* he corrected himself grimly. Just Lily, his lost love.

The ballroom glittered in the reflected light of crystal prisms dangling from massive chandeliers. In keeping with the season, the refreshments were displayed on sideboards decorated with cornucopias overflowing with fruits and vegetables. Behind a screen of potted plants, a small orchestra played, and whirling about the parquet floor were men in evening dress coupled with women in a kaleidoscope of colorful ball gowns. Uncle Henry and Aunt Lavinia had spared no expense in making this event memorable. Lily's head swam with the many people to whom she'd been introduced, including an outrageous number of unattached gentlemen. She danced now with Lionel Atwood, whose father was an important St. Louis financier. Thanks to the dance master Aunt Lavinia had engaged for her, Lily could make conversation without undue worry about the placement of her feet.

"Miss Kellogg, what are your impressions of our fair city?" Atwood had an athletic, rapierlike body, a chiseled face, dark hair and a waxed mustache in which he took obvious pride. Lily found him quite handsome, more than some of the other men clamoring for her attention.

"It is a wonder, sir. I am enjoying discovering more about it."

"Splendid." He led her on a dizzying series of steps, ending with a flourish near a secluded alcove just as the music stopped. "St. Louis must provide a welcome contrast to the frontier."

"Certainly there are many more amusements here." He would not make her disparage her upbringing.

He smiled down at her. "Of which I hope to be one. I am most eager to hear about the red savages and why our army has not yet succeeded in subduing them." He sniffed. "It's a national disgrace."

She thought of the times she had watched the troops ride out and of Caleb lying wounded in the hospital. "It is not as easy as it might appear from a distance."

"With your permission, I should like to call one afternoon this week. Perhaps then you can tell me more."

Lily had no sense that she would be able to bring truth into play, given the man's preconceived notions. She was grasping for a delaying tactic, when Aunt Lavinia swept up to them. "Lionel, Lily. How lovely your names sound together."

Lionel smiled smugly. "I was just asking Miss Kellogg if I might call on her this week."

There was no mistaking the gleam in Aunt Lavinia's eyes—this was good news to her. "But, of course, my dear boy. Just send your man around with a note so that we may properly receive you."

Lionel picked up Lily's hand and bent over as if to kiss it. Yet his lips hovered above it. "I shall eagerly await our conversation." He straightened to his full height and then excused himself, leaving the two women alone.

Lily felt Aunt Lavinia's fingers digging into her arm. "Well done, Lily. I do believe you have enchanted the most eligible bachelor of the season." She gazed out over the crowd, crooning softly, "What a match that would be!"

The rest of the evening passed in a daze. Never had Lily imagined so elegantly dressed a crowd or been the object of such attention. It was both heady and daunting. By evening's end, more than one of the young men had mentioned calling on her. Yet it was difficult to assess the difference between their genuine interest and social duty. Courtship here apparently involved both a language and an etiquette, the permutations of which seemed beyond her grasp.

In the wee hours of the morning when the last guests had finally departed, Lily escaped to her bedroom where the maid assisted her out of her gown and took down her hair. When the young woman picked up the silver brush, Lily reached for it. "It's late. Go on to bed. I'll do it." The maid's surprised look let Lily know she had made yet another gaffe, but she craved solitude in which to reflect on the evening. That was not to be. With the merest rap on the door, Aunt Lavinia, clad in her dressing gown, breezed into the room and took the chair nearest Lily.

"You were a sensation, my dear." Aunt Lavinia's eyes glittered with approval.

"If in any way that is so, the credit goes to you. I can't thank you enough for all you have done for me."

"It's as Mathilda would've wished."

At her mother's name, Lily stopped pulling the brush through her curls. "I do not want to disappoint her—or you."

"With no daughter of my own, having you here and being able to introduce you to the best people is quite special. And what Mathilda wanted for you." Then her aunt stood, came close and picked up the brush. "Let me," she said, smoothing the hair off Lily's forehead. "As you can see, I am surrounded by every object money can buy. Henry has been quite indulgent with me and I am grateful to him."

Lily waited, sensing that words were being left unsaid. Though polite and deferential to one another, Lily had seen little affection pass between her aunt and uncle.

"He knows how dear your mother was to me and will spare nothing for you to have a lavish and successful season."

"Successful?"

Aunt Lavinia maintained even brushstrokes. "Of course. Finding you the most advantageous match."

Lily had a sudden impression of herself as chattel.

"You have made a marvelous first step. Lionel Atwood would be a most suitable husband. His prospects are boundless."

What about the museums she had yet to see? The lectures she was to attend? The public library she might now be forbidden to visit? "Husband? It's too soon. I had thought to do and see so much and—"

"Nonsense. There will be time for other pursuits after you are comfortably settled. If a wife is discreet, a man generally will overlook her intellectual pretensions." She set down the brush and patted Lily's head.

"For now, you just concentrate on your young men. Particularly Lionel. Henry would be so pleased with that alliance."

Once her aunt had left the room, words, none of which made any sense to Lily, whirled about her—*successful season, advantageous match, prospects* and, worst of all, *alliance*. Is that how the Duprees saw her? As their representative in an *alliance?*

One word, she noted, had never been uttered. *Love.* It seemed to Lily a rather important oversight.

Throughout the month of November and into early December, hardly a day had passed without a social engagement of some kind—teas, concerts and balls. At first each new event had delighted Lily whether it was sitting, breathless, in a theater box, thrilling to an opera singer or dining on a sumptuous seven-course dinner served by footmen. No matter what surprises her social schedule presented, she would never become accustomed to the elaborate ritual of her toilette. Aunt Lavinia had made it clear that a lady never received company nor left the house until dressed in the appropriate gown and with every hair in place. Some mornings Lily longed to throw on an old gingham dress and tuck her hair into a bun as she had done every day of her adult life up until now.

Among her suitors were several socially charming yet intellectually dull fellows, but, gradually, Lionel Atwood had outpaced them until it was obvious he regarded himself as the front-runner for her affections. She had no trouble understanding why her aunt and uncle favored him. He was polished and urbane—a Harvard graduate and heir to his father's banking and financial empire. The mystery was why he preferred her. Following their several conversations about the settling of the West, Lily suspected she presented a novelty—an unpolished gem. Just last night in his carriage returning from a play, he had said, "Surely those barbarians have no understanding of civilization."

"It depends upon what you mean by *civilization*," she had countered. "While we might regard their living conditions as primitive, Indians have every bit as much sense of family as we do, as well as strong tribal loyalty."

"But aren't they filthy?"

"No more so than anyone who lives close to nature. The buffalo hunters, for instance."

"That's different."

Lily failed to see how, but kept that opinion to herself. "Some are talented craftsmen. Their beadwork and pottery are exceptional."

"Perhaps they should pick up their tepees and go someplace where they can indulge those pastimes and quit harassing our supply routes. The government is supposedly in the process of relocating these people. Not quickly enough, apparently."

Helpless to overcome his disdain, Lily could at least attempt to ameliorate it. "Had you been at Fort Larned these past few months, you would have witnessed the noble efforts the military is making to control the situation."

"Too bad they didn't employ the same strategy as at the Battle of the Washita River."

Lily's mouth went dry. From Caleb, she knew what a ghastly chapter that had been in military history—and how scarred he was by the event. "Sir, in the interests of friendship, I believe we should find another subject to discuss. That battle was a massacre, and those who fought it must live forever with their shame."

Lionel turned to look at her in the faint light of the passing streetlamps. "Whose side are you on?"

"I don't see why I must pick sides. There is good and evil in all of us."

He had patted her hand. "My dear, you are such an idealist." It didn't sound like a compliment.

Recalling the conversation the next morning, Lily tried to rationalize Lionel's remarks. He shared the prejudice of so many of his class, especially those geographically removed from the problems of the West. He had no experience with the complexities of subduing a people spread over thousands of miles who were doing nothing more than protecting and defending lands they regarded as their own. More almost than his ignorance of the realities, she was bothered by his condescending attitude, as if she could have nothing of value to contribute to the topic.

Yet the man had his redeeming qualities. He was unfailingly solicitous of her and seemed to take pride in entering a room with her on his arm. He was generous with gifts of flowers and jewelry and had helped to ease her into several challenging social situations. There was much to like about him, and she promised herself to focus on those qualities.

He was picking her up this morning for church. Lily enjoyed this element of St. Louis life. Sunday services at the fort had been hit-and-miss, dependent upon the presence of a chaplain or the availability of the commanding officer. The Duprees and Atwoods attended a large Episcopal church with beautiful stained-glass windows and a massive pipe organ. If grandeur had anything to do with God's favor, and she doubted it did, this congregation was blessed.

Standing at Lionel's side as they sang the opening hymn, she could almost picture herself as his wife. He tucked an arm around her waist and his pure tenor soared with the words, "Faith of our fathers, living still…" The sermon was uplifting, and the formality of the service impressive.

Outside the church afterward, she asked Lionel how long he had been a member.

"Since childhood."

"Religion must be an important part of your life."

"In what way?"

She opened, then closed her mouth. Had he not understood the simple question? To cover the awkward silence, she stammered, "Well, in all ways. Providing support in challenging circumstances and comfort in times of distress or grief."

"I'm sure it offers those amenities for many."

Amenities? Blessings, rather. "But for you?"

"I enjoy the aesthetics and the associations I make with the people."

"Membership is beneficial for your business, then?" Only with great restraint did she withhold her sarcasm.

"That's a bit crass, Lily, even if there is an element of truth in it. Let me reassure you that the Lord is still knocking at my door. I just haven't quite let Him in, yet."

Lily sighed with relief. She couldn't fault him for resisting God's call so long as he was receptive to it. Admittedly, she herself was not without an occasional question.

During the drive home, he took the liberty of holding her hand. "I presume you know how very fond of you I am."

Lily lowered her head to avoid his direct gaze. "You have been most courteous in escorting me about the town."

"It's more than courtesy, my dear. I enjoy showing you off." He tilted her chin so she could not avoid his chocolate-brown eyes. "You are quite beautiful, my dear. Any man would be proud to have you on his arm."

Here it was. All the sophisticated flattery and flirtation she had so long imagined, falling from the tongue of a handsome man practiced in the art. "Lionel, you make me blush."

"That is one reason I am so fond of you. You have none of the pretense or coyness of other women, whom, to be frank, I find boring."

"I often feel like a sparrow among the peacocks."

"Nonsense." He raised her gloved hands to his lips. "You are a rare, exotic bird, whom I treasure."

Oddly, her heart continued to beat at its normal rate. Her breath came easily. Why wasn't she ecstatic with joy to have such a sought-after bachelor singing her praises?

"May I?" And before she could stop him, he leaned forward and brushed his lips across hers, his mustache tickling her skin. He leaned back, then, smiling at her. "As delicious as I imagined."

She couldn't have written the dialogue any more effectively had she been Miss Austen or Miss Brontë, yet strangely, it had none of the power to move her as the novels had. The question boiled down to this: Could she will herself to love Lionel Atwood?

* * *

Astride the bay gelding he had bought in Independence, Caleb stared across the snow-covered Flint Hills, marveling at the sheer expanse of land. Three nights before, a powerful north wind had swirled down upon the ranch, bringing with it the first blizzard of the season. Only today was he able to make his way into the Cottonwood Falls post office where a week's worth of newspapers and mail had accumulated, including a letter from Will Creekmore.

Caleb had hoped Will's message would include word of Lily, but, instead, it was primarily an account of the diminishing number of military engagements at Fort Larned and one sentence extolling Fannie's virtues as a wife. He hadn't really expected Will to comment about Lily, nor, did he suppose, would it have made any difference. He guided his mount around a drift even as he reproached himself for letting Lily creep into his thoughts, as she did so maddeningly often. Foolishly, he had expected the change of scenery to help. He knew he needed to give her up, but knowing that didn't make it easier.

After stabling his horse, he walked toward the ranch house, a two-story frame-and-stone dwelling Seth and his father had built. The front porch had a sweeping view to the southwest. The rear was sheltered by a low hill and several cottonwoods and elms. Caleb stepped into the warm kitchen, eased out of his boots and laid the mail on the rough wooden table.

Sophie, her freckled face flushed, stood at the stove, stirring a delicious-smelling batch of beef stew. "Anything for me?"

"What were you expecting?"

She pursed her lips as if deep in thought. "Oh, maybe a billet-doux from the marquis or a proposal from the duke."

"Will you settle for the *Kansas City Times?*"

She faked a pout. "You're no fun."

"No, I guess I'm not." He'd intended the words jokingly, but they came out flat.

She set the spoon on a rest and turned to face him. "We need to talk. Sit down there—" she gestured at the table "—and have a cup of coffee with me."

He wanted to slither away, but he knew his sister. She was a woman on a mission. She served him, then sat down across from him. "You know I love you."

"I do. However, I sense a *but* coming."

"But—" she grinned by way of emphasis "—you've got something on your mind and whatever it is has stolen away my brother. You remember him? The kind, funny, lovable fellow I adore?"

He made a play of looking around the room. "Hmm. He doesn't seem to be here."

"Well, I want him back." She reached across the table and captured both his hands in hers. "You may not want to talk about this with Pa or Seth, but I can be relentless. I've waited long enough for you to broach the subject. Your time's up. Tell me about her."

He was trapped, not only by Sophie's hands, but by her penetrating look. His sister had always known him better than anyone else. "It's that obvious?"

She looked at him as if he'd just asked the world's dumbest question. "Spit it out, brother."

He disengaged from her grasp and, with a sigh, leaned back in his chair. "Her name is Lily Kellogg."

"Seth told me about her. Said you'd asked her to

marry you. That's serious business. Where is this Miss Kellogg who has stolen your heart?"

Slowly, reluctantly, he told her about Lily's dream of visiting St. Louis and his final, heart-wrenching view of her outside the Dupree mansion.

Sophie's eyes never left his face. When he finished, she nodded several times. "You love her still."

It wasn't a question. It didn't need to be. Sophie listened with her heart. "Yes."

"Did you have reason to believe she could return your affection?"

"Once I did."

Sophie picked up her coffee cup and stared into it, as if it were a divining pool. "You were right to let her go."

His head snapped up. "How can you say that?"

"She had to try it."

"It?"

"The fancy life in the big city. She would never have been happy wondering if she had missed out on that adventure."

"Small comfort," he muttered.

She eyed him over the top of her cup. "I believe it is. Now listen to me, Captain Caleb Montgomery, stormer of fortresses and leader of men, are you surrendering or is she worth fighting for?"

His sister had always had a strong will, and he felt himself being propelled along by it. "I will never love another woman the way I love her."

Sophie whooped, set down her cup and gave the table a tattoo with the flat of her hands. "Aha! I thought so. Your Lily must be quite a gal. So count me in!"

"For what?"

"Our strategy. I'm tired of you moping around here.

You are going to win her back, and I am going to help with the battle plan. 'Faint heart ne'er won fair lady.'"

Caleb felt his face relax into a smile. Sophie was a force of nature and he trusted her mightily. He couldn't explain it, but once again a ray of hope lightened his gloom. He corrected himself. More than hope. Determination.

Chapter Sixteen

Dressed in a plum-colored afternoon dress, Lily sat by the cozy fire in the parlor awaiting Lionel's visit. Ever since the New Year's ball held in his parents' home, he had grown increasingly attentive, squiring her to a concert by a noted tenor and treating her to several drama productions. She exulted in each exposure to such cultural events. Yet the highlight had come not with Lionel, but rather with Uncle Henry when he escorted her to a scientific lecture concerning Charles Darwin's controversial *On the Origin of Species*. There was no particular in which her fancies had gone unmet. She should be basking in contentment, but despite all she had been given and had experienced, she was aware of a void that went beyond missing her family.

In such moments she often thought of Caleb. Wondered what he was doing. If he was happy. At the same time, though, she recalled the brutal conditions on the frontier, especially in this season of icy blizzards and bone-chilling temperatures. Surrounded by creature comforts, her every need anticipated and met, she dismissed such idle speculation. She had made her choice.

In the distance she heard the butler greet Lionel and stood to welcome him. He entered the room, cheeks pink from the cold, and went to the fire to warm his hands before turning to clasp hers. "Let us find hope in the words of John Keats. 'If Winter comes, can Spring be far behind?'"

"Shelley," Lily found herself saying before she could stop herself.

"Shelley? My dear, you are mistaken."

Lily knew she was not and dared to correct him again. "Percy Bysshe Shelley. 'Ode to the West Wind.'"

Cocking one eyebrow, Lionel released her hands and laughed. "Silly goose. Who went to Harvard, you or me? I remember well. John Keats penned those immortal words." He ushered her to a love seat. "Never mind—" he sat beside her "—spring will bring not only temperate climes but beauty."

Lily did not appreciate being patronized, but decided pressing her point would gain nothing. She couldn't help thinking that Caleb would have known the difference. "Do you think it will snow soon?"

"I pray not. The town comes to a standstill, especially if there is ice." He leaned forward ingratiatingly. "Before that happens, I want to take you to an exhibition of paintings opening at my club Saturday."

"I should like that very much."

"I will call for you at two and perhaps we can stop afterward for an early supper at a highly recommended new café." He leaned forward and kissed her cheek. "I so enjoy showing you off."

She stifled the feeling of being objectified. After all, she had always dreamed of a man who would appreciate her and court her with devotion. She smiled coquettishly. "I shall do my best to live up to your expectations."

He beamed at her. "You always do. Few men can boast of having such a beauty on their arms."

"And what of brains?" she urged.

Again, he laughed. "Brains? What need have you of those pesky things? Leave that to me. Men are trained for the intellectual side of life. Women have their place in the home and as complements to their husbands."

Lily winced. She knew that such role expectations existed in society and had even seen them acted out by her aunt and uncle, but she had never before heard them so baldly expressed. Could she be the mere ornament of a man? But what was the use of confronting Lionel now? She usually enjoyed his company and thrived on the fascinating places he took her. Theirs was a relationship of mutual benefit. It wasn't as if they were engaged, she reminded herself.

"Lionel, you are somewhat old-fashioned, I suppose."

"Spoken like a freethinker, which I devoutly hope you are not."

"No, not a freethinker, but I do enjoy a spirited discussion of contemporary issues."

"At the appropriate time, my dear. In private."

It wasn't exactly like being muffled. Perhaps he would be open to serious conversations so long as others were not involved. She mentally shook her head. She was a long way from home.

After Lionel departed, Lily retreated to her room and picked up the most recent letter from Fannie. As she read, a wave of homesickness caught her by surprise.

Dear Lily,

I have much to tell you, but first, I hope you know how much all of us miss you. Yet we revel in your accounts of the places you are going and the sights you are seeing. It is a joy to picture you in your fine gowns living in the comfortable home you describe. How generous of your aunt and uncle to treat you with such affection!

Your father and Rose are in good health and spirits. Will and I continue to thank God for our blessings. Indian activity has subsided during the winter, so we are able to spend more time with one another. Yet the weather has taken its toll on the men, and I am very busy at the hospital. But, oh, Lily, how I love learning about medicine and being of help to your father, so devoted to his patients.

Lily laid the letter aside and gazed out the window at the bare branches scraping against the mansion's exterior. An ache of longing filled the pit of her stomach. The hospital. Once, she had felt useful, valuable. Her next thought struck her with the force of a blow—when had she experienced that kind of fulfillment here in St. Louis? She had been so caught up in the whirlwind of Aunt Lavinia's social agenda that she had not taken time to reflect on what she might be missing. In memory came the sights and smells of the hospital, the gratitude of her patients, her sense of satisfaction in her duties.

How could any number of exhibitions of paintings with Lionel compare?

* * *

Saturday morning as Lily was getting dressed for her outing with Lionel, Aunt Lavinia entered the room, shooed the maid away and perched on the crewel-covered bench at the foot of Lily's bed. "Tell me, dear, how are you enjoying our winter pastimes?"

"From *The Taming of the Shrew* to yesterday's band concert, I count myself among the most fortunate of young ladies, thanks to you."

"It is you who have given us the pleasure. I know Mathilda would be enormously pleased with how you are blooming in this setting." With her bejeweled fingers, she adjusted the large cameo hanging from her neck. "She would be pleased, as well, with the attentions of Lionel Atwood."

Intent on inserting her earrings, Lily waited, sensing her aunt had more to say.

"He seems very fond of you."

"He has been most kind."

Lavinia cleared her throat. "Perhaps he is more than fond."

Lily wheeled around. "Whatever do you mean?"

"I wasn't going to tell you, but perhaps it will be helpful for you to know. He has spoken with Henry."

Lily drew a quick breath. "'Spoken?' Surely you can't be serious…"

"Yes, I believe he intends to ask you to marry him."

Lily gasped. "No. I mean, we hardly know each other that well."

Lavinia waved her hand in dismissal. "You know him as well as any bride can know her intended before the wedding. My dear, any true marital relationship develops after courtship. Most brides take their husbands on faith."

Lily was appalled. *Take a husband on faith? It sounded no better than an arranged marriage.* "Aunt Lavinia, I am at a loss for words…"

"How many young women of your set will envy you your good fortune in bewitching Lionel. Why, I can see it now. A late-May wedding. The peonies will be in bloom and roses, too. A reception in our garden, and—"

"It's too soon." Lily could scarcely breathe. "I need more time with Lionel. I must sort out my feelings."

Lavinia rose to her feet. "Nerves, dear. We all have them, but, rest assured, you could not make a more promising match. What a delight it will be to host your wedding, and, of course, we must invite your father and sister."

"Stop!" Lily tried to soften the panic in her voice. "Lionel hasn't even proposed yet."

Lavinia smiled confidently. "He will." Her aunt stood, kissed her on the top of the head and repeated the ominous words. "He will."

After she left the room, Lily sat, hands folded in her lap, studying her reflection in the dressing table mirror. She hardly recognized the woman staring back—hair curled atop her head in the latest Parisian fashion, diamond earrings twinkling in the morning light, the rich peacock-blue fabric of her dress showing off her tiny waist. She glanced at her hands, pale and smooth, her nails buffed just so. Nothing about her reflection recalled the dedicated nurse enduring the hardships of life on a military outpost. She turned away from the mirror and stared into space. Did she even know who she was anymore?

The day was bitterly cold, but clear, and the bare mounds of the Flint Hills stretched to the horizon. Caleb and his father worked side by side digging stones for a pathway between the house and barn. The team of horses hitched to the wagon waited patiently as the men slowly hefted flat rocks onto the bed. Near noon, Caleb watched his father remove his hat and wipe away the sweat on his brow. The man was no longer young, but still worked like a strapping lad. "Let's stop for lunch, son," he said.

From the wagon seat, Caleb retrieved the packet containing slices of fresh baked bread slathered with apple butter, beef jerky and a chunk of cheese and settled on a nearby boulder next to his father. They ate in silence until his father spoke matter-of-factly. "You're having the nightmares again."

Caleb lost his appetite. When he had first returned home, the dreams came intermittently, but had ceased in recent weeks until the night before when they had returned with a vengeance. "I had hoped no one noticed."

His father chewed on his jerky. "I reckon you came by them honestly. A man can't witness what you undoubtedly have and remain untouched."

Fleeting images of bloodshed passed through Caleb's mind. "I can't forget."

"Nor should you. I had hoped, though, that you

would find peace with regular physical exercise here in God's country."

"I'll be fine."

"Are you so sure? Sophie tells me you might have something else on your mind. *Someone.*"

Caleb grimaced. Count on Sophie to spill the beans, although he suspected Seth also might have blabbed. "I'm dealing with it."

"Heartbreak is a difficult thing." His father gazed beyond the wagon, seemingly in another world.

Minutes passed while Caleb worked up the nerve to ask the difficult question. "Why didn't we ever talk about Ma?"

His father's jaw clenched. "I couldn't, son. Maybe it would've helped us all if I'd been able to." His gnarled hands restlessly folded the oilcloth that had held their food. "But, you see, a part of me died with her. I loved that woman beyond reason. Nothing in my lifetime will be worse than losing her, except now if I lost one of my children. I have tried to be the best father I can be to Sophie. She is precious to me, but everytime, *everytime* I look at her, I see your mother and remember that awful night when she breathed her last."

Caleb studied his father's face, set like the very rock upon which they sat, and he understood that the man's tears had been there all along, dammed up by his need for control. "She was a wonderful mother."

"And a blessing as a wife." Then his father wrapped an arm around Caleb's shoulders and uttered words Caleb knew he would never forget. "Son, if you have found that kind of love, go after it. Your agitated spirit will never find peace until you become one with the woman God has sent you to love. Never mind where she is or what has come between you." Then his father abruptly stood and finished in a husky voice. "If you love her, fight for her, son. Whatever it takes."

Caleb got to his feet and breathed in the pure fresh air of the prairie. *Whatever it takes.* He knew now, more powerfully than ever before, that Lily was his other half, and fight for her he would, no matter what the challenges. Come spring and better weather, his and Sophie's plan had to work.

The art exhibition was breathtaking. So engrossed was Lily in examining each painting in detail and then standing back to admire the totality of the artist's concept, that Lionel grew impatient, often withdrawing his watch from his vest pocket to study the time, as if by that act he could hasten their departure. They had arrived at his club at the height of the showing, but now the crowds had dwindled and winter dusk was settling in.

"Could we go now, Lily?" He stood with his back to the wall, ignoring the art on display. "We will be late for our supper at Café Maurice."

Lily took one last glance at the remarkable painting before her, then faced him. "I'm sorry, Lionel, but this afternoon has been a sheer delight. Such talent beggars the mind."

Lionel concealed a yawn. "So glad you enjoyed it, my dear. Now let's be off."

In the carriage Lily shook off the sense that Lionel had been bored. Perhaps she had lingered a trifle beyond the hour he had expected to leave, but it had been difficult to tear herself away. "Thank you for a lovely afternoon and for being patient with me."

"The art I studied today wasn't a framed piece on the wall. I had the leisure to study you."

She blushed with the thought that she had been the object of such scrutiny. "Sir, you are quite a flatterer."

"Flatterer? I think not." He gathered her gloved hand in his. "Would that I might always have the pleasure of your beauty." He sank back on the cushion, a satisfied smile on his lips. "One day soon, perhaps."

Lily froze. Was he referring to an imminent proposal? *Not today, oh, not today.* "I hope you do not regard me merely as a possession to be acquired."

He laughed then, a sound that relieved her tension. "Hardly. There is your lively spirit to be taken into account, as well. In short, Lily, you intrigue me."

She had never thought of herself in that light. For an uncomfortable moment, she recalled this morning's reflection in the mirror—a young lady of fashion, bedecked in the best money could buy, prepared to set forth on a romantic conquest. What did that woman have to do with Lily Kellogg? In a flash of insight, she realized that the Lily in the carriage was an actress playing a part on the stage of St. Louis.

When they arrived at their destination, the carriage drew to a stop and Lionel handed Lily down. The sidewalk bustled with people going home from work, and the street was crowded with carriages and wagons. The setting sun created a glare, and the cold caused Lily to gather her mantle about her. Across the way she noticed several former slaves unloading barrels and crates from a dray and carrying them into a dry goods store. Just then, their driver yelled, "Runaway, runaway!" Lionel grabbed Lily and pressed her against the side of the carriage.

The rattle of wheels, the cries of bystanders and the neighing of horses filled her ears. Careering down the street toward them came a wagon drawn by frightened, out-of-control horses, their nostrils flaring, their eyes white with panic. People ran for cover and other vehicles drew to the side. Now the wagon was upon them, and Lily felt the swoosh of the horses as they passed and heard the crack of the driver's whip. Then she heard a sickening thump, and all the breath went out of her. The wagon was long gone, but lying on the street was a limp body. A barrel rolled and bounced in the silence that had fallen over the onlookers.

Without a second thought, Lily tore herself from Lionel's grasp, ignored his "Lily, get back here now!" and raced for the victim, who had been unloading the dray. "Don't touch him, miss!" cried one; "Leave him be," yelled another. No one approached to help her. Heedless of her fancy gown, Lily knelt beside the man, feeling for a pulse. With a spasmodic jerk, he gasped for air. He was alive, but Lily didn't like the looks of the head wound gushing blood onto his black skin. She lifted her skirt and ripped a strip of cloth from her petticoat, then folded it and applied pressure to the wound. "Call a doctor," she shouted to Lionel. Instead, he rushed forward and tried to pull her from the man. "Come away, Lily. This man is beneath you. Leave him. Someone will attend to him."

"He could die," Lily muttered, squirming away and renewing her efforts to help the victim.

"Let him," Lionel said. "This has nothing to do with us."

Lily looked at Lionel as if she had never seen him

before. "It has everything to do with us. He's a human being."

Lionel's dark eyes burned with a banked fire. "*Now,* Lily. We're leaving."

Ignoring him, she leaned over her patient and spoke softly in his ear. "Stay with me. You've a nasty wound, but we're taking care of you."

Lionel backed away, and out of the corner of her eye, Lily noticed that still no one had come to her assistance. She glanced around at them. "What's the matter with you people? Somebody help me."

After long minutes, two strong lads approached. "Doctor's comin', miss. We'll take him to the saloon, lay him out on a table. This is no place for the likes of a lady."

She rocked back on her heels, uttered a short prayer for the victim and then stood. "Thank you. Keep pressure on the wound."

Oblivious to the blood splattered on her dress and gloves, she watched the two carry the man off. Why had others ignored the situation? Didn't they see his blood was as red as theirs? She nearly wept with the injustice of it all, and thoughts of Moses threatened to break her completely apart.

Finally, utterly spent, she turned toward Lionel, who waited stony-faced beside the carriage. "Get in," he barked.

He helped her in, pulled himself up and gave orders for the driver to take them to the Duprees'. Hell would freeze before Lily would utter the first word to him.

After several miles, the silence unbroken except for the clop of hooves and the creak of leather, Lionel finally spoke. "What in the name of God were you thinking?"

"It was exactly in the name of God that I *was* thinking. A life hung in the balance." She sighed sadly, knowing that nothing she said would touch him.

"Who do you think you are? Florence Nightingale?"

"As a matter of fact, yes. I am a nurse."

"Not here, you're not. Do you have any idea how you've humiliated me? Demeaned yourself?"

"What? By trying to save a life?"

"Ladies of your social class are not nurses, and they most certainly do not touch strange men, especially of the ilk of that no-account."

Why had she even tried to get Lionel to see reason? Was he really that caught up in status and prestige? Worse yet, were the social mores of his class such that human life was inconsequential? She could see no point in prolonging their conversation. She didn't know with whom she was more disgusted. Lionel or herself. When had she lost sight of what really mattered? It certainly wasn't finery and balls and palatial houses. Nor, God help her, one's social standing.

Lionel held himself still as a graven statue until they mercifully arrived in front of the Dupree mansion. Stiffly, he did her the courtesy of escorting her to the door. There he dismissed her with one curt sentence. "You have gravely disappointed me, Miss Kellogg."

Lily waited until the door closed behind her, then sank to the cold marble floor, shuddering with the enormity of the events of the past half hour. The accident had happened in a split second, but the ramifications reverberated in her head like thunder. Anger, indignation, bafflement—it was all overwhelming. But in no corner of her brain could she rationalize that she should have acted differently. A human being was hurting and needed help which was not forthcoming from others. In no world could she have stood idly by and watched the man suffer. If Lionel was horrified, so be it.

In another part of the house she could hear the tinkle of goblets, the clink of silverware and the quiet shuffle of servants moving between the kitchen and dining room. Dinner. The aroma of roast beef wafted under her nose, and a spasm of nausea caused her to get to her feet and flee to her bedroom. There, she threw herself across the bed and lay in the dark, a whirl of questions giving her no peace. How could she have seriously entertained Lionel Atwood's attentions? Today's actions would surely dash Aunt Lavinia and Uncle Henry's plans for her. She smiled bitterly. The much anticipated *alliance*. How would they react? Would they share Lionel's disappointment in her? It seemed that her every basic instinct was at war with the society in which she found herself. The society she had coveted.

She rolled over on her back, shielding her eyes with her forearm. There was one silver lining. For the first time since arriving here, she had done something truly useful. She had once more become a nurse. In that same act, though, she had also been confronted by the bigotry that surely could play no part in God's plan. Yet all in all, she felt more alive, more herself than she had in months.

There came a light tap on the door, and her maid called out, "Miss, are you all right? Is there aught I might do for you?"

Lily raised her head to be heard through the door.

"Please ask my aunt to come to my room at her convenience." It was best if Aunt Lavinia heard the story from her rather than from Lionel. Lily knew the conversation would not be pleasant, but better to get it over with as soon as possible.

She stood up, then glanced down at her dress, which bore mute testimony to the violent scene in the street. The maid had gone, but Lily had spent years dressing and undressing herself and managed to step out of the bloodstained gown and slip into a robe. Near the window were two chairs. Lily sat down in one to wait, all the time wondering what she had found so appealing about St. Louis society that she had left her family, denied Caleb and abandoned the nursing that gave her life purpose. She had some serious thinking to do.

She was so engrossed in her thoughts that she didn't hear Aunt Lavinia knock and only roused when she heard, "Why are you sitting here in the dark?"

Lavinia moved to the bedside table and turned on a single gas lamp.

"I have something to tell you. Please, come sit with me."

Lavinia, her brow furrowed quizzically, took the chair across from Lily's. "Are you ill?"

"No." Lily fingered the silken tie of her robe. "I have done something I believe to be right, but which I fear will be upsetting to you." Then drawing a deep breath, she launched into details of the accident and her own part in tending to the former slave's wound.

Lavinia listened without interruption, although Lily observed the sag of her aunt's shoulders when she described the victim. "Oh, child" was all she managed when Lily concluded with Lionel's unforgiving reaction. "I'm afraid you have jeopardized your chances with Lionel."

"I have no doubt of it." Lily raised her head in defiance, far more concerned about the fate of the victim than Lionel's pique. "Mr. Atwood and I come from two different worlds, and I have concluded I have no desire to be any part of his."

"But surely—" her aunt sputtered the words "—you understand that it is not merely Lionel of whom we speak. Hobnobbing with inferiors is just not done. Touching such a person, bloodying yourself—why, it's unthinkable behavior. If word of this gets out, you will become a social pariah."

Lily gritted her teeth. She had not realized how ingrained the mores of Lavinia's class could be. "I know you're disappointed in me. I am grateful for all the many opportunities you have provided, but I fail to understand people who put self-perceived propriety above human decency."

Lavinia heaved a sigh. "My, you are your father's daughter."

"And proud of it."

Lavinia sat back in her chair, hands folded in her lap, deep in thought. Finally she spoke. "Lily, I love you. I always will. Yes, you have embarrassed Henry and me, and I have no doubt rumors of your outrageous behavior will spread. However, we will hold our heads high and proceed as if nothing has happened. Perhaps other swains will appear. It will take time for gossip to die down. Meanwhile, I ask you to act with decorum and abide by the customs of polite society." She leaned forward and fixed a piercing gaze on Lily. "Do I have your promise?"

Once again this day, Lily felt as if she were sacrificing an essential part of herself, but after all the Duprees had done for her, it was fair of them to ask. "Yes, Aunt Lavinia."

Even as she uttered the word, Lily knew the time would come when she could no longer stay in St. Louis. Worst of all, she was slowly coming to the realization that she had burned the only bridge that really mattered—Caleb.

Chapter Seventeen

Lily slit open the envelope the maid had deposited on her desk and withdrew a card laced with pink satin ribbon. Beneath the words Happy Valentine's Day, a rosy-cheeked cupid holding a bow and arrow smiled up at her. The verse read, "When Cupid's arrows pierce your heart, / You'll know my love though we're apart." On the back was a note in her sister's spidery handwriting. "I miss you and hope you are finding true love in St. Louis."

Lily clasped the card to her chest, a surge of homesickness and guilt sending an ache throughout her body. If Rose only knew. Lily had utterly failed in her ambition to become a sophisticated, sought-after young lady. It was no surprise that Lionel had dropped her, barely acknowledging his acquaintance with her when their paths crossed, and word of her serious faux pas had obviously spread. The only person now who could remotely be called a suitor was a doughy-looking young man with rosy cheeks and plastered blond hair whose father owned a brewery. As for her would-be female "friends," now only their mothers called on Lavinia, always ready with an explanation why their daughters had been unable to accompany them.

Lily set the card back on the desk, acknowledging that essentially she was a social outcast. All the more reason why she longed for her sister's comfort and reliability and her father's steadfast devotion. Like a bird in a cage, she was without options. Her father had decided to leave the army in the upcoming summer and set up a small medical practice, but had not yet decided where to relocate. Until such time as those plans solidified, Lily was stuck in the luxurious prison of the Dupree mansion.

Odd. At one time she had thought of Fort Larned as a prison. She had chafed under the wilderness hardships, barely tolerating the extremes of weather, the wild winds, gritty dust clouds and vermin of all descriptions. Yet she couldn't help thinking that instead of finding her niche here in the city, she had merely traded one wilderness for another—this wilderness characterized by snobbery, hypocrisy and indifference to human suffering.

She had never felt so alone. Oh, Uncle Henry and Aunt Lavinia cared for her, but they no longer sought out places to take her to show her off. The family's social outings had been curtailed, and Lily knew she was the cause. It was Aunt Lavinia's way of "lying low" and waiting for the gossip to subside. Lily shook her head. And all because of one humanitarian impulse on her part, an impulse she would act upon again in the same manner.

What would Caleb say about her actions? Would he, too, condemn her impulsivity, or would he join her to relieve another's pain? In her heart, she knew the answer. The two of them had often discussed God's role in human suffering. She was coming to believe that much of human struggle was self-inflicted. God didn't start wars; mankind did. Nor did God create barriers between different kinds of people. It was up to each person to exercise free will and make loving, compassionate choices. For the first time that day, Lily smiled. Maybe, just maybe, by going to the poor man's rescue as he lay in the street, she had pleased God.

Fierce March winds swirled around the ranch house and sleet clacked against the windowpanes. Seth rose from his chair to set more logs on the fire while Sophie and Pa bent over the chessboard, locked in fierce competition. Caleb moved closer to the flame, the better to read Mark Twain's *The Innocents Abroad,* travel adventures that sometimes made him chuckle aloud. He had needed laughs during these short winter days and long nights when, more often than not, he fell into bed exhausted from his labors. His nightmares had subsided, perhaps as a result of fresh air and hard work. Between them, he, Seth and Pa were creating a cattle operation that held great promise. Yet while it was a blessing to be with his family, something was still missing, and he intended to do something about that.

"Mate!" Sophie cried in triumph.

Pa grunted. "Well, I'll be hornswoggled if this pollywog didn't beat me."

"I would never count her out," Caleb said.

"It doesn't hurt that she has us menfolk wrapped around her little finger," Seth agreed.

Sophie batted her eyelashes. "My, how you do go on."

Caleb studied his sister, suddenly struck by the fact that she was no longer all tomboy. She still had a head of flyaway red curls, but her body was more woman-ish and her freckles seemed to have faded some. How had he not noticed? He figured soon they'd have to be protecting her from the area bachelors. How many such single men were even now clustered around Lily, beguiling her with sweet talk and showering her with extravagant gifts? He closed his book in disgust. He could not let himself think like that. He had to remain positive.

Sophie set the chess pieces back in their box and then turned her chair to face Caleb. "I reckon now that spring is soon upon us that it's time we told Pa and Seth about our plan."

Caleb's stomach churned. To say it out loud might sound foolish and make him out to be some wild-eyed Don Quixote on a futile quest. "Maybe."

"No 'maybe' about it. We are all in this together." She glanced around at the men, then grinned impishly. "Raise your hand if you want to make Caleb happy." She glared at Pa and Seth until slowly each raised his hand. "And in one word, what will it take to accom-plish that?"

Caleb blushed mightily when all three shouted, "Lily!" He had hoped that, by and large, he had con-cealed his longing for her.

Then Sophie launched into the details of their scheme, which filled Caleb with hope while at the same time scaring him with its finality.

Sophie leaned forward and placed a hand on his

knee. "Truth to tell, we're doing this as much for ourselves as for you. Your hangdog lovesickness needs a cure. Sometimes you're not exactly pleasant to be around."

Seth nodded vigorously. "I love you, brother, but sister has the bead on you. I met your Lily, you remember, and I can understand how you could be right fond of her. But you're a soldier, so forward, march!"

Pa got to his feet. "Gonna check on the livestock," he said, putting on his coat.

"I'll come with you." Caleb needed air…and the reassurance of his father's counsel. As they strode toward the barn, trailed by a pair of mixed-breed ranch dogs, neither said a word for the howling of the wind.

Inside, the odors of hay and warm animal flesh greeted them. Holding his lantern high, Pa moved from stall to stall, Caleb trailing him. "All's well," he said, coming to the end of the barn.

"Is it?" Caleb faced his father. "Is what Sophie and I are proposing crazy?"

Pa set the lantern on the floor, sat on a wooden crate and gestured at a nearby hay bale. "Sit."

Caleb did as he was told, then waited for his father to speak.

"When I first met your ma back there in Missouri, I was barely eighteen, wet behind the ears and awkward as a newborn calf. Everytime I saw her, my throat would get all tight and I couldn't get a word out. Even then I knew I was meant to be with her, to be her man. So I kept hangin' around. To this day I don't know what she saw in me, but together we were somethin'. More than either of us could have been on our own. That kind of completion, son, that's love. That's what your mother and I had, and that's what I want for all you children." Then he stood and led the way to the barn door where he paused and turned to Caleb. "I love you, son."

Caleb embraced his father, so choked up he could barely get out the words. "I love you, too, Pa."

Lily stepped around the piles of dirty snow lining the sidewalk outside the church. A charcoal haze hung over the city, and looking around, she noticed the bleak window-eyes of the brick row houses across the street. An unseasonal late March storm had taken the city by surprise. It was hard to believe spring was just around the corner. Sometimes she doubted that even flowers would perfume the air, so often befogged with smoke. St. Louis was not the alabaster city of her dreams, but a gritty, noisy mecca of commerce.

"Lily, dear, do come on. We shall be late for the restaurant." Aunt Lavinia stood by the carriage, her expression one of disapproval.

Lily hurried toward her, aware that once again she had disappointed her aunt. No matter what she did these days, she seemed to fall short. Just an hour ago as she was entering the church, Lionel had cut her dead and behind her she had heard Aunt Lavinia's tsk-tsk. Throughout the service, she was aware of thin-lipped dowagers studying her from beneath their bonnets and prissy young ladies studiously ignoring her. How long could these people censure her? She wasn't sure she wanted to know the answer.

Somehow Lily endured lunch at the highly touted restaurant, where elegance of food presentation outweighed taste. Other than these Sunday outings, she contented herself with the piano, needlework and reading. Although Aunt Lavinia had never again spoken to her about the sanctity of Uncle Henry's library, by tacit agreement, Lily was permitted to peruse the volumes stored there. With each advancing day, her restlessness grew, akin to that she had experienced at Fort Larned. Then, that restlessness had had a foreseeable end—her visit to St. Louis. Here? Nothing. At least not until her father and Rose were settled and she could join them. She steadfastly refused to name the other cause of her restlessness. Even saying Caleb's name filled her with fierce longing and unutterable regret.

Riding back home in the stuffy carriage, Aunt Lavinia and Uncle Henry were silent. Lily studied them, noting how apart they seemed—like a pair of bookends separated by their individual busy lives. They were civil to one another, and each seemed proud of the other, but where was the joy? Why, even their bedrooms were separate. Was this what marriage was like? Giddy first love replaced by tolerant acceptance?

Fortunately when they returned home, Aunt Lavinia withdrew to her boudoir with a headache, so Lily was free to curl up in her room with the delightful new book she had just started, *The Innocents Abroad.* Mr. Twain had such a droll way of poking fun. She almost laughed aloud as she read about the ignorance of the smug, ill-informed tourists. She had just finished a chapter and moved to the window to note with pleasure that the clouds had been replaced with sunshine when her maid knocked and entered. "Miss, you have a gentleman caller."

Please, not the brewmaster's son, she thought to herself. "I am not expecting anyone."

"He said as much." The girl screwed up her face. "But then he added the strangest thing."

"What was that?"

"Well, miss, these are his very words. 'Ask Miss Lily if she needs to be saved from snakes.'"

Lily's hand flew to her heart and fireworks exploded in front of her eyes. "Caleb? Caleb?" She nearly knocked the maid down as she ran past her, into the hall and down the stairs to the foyer, where she stopped cold, questioning the evidence before her eyes. There stood a handsome young man with warm hazel eyes, curly hair and broad shoulders dressed in a dark brown suit. Once more she croaked, "Caleb?"

He never stopped gazing at her as he crossed the floor, took her in his arms, folded her against his chest and whispered, "Lily, my dearest Lily."

So long as he lived, Caleb would never forget this moment. Holding her, breathing in her lilac scent, feeling the wisps of her gold-spun hair tickle his cheek, hearing her whisper his name over and over again, he gave a mental nod to his father. Lily Kellogg completed him.

After moments when nothing sounded but the steady ticktock of a grandfather clock from the next room and the two remained locked in an embrace, Lily finally stepped back, her blue eyes luminous with tears. "I can't believe it." She clasped his shoulders as if to assure herself he was real. "How did you get here? When? Oh, my, I'm flustered with so many questions."

He looked about, then said, "In a house this big, could we locate a quiet corner where we might talk?"

A joyful giggle escaped her. "I imagine we could find one." She pulled him along after her. "Oh, Caleb, there's so much I want to know."

"And so much I want to tell."

After they were settled on the love seat in the parlor, she covered his hand with hers. "I've missed you."

"And I, you." He wanted a few minutes to savor his welcome before he presented his case, so he bought time by telling her about the ranch and giving an account of his travels.

When he finished, Lily said, "This is a delightful surprise. Are you here on business?"

"Yes, but not the kind you mean." With one finger, he reached out and tilted her chin, so she was looking straight at him. "I've come for you."

Her eyes widened. "I don't understand."

"Every hour without you has been torture. That day you left me on the wharf and climbed into your aunt's carriage was the lowest point of my life. Yet I knew you had to come here—" he gestured around the opulently appointed room "—and see for yourself. What I'm hoping is that your curiosity has been satisfied in a way that has given you much pleasure, but that you might now be ready to entertain a marriage proposal."

Her hand fluttered to her heart. "I don't know what to say."

"Hear me out, dearest. I cannot give you what you have here. If it is culture, fine clothes and posh society you crave, then you must deny my suit. What I *can* offer is a promising young cattle business, a welcoming family and…my heart. We once talked of dreams. Here is mine. You by my side, a home of our own and children to cherish."

"You honor me. I don't deserve a second chance." She threaded her fingers together in her lap.

"I sense some reservation."

She nodded almost imperceptibly. "I don't know where I fit. I've learned I'm not cut out to move in these rarefied circles, but I don't know where I *do* belong." She raised her head and in her eyes, he read both pain and honesty. "Kansas was difficult for me. The constant spring winds grated my soul and there was no keeping up with the dust. The scorching heat and the freezing cold brought unrelieved misery. I don't know if I can go there again, even with you."

"You forgot to mention the snakes," he said dryly. He slumped. There was no way he could alter the forces of nature. "That's the choice, isn't it? I'm committed to the ranch and, frankly, to what I see as the beauty of the Flint Hills. I love you, but I don't want you to marry me because you have no other options. Even though I didn't want to lose you to St. Louis, I knew you had to have the experience so that if we got together later, you wouldn't resent me for holding you back. I feel the same way about our potential marriage. If you say yes, you must say it with the conviction that you will never blame me for the place we live." He paused to get a breath. "It's all or nothing, Lily."

"Would it be ironic to say I need time to think?"

He tried to keep bitterness from his laugh. "I expected as much." He rose to his feet.

"Must you leave so soon?"

"I have accomplished what I came to do. I'm needed at the ranch and must hasten home. Walk me to the door?"

She gripped his arm and suddenly she seemed frail to him. "You really came all this way just for me?"

"I'd walk the world for you, Lily."

They had reached the front hall. "What happens now?"

"You do whatever thinking you need to do to come up with an answer."

"How will I get in touch with you?" There was a frantic edge to her voice.

He reached in his jacket pocket and pulled out an envelope. "This is a letter for you from my sister, Sophie. You will find our address enclosed." Just as he handed it to her, he sensed another presence. Looking up the stairs, he saw Lavinia Dupree standing on the landing.

"Who is this gentleman, Lily?" She began her descent. "I hope you have not been entertaining him without my permission."

Caleb bit his tongue and bowed slightly. "We met on the wharf, Mrs. Dupree. I am Caleb Montgomery, retired captain of the United States Army."

"I remember now. You escorted Lily on her trip to St. Louis." She looked from Caleb to Lily. "But what on earth are you doing here now, young man?"

"I have come in the expectation that Lily might agree to become my wife."

If the situation hadn't been so serious, Caleb would have laughed aloud at the way Lavinia drew back in horror, her bosom heaving. "Lily!" was all she could manage.

"The captain was just taking his leave, Aunt Lavinia. You and I will talk later. Right now, I am walking him out to his cab." Without a backward glance, Lily sailed defiantly out the door.

At the cab, he held her once more, shielding her from the cold. "Please, Lily, give us a chance." He uttered a silent prayer, then said, "I asked you this question months ago, and I ask it now for the final time, because after today, you will see me again only if it is your choice. Here is that question." He stepped back to plumb the depths of her eyes. "Can you say in all honesty that you don't love me?"

She drew a gentle hand across his cheek. "Dear Caleb. It is a valid question. And you will have an answer."

He hoisted himself into the cab. Unable to say goodbye, he simply said, "Until we meet again."

Clutching Sophie's letter, Lily dashed by her aunt with a curt "Not now," and headed for the privacy of her bedroom. In the past hour she had run the emotional gamut from surprise to delight to confusion and loss. It was hard even now to believe Caleb had actually been here, that he had made a difficult journey simply to see her, that he had persevered in his proposal and then left as unexpectedly as he had arrived. His appearance seemed incongruous, his simple clothes and unaffected air at odds with the grandeur of the place. Oddly, he had seemed more at home, more comfortable than the preening Lionel ever had. Caleb displayed a confidence that went far beyond others' opinions of him. Why hadn't she let him sweep her off her feet, rescue her once again? It would've been so easy to tell him she loved him, to say "yes," but she had decided long ago that she would never promise herself to a man, to Caleb, unless she could do so without reservations. He deserved that. If she were to join him in the Flint Hills, she would have to embrace his world rather than criticize it. Both the wilderness of Fort Larned and the alien wilderness of St. Louis society had been difficult. Was she brave enough to face yet another on the prairies of Kansas?

She also had Aunt Lavinia and Uncle Henry to consider. They had been more than generous to her and, indeed, had fulfilled all her dreams of city life. If she accepted Caleb's proposal, would that be a slap in the face to them? Their world was far different from anything she had experienced before, and she didn't want to hurt them, but the fact was, this was not her world.

Then there was Caleb. So steadfast, so true. She could never doubt his love. He had demonstrated it again and again. Yet in his final words to her, she recognized he was losing patience. She would not have another chance. Sitting by the window, she picked up Sophie's letter. Caleb had always told her she would like Sophie, and as she read her words, Lily knew he had been right.

Dear Lily,

I know this is an irregular way to introduce myself, but I want to offer you some food for thought. It is not my intention to meddle in your business, though perhaps I am. My brother is very dear to me, and when he suffers, I suffer. And he is suffering. From love of you. I don't

suppose I need to catalog for you his fine qualities, though I will mention one. Devotion. If you
should accept his proposal, you would never have
cause for distrust. He will cherish you beyond
measure.

As for Pa, Seth and me, we would welcome
you warmly and embrace you as sister and daughter. Personally, I long for the kind of friendship
we two women might enjoy on the prairie.

Yet Caleb has told me about your reservations. Leaving all that is familiar for a strange
place which, like Fort Larned, is subject to the
extremes of weather and climate might prove
difficult. That we cannot change. But I can assure you that we will do our utmost to make you
comfortable. And think of the garden you and I
could create! Oh, and I promise to take care of
any menacing snakes.

Lily stopped reading, picturing in her mind Caleb's
family and his irrepressible sister. Already Lily felt a
bond of sympathy with this plucky young woman who
seemed to make the best of life and cared so deeply.
Sophie's next words bowled her over.

Here is my proposal. Seeing is believing, they
say. Why don't you come try us out? Caleb will
send money for you to take the train to Kansas
City where I will meet you and accompany you
on to Cottonwood Falls and the ranch. Spend
time with us, with the Flint Hills and, above all,
with my darling brother. Then make your decision. Because I warn you—unless you want

to experience the wrath of Sophie, don't marry
my brother unless you love him unconditionally.
Here's what I think: How could you not?
With high hopes,
Sophie

The generosity and enormity of Sophie's offer
stunned Lily. Yet it made perfect sense. She didn't have
to commit to the unknown. She would have the chance
to experience the Flint Hills wilderness. And the lure
of Caleb was intense. When he had driven off in the
cab, a wave of loneliness had engulfed her.

She reread the letter, smiling at the exuberant, no-
nonsense tone. Lily knew she would treasure Sophie's
friendship, particularly after the affectations of the
young ladies she had met in St. Louis. She sat a bit
longer pondering the events of the day and praying for
guidance. Then, knowing she could delay no further,
she made her way to her aunt's room.

Lavinia sat at her dressing table, trying on and then
discarding jewelry. Holding two necklaces, she turned
to Lily. "Which do you think? The topaz or the amethyst?"

"They're both exquisite."

"The amethyst, I think." Lavinia fastened the gem
around her neck and then said with asperity, "What
exactly was that about this afternoon?"

Lily sat down on a nearby slipper sofa, clasping her
icy hands in her lap. "You heard him. Caleb Montgomery has asked me to marry him."

"What kind of prospects does he have, pray tell?"

"He owns a ranch in Kansas, along with his father
and brother."

"A ranch!" Lavinia couldn't have sounded more shocked if Lily had told her Caleb was a pirate. "Lily, dear, that will never do."

"Perhaps it will."

"Are you out of your mind, child?"

"I love him, Aunt Lavinia. He's been the only one ever since I met him. I admit that, like you, I am hesitant about what life on a ranch would be like, but his family has kindly invited me to visit so that I can make my own determination."

"It's out of the question." Lavinia's jowls quivered.

"His sister will accompany me on the journey from Kansas City, and Caleb is paying for my travel."

"This is crazy talk. I forbid you to go."

"I am of age, Aunt Lavinia, and not a captive here. I am going."

Lavinia threw up her hands. "You're just like your mother."

"Whatever do you mean?"

"No matter how I tried, there was no talking her out of marrying Ezra, nor dissuading her from traipsing about the country with him. She would have followed that man into the jaws of hell."

"That's the kind of love I hope to find. Why is following my heart wrong when it feels so right?"

"There is much more to what you call love, my dear, than feelings."

"What, for instance?"

"Knowing your situation is secure. Never wanting for fine things. Moving among the best people."

"Forgive me, but that sounds more like a business relationship than a marriage."

Lily noticed her aunt's fingers trembling. "You are

so naive," she rasped. "I shouldn't be surprised. Your
parents were the exception to the rule."

"Rule?"

"That few marriages are made in heaven." Lavinia
lowered her head, pleating and repleating the folds of
her skirt.

Lily waited, not knowing what to say but sensing a
kind of cataclysm within her aunt.

Then Lavinia leaned back in her chair and fixed her
eyes on Lily. "You're determined?"

"Yes."

"Then I will not argue further." She seemed to wilt
with that concession and sat wordless for a time. "I
only hope you know what you're giving up."

Lily admitted she'd disappointed her aunt, but there
was no turning back. "Thank you for all you and Uncle
Henry have done for me. I shall always be grateful."

"You have made us very happy." The older woman
fiddled with the amethyst, and Lily was shocked to
see her eyes glaze with tears. "It isn't always so with
Henry and me."

"But you are adored, Aunt Lavinia."

"Oh, yes. 'Adored.' But am I loved?" She shook
her head sadly, and Lily heard bitterness tinge her
aunt's voice. "There is a gulf between being adored
and being loved. I have been pampered and appreciated, but loved? I think not."

Lily was appalled by both her aunt's confession and
by the forlorn look on her face. Gone was the confident
woman in control. "I had no idea."

"I don't intend to shock you, but marriage is a complicated arrangement. I settled, Lily, and to all outsiders, it must look as if Henry and I are devoted and

content." She leaned forward and grasped Lily by the shoulders, her words falling with the force of a hammer. "Don't settle, Lily, whatever you do. Don't settle, as I did. Go." She waved her hands in dismissal. "Go find your Caleb."

Chapter Eighteen

Excited by the novelty of railroad travel, Lily watched the countryside roll by at astonishing speeds, green trees and fences blurring with the expanse of the Missouri River. The staccato rhythm of the wheels on the railroad track sang an insistent song: *Ca-leb, Ca-leb, Calebcalebcaleb.* Following his St. Louis visit, a flurry of correspondence had ended in the arrangements for this day. With the recent advances in rail transportation, he had not wanted to wait for her to make the slower river voyage. This very evening she would alight in Kansas City to be greeted by Sophie. In mere hours she would be lifted from Aunt Lavinia's world into Caleb's. She gazed at the distant riverbank. Could his world become hers?

Pondering that question, she recalled Aunt Lavinia's final words to her on the train station platform. "Be open to all the possibilities, Lily. As I know all too well, no joy is to be found in stubbornness, nor, as your mother proved, is there any hardship love cannot overcome."

The acrid cinder odor and the swaying motion of the train did nothing to ease the nervousness that had settled in her stomach. Yet it was a good kind of edginess, born out of anticipation and hope. She reached in her pocket and withdrew an oft folded and refolded letter from Caleb, the first after he received word she would come visit.

My dearest Lily,
You cannot know with what elation I received your recent letter. You are coming! My family thinks I've gone daft with the excitement of it. Although I harbor high expectations, let me assure you that I know the visit in no way entails a promise of any kind on your part. Yet I long to share with you the special nature of my home and pray that you will be able to see it through my eyes. Once again, let us be honest with one another, for we cannot go forward with secrets or reservations.

I am counting the days until I see you, beloved.
Yours devotedly,
Caleb

During the train trip Lily prayed for the openness Lavinia had urged. If only she could embrace the Flint Hills wilderness the way she longed to embrace the man she loved… She was realistic enough to know that happiness would result only from a shared vision of their future. She laid her head back and, rocked by the motion of the train, allowed her eyes to drift shut.

She was awakened by the soft voice of a porter. "Ma'am, Kansas City be the next stop."

Every nerve in her body came alive as she fumbled with her hat pin in her haste to ready herself for meeting Sophie, who also had been corresponding with her. The train slowed, snorting and puffing its way to the depot, then hissed to a stop, throwing Lily forward in her seat. A small crowd waited on the platform, and as Lily scanned those greeting the passengers, she saw her—Sophie! Tousled red curls, just as Caleb had described, a trim, shapely body clad in a simple dress and a smiling face dusted with freckles.

No sooner had Lily stepped off the train than Sophie came running toward her and engulfed her in a hug. "You have to be Lily! I'd have known you anywhere. Welcome, welcome! We are all so delighted that you agreed to come."

"I am grateful for the invitation."

Sophie pulled away and stood beaming at her. "How I wish Caleb were here to share this moment, but very soon I shall witness your grand reunion." She clasped Lily around the waist. "Now then, let's gather your bags and catch a cab to the hotel. We'll spend the night and then tomorrow get on the stage and then…"

Lily couldn't help smiling, pulled along into the future by Sophie's chattering account of their plans.

Clutching a bouquet of lilacs, Caleb paced the boardwalk outside the general store in Council Grove, willing the arrival of the stagecoach from Kansas City. Nearby loomed the towering oak tree that gave the town its name. Under its shade the Osage Indians had signed a treaty granting right-of-way for the Santa Fe

Trail. The town bustled with Saturday business. Loafers gathered on corners to jaw and spit tobacco, while children darted in and out among the men and women intent on their shopping. Caleb thanked God for this mild, sunny May day to welcome Lily. Now that his and Sophie's plan was in full swing, he was questioning it. So long as Lily hadn't yet rejected the Flint Hills, he could live in his dream, but if she did…?

From the edge of town, came the excited cry, "Stage is a'comin'!" Heeding the announcement, small boys ran to greet the coach, now visible and rumbling toward its stop in front of Caleb. First out was a large, stern-faced woman, taking her sweet time. Then he saw his Lily—her bonnet slightly askew—her eyes searching the onlookers. He stepped forward just at the moment she spotted him. He would never forget her gasp of pleasure nor the sunshine of her smile as he handed her the bouquet and drew her into his embrace. Their simultaneous "Lily" and "Caleb" mingled in his ears as he held her, still trying to convince himself she was actually here.

"Hey, brother. What about me? Do I count?" Sophie's teasing giggle caused him to reach out and gather her into the hug.

After retrieving their baggage, Caleb led them down the street to the hotel he had booked for the night. "You two freshen up and then we'll have dinner. We need to get a good night's sleep before we set out for home."

"How far is it?" Lily asked.

"About nineteen miles. The ranch is just this side of Cottonwood Falls. We'll have a long day."

"With our chatting, it will pass in a flash," Sophie

said, linking her arm through her brother's. "We'll give Lily a regular tour."

"I'll look forward to that." Lily beamed up at him, her eyes dancing. "I'm so happy to be here." Then under her breath so only he could hear, she added, "With you."

Caleb had not exaggerated. It had been a long day riding through the rolling hills, but he and Sophie had entertained her nearly the entire route with amusing stories of their childhoods, recitals of their neighbors' backgrounds and a botany lesson concerning the area flora. Finally, they started up the road to the Montgomery Ranch. Sophie raised her arm and pointed. "There," she said with a contented sigh. "That's home." The last rays of the setting sun slanted across the meadow highlighting a two-story stone house sheltered by a hill and overlooking a prairie panorama. Beyond it was a huge stone barn and corral.

Lily sensed Caleb studying her for a reaction. She touched his arm. "It's far grander than I had imagined." Knowing they were nearing the barn, the wagon team broke into a trot. As they approached the yard, Lily noticed the colorful flower garden bordering the front porch and the large vegetable patch a few steps from the kitchen door. The Montgomerys had obviously worked hard to create such a welcoming home. The last of the day's sunlight reflecting off the tall, narrow windows was like a whispered blessing.

Seth and a tall, weathered man came outside the barn, both waving their arms aloft while two dogs danced around them. Lily was seized with momentary jitters. She had met Seth, but she so wanted to make a good impression on Caleb's father. Caleb handed the two women down from the wagon bench, setting Lily down gently. "You know my brother, but this is my father, Andrew Montgomery."

Lily felt her hands grasped in Mr. Montgomery's large, worn ones. "My dear, we have awaited your arrival with much happiness."

"Thank you for inviting me."

Caleb's father chuckled, then winked at his son. "What could we do? He held a gun to our heads."

Momentarily disconcerted, Lily wondered what to say, but then when all three Montgomerys laughed, she realized Caleb's father was teasing.

That was by no means the end of the joshing. This family was such a departure from the formal Dupree household that it took Lily a while to relax and relish the give-and-take of an affectionate, happy family. The first time she managed to make a joke, they acted as if she had won a blue ribbon at the county fair. In the first few days, she and Caleb walked or rode horseback around the countryside, lush with blue-green grasses undulating in the wind.

Awakening one morning late into the second week of her visit, she was charmed by the melodies of a variety of birds, all trying to outdo one another. She had attended several concerts in St. Louis, but none had brought her the pleasure of this natural symphony. Gathering the blanket around her, she went to the bedroom window and opened it to a breeze fragrant with dewy grass, honeysuckle and wood smoke. Caleb had been gentle with her, giving her time and space to adapt to this new environment. She was grateful to Aunt Lavinia for once again calling in the dressmaker, this time to equip her with a wardrobe more suitable for the frontier. Already she and Sophie had spent hours together, weeding and planting in the garden and cooking. To her surprise, Lily found she enjoyed the food preparation Rose had customarily done. If she did say so herself, she was turning out light, feathery biscuits the menfolk seemed to enjoy.

One day Andrew Montgomery took her aside and walked her out to a pasture where he explained about cattle breeds and the seasons of ranch life. As they strolled home, he spoke about Caleb. "He is a fine son, a good man. His mother's death was hard on him, and the little I know about his war experiences sounds like it could do a fellow in. You probably are aware, too, that in the midst of that conflict, he got his heart broken."

"I know about Rebecca."

"Well, I reckon that match wasn't meant to be." He stopped walking and faced her. "Lily, I'm hoping this one is. Whatever you decide, though, make sure it's final and forever." He took off his hat, then repositioned it on his head. "Caleb can't take much more sorrow."

Lily nodded, too moved to speak. She guessed Andrew Montgomery also had experienced more than his share of heartbreak.

The second Sunday after her arrival, the men harnessed the buggy for Lily and Sophie and rode alongside them for the two miles to the community church. The white clapboard building with a small steeple surmounted by a simple cross was set on a corner near the general store. Horses, buggies and wagons pulled up to the hitching posts or stopped along the side of the street disgorging whole families of settlers who greeted each other with happy voices or claps on the back. In the first five minutes, Sophie had introduced Lily to several women who clucked over her and smiled their approval. Finally it was time to settle on the plain wooden benches, so different from the carved, high-backed pews of her St. Louis church.

Caleb stood aside to let the two women enter the row first before taking his place next to her. Nestled between the brother and sister, Lily glowed with a comfortable sense of belonging. When they stood for the first hymn, Caleb tucked a hand beneath her elbow and leaned closer to share the hymnal with her. When the congregation began singing and she once again heard Caleb's melodious voice, she could hardly squeak out the words, so perfectly did they pertain to the two of them.

> "Blest be the tie that binds
> Our hearts in Christian love.
> The fellowship of kindred minds
> Is like to that above."

With her free hand, Lily slowly withdrew her handkerchief, knowing she would soon need it. Verse two began and Lily couldn't sing at all as her eyes sought Caleb's while he sang tenderly as if only to her.

> "Before our Father's throne
> We pour our ardent prayers;
> Our fears, our hopes, our aims are one,
> Our comforts and our cares."

Lily bowed her head and softly blew her nose. *Our fears, our hopes, our aims are one, Our comforts and our cares.* She thought of her friend Fannie who knew the truth of those words, of her father and mother who had lived them and of the man beside her who loved her with all his generous heart. With newfound clarity, she realized she could not go through life without him. She caught her breath, then looked up to find him studying her with blinding affection.

After a picnic lunch on the green beside the church, one by one, the families began hitching up and leaving. On their way back to the ranch, Seth commented about the gathering clouds. "Mighty tall ones. Storm's a'comin'."

Sophie shook the reins, urging the horses into a quick trot. Seth and Caleb rode ahead to check on the stock and get the barn closed. The air carried the metallic hint of rain, and off in the distance a bolt of lightning speared the darkening sky. By the time the others reached the barn, secured the buggy and stabled the horses, rain had started to fall. Sophie and Lily raced for the house, belted by increasingly powerful gusts of wind. Shivering, Lily went to retrieve a shawl. When she came back into the kitchen, Sophie had stoked the fire and put on the kettle for tea.

Caleb was the first of the men to arrive back at the house. "This is going to be a whopper." He stood near the stove, drying his hands. Soon he was followed by Seth and Andrew. When they entered, the fierce wind nearly ripped the door out of their hands. Somewhere close by, Lily heard a loose gate whipping back and forth, and peering out the window, she saw bean plants lying flat, beaten down by the wind and rain.

When the wind died and there was a sudden lull

in the rainfall, Andrew moved into the front room to look out to the southwest. "I don't like this," he said. The others joined him. Outside, the sky had taken on a sickly mustardlike hue and the distant clouds were roiling and becoming convoluted as if they were rapidly outgrowing their bounds. Then out of one of the clouds emerged a wide corkscrewlike tail moving like a ravaging beast toward the ranch, accompanied by now deafening winds. Andrew pivoted quickly and shouted, "Cyclone! Get to the storm cellar."

Watching the terrifying cloud-creature advance, Lily went numb. She had never been more afraid in her life. "Lily!" Caleb grabbed her arm. "C'mon." He pushed her in front of him out the back door where his father stood holding open the cover of the storm cellar. From below, Seth reached up and lifted her into the earthen cave, then Caleb and Andrew jumped in, pulling the heavy cover shut behind them. In the dark, Caleb found her and nestled her close, his warmth quelling her trembling. The dank quarters smelled of fresh earth and above them they could hear the thrashing and thumping of a violent wind.

Sophie lighted a candle, throwing shadows into the corners. On each grim face, Lily read concern. What damage might such a storm inflict upon all the work these three had expended? Lily reached out and touched Mr. Montgomery's hand. "Might we pray?" He nodded, managing a half smile.

She sought the words. "Dear God, in Your mercy bless this ranch and those who have toiled so diligently to produce its bounty. Spare us and this place that we may go out from this shelter to continue the good work You have begun in us." Before she could say "Amen" a particularly loud thump caused her to jump. "Amen," the others echoed. Then they sat quietly, each lost in thought. After what seemed a long time, the winds died. Andrew withdrew his watch and leaned close to the candle, checking the time. "We'll wait five more minutes. Then I'll check outside."

When at last he opened the shelter door, a welcome rush of fresh air greeted them. The men left first, then assisted the women to the surface. Lily gasped. All around them were downed trees, shingles and broken fence posts, but, blessedly, the house and the barn still stood. "Praise be," Andrew muttered.

Before leaving to assist his father, brother and sister with the cleanup, Caleb ushered Lily into the kitchen. "You can help by fixing supper." He lingered there, seemingly reluctant to leave. Then staring at his feet, he said quietly, "I guess your worst fears were realized this afternoon."

She was speechless. He had voiced exactly what she was thinking.

"I don't know how to make it right. You saw what happened, Lily. There's no way I can control events like this. Cyclones, prairie fires or blizzards, it doesn't really matter. Life on the prairie is perilous. The most I can promise is to try to keep you safe." He looked up then, his face pale, his eyes reddened with regret. "I reckon you'll want me to make arrangements for you to leave."

She thought about the inconveniences, the deprivations and the outright dangers. Then about these four dear people who had shown her nothing but acceptance and affection. About the one who loved her. Then a surprising insight came to her. In that storm shelter, she had not been afraid. How could she be, surrounded by the Montgomerys and comforted by prayer? With an ecstatic sigh, she realized *I am home. At last*.

"Caleb, dear, I think that might be a bit premature. I haven't even seen my first snake."

He looked at her with dawning incredulity.

"Besides," she continued, quoting the hymn, "'our hopes, our fears, our dreams are one, our comforts and our cares.'"

Beautiful weather followed the storm—warm days and cool nights with the gentlest of breezes teasing the petals of the roses climbing the trellis beside the back door. Lily and Sophie had toiled in the garden to set things to rights while the men had checked on the cattle, repaired the roof, trimmed tree limbs and sawed broken trunks into firewood. A week after the storm, Caleb approached Lily early in the evening. "The almanac predicts a full moon tonight. Might I invite you for a buggy ride? I have something to show you."

Lily smiled. She had enjoyed watching him these past few days, looking at her when he thought she wouldn't notice as if checking to be sure she was still in residence. "I would like that. Let me get a wrap."

She trembled with delight when he spanned her waist with his warm hands and lifted her onto the buggy seat. He climbed up beside her, gathered the reins and clucked to the horse. She laced her arm through his and snuggled close. Neither the horse nor the buggy occupants seemed in any hurry.

"Where are we going? What is it you want to show me?"

He chuckled, a warm, throaty sound. "There's that

curiosity of yours rearing its saucy head. Can't you wait to be surprised?"

She grinned. "It's not easy." She moved away from him briefly. "But I do like surprises, sir."

They rode in silence for several minutes, watching while the fading sun slipped behind the faraway hills. The only sounds were the regular clip-clop of the horse's hooves, occasionally punctuated by the call of a mourning dove. They began an ascent through a patch of trees and emerged on top of one of the lower hills. Caleb stopped the buggy at a point where it faced east. Below, a lazy stream wound its way among the rocks. "Do you like this view?"

"It's beautiful," she said, and in her heart she knew it was so. "Your Flint Hills are beginning to charm me."

He cuddled her closer. "Just you wait," he whispered.

Almost without warning, an orange ball rose in front of them glazing the landscape with moonlight. Lily shuddered with delight. "Caleb, I've never seen anything more lovely."

"I have," he said softly. He turned and gathered her in his arms. "You."

In the pause that followed, she thought she might expire if he didn't kiss her, but then his lips lowered to hers and all the moons and suns and stars in the skies couldn't ignite in her the sheer joy of his kiss. "Oh, Caleb," she murmured when they parted. She drew his face to hers to repeat the bliss.

Abruptly, he leaped from the buggy and came around to her side to help her down, pausing in that effort for yet another kiss. Then he took her hand and walked her a ways down the hill. Locating a flat rock, he sat her down. "It's time," he said quietly.

Lily glanced up at him, dismayed by his serious expression.

"I need your answer, Lily. You have been here long enough to know your mind, and I cannot go on living beside you, all the time wondering whether you will stay. Either you love me enough to endure what you call a wilderness or you don't."

She rose and took both of his hands in hers, gripping with all her might. "I know all about wildernesses now. I've lived in them. Here is what God has revealed to me." She drew in a quick breath. "A wilderness, my dearest love, is any place without you."

He reeled a bit, then cupped her face in his hands, searching her eyes. "Does that mean you can't say you don't love me?"

"I could never say that because it would be dishonest. I, Lily Kellogg, love Caleb Montgomery with all my heart."

She was crushed then in his embrace, and if she didn't know better, she would think he was stifling a whimper. Finally, he whispered, "I've waited so long for you." He drew back and held her by her arms. "Now then, *please,* do me the honor of becoming my wife."

Arms outspread, she whirled around and around, shouting to the moon resting over their heads, "Yes, yes, yes!"

After more kisses, she looked up at him, her expression turning serious. Her next words, she knew, had to be said. "Caleb, before we say anything further, I want you to know that I understand, as much as it is possible for a woman, how your experiences in battle have affected you and how they will always haunt you. You did what you had to do then, but this is a new day. God knows your heart, and I know your heart. You are a good man. On this earth, we will never escape the bad things that happen or fully comprehend God's plan, but perhaps we can agree to live each day in the hope of His grace."

Caleb placed his hands on her shoulders and fixed his eyes on hers. "You are part of His plan. Right now, that's proof enough for me. Faith will grow as, together, we put our trust in Him."

Sensing, the need for a lighter mood, she said, "You mentioned a surprise. Is it time now?"

"Follow me." He took her hand and led her around a large clump of bushes. "There," he said, pointing to a stone foundation.

She walked closer to examine it. "What is it?"

"Our house."

"Our house?" She spun around, her hand to her mouth.

For a brief moment, he looked dubious. "You did say you liked the view."

"Yes, but—"

"Hoping for the best, in my spare time, I've been working on it. Here is where our dream can begin— having babies, raising a family, growing old."

"It's perfect," she said, and knew it was so.

"Perhaps I can make it a bit more perfect," he said grinning mischievously.

"It couldn't be."

"You doubt me, Miss Kellogg? I have one more surprise for you." He reached in his pocket and withdrew an envelope. "Read this."

Had it not been for the light of the full moon, Lily could not have recognized her father's bold hand nor read the astounding message.

Thank you, Caleb, for your kind offer to establish a medical practice in Cottonwood Falls. Rose and I have discussed the situation, so if, as I suspect she will, Lily accepts your proposal, we will make plans to relocate near you later in the summer.

Lily sank to the grass, dumbfounded. Gathering her wits, she said, "You've planned this all along?" She shook her head in bewilderment. "How did you know I would say yes?"

"I didn't, but prayer can work wonders." He held out his hand and assisted her to her feet.

She leaned against him, knowing she would always feel safe in his arms. "Captain, you have thought of absolutely everything."

"Caleb," he reminded her with a lilt in his voice.

She laughed out loud. "Oh, yes, *Caleb*. My darling, dearest man. Caleb." *The love of her life.* It hadn't been an easy journey, but Fannie had been right about love. When a woman knows, she knows. And, thanks be to God, Lily knew.

* * * * *

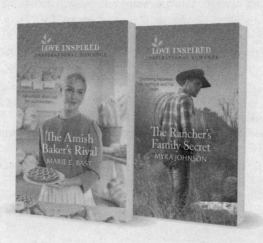

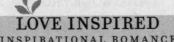
"Oscar will be perfect for your needs," Ruby assured Aaron, reaching down to scratch the poodle's head.

"That froufrou dog? No way, ma'am. Not gonna happen."

"Excuse me?" She'd expected him to hesitate but not downright reject her idea.

"Look, Ruby, if you like Oscar so much, then keep him for yourself. I need a man's dog by my side, not some… some…"

"Poodle?" Ruby suggested, her eyebrows disappearing beneath her long ginger bangs.

"Right. Lead me to where you keep the German shepherds, and I'll pick one out myself."

"Hmm," Ruby said, rubbing her chin as if considering his request, although she really wasn't. "No."

"No?"

"No," she repeated firmly. "First off, we don't currently have a German shepherd as part of our program."

"I'd even take a pit bull." He was beginning to sound desperate.

"Look, Aaron. Either you're going to have to learn to trust me or you may as well just leave now before we start. This isn't going to work unless you're ready to listen to me and do whatever I tell you to do."

His eyebrows furrowed. "I understand chain of command, ma'am. There were many times as a marine when I didn't exactly agree with my superiors, but I understood why it was important to follow orders."

"Okay. Let's go with that."

"For me," Aaron continued, "following orders is black-and-white. My marines' lives under my command often depended on it. But as you can see, I'm having difficulty making that transition in this situation. We're not talking people's lives here."

"I disagree. We're very much talking lives—*yours*. You may not yet have a clear vision of what you'll be able to do with Oscar, but a service dog can make all the difference."

"Yes, but you just insisted the best dog for me is a *poodle*. I'm sorry, but if you knew anything about me at all, you'd know the last dog in the world I'd choose would be a poodle."

"And yet I still believe I'm right," said Ruby with a wry smile. Somehow, she had to convince this man she knew what she was doing. "I carefully studied your file before you arrived, Aaron, and specially selected Oscar for you to work with. I'm the expert here. So how are we going to get over this hurdle?"

"I have orders to make this work. How will it look if I give up before I even start the process?" He shook his head. "No. Don't answer that. It will look as if I wasn't able to complete my mission. That's never going to happen. I'll *always* pull through, no matter what."

Don't miss
The Marine's Mission *by Deb Kastner,*
available July 2021 wherever
Love Inspired books and ebooks are sold.

LoveInspired.com

LIEXP0621

LOVE INSPIRED
INSPIRATIONAL ROMANCE

UPLIFTING STORIES OF FAITH, FORGIVENESS AND HOPE.

———————

Join our social communities to connect with other readers who share your love!

Sign up for the Love Inspired newsletter at **LoveInspired.com** to be the first to find out about upcoming titles, special promotions and exclusive content.

———————

CONNECT WITH US AT:

f Facebook.com/LoveInspiredBooks

🐦 Twitter.com/LoveInspiredBks

Facebook.com/groups/HarlequinConnection

HARLEQUIN

Heartfelt or thrilling, passionate or uplifting—Harlequin is more than just happily-ever-after.

With twelve different series to choose from and new books available every month, you are sure to find stories that will move you, uplift you, inspire and delight you.

SIGN UP FOR THE HARLEQUIN NEWSLETTER

Be the first to hear about great new reads and exciting offers!

Harlequin.com/newsletters

Get 4 FREE REWARDS!

We'll send you 2 FREE Books plus **FREE** 2 FREE Mystery Gifts.

Love Inspired books feature uplifting stories where faith helps guide you through life's challenges and discover the promise of a new beginning.

FREE Value Over **$20**